*T*here's a storm brewing in the quiet town of Litchfield. A whirlwind of media attention, political debate, and anger is about to sweep through and hold the fate of three women captive.

In the eye of the storm are sixteen-year-old Clara Mahoney, a lonesome girl living in a family strained by autism; Pia Fernandez, a battered wife who wants only to escape her abusive husband; and, Loren Elliot, a forty-three-year-old who can barely make ends meet with two kids in college and a husband who just lost his job.

Though these women are very different, they have a great deal in common. They are each unexpectedly pregnant, scared, and in positions where they cannot devote themselves to a child. And, they all have appointments at the same abortion clinic in Litchfield.

But getting there won't be easy. Anti-choice forces—headed by a vain socialite and a self-indulgent priest—are mounting a demonstration against the clinic. Can these desperate women brave the chaos? Or will they let the public debate dictate their private decisions?

An easy read that raises hard questions and then answers them in a compelling way, *The Recovery Room* is a book every woman should read.

❧

THE RECOVERY ROOM

A Novel

❧

ANN ORMSBY

ISBN: 0615728944
ISBN 13: 9780615728940
Library of Congress Control Number: 2013949940
Great South Bay Press, Westfield, NJ

Larry ❧ Charles ❧ William

"No woman can call herself free until she can choose consciously whether she will or will not be a mother."

Margaret Sanger, Founder, Birth Control Federation of America, Later renamed Planned Parenthood Federation of America

$\mathcal{O}$ N E

❧

$\mathcal{T}$he recovery room at the clinic out on Route 54 had eight small stalls, each just big enough for a bed and the nurse to stand beside it. The room was kept very cold, so the women were all swaddled in cotton, waffle-weave blankets that were heated in a large warming cabinet at the back of the room. The nurses had a special way of replacing the used, cool blankets with new, hot ones without ever exposing the women to the cold air. Yellow curtains with white and blue flowers surrounded each bed for privacy. Patty, the head nurse, had chosen yellow because it was hopeful. She had said it made her think of the sunrise.

On this particular morning, two women were already in recovery. Now, just being wheeled out of the procedure room and down the hall to the recovery room, was a young girl, Clara Mahoney. She was only 16 years old, and the man who had come with her was in the waiting room pestering the receptionist.

"How is she? Is it over yet?" he had started asking, about ten minutes after Clara had been called in by the nurse.

"No, not yet. Sit down. Relax. She'll be fine," said Kathleen, the receptionist, hunching over her paperwork.

Michael Russo could not sit down. He stood in front of the nurse's window, craning his neck to see into the inner depths of the clinic. Frustrated by the floor-to-ceiling file cabinets blocking his view, he turned on the heel of his army boot and started to pace in front of the first row of chairs lined up auditorium-style in the large room. His black hair, slick with gel, glistened under the harsh fluorescent lights and the smell of disinfectant filled his nostrils. He was oblivious to the stares of the other patients, who worried that he would stomp on their feet as he assaulted the gray, industrial-grade carpet. A young man with crossed legs and a book in his lap cleared his throat as Michael marched by. Their eyes locked for a moment and Michael sat down, pulling on his mustache. Feeling as if the situation were out of his control, he rested his head on the back of the chair and forced himself to silently count, visualizing each number behind his closed eyelids.

Michael had met Clara two months earlier. It had been a warm spring night, one of the first of the season when the air smells sweet. After work he had headed to The Sportsman, the one working-class bar in town. When he walked in, he saw his buddies playing pool in the back but decided to have a quiet beer first. Jay, the bartender, flashed his crooked smile and gave him a draft Budweiser. Michael usually knew everyone who hung out at the bar, but there were some new faces there that night. Young faces. A whole pack of little girls. He saw them, five or six of them stuffed into one of the wooden booths by the jukebox. He scanned the table of silky hair and spaghetti straps. The girls' slim, tanned arms glowing from the light of the candles. Their silver jewelry shimmering. He chuckled at his interest in these girls and looked away. He took a long pull on his beer. Okay. Who was that at the pinball machine? Long legs. Tight blue jeans and a soft, loose blouse. Curly dark hair fell almost to her waist. He couldn't see her face. He grabbed his Bud and walked over to the pinball machine. As he did, she lost her ball.

"Damn!" she swore, banging the top of the game with her fist. "I didn't get the highest score," she said to no one in particular.

He leaned on the Ms. Pac-Man game next to the pinball machine she was playing and watched her with amusement. "I'll play you. I have the second highest score on that machine," he bragged.

She turned to look at him. She was still pouting over her lost ball. His heart skipped a beat. She was almost ripe, still a girl, just moments away from being a woman. Minus the eye makeup she would be fabulous, he thought. Her lips were so pink and so full, he stared at them and his mouth ran dry.

"Okay, but I warn you. I'm good," she said slightly slurring her words and holding out her hand for him to give her coins for a new game. He laughed at her presumption, but reached into his pocket and pulled out a handful of change. She picked out two quarters and put them in the machine. His palm tingled when her soft fingers touched it. She had made no attempt to introduce herself, being more interested in playing pinball than in meeting him.

"Ladies first," he said, but she was already pulling the lever to play the first ball.

Michael was fascinated. Of course, he was 23 and this girl was way too young for him, but it was only a game of pinball. He watched her manipulate the flippers. She was pretty good. He hoped he could beat her. After three humiliating games for Michael, he wanted to stop playing. "Let's get a drink," he suggested.

"Can't stand to lose again?" she taunted. She smiled at him in a slightly condescending way, her eyes twinkling. He noticed that she had two deep dimples.

"I'm letting you win," he lied, and laughed at himself. He took her arm and guided her to where he was sitting at the end of the bar.

"Really?" she laughed at him, but allowed herself to be escorted to a bar stool with a dirty, red leather seat. Clara, never having been in a bar before, was amazed at all the tools the bartenders used to make drinks. She watched Jay, the bartender, pour liquor from exotic-looking bottles into shot glasses and stole a cherry from the plastic box containing sticky fruit and sour lemons. At the center of the bar was a row of beer taps. Michael was amused by her interest in these common things.

"Don't get out much?" he asked. Immediately, Clara's face changed. She frowned slightly. "It's okay," he said, smiling. He ordered another beer for himself and a Tequila Sunrise for her. She already felt more than a little giddy from the first one. She took a sip from the tiny cocktail straw and looked up at him as she did. She had just begun to realize her affect on men and, like a child with a new toy, she played him. He was amused but excited by her at the same time.

"What's your name?" he asked.

"Clara."

"I'm Michael."

"You really suck at pinball," she said with a smile, fixing her eyes on him. He looked over at Jay, who tipped his chin toward Clara and smiled. Michael tipped his chin back.

She finished her drink. "I need'a go see my friends." She pointed to the table of girls that now had a ring of young men standing around it. "Thanks for the drink, Michael." She touched his shoulder and he flinched. She laughed. He watched her walk over to the table and join the other girls, noting that she was greeted by warm hellos from the men.

"Jailbait, that one," said Jay.

"All of them," said Michael. "Don't you proof these girls? How are respectable men supposed to relax and just have a drink?" Michael laughed. "I should call the police."

"Ha, ha," said Jay.

At that point Michael's friends had finished playing pool and came over to chat with him. As the night wore on, he couldn't stop himself from looking over at Clara. He was never able to catch her eye. He wished she would play pinball again. While his friends talked of their day, he could hear her laughing in the background. Not being able to help himself, he glanced in her direction and saw her look up at one of the guys with the same alluring look she had given him earlier. Michael felt his cheeks grow hot.

Meanwhile, Clara was enjoying herself, flirting with the young men at the table, but for some reason she peeked over at Michael to see if he was still there. She knew that if she went over to play pinball, he would come to her. She thought he'd drive her home if she asked him. A rugged young man bought her another drink. Very drunk at this point, she suddenly felt as if she had had enough and tried to look at her watch, but the room was too dark.

"I'm gonna go home, Lin-na," she said abruptly to her friend, her words slurring into one big sound. Linda, equally as drunk, ignored Clara and laughed as one of the young men kissed her ear. Clara rose unsteadily and walked over to Michael. "Take me home," she demanded. Michael's friends howled with laughter as Michael quickly stood up. They slapped him on the back and hooted. "They're just jealous," she said. It came out "ja-wus." He laughed and put his arm around her to hold her up.

They walked outside into the parking lot to his red Mustang, and he helped her into the passenger seat. He ran around to the other side of the car and jumped in. After he put the key in the ignition, he looked over at her and saw that she was leaning back against the black leather seat with her eyes closed. Her lips were slightly parted, and he realized that she had passed out. He didn't know where she lived, and he didn't want to deliver her in this condition to her parents. With his luck, her father was a cop.

It was 11 p.m. according to the dashboard clock. Did she have to be home at midnight? He vaguely remembered midnight being the magic curfew hour. He decided to take her to his apartment and let her sleep for an hour. Driving through the quiet streets of Litchfield, she never moved. He parked his car in the lot in front of his apartment building and carried her up the stairs to the second floor. She was light, but her long legs kept hitting the wall and he hoped that snoopy Mrs. Stockwell, his neighbor, didn't see him carrying a drunken teenage girl into his apartment.

When he reached his door, he put her down, and then swung her over his shoulder so he could find his keys. Once inside, he put her on the couch and rolled up an old sweatshirt to put under her head as a pillow. She was totally unconscious. He felt kind of nervous, as if he were kidnapping her. If she had been five years older, it would have been different. He went into the kitchen to grab a beer. When he came back to the living room, he decided to watch television and wake her up in an hour to take her home. She was taking up the whole couch, so he lay down on the floor in front of her and turned on a rerun of *Seinfeld*.

Bored and stuck in his apartment, he turned around to look at the sleeping girl. He ran his finger down her cheek, noticing how rough his own skin looked next to hers. He wanted to wake her up. Without thinking, he leaned over and kissed her on the lips. She turned her head a little and a silky strand of hair fell across his hand. Rising up on his knees, he leaned down, breathing in her apple-scented shampoo. He kissed her again, this time with more force. He felt himself stirring, but since she did not respond, he turned abruptly, sat back down, and looked at the television.

Seinfeld segued into *Friends*. He watched the show as long as he could and then turned back to the girl. She opened her eyes and he rose up on his knees to look down at her. She stared up at him, her gaze looked unfocused. Bending down, he kissed her, forcing his tongue in her mouth, and his hands reached under her shirt before he could stop himself. She didn't scream or struggle, but lay lifeless, as he climbed on top of her. He took her silence as submission. When he rolled over on his side to unzip his jeans, and then hers, she kept her eyes closed, arms stiff at her sides. She didn't stop him, but she did nothing to help him, as he struggled to pull her tight pants off. The skin on her thighs was so soft, and the smell of her hair was so over-powering, that rational thought left him.

Clara didn't know what to do. Panic bubbled in her chest, draining her of the ability to move. At first, her Tequila-soaked brain tried to comprehend the dim light, the laugh track from the television, the unfamiliar smell of masculine sweat mixed with beer, and the freckles on the shoulder above her, gyrat-ing. Gradually, she became alert, her survival instinct kicking in, and she knew she needed to pull herself together, to get out of the apartment. She didn't know this man. What else would he do to her? He didn't seem hostile or angry, but he was very strong and heavy. She could feel the hard muscles in his arms, chest, and thighs crushing her. His body shuddered, and he moaned, his face buried in her neck. She suddenly felt like she couldn't breathe. Tears started to stream down her cheeks.

He picked up his head when he heard her sniffle. "It's okay, Clara," he said softly. "Did I hurt you?" She winced when he said her name, and looked at him with frightened eyes. Michael's gut twisted. "I'm sorry," he whispered, putting his fingertips on her cheek to hold her face where he could see it. When she didn't answer, he asked more urgently, "Are you okay?"

"My parents…are waiting for me." She choked on her words, and then, afraid he might take this as a threat, she added, "I won't tell them."

Thinking fast, he said, "No, they would be angry at you for getting so drunk. You shouldn't tell them."

She finally steadied her voice and said, "I want to get up." Michael rolled off her toward the inside of the old gray velour couch, pulling his jeans up to cover himself.

She sat up quickly. "Yes. Can I use the bathroom?" she asked, grabbing her pants and underwear, which had fallen on the floor. He pointed to the door across the room. She got up, naked from the waist down, and walked to the bathroom.

Michael put his head down on the old sweatshirt he had made into a pillow for Clara and closed his eyes. *Shit. This could mean all kinds of trouble.*

In the small, dark bathroom that smelled like sour towels, Clara collapsed onto the toilet. She urinated and tried to wipe away the mess between her legs. Then, she hurriedly pulled on her underwear and her jeans. As she did, her cell phone fell out of the pocket, and she saw that it had run out of power. Taking some toilet paper and wetting it, she tried to fix her smudged eye makeup. As she ran her fingers through her hair to smooth it, she thought of her mother, who would be waiting up for her. She wanted to seek comfort in her mother's arms, but quickly realized she could never tell her mother the truth. It would be the crushing blow. Her mother wouldn't be able to endure it. Both of her children ruined. No, Clara had always been invisible, and what had happened here tonight would not change that.

When she was done, she came hesitantly out of the bathroom. "Can we go now?" she asked awkwardly, standing in front of the man. Gone was the bravado and confident attitude he had seen in the bar. She looked vulnerable and frail.

"Sure. Let's go," he said, using the remote to turn off the television and getting up from the couch. He took a step toward her to comfort her, but a flicker of fear crossed her face and he thought it was better to just get going. They left the apartment and got into his car. Once they were out of the parking lot, he asked tentatively, "Are you okay?"

She sensed he needed reassurance of some kind, so she said, "Yes. I'm okay," and gave him directions to her house in Sunken Meadow, an exclusive area of town. Ten minutes later, they pulled up in front of a white six-bedroom house with a three-car garage. Lights were on at the front door and glowed through the large front windows. Fancy landscaping ran across the front of the house and down the side yard to a high wrought-iron fence. Michael heard himself swallow hard. He was a carpenter who lived in a tiny apartment.

"Listen, you had birth control, right?" he asked.

"No," she said.

*T*wo

❧

*F*ather Thomas O'Malley wished he could jog in shorts, but he didn't think that would send the right message to his parishioners. With a sigh, he pulled his maroon sweatpants with "Harvard Divinity" emblazoned up one side onto his long, muscular legs and tucked his thick, curly hair under a visor from last year's youth mission. He liked to start every day with a five-mile jog, early in the morning, in Town Hall Park.

Father O'Malley exited St. Raymond's rectory into the bright sunshine of the June morning. He breathed in deeply, smelling the intoxicating scent of the honeysuckle that grew all over the church grounds. He jogged down the small hill to the sidewalk and turned right to run down Grant Avenue, the main thoroughfare in town, passing small mom-and-pop shops, restaurants, the town diner, the library, and the firehouse. On the other side of the street were the train tracks, which cut the town in two. At the far end of the avenue was Town Hall Park, ten acres of wooded grounds, tennis courts, soccer fields, playgrounds, and a bandstand. In the southeast corner of the park stood the Litchfield Town Hall, surrounded by a black wrought-iron fence.

Mayor Antonio Ceravolo arrived at the office each morning at approximately 7:00. Glancing at his watch, Father O'Malley rounded the turn in the jogging path, and saw Town Hall with its white clapboard steeple rising out of the trees up ahead. 6:45. He had this mental game he played every morning: Would he run by Town Hall before Mayor Ceravolo bounded out of his shiny sedan? *Didn't win today.* As he came up to the fence, he saw the mayor helping someone out of the car. Father O'Malley squinted to see who it was. One shapely leg, with pump, emerged from the black car, and then another, before Patricia Castellano, the mayor's sister, lifted her face to smile up at her big brother.

"Damn," swore Father O'Malley under his breath, but before he could turn around and run in the other direction, she had spotted him.

"Father," she called, as she waved her manicured hand. "Good morning! How are you? Come have tea with us." Mayor Ceravolo turned, still holding his sister's other hand. His face stiffened when he saw the priest.

Father O'Malley took that as his cue to beg off. "Good morning, Patricia, Mayor Ceravolo. I'm sorry. I have the Sweeney funeral at ten. I have to get back to the church to see that everything is in order," he called. "Another time." He smiled, but did not wait for a response, continuing to jog past the driveway that led up to Town Hall.

Why was Patricia with the mayor? Father O'Malley pondered this as he continued his run around the park. Were they discussing the demonstration? He hoped not. It was getting too big, too fast. They were siblings, so maybe they were just having breakfast to discuss family things, or maybe she was spearheading another committee, or hosting a fundraising dinner. Father O'Malley shook his head and tried not to think about Patricia. Patricia—and all of her plans—as he continued his loop around the park.

$\mathcal{T}$ H R E E

$\mathcal{O}$

$\mathcal{P}$ia Fernandez woke from a fitful sleep, turned her head to the other side of the bed, and was relieved to see that Eduardo, her husband, wasn't there. She took a deep breath, feeling the oxygen waken her brain, and took a moment to enjoy the silence. She lay very still, listening, but she heard no movement in the house and prayed that he had already left. But why did he leave so early without waking her? It gave her an unsettled feeling as she got up and went into the adjoining bathroom to shower. The hot water raining down on her back felt good.

She got out of the shower and started to comb her hair. Trying to look in the mirror, she found her face partially obscured by the fog from the hot water. She took her towel, wiped a spot clean, and studied her face. Her fingers went automatically to the reddish-purple bruise on her cheekbone. Her eyes traveled down to her arms, where five grape-size marks wrapped around both of her upper arms. *Presents from her loving husband.* After having this thought, she was seized with panic. What if he knew she was being insolent? *Pia, get a grip. He's not in your mind.* Shrugging, she took the towel and wiped the rest of the mist from the mirror. Where was her makeup bag? She glanced at the clock. She still had a few minutes before she had to wake the girls. Cover-up, foundation, powder. She lined them up in front of her. She bought these products like other women bought milk. They were always on her shopping list. In the summertime it was worse. But the marks on her arms were high up this time. She went to her dresser and pulled out a T-shirt with sleeves to the elbow.

Then, after returning to the bathroom, she quickly and expertly covered her bruised cheek. She sighed as she returned the makeup to the cosmetics bag, and left the bathroom without giving herself another glance. Pia's mind flipped through the various places that Eduardo could be as she walked down the hall to wake up Maria, 15, and Carmen, 9, who shared a bedroom. Carmen had insisted on moving into the extra twin bed in Maria's room last year. She said "sounds scare me in the night."

"Time to get up, sweetie," Pia said, as she gently touched Maria's shoulder. Maria opened her eyes and Pia smiled down at her older daughter. When Pia looked at Maria she always felt like she was looking at a younger version of herself. An undamaged version. She turned and roused Carmen, who was also dark and had Pia's heart-shaped face.

Confident the girls were awake and wouldn't fall back to sleep, Pia went downstairs to start breakfast. Coffee, orange juice—no pulp—Cheerios, milk, two ripe bananas. Pia put two pieces of whole wheat toast in the toaster for herself. It was the only breakfast she could keep down. She was getting silverware out of the drawer when Maria straggled into the kitchen, looking glum, the hood of her dark-blue sweatshirt pulled up over her head, and just a hint of short shorts showing underneath. Mother and daughter exchanged a look before they heard Carmen bounding down the stairs, and then they watched her skip into the bright-yellow kitchen. Carmen ran over and hugged her mother, and then sat down, poured herself a heaping bowl of Cheerios, grabbed a banana, and started eating with relish. One bite of banana. One spoon of Cheerios.

"Maria, it's a little warm this morning for your hood," Pia said, as she carried her dry toast to the table and sat on the bench in front of the window with Carmen.

Maria was intently moving her Cheerios from one side of the bowl to the other. "Is it?" She asked with an edge.

Pia studied Maria with pain in her eyes. "Yes, look, the sun is shining. It's beautiful," she said, pulling the curtain back to look out.

"How do you do it?" Maria asked suddenly, her eyes flashing.

"Maria, let's not get into it," Pia said firmly.

"Get into what?" asked Carmen.

"Nothing," Pia said quickly.

"Right, nothing," echoed Maria.

At 15, Maria was quickly becoming a woman. She was smart and quick, and Pia knew that Maria had noticed her mother's black-and-blue marks, and her father's temper. Pia had noticed something even worse than her own bruises. She had watched from the darkened doorway to the family room last weekend, as Eduardo had taken off his dirty socks, thrown them on the floor, and then called Maria and told her to come and pick them up.

"Maria, clean up the mess in here," he had called to her, with a bottle of Corona in his hand. Then he had laid his head back against the couch and watched his daughter bend down to pick up his soiled socks.

The thought of it made Pia sick. To wash the image out of her mind, she said, "You have dance today, Carmen. Do you have your dance bag?" As she looked at her younger daughter for an answer, they heard a car door slam, and footsteps on the gravel in the driveway. Pia and Maria grew still.

"It's upstairs. I'll go get it," said Carmen, who jumped up and sashayed out of the kitchen.

"Where was he this morning?" whispered Maria.

Pia just shook her head and silently mouthed, "I don't know." They listened to the sound of the footsteps growing louder.

"Maria, go and help your sister."

"No," said Maria calmly. "I'm not leaving you alone with him. If you think I don't know what's under..." As she spoke, the door flew open and Eduardo stomped in, wearing his heavy boots. When he saw Pia sitting with Maria, he stopped and looked at them. Then he smiled. A twisted, taut grimace.

"Okay then, Maria," he said with a dark and ominous tone, "take out the fucking garbage," emphasizing the last two words. "Earn your keep around here, you lazy..."

"Eduardo. Leave her alone. Maria, do as he says and then go help Carmen." Pia stood up, placing herself between her husband and her daughter. "Eduardo. Where were you? Do you want..."

"Shut up!" he said, as he walked through the kitchen to the stairs.

"Hurry, Maria. Just do as he says, then get Carmen and go outside and wait for the bus." Maria gave her mother a disgusted look, but went over to the garbage can and started to pull the plastic bag out of the container. It was full and she had to work it back and forth to get it free from the can. Pia went over to help her, wondering where Eduardo was. She hoped he wasn't with Carmen. Filled with fear, she used all her strength to pull the bag free, handed it to Maria, and went into the living room to look up the stairs.

On the landing at the top of the stairs, she saw Eduardo, stroking Carmen's face and looking down at her like he was the most adoring father. "I only stay here for you, *mi amor*. Your mother does not love me, and I would leave if it wasn't for you. Do you want me to leave, *mi amor*?" Pia heard him ask.

Pia watched them and remembered that when she and Eduardo first met he had called her *mi amor*. That was long before Carmen was born and the beatings had started. During the night it was the worst. If Eduardo was woken by the baby's cries he would get furious. First, he would yell at Pia. "Shut that fucking kid up!" The sound of his angry voice would make the frightened baby scream louder until she passed out from exhaustion. Then Eduardo would be aroused. He would want Pia to have passionate sex with him. If Pia didn't live up to his increasingly violent fantasies, he would slap her. Over the next year, his open hand closed into a fist. This became a pattern, and Pia wanted to take her babies and run away, but she was afraid of Eduardo tracking her down and hurting the girls. She had no money of her own and nowhere to go.

"Carmen, the bus is coming. It's time to leave." There was a quaver in Pia's voice. Eduardo looked down the stairs at his wife. He still held Carmen by the shoulder. The small girl looked like she was about to cry. "Eduardo, let her go!" Pia yelled. Eduardo checked himself and let the girl go. "Come. Carmen. I'll take you in the car," said Pia, holding out her arms for the girl to come to her. Carmen hesitated, looking from parent to parent, but then came down the stairs to her mother.

"Come right back, Pia," snarled Eduardo. Each word inflicted a staccato blow on Pia's back as she hurried Carmen toward the back door.

That night, as Pia lay in bed nursing new wounds, she knew what she had to do. She would make the appointment in the morning.

$\mathcal{F}$OUR

જ

$\mathcal{C}$lara Mahoney parked her bicycle at the bike stand at the pharmacy in Wheatley, the next town over from Litchfield. She pulled her hair into a high ponytail with a Scrunchie, letting the air cool the back of her neck. She entered the pharmacy and went first to the magazine stand and reached out for the first glossy cover. *Glamour.* She tucked it under her arm and started to read the signs at the top of every aisle. Deodorants. Greeting Cards. Feminine Products. Feeling like a criminal, she walked down the feminine-products aisle, looking for the pregnancy tests. Using her peripheral vision as best she could, she scanned the boxes and tubes. There. Two entire shelves. She looked up and down the aisle to make sure she was alone, before she reached out and picked up the first box. Not able to understand the directions, she put the box back. She read another and another until she found a simple one in a pink box. Plus sign for pregnant. Minus sign for relief. Tucking it under the issue of *Glamour,* she went to wait in line. In front of her was a young mother with a baby and a little girl. Clara looked at the baby, who raised her little arms, giving off whiffs of baby shampoo and talcum powder. Clara grimaced at the child, and the baby frowned.

The young mother shifted the baby from hip to hip to get to her purse. The child pulled on her mother's hair, forcing the woman to sit the baby on the counter to disengage the small fingers from her curls. All the time, the baby gurgled and drooled, staring at Clara. Finally, the mother handed her debit card to the cashier, who completed the transaction. The woman grabbed her package, picked up the baby, reached down for the little girl's hand, and moved out of the line. Clara quickly put the box, with its protective covering of *Glamour,* on the counter. Although the air conditioning was on high, she started to sweat. The ancient cashier, every movement accompanied by a groan and then a rest, pushed her rimless glasses up on her nose and reached out for the magazine and picked it up. Clara could hear the people piling up behind her: men's voices, women's voices, a crying baby. She could feel her heartbeat in her ears. *Swush, swush, swush.* The cashier looked at the cover of *Glamour,* leaving the pregnancy test exposed on the counter. Clara fought the urge to turn around and see if she knew anyone in line. After ringing up the magazine, the cashier licked her arthritic fingers to separate the plastic bags and slid the magazine into the top one. She picked up the pregnancy test and began to search each side for the bar code. Clara bit her lower lip to keep from screaming.

"That'll be $22.99," said the cashier. Clara held out two twenties that were wilted and slick with perspiration. The cashier peered over her glasses, looked at the money, and then looked up at Clara. In the instant that their eyes met, Clara felt that the cashier was judging her. She waited for her change, scooped up the plastic bag, stuck it in her backpack, and quickly exited the store.

Keeping her head down, she jogged over to the bike rack and pulled out her bike. As she threw her leg over the seat, she looked down at her crotch, hoping to see a red stain. She was two weeks late. She was sure that she had had her period the day of the last unit test in math. She had never been late before. No stain. She got on the bike and started the long ride home.

Taking the back roads on her return to Litchfield, she started to think about her family. She loved her mother so much. Her sweet, sad mother who was so overwhelmed by her oldest daughter's problems that she might have a nervous breakdown if Clara told her the truth about her own problem. She didn't want to cause her mother any more pain than the constant turmoil that a severely autistic child causes to the entire family. Clara had gotten herself into this mess and she would not add to her mother's burden. While her mother was the center of the household, Clara's father lived in the shadows of the family. A workaholic who came home late, ate something, and headed into his home office. His "man cave," her mother called it. When Clara was younger, he would spend time with her on Saturdays, but that had stopped when she was nine or ten. Now, he gave her money and had taken her to get her driver's permit but had not suggested they go out on the road together.

The year that Clara was born, Agnes had been diagnosed with severe autism. Agnes was three at the time. The only life that Clara knew was one in which Agnes and her problems came first. Clara's earliest memories were of Agnes down on all fours, banging her head on the floor and groaning. Any time the family had to do something or go somewhere, Agnes would throw a temper tantrum. Now, at 19, it was clear that Agnes would never be any better. Clara's father and mother were constantly fighting about how to handle Agnes.

From a very early age, Clara had learned to take care of herself. She never ran to her parents when she fell off her bicycle, needed help with homework, or wanted advice when she had a spat with a friend. They never provided her with any unsolicited advice, either. She never gave them any cause for concern, she never got into trouble at school, she always got good grades, she had friends. She was a model daughter. Or, so her parents thought. She knew that there was no room in their lives for her little problems, so now that she had a potentially life-altering problem, she knew she had to take care of it without their help. She just didn't want them to find out. She wanted to be the daughter without problems.

Clara's relationship with her older sister was complex. She felt love, fear, jealousy, sadness, and anger. The house was always tense. They were always waiting for something bad to happen. Clara's ears were always on alert. Always waiting for Agnes' tirades to start. Banging. Scuffling. Jumping. Flapping. Her mother pleading. Her father yelling.

There were a few happy moments. Dessert time was Clara's favorite time. Scenes from the night before floated into Clara's mind as she pedaled. *Agnes sat at the kitchen table waiting for Clara to get the pudding out of the fridge, sitting still as Clara heaped huge scoops of chocolate pudding into their favorite bowls. Agnes grinning as Clara broke a banana off the bunch and clapping as Clara sliced the banana, placing the pieces in rings on top of the pudding. Agnes, who rarely made eye contact, looked up at Clara then, with excitement in her eyes. Clara smiled. Agnes smiled. Clara laughed and looked at her mother—whose eyes were brimming with tears—and for that moment, everything was okay. They were almost normal.*

Back into Litchfield, Clara rode by Town Hall Park. Pedaling faster and faster, she just wanted to get home and go upstairs to the bathroom and lock the door. As she rounded the corner, she saw her mother's van in the driveway. She and Agnes would probably be in the backyard. Clara decided to go in the front door. Leaving her bike in a heap on the side of the house, she cautiously walked to the front door, turned her key soundlessly, and entered the cool foyer. Hearing nothing, she bounded up the stairs and into the hall bathroom, quietly pushing the lock. She leaned on the door and closed her eyes for a minute to steady herself, then took the test out of her backpack.

Her hands shook as she read the directions. "Point absorbent tip downward in urine stream for 5 seconds ONLY. Wait two minutes. A blue line will appear in the control window indicating the test has worked." Clara heard the tantrum start as she pulled her shorts and panties down. She continued reading, "A "+" in the result window indicates a positive result." At least her mother wouldn't come looking for her.

Okay. Here goes. Maybe she was wrong. Maybe she could breathe easy in two minutes. Suddenly, her stomach lurched and she felt the need to vomit. Just nerves, she tried to tell herself. She sat on the toilet. When she looked down to position the wand, her long hair, which was all disheveled, half out of the Scrunchie, fell in front of her face and blocked her view. She stood up to fix it. She had started to sweat. She pulled off her T-shirt for air and looked down at her full breasts, bursting out of her Maidenform bra. Panic ripped through her chest and constricted her throat. She started to hyperventilate and reached out to the counter to steady herself. Her symptoms were unmistakable but just to be sure, Clara sat down on the toilet and peed on the wand. Taking action seemed to calm her as she watched the "+" form in the window of the wand. She straightened her shoulders and took a deep breath. Determination pushed fear out of her mind, and she knew what she had to do, and she knew she needed his help. There was no one else.

F I V E

*P*atricia Castellano's new ebony Jaguar XKR Coupe
gleamed in the bright sunshine as she pulled up across
the street from her office, above the diner in downtown
Litchfield. She just had time to fix her lipstick before her interview with Channel 6. Patricia loved nothing more than seeing
herself on television. A close second was seeing her photograph
in the newspaper. As she slammed the car door and hurried
across the street, Lee Laquess and Simon Wong peered down
from the office window and watched their boss arriving, her
hips swaying in her usual exaggerated manner as she teetered
on her stiletto heels. She would be there in a matter of minutes.
They gave each other a look to fortify themselves and then went
quickly to their desks. Lee, Patricia's publicist, picked up the
phone, although it did not ring, and Simon, her assistant, put
on his glasses and turned to page 34 of the latest Guttmacher
Institute report on abortion rates in New Jersey.

Patricia had three employees at Stand Up for Life. Lee was
a 24-year-old college dropout, who was nonetheless a gifted
writer. Simon, a Chinese-American graduate of community

college, was smart but unmotivated. Although Patricia had no idea, the two men were lovers and were secretly horrified by what her organization stood for. Their fear and loathing of Patricia bonded them together even more than their intimate relationship. The third employee was Sandra Stett, a southern transplant, whom Patricia had met at a book club meeting. Sandra shared her pro-life views and was an experienced fundraiser.

As Lee and Simon sat, waiting to begin their fake tasks, they could hear Patricia's voice talking into her cell phone. As the door swung open, she filled the doorway with her big hair, big breasts, and big jewels. Without a pause in her conversation or a nod to either Lee or Simon, she went directly to the mirror over the credenza in the waiting room and smoothed a ruffled bang, righted an earring, and checked her teeth for lipstick. When she was perfect, she walked over to Simon's desk and, without making eye contact, extended her hand to Simon for her mail. As he reached up with the file, she changed her mind and walked away. Simon stuck his tongue out at her back and Lee gulped back a giggle.

"Helen, honey, I just want to bring you up to speed," she continued. "I like to talk in person. The phone is so cold." Pause. "Well, we can meet here, at my office, or we can have lunch at Chez Cecile," she said with a perfect French accent. "They do a *crepe poulet avec haricots verts* that I just know you would adore. *C'est magnifique!*"

Lee got up and went over to stand next to Patricia and tapped his finger on his wristwatch. The Channel 6 reporter would be there any minute.

"Noon tomorrow?" As she listened to Helen's response, Patricia gave Lee a wicked look, squinting her bright-brown eyes and puffing out her chest. With one defiant forefinger to his watch, he went defeated back to his desk.

"Fabulous. I'll see you tomorrow. *Ciao.*" She clicked her phone shut with such force that both young men jumped.

Throwing the phone on Lee's desk, she snapped, "Do *not* ever interrupt me when I am on the phone. Do you understand?"

"I just…" stammered Lee.

"I *do not care*. Do you think that I do *not* know what time it is? Do you think that I need *you* to keep time for me?" she roared at Lee, who couldn't muster the courage to reply. Patricia sucked air in through her nose, closed her eyes to calm herself, smoothed her skirt, and went into her office.

Simon silently mouthed the words, "Are you out of your mind?"

Lee just stared at Simon with pursed lips.

At exactly 10 a.m., DeShawn Fletcher, the New Jersey reporter from Channel 6, opened the door and took a look around the peach-colored waiting room. Patricia had redone the dingy space when she had started the organization five years before. Pastel paint, soft lighting, and oriental carpets. Fresh flowers were delivered daily and came with cards signed "Love, Salvatore." Salvatore and Patricia had been married for ten years, and their wealth, stock, bonus, and options from Goldman Sachs seemed to make them both happy. "Hey Lee," DeShawn said with a big, friendly grin as he held the door for his cameraman. "How ya doing, man? You look a little sick."

Lee shook himself and found the inner strength to do his job. "No, no. How are you, DeShawn? Just ate too much. I have to stop going to the diner on my way up." He reached out to shake hands with DeShawn. "You remember Simon?"

"Simon, hey, sure. How ya doing, Simon? And this is Joe, my cameraman." With hellos all around, Lee looked over at Patricia's closed door. Experience had taught him that she would emerge from behind the closed door as the most gracious woman known to mankind. The blazing brown eyes would be soft and inviting, the perfectly outlined snare and bared teeth would be set in the most dazzling smile, and the rasp of her tantrum would be replaced by a soft, melodious voice. He told DeShawn to wait, summoned his courage, and went to knock on Patricia's door.

But, as he walked with trepidation toward the inner sanctum, the door swung open and Patricia burst forth in a cloud of perfume and hair spray. "DeShawn!" she exclaimed, holding out her hand in a welcoming gesture. Lee and Simon exchanged a knowing look as Patricia started to work her magic on the reporter.

"DeShawn, you handsome man," she crooned. "Have you been working out?" Patricia reached out and gently squeezed the biceps of DeShawn's left arm and opened her eyes wide with approval, turning her head to the side and nodding. If black men could blush, DeShawn would have been pink.

"You are a bad woman," said DeShawn, looking down and shaking his head.

"Where are we set up, Lee?" asked Patricia, turning her sweetest smile in his direction.

"I thought we would do it in the blue room to offset your jacket," Lee stammered, pointing the way with a very limp wrist.

Patricia arched one eyebrow at Lee. "The blue room would be perfect. Will you be shooting B roll?" she asked, as she hooked her arm through DeShawn's and started toward the inner office.

"Joe, are we shooting B roll?" DeShawn asked his cameraman.

"Of course, why would you worry your handsome head over technicalities?" Patricia asked DeShawn. "Joe, you really need to get DeShawn on reaction. Your viewers need to see this man!"

"I think you should sit in the Queen Anne, and DeShawn in the ladder-back," opined Lee, as they stood in the blue room determining how to set up the interview. Another lift of Patricia's brow and Lee silently motioned zipping his lips and went into the front office, where Simon patted him on the shoulder.

"So, I'll open with a broad question and we'll take it from there. Okay?" asked DeShawn, trying to look comfortable in the chair, which was clearly too small for his long limbs.

"That sounds fabulous. Give me a minute. Lee, where are you? My hand mirror," she demanded. Lee ran in with the desired item. "How am I?" Patricia looked at Lee for his appraisal.

"Almost perfect," ventured Lee. "Smooth that bang," he pointed.

"Yes. Is my jacket riding up?"

"Sit on the back," said Lee. Patricia pulled the back of her jacket down under her bottom, leaned in slightly to DeShawn, and lifted her chin.

"I'm ready any time you are, Mr. Fletcher," she said with a professional air, handing the mirror back to Lee. Joe had positioned his tripod behind DeShawn.

"And we are rolling," said Joe.

"This is DeShawn Fletcher, News 6, and I'm here now with Mrs. Patricia Castellano, Executive Director of Stand Up for Life, in downtown Litchfield, New Jersey. Good morning, Mrs. Castellano. So, your organization will be celebrating its fifth anniversary soon. Please tell our viewers about it."

"Good morning, Mr. Fletcher, and thank you for coming over. We, at Stand Up for Life, will be celebrating an important anniversary later this month. Five years ago, after my twins were born, Salvatore, my husband, and I started this nonprofit organization to speak out about the sanctity of life." Here Patricia paused, looked straight into the camera, and gave the viewers a chance to admire her angelic commitment. "We believe that every baby, every senior, and all of us in-between have a right to live our God-given life. No one but God himself should make the decision to end a life. We have partnered with St. Raymond's Church here in Litchfield to speak out for the unborn." As Patricia spoke into the camera, DeShawn nodded, hanging on every word.

"How will you be celebrating the organization's anniversary?" asked DeShawn.

"Mr. Fletcher, I'm glad you asked, because I want everyone in Litchfield to know that out on Route 54, at the edge of

Country Club Road, there is an operating abortion clinic, and we want to reach the women who are right now considering using those services. We are planning to be on site outside the clinic on Saturday, June thirtieth, to expose what goes on behind the clinic's doors. We feel that it's time to speak out more openly about what's going on right here in town."

"So, you will be demonstrating in front of the clinic? What time do you plan to start? And who will be with you?" asked DeShawn.

"I don't really want to say we're demonstrating. I want to say we will be educating the community that morning. We will begin gathering at 9:00. We want to spread the word in an effort to save innocent human lives. The protection of life is fundamental to the common good. We will be led by Father Thomas O'Malley of St. Raymond's, and I want to invite the entire Litchfield community to come and hear this important message."

"What are the top two factoids, if you will, that you would like our viewers to know, Mrs. Castellano?"

"The number one thing that I want the people of Litchfield to know is that New Jersey has the second-highest abortion rate in the nation among underage girls. These girls are babies themselves, who cannot make these life-changing decisions alone. People should know that there are no parental consent restrictions in New Jersey. And secondly, people should understand that abortion kills children. We don't like to think of it in those terms, but that is essentially what it does. I want people to think about that."

"Interesting. Well, I want to thank you, Mrs. Castellano, for your time."

"The pleasure is mine," smiled Patricia.

"And, it's a wrap," said Joe. "Stay where you are, both of you, and smile at each other for B roll. Now, look serious. Fletch, shake your head. Now nod. And we're done."

"Perfect on the first take," said DeShawn, looking at Patricia with admiration.

"I don't want to waste your time," said Patricia, standing up and offering her hand to DeShawn. As soon as the camera was switched off, she had changed again into a businesswoman eager to get back to work. "Lee will see you out and give you additional information. Thank you for coming."

S I X

❦

*M*ichael couldn't get Clara out of his mind. He thought about going to her house and knocking on the door. *"Yes? Are you here to fertilize the lawn?"* Michael could hear her father saying. He did drive by more than once, hoping she would be outside, and when he went to The Sportsman, he always hoped she would turn up. Weeks passed, and still, he wanted to see her. The memory of her made him feel nervous and excited at the same time.

Then, one weekday night, when he walked into the bar, there she was. He quickly scanned the room for her pack of friends, but she was alone. She had come to see him. He could feel it. As he walked down the bar to where she sat, she watched him coming toward her, and he saw fear and pain in her eyes. What was she doing here? When he reached her, he sat down on the stool next to her. She turned her head and looked straight ahead.

"Hi," he said cautiously.

She closed her eyes, gathering her thoughts, and then looked directly at him. Gone was the wild eye shadow. Without it she looked very young and vulnerable. Gone was the confident attitude. "I need to talk to you," she said, her voice sounding shaky.

Noticing that Michael had come in, Jay, the bartender, came over to give him a beer.

"Hey, this Bud's for you," Jay smiled. "She's been waiting for you. Haven't you, babe?"

She tried to smile at Jay. "Can we go outside?" she asked, looking at Michael.

"I'll be back for the Bud," Michael said to Jay, as he followed Clara out of the bar. They walked out into the sandy parking lot and he headed toward his Mustang.

"Do you want to sit in the car?" he offered.

"No," she said, looking down and touching a rock in the dirt with her sneaker.

He leaned against the Mustang, crossing his muscular arms over his chest, and ventured, "How've ya been?"

"I'm pregnant," she stated flatly, staring down at her sneakers. He noticed her lips trembling.

Michael felt his whole body tense up. He started to sweat and reached up to push his thick hair off his brow. "It's mine?"

As if he had hit her, she reached out to the car to steady herself. "Yes."

He believed her. She started to cry, covering her face with her hands. Her thin shoulders convulsed with her sobs. He wanted to comfort her. "We'll take care of it," he said and reached over and put his hand on her shoulder and then smoothed her hair. This made her cry harder. He tried to calculate how long it had been since they met in the bar.

"I can't let my parents find out. They have enough problems. It would kill my mother. I don't want a baby. I can't take care of a baby. I'm only sixteen. I go to high school. I don't even drive yet. I had to walk here," she cried. Her nose was running and she wiped it on the back of her hand.

Michael tried to pull her toward him to hug her, but she stiffened her spine and leaned away from him. His eyes darted to the road. He was afraid someone would see them like this in the parking lot.

"I'm glad you came to me. We're going to fix this," he said. "Don't worry. I'll pay for everything. We'll go to the clinic." She looked at him and his face looked genuinely concerned. His black eyes looked pained and he was chewing on the inside of his mouth. He tried to smile at her to let her know everything would be all right. She noticed that his teeth were crooked.

"I'm really scared," she murmured. Her beautiful pink lips were pulled down in the saddest frown Michael had ever seen. Tears flowed down her smooth cheeks. Her long dark eyelashes were clumped together in little cones.

"I know. I'll call and find out what to do. Don't worry. We'll take care of this. No one will know. Okay?" He looked over at her and her chin fell to her chest. She started to cry, deep throaty wails. He felt terrible. He went and opened the back door of the car, fumbled around in the garbage on the floor, found an unused McDonald's napkin, and brought it to her. He never wanted to hurt her. Plus, if her parents found out, they could press charges. They needed to fix this. For her and for him.

They leaned on the car until finally, she had no more tears.

"Do you want to go to my apartment to wash your face?"

"No," she told him firmly. A look of panic flickered across her face.

"Do you want to go home?" Michael didn't want her to go back in the bar. He wanted some time to think.

"Take me to my friend Linda's house. She lives on South Drive."

"Okay."

She had to sweep a pile of garbage off the passenger seat to get into the car. The smell of old French fries made her queasy as they headed into town. As he drove to South Drive the houses got bigger and bigger and the lawns greener and greener. Michael wondered why these girls had ended up in

The Sportsman that night. Why would girls who live in fancy houses with fathers who wore suits go to The Sportsman to hang out with guys like him? He wanted to ask Clara that question, but when he turned to look at her, he snapped back to reality. Her eyes were swollen from crying and her lips quivered as she tried to gain control of herself.

He wondered why she didn't turn him in. Why she didn't cry rape and accuse him. It was his fault. Wasn't it? She was sleeping and he should have left her alone. He was glad she said she couldn't go to her parents. He would take care of her and no one had to know.

"How are you feeling? Physically, I mean…," he asked.

"Sick. I throw up all the time. I have morning and night sickness. It sucks," she said accusingly.

"Well, it'll only be a week or so. Do you think you can make it?"

"What choice do I have?" she turned to look at him and their eyes met. He wanted to tell her how sorry he was. He wanted to explain to her that he hadn't meant to hurt her. He wanted to protect her even though he knew he was the one who had done this to her.

She rode through the streets in his car knowing that for now she was dependent on this man. At the same time that she had to protect herself from him, she also had to make him want to help her. She needed his money, and she needed him to take her to the clinic. It was a hard line to walk. She wanted to scream at him. To blame him for what he had done. She hated and feared him, but she needed him. Who else would help her? She dreaded the time she had to spend with him, but her fear of her parents finding out she was pregnant was so great that when she thought of it she shuddered. She literally shook with fear. She had to keep him on a string until this was over.

Michael pulled over in front of the large house that Clara pointed to, and he took in the size of the property, the three cars parked in the driveway, and the ADT home-security sign meant to keep people like him at bay. All of these signs of money and power made him jittery. He was more comfortable in surroundings that he understood, like The Sportsman and the Green Street Apartments.

"I'll find out what we need to do," he said, pushing a stray curl back from her eye. "Okay, little girl?"

Clara winced at this endearment, but quickly closed her eyes and tried to center herself. *Be nice*, she told herself, *you need him.* "Yes. Let me know what you find out. Here's my cell number," she said, and waited for him to get his cell phone out of his black jeans.

After she gave him the number and he typed it into his phone, she tried to manage a weak smile as she got out of the car. "See you," she said.

"Everything will be okay. You'll see," he said, as she walked away.

S E V E N

$\sim$

$\mathcal{B}$oth Loren and Peter Elliot couldn't wait to get home to tell each other their news. Not because either of them had good news, but because after 23 years of marriage they were used to discussing things with each other. Loren and Peter seemed to be cut of the same cloth. Their friends always told them how compatible they were, and it was true. Nine times out of ten they saw things the same way. Now, driving home, Loren was not quite sure how Peter was going to take this news. She was 43 years old. He was 47. How did this happen?

Peter left the parking lot of Litchfield High School, where he had taught for 20 years. He felt like he was in shock. He couldn't really concentrate on driving. Maybe he should pull over and call Loren. No. She would be driving now and she didn't like to talk and drive. He couldn't believe that he had been RIFed. RIFed. What a horrible-sounding word. The teachers all said RIFed for "reduction in force," and it meant that even though he had tenure, if the school district needed to make cuts in the budget, they could cut a whole program, and teachers with tenure could be let go. Peter taught Mandarin

Chinese and next year it would not be offered. His job. His family's health insurance. Gone. Teachers were being RIFed and programs were being cut all over the state. Where would he find another job? What could he do besides teach? Translate? What would Loren say? Maybe the paper would take her on full-time instead of freelancing. He needed to get home.

Across town, Loren was thinking about how much things had changed since Marshall and Emily had been babies. One young freelancer at *The Press* ordered all her diapers and formula online. That would make things easier. Loren thought about that young mother and then looked at her reflection in the rearview mirror. There were only a few streaks of gray in her auburn hair, and the freckles across her nose gave her face a youthful look, but, still, she felt too old to be a new mother. Marshall was 22 years old. People would think that she was the baby's grandmother when they all went to the park together. When the baby was five, starting kindergarten, she would be 48. Peter would be 65 when the kid went off to college. Jesus, how had this happened? She always used that messy diaphragm. What would Peter say? Would he want another baby?

While Loren thought of diapers and kindergarten, Peter was wondering how they would continue to pay two college tuitions for Marshall and Emily next year. With financial aid and scholarships they didn't pay the full freight, but now Peter didn't even know if he could put together the money to keep them both in school. Marshall would be a senior at New York University, and Emily a sophomore at The College of New Jersey. Marshall had started talking about graduate school and Peter had told him to look into a fellowship or a loan. Now he couldn't even guarantee that Marshall could finish his undergraduate degree. Emily had been chafing at the bit to take a year off and travel. Maybe now she would have to take a year off and work.

Loren turned left off of Grant Avenue and headed south on Woods Avenue to the development of modest homes called

Sterling Heights. She and Peter had bought their three-bed-room split-level starter home 20 years ago, but had never been able to save enough to move up and out. As she pulled her tiny Honda Civic into their driveway, her stomach lurched and she felt the primordial urge to throw up. She winced.

Peter continued home as if on remote control. How could they discontinue Mandarin when the Chinese were going to rule the world in the future? Wasn't that short-sighted? Why teach Italian? The Italians were not going to rule the world. Rome had its chance. French? No way. Spanish? Well, they would all be speaking Spanish soon. Loren would be support-ive. He was sure. That was the only thought that kept him go-ing. He just wanted to get home to Loren.

Loren sat in the car for a minute, collecting her thoughts. Looking up at their house with the white shutters, she mentally noted that it needed a paint job. She turned off the car and sat, amazed by the fact that her body could still produce enough progesterone to make her want to throw up. *Must be having a boy.* She heard tires scraping the pavement behind her and looked in the rearview mirror to see Peter's black Kia pulling into the driveway. She felt kind of excited to tell him.

They both got out of their cars at the same time. Loren had a half-smile on her face as she turned to Peter, who looked like he was going to die. Loren forgot all about her news and said, "My God, Peter, what's the matter? Are the kids all right?" Loren held out her arms. "Peter, what happened?"

"I've been RIFed," he said, as he threw his arms around her and buried his face in her hair.

"You've been what?" she asked, hugging him without under-standing the problem.

"Reduction in Force. Essentially, I've been fired," he cried.

"Fired?" Loren asked, soaking in all the implications of that word.

"Not fired for cause. Fired because they're not offering Mandarin next year."

"Let's go in," she said.

They walked with their arms around each other up the front walk to the door. Loren searched in her bag for her keys. Her mind was racing. How would they live? All of their savings had gone to tuition for Marshall and Emily. Health insurance. Had they lost their health insurance? She found her keys and opened the door. They stumbled into the small foyer, Peter refusing to totally let go of her.

Loren took a deep breath. "Have we lost our insurance?" she whispered.

He nodded his head. She closed her eyes.

"Effective when?"

"The thirtieth."

Ten days. Loren swallowed a sob. She had ten days to figure out what to do about her own problem. Their problem. She hugged Peter to reassure him and decided not to tell him her news tonight.

$\mathcal{E}$ I G H T

$\mathcal{B}$ecause of her somewhat repulsive appearance, with the face of a mole and the body of a cartoon hippo, Helen Acker viewed the world as a nasty place. Her physical appearance brought out the worst in people. Back in high school, she had endured the snide remarks of the popular girls and all the boys. The locker room had been a torture chamber. With no friends, she had turned to writing and was now the best reporter on staff at *The Litchfield Press*.

Helen woke every day in a bad mood, and today was no different. As she got ready for work, she cursed herself for agreeing to have lunch with Patricia Castellano. And in some chic restaurant. The other patrons would look at them as if they were the beauty and the beast, and because Patricia was both beautiful and rich, a lot of people would stop by to pay homage. They would smile at Patricia and then recoil, as they glanced over at her lunch partner.

Helen liked being a reporter because she was in demand. She didn't have to actively pursue friendships because there was always someone who wanted to talk to her, and people never insulted her. People treated her with respect, and if they didn't, she always got the last word. In print. Patricia wanted her to cover some demonstration she was planning, so Helen knew she would be gooey-sweet and adoring. She would compliment Helen on a few specific recent articles in hopes of winning her over to her side. "*Helen, your piece on the new sewage tax was so insightful,*" she would gush. Patricia always did her homework. Helen admired that in a socialite. Should she let Patricia know she was pro-choice? Did it really matter? Helen was looking for the best story. She wasn't interested in promoting a cause.

Let's see. What to wear? The brown skirt with the gray shirt or the gray skirt with the tan shirt? As Helen stared at the dull contents of her closet, her eyes lit on the one article of clothing that wasn't the color of mud. Her mother had given her a salmon-colored man-tailored shirt two birthdays ago. The tags were still on it. She pulled it out of the closet, ripped the tags off, and put it on.

For the past five years, Helen had moved up the byline ladder at *The Litchfield Press*. She had started covering the senior center, moved up to entertainment, then the regional political roundup, and finally, onto the front page with breaking news. She covered the most important stories for *The Press*. Usually she spent her days at Town Hall in Room 6, where each media outlet had a desk. Hers was next to DeShawn Fletcher, the popular reporter from Channel 6. She liked to watch him and his easy way with people. He had a smile, a handshake, a wink, and a nod for every occasion. They both covered the Mayor, the Town Council, and the myriad of special-interest groups that showed up to either plead their case, celebrate a victory, or protest a wrong.

With a population of 60,000, Litchfield was a conservative, largely affluent town with no real poverty. It was an appealing choice for families, because it was located one hour from downtown Manhattan, had very little crime, excellent schools, and a vibrant downtown with a variety of restaurants, movie theaters, wine bars, posh shops, churches, and one seedy blue-collar bar. Most of the people living in Litchfield were there to raise their children and live a quiet life.

Helen had met Patricia—one of Litchfield's elite—a few years ago when Patricia had attended her brother's swearing-in as mayor of Litchfield. When the entire Ceravolo clan had stood at the front of the ceremonial room on the first floor of Town Hall, it was like an invasion of tall, raven-haired gods and goddesses who had descended from Mount Olympus. The four Ceravolo brothers and Patricia, with their spouses, and 15 or so children between them, had taken up half the room. Patricia had made it a point to get Helen and her photographer a front spot, so that Helen could cover the story and *The Press* would have a good photo for the front page.

Sucking in her bulging stomach, Helen tugged on the salmon-colored shirt to secure the last button, and went into the bathroom to search for the blush she had bought last year. There it was at the bottom of the catch-all drawer under the sink. She didn't really know how to apply it. She ran the brush over the rose-colored powder and then applied it to her cheeks where she thought her cheekbones were hidden under a layer of chubby skin. There. That would do. She grabbed her laptop bag and headed to *The Press* offices.

NINE

How to get the money and how to get it fast? That was Pia's problem. She had vowed to never again have one of Eduardo's babies, yet here she was, pregnant again. According to the Internet sites she had read, she needed $600 to fix her problem. Eduardo counted out the money he gave her to run the house, and the little she had hidden in the basement closet in a shoebox was not nearly enough. Insurance was out of the question because he would see the paperwork.

She needed to borrow the money from someone who had access to cash. Her friends would tell their husbands, and the husbands would surely tell Eduardo. She thought about her sister, Stella. Yes, Stella was her only hope. Stella and her husband George, who was a corporate lawyer, were rich, and Stella could go to the bank tomorrow and take out $600 and no one would question the withdrawal. Still, $600 was a lot to borrow, but she would pay it back little by little.

As Pia sat at her kitchen table, she stared out the window into the street. The sky was gray and it was raining. The wind tossed the long, thin boughs of the willow trees. Like beautiful strands of light, soft hair, they floated on the breeze. They soothed Pia's tormented mind. She had to get out of this relationship with this monster before he hurt one of her girls. Taking a deep breath to fortify herself, she decided that after this was over, she would go to her parents and tell them about her life. *God only knows if they will help me.*

She got up and went over to the kitchen desk, picked up the cordless phone, and dialed Stella's number. The sound of her sister's voice, when she answered, made Pia cry. Stella tried to comfort her. "Pia, what's the matter? I'm sure it's not all that bad. Are the girls okay?" asked Stella with concern in her voice.

"Yes," Pia whispered. "Can you come over? Don't tell anyone you're coming. Don't call Mom, okay? Come alone."

"Pia, you sound so weird. What's going on?"

"Just come. I can't say over the phone, and whatever you do, don't tell George or anyone. Just come."

"Okay. I'm coming. I'll be there in a few minutes."

Although it only took Stella 15 minutes to drive from Dorian Estates where she lived, to Chandler Hills where Pia lived, it seemed like hours to Pia. She was afraid her mother would come by or that Eduardo would show up. She stood in front of the living room window, looking out at the street searching for Stella's minivan. Finally, she saw it pulling up in front. She went to the front door to let her in.

Stella stepped into the front foyer, and Pia fell into her arms, crying and sobbing.

"What is it, Pia? You're scaring me. Tell me what's wrong," said Stella, hugging her baby sister.

"I'm pregnant again," Pia wailed.

Stella's face broke into a smile. "Oh, how wonderful! You silly. You're just feeling blue. You know that's normal," she said, pushing Pia away to arm's length to look at her face. But after looking at her sister's tormented face, she knew this was not normal. "Is there something wrong with the baby? Are you sick? Do you and Eduardo have money trouble? I know that the plant is not doing well. Mother told me. Are you afraid you'll lose the baby?"

"I wish I would lose the baby," Pia cried, pushing Stella away. They were the same height in bare feet, but Stella, as usual, was wearing three-inch heels, and she stumbled backward slightly when Pia pushed her.

"Oh, you're just overwhelmed. Maria is old enough to help with a baby. I know it's a lot of responsibility. I should know, with my five boys. You'll be fine. C'mon, let's sit down," she said, as she led Pia into the living room, where they sat down on the blue-flowered couch.

Pia bent her head down, her shoulders hunched over, and shook her head with closed eyes, her long black hair falling in front of her face. Finally, she looked up and said, "Stella, you must listen to me. Eduardo is not who you think he is. He beats me. He's mean to me. He looks at Maria with longing. I must get away from him, and I can't be pregnant. I'm getting rid of it. I can't bring another one of his children into the world. I won't do it. I have to protect the two I already have." Pia's face was mottled pink and white from crying, and her eyes were filled with terror, as she searched for a tissue in her sweater pocket.

A look of shock and horror appeared on Stella's face. "He beats you? He looks at Maria? What? When did this start?" Stella couldn't process what Pia was telling her. Eduardo had never been her favorite person, but she had never imagined that he was violent or that he would hurt his own children.

"Years ago. I couldn't tell you. I couldn't tell anybody. He says terrible things in front of the girls, and the way he looks at Maria, I don't trust him. I want to get away, but first I need to take care of this pregnancy and I need money. Will you give me $600? As a loan, I mean." Pia looked at her sister intently, her eyes rimmed in red from crying.

"It's so much to take in. I thought you were happy."

"I put on a good face for the family, but here, at home, I am miserable. The girls are miserable. After I deal with this, I will go to Mother and talk to her, but what I'm going to do she would never sanction. How can I leave when I'm pregnant? And then if I have the baby I won't be able to work." Pia was angry now. She broke free of Stella's embrace, stood up, and paced across the Oriental carpet.

"Why didn't you go to Mother before? Or come to me?" asked Stella.

"It's not that simple. I'm afraid Father will stand by him. He will say he is my husband and I must submit to him." Pia stopped pacing and stood in front of Stella with her hands on her hips. "Don't you think that is what he will say?"

Stella did not answer right away. She looked deep in thought, a frown pulled on her pretty face. "He might," she finally said.

"He will. I have thought about it a lot. But if I am strong—which means not being pregnant—maybe I can make him understand. Or I will leave and get a job to support the girls. Or I'll run away. But first, will you loan me $600?" Pia begged. Stella reached up and took her sister's hand.

"Yes. Yes, I will give you the money. Don't worry about paying it back, but are you sure you want to do this? Get…rid of the…it…I mean…"

Pia fell to her knees and buried her head in her sister's lap. "I don't know what else to do. I don't want it. Not now. Not with him," she said between sobs.

"Okay. There, there. The girls will be home soon. Let's get you cleaned up." Stella stroked Pia's hair. "I'll help you. I'll give you the money. I'll go with you."

"Thank you, thank you," said Pia.

$\mathcal{T}$ E N

⚛

$\mathcal{M}$ ichael couldn't sleep or eat. *Classic.* If he didn't know better, he would have thought he was falling for that little girl. *Get a grip, man, she's a kid. Jailbait.* But, when he closed his eyes, he could smell her apple shampoo. Feel the smoothness of her thighs. He needed someone to talk to. Someone who might relieve his guilt. Reassure him that he was doing a good thing by taking care of her. Part of him wished that she had never come to the bar that night, but another part of him just wanted to be with her. He couldn't talk to Jay or any of the guys. He didn't want them to know what had happened. He thought about going to talk to Father O'Malley.

Thomas O'Malley had lived next door when Michael was growing up and had dated Michael's older sister, Stephanie. Michael knew they used to neck out on the hammock in his backyard. He vaguely remembered a lot of screaming and door slamming after Stephanie stayed out all night at the senior prom, and as a result, Stephanie was sent off to their grandma's house in Florida after graduation. Thomas had already been accepted at Harvard, and Stephanie met a boy on the beach, married him the next year, and rarely came back to Litchfield.

Michael could never understand why any man would want to be a priest. It seemed downright unnatural to him that a man would want to live without having sex with a woman. He assumed that Father O'Malley and Stephanie had slept together. He assumed that was why she had been sent away. He assumed that Father O'Malley had fooled around at college and over in Africa during his Peace Corps days. He wondered what had made a good-looking guy like Father O'Malley take a vow of celibacy. It just didn't make any sense.

After Michael graduated from high school, he did odd jobs around town. Burger King. Landscaping. Until Father O'Malley hired him to help out around the church. One of Father O'Malley's hobbies was carpentry, and he taught Michael everything he knew. Michael remembered the priest teaching him how to use the lathe in the church's workshop. He loved the way the workshop always smelled sweet from the freshly cut wood. "Keep your elbows braced against your body," Father O'Malley patiently instructed Michael. They had made all the spindles to support the new handrail on the rectory staircase. He had showed him how to use the chisels and the gouges. "Not too deep. Keep the pressure steady," he would say, looking over Michael's shoulder as the younger man cut the grooves into the wood.

Over the next three years, he spent a lot of time with Father O'Malley and discovered many of his secrets. Like the fact that he drank too much sometimes, and that he was overly concerned with the way he looked. Michael also knew a much darker secret that he stumbled upon one night, when he went back to the rectory to collect a backpack of work clothes that he had left in one of the upstairs bedrooms. Father O'Malley never locked the back door, so Michael slipped in without knocking and was taking the stairs two at a time, when he heard a sound. Stopping mid-jump, he listened. Giggling. He heard giggling.

Female giggling. Like being-tickled-giggling. *What the hell? Who was that? Maybe Father O'Malley had a family staying with him.* He continued to the top of the stairs, and all was dark. Father O'Malley's room was the first door on the left. Now, Michael heard Father O'Malley's deep laugh join the giggling from behind the door to his room.

Michael didn't know what to do. He was paralyzed for a moment, and then he quickly went down the hall to the bedroom where his backpack was, picked it up, and quietly retraced his steps down the hall, down the stairs, and out the back door. That was the night that Michael realized that Father Thomas O'Malley did not always sleep alone. That was one of the reasons why he wanted to tell the priest about Clara. Michael thought he would understand, and he knew O'Malley couldn't tell anyone. Michael didn't need Father O'Malley to tell him what to do. He just wanted to unburden himself. Not of the whole truth. Not that he had forced himself on a drunken girl who had passed out. He would say it had been consensual, but that she was only 16, and since he was 23, it could be misconstrued.

The next morning he went to the rectory. It was Saturday, and he knew that Father O'Malley always spent Saturday morning working on his homily for Sunday's sermon. When he arrived at the rectory, he went straight to Father O'Malley's office. Peering through the small window in the door, Michael could see the priest sitting at his desk, working on his laptop. Michael knocked and saw Father O'Malley look up and gesture to come in.

"Hey, Michael. How are you, buddy? It's been too long." Father O'Malley got up as Michael entered the office, and the two men hugged.

"Thomas. I mean, Father. How goes it? Do you have a few minutes?" asked Michael.

"Of course. Sit down. How've you been? How's your mom?"

"She's fine. Everyone's fine," said Michael distractedly, as he tried to settle into the chair in front of the priest's desk. Father

O'Malley could tell that something was bothering Michael, but experience had taught him that people had to get comfortable before they opened up to him, so he waited until Michael was ready.

Michael suddenly felt very nervous as he looked at Father O'Malley's familiar face. His throat was parched. He couldn't stop his leg from bouncing up and down, and he couldn't find the words to start his story.

"Ah…you have a bottle of water, Father?" he finally asked.

"Yes, let me get you one." Father O'Malley went and got two bottles of water and gave one to Michael. "I want to show you something before you go, after we talk. I've rebuilt the cabinets in the hallway on the first floor of the school. I could have used your help. It was a big project."

"All those cabinets? Yeah, that's a big job," said Michael. "Yeah, you can show me on my way out. So, here's the thing… there's this girl. A young girl and she's in trouble." Michael stopped here to look up at Father O'Malley to see his reaction.

Father O'Malley looked at Michael with concern. His deep blue eyes were reassuring as he said, "Go on."

"See, the thing is, we're gonna take care of it, you know, but I think I might be in love with her and she's 16 years old." Michael talked faster and faster. "I think about her all the time. I can't stop. She's like the most beautiful thing. And I didn't want to hurt her. It just happened. You know? And now, she's like, afraid of me. You know? And it makes me feel bad."

Father O'Malley listened, never letting his gaze wander from Michael's face. "Are the two of you dating?" he asked.

"Well, no. See, her and her friends showed up at The Sportsman one night and we got drunk and I took her home with me. I didn't see her again until she came looking for me one night. She lives over on Seward's Mill Drive. In one of those houses with the three-car garages. I don't think her father would want to see me picking her up for a date."

Father O'Malley was nodding his head. He wondered if the girl worshipped at St. Raymond's. "So, you say she's in trouble?"

"Yeah, in trouble." Michael looked Father O'Malley boldly in the eye. "We need to fix that."

"I see."

"I just need someone to talk to. I thought since you…"

"Michael, you know the Church doesn't condone, shall we say, 'fixing' the problem," interrupted Father O'Malley. "Has she considered having the baby and giving the child up for adoption?"

Michael began to feel a little queasy. He felt the blood draining out of his cheeks. He hadn't thought about the Catholic Church's stance on abortion. He really just wanted Father O'Malley to make him feel better. He started to feel sorry that he had come to the church.

"Listen…Father… I didn't come here to debate what we're doing to fix the problem. I really came here just to have someone to talk to. That's all. I'm not looking for your approval or anything like that. I just thought I might feel better if, you know, I could tell someone."

"I'm glad you came, Michael. You can always talk to me. I can see that you care about this girl. Has she considered telling her parents?" Father O'Malley asked.

"No, she says she can't. She really doesn't want them to know, and I don't think it's a good idea. You know, I think I gotta go." Michael stood up.

Father O'Malley stood up too. "Michael, don't go. Let's talk it through. I just don't want the girl to get hurt. To do something she might regret."

"No, I think she's already done that. Anyway, I'll see you around. I'll stop by another time and see the cabinets." Without waiting for a response, Michael bolted out of the office and out of the rectory.

ELEVEN

❧

The Elliot's family room needed new couches. The cushions sagged where Peter and Loren sat together night after night, watching their favorite shows. On the night after Peter was RIFed, as they sat waiting for the commercial to end and the show to start, Loren tried to lighten the mood by quipping, "I'm miffed that you were RIFed," but by the look on Peter's face she knew it was too soon. She still hadn't told him about her condition, but she planned to immediately following the show. As Hugh Laurie and Lisa Edelstein flirted shamelessly on the screen, Loren thought about how to tell Peter. He was so upset about his job situation that she couldn't bear to add to his misery.

She thought back to the day she found out that she was pregnant with Marshall. "We're having a baby. Our family's growing!" She remembered Peter saying when she told him. Now, with Peter's job prospects so grim, how could they afford to have another child? She was going to talk to her editor about a full-time position, but she didn't think one was available. Also, with Marshall and Emily grown, how could she and Peter go back to diapers and all-nighters? Would they be too old to ever put this baby through college?

Peter got up to go to the bathroom, and she watched his retreating back. His steps were hesitant, uncertain. Like he couldn't remember where he was going. His shoulders were hunched like he had suddenly developed osteoporosis. He held his arms rigid and slightly forward of his body. *My Frankenstein.* Maybe she shouldn't tell him she was pregnant. Just go and get it done. Like it never happened. If no one else knew, was it real? That would almost be easier, except she had never lied to him before. Maybe about stupid stuff like the cost of a shirt or the fact that she didn't really like his penne vodka, but not about anything like this. No. She would tell him when he got back. She couldn't wait any longer. Not with their health insurance being canceled in nine days.

The sound of the toilet flushing filled the house. All of her senses were amplified as she watched him amble down the hall toward her. He was a large man with a bald head and a round face. Usually, when he smiled, his whole face lit up, but now his mouth was pulled down in a frown, and his bright eyes were dull and listless. She didn't think he had showered today. Mustard had dripped down the front of his T-shirt.

"Honey," she said, as he sat down beside her. "Honey, you know I love you and we are going to get through this." She saw tears start to well up in his eyes. She took a deep breath. "But there is something I need to tell you." Her serious tone was making him very nervous. Too nervous to speak.

"See, I don't know how this happened but...I'm pregnant." She looked hard at his face to watch his reaction.

First his face went totally blank, and then he started to laugh. Not a hearty laugh, but a sarcastic, *I can't believe you would say that when I'm already suffering* kind of laugh. "Oh, that's a good one," he finally said. Loren realized he thought she was kidding, and for some reason this made her mad.

"I'm not kidding," she said flatly with an edge.

He looked at her to see for himself that she was not kidding. He could tell she was not. She watched his face register his emotions like a mood barometer at the amusement park. She saw the red arrow go from disbelief to shock to anger to pain.

"I know what I have to do. I'm going to make an appointment tomorrow at the clinic," she started.

"The clinic?"

"To...you know...get rid of it." She couldn't bring herself to say the "a" word.

Peter laid his head back against the faded couch. He closed his eyes. Maybe if he went to sleep, when he woke up, he would have his old life back.

"Peter, are you all right?" As she waited for him to answer, the phone rang. She got up to get it. As she did, a wave of nausea caught in her throat and she gagged. Peter shot upright.

"Loren?" was all he said. The phone rang again.

"I'm fine." She breathed in through her nose. "Hello?" Pause. "Hi sweetie." She silently mouthed to Peter that it was Emily. She listened. "Tomorrow? They want you to start tomorrow?" Pause. "That's so exciting!" Pause. "Yes, I'll tell Dad." Pause. "I love you too. Okay. Okay. Bye." Loren put down the phone.

"That was Em. She got a summer internship at the paper."

"With or without pay?"

"She didn't say...listen, Peter, let's just go to bed. Everything will look brighter in the morning."

"Why do you think that?" asked Peter, as he got up and headed haltingly toward the stairs without waiting for an answer.

Loren went into the kitchen and cleared the rest of the dishes from the table. *Let's try to focus on the positives.* She and Peter and the kids were all healthy. The kids were doing well. Marshall had a job in New York for the summer, and now Emily had this internship. She hoped a paycheck went along with it. Peter would rally and get another job. She would take care of this and move on. Another wave of nausea rose up in her throat, and this time she let it go and threw up all over the dirty dishes in the sink.

TWELVE

ome people say that walking clears their heads but Clara always felt angry when she was walking. She would start out walking the dog with a clear head, and then angry thoughts would emerge with each new step. In her mind were all these competing people. Their voices. Their faces. Her mother. Her father. Agnes. Linda. And images. The man. His massive shoulders. His massive other parts. The soiled bathroom. She shook her head to thrust these thoughts out.

She walked down the sunny street, ostensibly on her way to Linda's house, although she wasn't sure that she really wanted to see Linda. Spiro Agnew, her father's big standard poodle, pulled on his leash as she walked by Sunset Park, the small park with the pond, down the street from her house. When there were ducks in the park, Spiro liked to run at them and bark. Clara looked down at Spiro and wondered if he liked to wear his coat all sheared so that he had a big pompadour on his head, a ruff around each delicate ankle, and a silly pom-pom on the end of his tail. She thought that he secretly felt ridiculous and wished her mother would leave him unshaved.

Her mind wandered back to her crisis. She looked down at her massive breasts, thinly veiled in her white ribbed tank top. When she got home, she had to change her shirt to something looser. She felt sweaty and her boobs were popping out of her small bra that usually fit her just fine. And they hurt. When Spiro pulled on the leash, pain shot through her engorged chest.

Visions of the procedure kept popping into her mind. She imagined herself on an operating table. Lying on crinkly white paper. Her feet would be cold. Would the doctor be a man or a woman? She hoped a woman. Would it hurt? She had looked it up on the Internet and it had said there might be cramping afterward. Afterward. If she could only hang on until afterward.

As Clara continued to walk around the neighborhood, she was so deep in thought that she was oblivious to the beauty of the chemically enhanced lawns, extravagant beds of annual flowers that were planted each spring, expensive cars that shone in the bright sunshine in the long driveways, and the houses themselves. Massive tudors and center hall colonials with tall columns. Each house was unique. Not like the developments in Chandler Hills where only the paint colors changed, but the structure of the houses was the same.

Images of Michael kept popping into Clara's head. She didn't even like to think of his name. She tried to push the thoughts away, but they boomeranged right back. Thoughts of his thick tongue in her mouth wormed their way into her brain. His weight on her body. The freckles on his shoulder. His masculine smell. Yick. She couldn't bear it.

She hadn't been a virgin. She had been violated before. Willingly violated. It had happened on her way home from a New Year's Eve party she had gone to with Steve Clark, whom she had adored for as long as she could remember. Tall. Blond. Captain of the swim team and president of the National Honor Society. Her mother had approved. When he was driving her home, they had stopped at his house and found it empty. His parents were at a neighbor's party. She wanted him and he had worn a condom. The next day at school he didn't even say hello.

After the night with Steve, Clara had guarded herself mentally and physically. She knew boys admired her, but until The Sportsman she hadn't really tried the flirting game that her girlfriends all found to be so much fun. She cursed herself for going to the bar. *Damn, Clara, why did you go there?*

Yet, he was going to help her. Thank God for that. Where would she get the money without him? She had also looked that up on the Internet. $600. Where would he get $600? He didn't look rich. His apartment had been small and dingy. She hoped he could get $600. He must work. She wondered where. Clara didn't see the red Mustang until it pulled up next to her. She jumped when he called her name.

"Clara."

She couldn't believe that he would come to her neighborhood in broad daylight.

"What are you doing here?" she whispered, bending down to look in the window of the car. Spiro jumped up and tried to lick Michael's face.

"I just wanted to let you know that we have an appointment for Saturday morning. You have to go to mandatory counseling a week before. Where should I pick you up?" asked Michael, trying to push the large dog out of his face.

"Spiro. Cut it out." Clara yanked on the dog's leash. "Heel. Heel. You stupid dog," Clara yelled.

"Spiro?" Michael laughed. With his dark sunglasses, jet black hair, mustache, and tight T-shirt, he looked so macho. Clara was used to the sandy-haired boys with popped collars on their Abercrombie polo shirts. She knew the vintage red Mustang would cause people to stare.

"What time?" she whispered.

"Why are you whispering? Ain't no one else here."

"I don't know. You shouldn't come here. I'll meet you at the tennis courts at Town Hall Park. What time?"

"I'll pick you up at ten. How are you feeling?" he asked, looking genuinely concerned.

"I'm okay," she said. All of a sudden, she was very aware of her bulging breasts, her thin T-shirt, and her short pink shorts with the sailor buttons. Her long hair was pulled back in a ponytail, and she wore sunglasses with white heart-shaped frames. "I have to go." She pulled the leash and Spiro fell in line beside her.

Michael watched her walk away. He loved the way she walked. Her tall, slender form. He took out his cell phone and took her picture as she walked away. He thought he would love a photo of her face. How could he get one? She had rounded the corner. She was going back to her house. Maybe on Saturday she would let him take a picture. Probably not, he thought, as he pulled away and turned in the opposite direction toward the center of town.

$\mathcal{T}$ H I R T E E N

$\oint$

$\mathcal{D}$r. Amy Friedberg was raped when she was 15 years old by her new stepfather. Luckily for her, her mother arrived home just in time to catch him holding her down on the living room couch as she kicked and screamed, her face bloody and her skirt torn. There was no gray area. It was rape of a minor, no matter what he tried to say at trial, and he was sent to prison for 10 years. When Amy discovered she was pregnant the following month, her mother took her to the local clinic, where a quick procedure was performed, and she went home to try to put her life back together. After years of rape therapy, she graduated valedictorian of her high school class and went to the University of Pennsylvania undergrad and then on to medical school.

She knew from the time she left the clinic that day that she wanted to help other women, especially young girls, get a second chance when it seemed that the walls were crashing in. While she was at school in Philadelphia, she spent time volunteering in a domestic violence women's shelter and at the local Planned Parenthood clinic. Through the years, she met and counseled hundreds of women, and offered them a quick and permanent solution to a life-altering problem.

After med school, she knew she couldn't go back to Long Island, where everything had happened. First, she moved to New York City and spent 10 years working up in the Bronx, where it was not uncommon for 17-year-old girls to be the mother of three. She saw the cycle of poverty descend on those babies from their first breath. Drugs, poverty, prostitution, gangs, jail, violence, pain—this would be their plight. Seeing this level of hopelessness day in and day out finally took a toll on Amy, and she started to look for a job in a clinic where the girls and women were middle class and had a fighting chance to get their lives back on track. After seeing an ad in *The New York Times,* she applied for and was offered the position of chief doctor at the Litchfield Women's Clinic, where she had been working for the last 10 years. Ten quiet years, until now. Until she heard a rumor that Patricia Castellano and her organization, Stand Up for Life, was going to demonstrate in front of her clinic. She had seen DeShawn Fletcher's story on Channel 6 last night, and Helen Acker from *The Press* had already called.

Maybe it had been a mistake, but Dr. Friedberg had agreed to meet with Acker. She didn't want her coming to the clinic and disturbing the privacy of the women who were there, so she had said they could meet in the small coffee shop next door. She arrived on time and the only other woman there, the only person in the shop, was a rather frumpy, colorless young woman wearing a salmon-colored shirt.

"Hi. Helen?" Dr. Friedberg said tentatively, as she approached the woman.

Helen looked up and saw a nice-looking, middle-aged woman with wavy brown hair, hazel eyes, and glasses. She had a kind and generous smile with very straight, white teeth. The woman held out her hand. Helen, never graceful in social interactions, shook the hand once and withdrew. "Sit down," Helen said. Helen had just come from having lunch with Patricia

Castellano, who was all charm, and now this doctor was all business. Patricia's parting salvo, as the waiter in the expensive French restaurant swept away the bread crumbs on Helen's side of the table, was, "What kind of woman would spend her life disposing of other women's babies?" Helen thought about this now as she took the measure of Dr. Amy Friedberg. Competent, intelligent, efficient. Helen also sensed annoyance at having to meet with a reporter. The doctor was clearly not looking for the spotlight. She probably just wanted to do her job.

"Do you want coffee?" asked Dr. Friedberg.

"Okay."

After Dr. Friedberg ordered two cups of coffee, Helen reached into her purse and pulled out a small tape recorder. "Do you mind if I tape our conversation?"

Dr. Friedberg considered her options. "Okay," she said hesitantly.

"Thanks. So, how long have you been working at the clinic?"

"If we can just back up a minute," said Dr. Friedberg. "What exactly are you writing about? The clinic and the services we provide, or the upcoming demonstration that you mentioned on the phone?"

"Well, both. Right now I'd just like to get some background, if that's okay."

Dr. Friedberg felt uncomfortable. She really wanted Helen and Patricia Castellano to go away. She felt that the clinic and the women she served would be better off. She decided to give as little information as possible.

"I have been at the clinic for ten years," she said.

"What services do you provide?"

"We provide a full range of reproductive health care."

"Including abortions?"

Dr. Friedberg hesitated. She didn't like Helen's brusque manner. "Obviously, our goal is to reduce the number of un-intended pregnancies, but at the same time, we provide safe, legal abortion services. It is a constitutionally protected right for women to make that choice, but I'm sure you know that, Helen," said Dr. Friedberg with an edge.

"Of course, I know it's constitutionally protected. I'm not suggesting you're doing anything illegal," said Helen, pushing her glasses higher on her nose.

Dr. Friedberg took a sip of her coffee.

"How many procedures do you perform in a given year?"

"I don't know those numbers off the top of my head. Listen. We're a private clinic, and as such, I do not have to give you any of that data. However, here are a few numbers for your story. One in three American women will have an abortion by the time she is 45-years-old. Seventy-eight percent of those women report a religious affiliation. 86% of them are unmarried. 57% of them are poor. 41% are white. 32% are black, and 20% are Hispanic. Those are some very interesting numbers." By the time Dr. Friedberg was done, the color had risen to her cheeks.

Even though Helen was taping the conversation, she was also making a few notes. When she was done, she looked at Dr. Friedberg and asked, "Are you familiar with the group, Stand Up for Life?"

"Yes," answered Dr. Friedberg. Helen waited for Dr. Friedberg to elaborate. The two women sat silently staring at each other. Even though Castellano was annoying, she was easier to interview than this doctor. Helen thought about telling Dr. Friedberg that she was pro-choice. That she was on her side. But, as an objective reporter, she couldn't.

"The executive director, Patricia Castellano, says her organization stands for life. That only God can take a life. Do you want to comment on her view?" asked Helen, looking at Dr. Friedberg with her small, birdlike eyes.

Dr. Friedberg paused to gather her thoughts. "I believe that every child who enters this world should have devoted parents. I do not believe that children should have children. I do not believe that women who are in abusive relationships should have children unless they are planning on moving out of that relationship. I do not believe that there is a God-given right to give birth to children who will live in poverty without the basic necessities of life. I believe that women should choose for themselves when to have a child. From what I've seen, unwanted children usually turn out to be unhappy and live terrible lives." As she heard her own voice, she knew she was saying too much. She shut her mouth and kept it closed, although there was a lot more she wanted to say.

Helen was rapt. *This is great. Game on!* Helen made a mental note to call Patricia for a rebuttal.

$\mathcal{F}$ O U R T E E N

🙋

$\mathcal{E}$duardo Fernandez sensed that his wife, Pia, was hiding something from him. Last night, on his way home from the paint plant where he worked for her father, he had stopped at the liquor store to buy a six-pack of Corona. He was thinking of sitting out back on his porch, the ice-cold beer feeling good on the back of his throat, the tart sting of lime that he liked to bite on the side. He wanted to have a drink before he had to listen to the annoying high-pitched voices of his wife and daughters at the dinner table. Maybe he would eat dinner out on the porch from now on.

As he was getting in line to pay at the liquor store, he ran into Stella. Before he realized who she was, he had been admiring her from the back. Pia's sister had always been a nice piece of ass, always making Pia look dowdy, he thought. As he sauntered over, boldly staring at her, she turned and looked at him. A windy cloud of emotion passed over her face. Anger whipped past, followed by disgust with a gust of fear.

"Eduardo," she stammered, looking downright sick.

"Hey Stella." He leaned in to kiss her cheek. They were family, after all, but she recoiled from him.

"I...I have a bad cold," she explained, putting her hand up to her mouth as she spoke.

He couldn't really say that she was rude, but there was something buried in the blackness of her eyes and the set of her mouth. Pia wouldn't tell her sister anything bad about him. Pia lived like a queen. She had her daughters. She had a nice house. He brought home a paycheck every week to pay for it all. Sometimes she got out of line, or she couldn't keep those brats quiet, and he had to show her who was the man of the house, but where would she be without him? She would have nothing. She would be nothing without him. No, he knew that Pia wanted her family to think that they were the perfect couple.

Still, he had this unsettled feeling. Tonight he would watch Pia and see if she acted strange. However, he wasn't going straight home. First, he was going to visit Casandra, his new girl. He had met her at The Sportsman, where he liked to go and drink with the guys. All the other bars and restaurants in town were family friendly, but The Sportsman was a working-class man's bar. A place where you did not bring the family.

A few weeks ago, he had been playing pool with a bunch of guys when Casandra and her friend Molly had come in for a beer. Tall, slim, and blond, with plastic boobs and big hoop earrings, she had caught his eye immediately. "I like your ink," he said, looking at the large tattoo of a rose on her arm. "I have others," she countered with a mischievous grin. One thing had led to another, and Casandra had invited him back to her apartment on Green Street. After that night, it had become a steady thing for Eduardo to stop by her apartment on his way home or meet her at The Sportsman after dinner and then go to her apartment. It turned out that she was only 22, with no kids, no responsibilities, and real talent in the sack.

Pia didn't seem to mind his coming home late for dinner or going out at night. Again, his mind rolled back to Stella.

Maybe she knew about Casandra and had told Pia, or maybe Pia knew and had told Stella. How could that be possible? Stella and her husband George ran in a different circle, going to expensive black-tie events and fundraisers, and Pia never went out at night. She was always with their girls. It bothered him that Pia was always with the children. It bothered him that they both looked like Pia, too. Dark hair and skin. Neither of them had his sandy hair or fair skin. Maybe they weren't even his, he thought, as he pulled into Casandra's parking lot.

He sat in his black truck for a moment. Boy, he was in a bad mood. Thinking about Pia and Stella and the kids had made him jumpy. Well, he could think of a few things that Casandra could do to cheer him up. She was always ready for sex, probably her finest quality, he thought. He got out of the truck and headed over to the stairs leading up to Casandra's apartment. He heard footsteps before he saw Michael Russo, whom he knew from The Sportsman, come bounding down the stairs, taking a few at a time. Michael smiled when he recognized Eduardo.

"Hey, *gumba*. What'cha doing here?" asked Michael.

Eduardo thought fast. "Ah, the super wants to paint the apartments, and he asked me to drop by and give a quote. I didn't know you lived here."

"Yeah. I've been here a couple of years. It's okay. I'm glad the super's thinking about painting. My apartment could really use a coat or two," said Michael in his easy way.

"Well, we don't have the job yet," said Eduardo.

"I'll put in a good word. I gotta go. See ya at The Sportsman. Going over later?"

"Maybe. I don't know. The old ball and chain may want me to put the girls to bed," said Eduardo with a smile.

"Yeah. Well, see ya'round," said Michael, as he headed to his car.

Great, thought Eduardo. He went up the stairs, making haste to be sure that he didn't run into anyone else. Michael was a regular guy and wouldn't gossip, but the encounter only added to his paranoia. With each step that he took down the dimly lighted outdoor hallway, he could feel the tension in his brain growing. Like a balloon filled with too much air, he started to feel tight, light-headed with irrational fury. He suddenly had the idea that Casandra was banging Michael, too. They lived in the same apartment building. They were about the same age. By the time he got down the hallway his head was swollen with jealousy. The blood racing through his ears made him feel dizzy. He banged on Casandra's door.

She opened the door wearing only her lemon-and-lime striped panties. A mental picture of Michael having just left Casandra's bed overwhelmed him. He pushed the girl into the apartment, practically throwing her clear across the room, kicked the door shut with his foot, and before he knew what he was doing, he had punched her in the face and kicked her repeatedly. She started to scream, and he had to shut her up. He bent down and grabbed her by the hair.

"Shut up, bitch. Stop screaming. I know you've been screwing Michael Russo. Shut up." He thrust her head down hard on the floor, pulling her back up by the hair to slam her again and again on the floor. Casandra, who had been waiting for Eduardo, looked up at him with frightened, puzzled eyes. She had no idea what he was talking about. He didn't notice the blood starting to ooze out from under her head as he spun around and stormed out the door.

$\mathcal{F}$ I F T E E N

$\mathcal{I}$t was a beautiful June day. The sun was shining and the hum of the cicadas rose and fell overhead from the depths of the lush trees. It was the perfect morning for breakfast on the terrace, but Patricia was so engrossed in her own image in the paper that she was unaware of the natural beauty around her. She sat in a large wicker chair, with *The Litchfield Press* spread out before her on the table. As Rosa, her housekeeper, scurried about, making ready for Patricia's meeting with Father O'Malley, Patricia looked up from the paper momentarily to ask, "Did you make the orange-cranberry muffins that he likes?" Without waiting for an answer, she continued, "and hazelnut coffee? He doesn't like classic roast. I'll let you know if he wants an omelet."

Helen Acker's article on the upcoming demonstration was in the morning's paper. Front page. *Bottom of the fold.* Patricia frowned. How could Darius Greeley, *The Press's* editor and publisher, put her photo bottom of the fold? Hadn't she and Salvatore chaired that boring dinner last year for his pet charity? What was it called? The Literacy Project? Teaching im-migrant seniors to read, or some such nonsense.

She continued to stare at her own image. It was a good pho-tograph, at least. She was standing in front of Town Hall on her way in to see her brother, Mayor Antonio Ceravolo. She was wearing a white-and-gold vintage Channel suit and a coordi-nating Hermes scarf. Her black hair was thick and shiny, and she had a determined, serious look on her beautiful face. She had purposely made the photographer meet her at Town Hall, instead of in her offices or at her home. She knew the photo would make Antonio crazy. In fact, she was surprised he hadn't called already.

The article was the first in a series that Helen Acker had told Patricia she was writing. She was going to explore the topic of a woman's right to choose, from various perspectives. This short article was really just a teaser to introduce the play-ers and pique the public's interest. First, Patricia was quoted in the article, and then Dr. Amy Friedberg, chief doctor of the Litchfield Women's Center. Patricia wondered what Dr. Friedberg looked like. She hoped she was plain. Patricia knew that it would just ratchet up the competition if Dr. Friedberg was also beautiful.

Patricia read the doctor's quote again. "I believe that wom-en should choose for themselves when to have a child." She uttered an involuntary guttural sound of disapproval. "Haven't they already made that choice when they get themselves preg-nant? They need to take responsibility for their actions. It's just wrong," Patricia declared out loud.

As Patricia sat, lost in her own thoughts, Rosa announced Father O'Malley, who came bounding out of the house onto the terrace.

"Good morning, Father. Thank you for coming all the way up here for breakfast. How are you?" Patricia asked, pointing to the chair next to her. "Please sit down. Rosa will be right out with your hazelnut coffee."

"Hazelnut! You remembered. Isn't that just like you, Patricia? Always the perfect hostess," said Father O'Malley, sitting down in his place and getting comfortable. Even wearing his priestly black suit with the white collar, Father O'Malley was a very sexy man, Patricia thought to herself. A slight smile wrinkled the corner of her mouth as she thought how she would probably be damned to hell if anyone knew she had just had that thought.

"Of course I would remember your favorite coffee," she said, as Rosa hurried in with a thermos of coffee and hot orange-cranberry muffins. "Do you want an omelet or just muffins?"

"Just muffins will be fine. Thank you, Rosa," he said, smiling up at the middle-aged Portuguese woman.

"Did you see the paper this morning?" asked Patricia.

"No, I haven't seen it yet. Is that it?" He pointed to the paper that Patricia had tossed in another chair.

"Yes, here." She handed the paper to him. "It's only a short teaser, really. The first large article will come out on Sunday. Has Helen called you for an interview yet?"

Father O'Malley finished reading the article. "This Dr. Friedberg here is quoted as saying that one in three women will have an abortion before the age of forty-five. That's astounding. Do you think that's true? Nice photo, by the way," he said.

"Thank you, Father." She paused for effect. "I do believe it's true. Many women use abortion as a means of birth control. They have no self control. That's the problem. And these young girls, these teenagers who have abortions without telling their parents? It's just too awful. I tell you. That's just because no one's watching them. A good mother would know what's going on with her daughter."

"Patricia," Father O'Malley paused. "Patricia, I've been thinking a lot about this event, and I'm not sure that I want it to be a demonstration. What we discussed was an event to raise awareness. Not a demonstration with picket signs and name calling. I think the congregation wants us to help women understand that there are alternatives."

"Thomas, I want you to know that I never called it a demonstration. It was that DeShawn Fletcher from Channel 6 who described it that way after our interview, and now people are calling my office to ask where they can sign up to picket. We keep telling them that we will be handing out educational materials, not picket signs. I'm not sure how to stop it."

Father O'Malley ate the hot muffin with large, juicy cranberries and looked out over the Olympic-size pool. He knew that many of his parishioners were closet choice supporters. *The silent majority.* It wasn't a subject that they liked to talk about, but it was a service that they used. He knew he had to walk a fine line here. Salvatore and Patricia were St. Raymond's largest donors, and Father O'Malley knew that he could not offend Patricia in any way. When she had asked him to get behind this event at the clinic, he had no choice but to support her.

"I'm planning to speak about the subject in my sermon on Sunday. I will try to calm the waters," he said, as he reached out for another muffin.

Patricia nibbled the fruit cocktail that Rosa had brought her. A little taste of the pineapple. The tip of the strawberry. She was constantly battling the extra 10 pounds she had gained during her pregnancy with the twins. She, too, was thinking of the fine line. She wanted massive press coverage, but even the thought of standing outside that dingy clinic in the hot summer sun was both intimidating and tawdry. She wished that she could do the pre-event publicity and that Father O'Malley would go out to Route 54. How to make him see that he needed to be the face on the day of the event?

"Father, how is your capital campaign going?" she asked. "Is Elsa Martinson still running it? It's so sad that she's all alone with those three children." At the mention of the Martinsons, she saw Father O'Malley stiffen ever so slightly. She studied his face.

"The campaign is going slowly. Yes, Elsa Martinson is the chair and is really an excellent fundraiser. It's just that the current economic situation is making people cautious." Father O'Malley realized that the Castellanos had not made a contribution to the campaign as of yet. He sat up slightly straighter in his chair. How much would Patricia and Salvatore give? He looked around at the exotic landscaping. The stucco pool house. The tennis courts. Four-car garage. He didn't think he'd ever actually seen a four-car garage before. Hmm. This could turn into a profitable breakfast.

Patricia's eyes, with the heavy coating of mascara, looked deep into the steely blue eyes of Father O'Malley. Dollar figures and images of demonstrators flew back and forth between the two players. Not a word was spoken as they reached a profound understanding. Patricia knew she would write a large check. Father O'Malley knew he would lead the demonstration. Breakfast was over.

SIXTEEN

❧

"No, don't come tonight," Father O'Malley said in a low voice into the telephone on his office desk.

Pause.

"I can hear you're upset. I think it's best that you not come here tonight."

Pause.

"Don't scream. We will find a way out of this situation."

Pause.

"Try to calm down. Try to stop screaming. Are you alone?"

Pause.

"Good. Try to find the strength to pull yourself together."

Pause.

"I'm here for you."

Pause.

"Please do not come here in this condition. No."

Pause. The person on the other end of the line put Father O'Malley on hold to take another call. He closed his eyes. He could not believe this was happening.

He listened. "She is? Okay. Come over."

SEVENTEEN

❧

*A*gnes had fallen asleep on the couch in the family room after dinner. Mrs. Mahoney and Clara sighed in relief when her regular breathing indicated that they might have a few hours of respite. Mrs. Mahoney always tried to keep Agnes on a strict schedule, and she knew that a few hours of sleep now would mean a hellish night when she woke at one or two o'clock, but she felt the need to spend a little time with Clara.

Mrs. Mahoney motioned to Clara to come outside on the back porch. She could keep an eye on Agnes and talk to Clara at the same time. Clara put down her magazine and followed her mother out onto the porch. Spiro Agnew followed them out and lay on the floor at their feet. Mother and daughter sat together on the old couch with the baby-blue cushions. Mrs. Mahoney couldn't remember the last time she and Clara had been alone for any length of time. She suddenly seemed to realize that Clara had been spending more and more evenings at home. She looked at Clara, who smiled sweetly at her. *Clara is such a good girl.* When she thought of Clara, she felt happy. She felt that life was good, normal. *Clara is a breath of fresh air.* A pang of regret washed over her as she realized that Clara would only be home for another year before she went off to college. She knew that the greatest gift you can give your child is time, and she had failed miserably in that regard with Clara. She wondered if Clara felt neglected, but she couldn't bear to ask her and hear that she did. Instead, she said, "So, how are you, honey? I feel like we never get to talk," as she reached over to gently touch Clara's tanned knee. "Did you go to the pool today with Linda? You're getting a good tan, but don't forget to put on sunscreen."

"I read an article that said that sunscreen was preventing people from getting enough vitamin D. The doctor in the article said that you should get fifteen minutes of sun on your legs each day," said Clara, as she stretched her legs out on the coffee table. Her mom stretched her legs out too. They had very similarly shaped legs, but Mrs. Mahoney's were milky white and Clara's were golden brown.

"I used to get a nice tan like that," said Mrs. Mahoney, pointing to the difference in the color of their skin. "I just don't have the time to get out in the sun anymore," she said sadly.

"Mom, you know," she hesitated, "there are nurses you could hire to help you."

Mrs. Mahoney looked at Clara and knew she was right. "It's just hard in the summer, now that school is out."

"Mom, it's hard all the time," Clara said, a sharp edge in her voice. A pent-up edge.

Mrs. Mahoney rested her head on the back of the couch. "I know, Clara. I know it's hard, and you are such a good girl. You never give me any trouble, and I want to thank you for that. I know Agnes is hard to live with."

Clara didn't really want her mother to sing her praises right now. "Do we have today's paper?" she asked, just to switch the topic of conversation.

"Yes, it's on the coffee table in the family room. Please be quiet."

Clara went in and got *The Litchfield Press*. Agnes was still fast asleep. She went to the kitchen and grabbed a box of Saltines to keep her nausea at bay and headed back to the porch. She took the Entertainment Section and handed her mom the front page. They read in silence for a few minutes, enjoying the simple pleasure of each other's company.

"There's a new Mexican restaurant in town. Do you think we can go sometime?" asked Clara.

Mrs. Mahoney looked stricken. "Ah, Clara, you know how hard it is with Agnes."

"You know, Mom, we've never gone to Disney, or on any vacation for that matter, or to a restaurant or a movie, because of her," said Clara, frowning. "Just once, I want to be the girl who did something first. When the girls ask, '*Have you been to Pancho's?*' I want to say, '*Yes, and isn't it great?*' Just once."

"I know, Clara. I know, and I'm sorry. Let me see if I can work something out and we'll try to go to the Mexican restaurant." She tried to smile, but her mouth wouldn't cooperate.

Mrs. Mahoney wondered if Clara could remember the last time they had tried to go out as a family. It was years ago. Clara was six, Agnes nine, and they had decided to go to McDonald's for lunch. Mr. Mahoney had gone to stand in line to order the food, and Mrs. Mahoney had taken the girls into the ball room. This was the super McDonald's with the jungle gym built around a huge pit with colored balls. After jumping into the ball pit, the tiny bodies would sink into the balls with sounds of hollow plastic rubbing on hollow plastic, and with squeals of joy and trepidation, the kids would disappear into the tunnels, ropes, and secret forts. Mrs. Mahoney had meant to keep Agnes with her while Clara ventured into the maze, but before she could stop her, Agnes had darted up the gang-plank-like ramp and disappeared into a swirl of rope, plastic, and netting. There were four separate exits to the maze. Mrs. Mahoney left Clara and started to run from one exit to the other, screaming for Agnes. Clara climbed into the maze and fell into the ball pit, where a boy did a cannonball onto her back. Clara was screaming in pain, Mrs. Mahoney was screaming for Agnes, Agnes was curled up into a ball behind Ronald McDonald's head, and management finally had to evacuate the jungle gym, so that Mr. Mahoney could go in and find Agnes and Mrs. Mahoney could dig Clara out of the balls. Mr. Mahoney had screamed the entire way home, with Agnes howling and shrieking and Clara crying.

Mrs. Mahoney turned back to the paper and tried to redirect the conversation. "This Patricia Castellano woman. The mayor's sister? She's really attractive. Isn't she?" she asked, holding up the photograph of Patricia on the front page.

"She's very pretty," Clara said curtly.

"She runs this organization in town, Stand Up for Life," said Mrs. Mahoney.

"What's that?" said Clara, still with a hint of annoyance.

"It's a pro-life group. Do you know about that? Pro-life versus pro-choice?"

"Yeah...they taught us about it in health class." Clara hesitated and then asked, "How do you feel, Mom? Are you pro-choice?" Clara held her breath.

"Of course, honey. I don't believe in women having children they don't want or can't take care of. Having a child is a very serious thing. This woman should mind her own business. That's what I think. She's talking about holding a demonstration at the clinic out on Route 54. She shouldn't be meddling in the lives of women she doesn't know."

"What's the name of the clinic?" asked Clara, her stomach suddenly churning. She had to breathe through her nose to stop from retching.

"Clara. Are you all right? What's the matter?"

"My cracker just went down the wrong way."

"Well, breathe through your nose."

"I am."

"Mooom." The call was loud and panicked and came from the family room. "Mooom!" screamed Agnes.

"Oh God! Clara, are you okay?"

"Yes, I'll be fine. Go," said Clara, who was anxious to see her mother leave so she could read that article herself.

$\mathcal{E}$ I G H T E E N

‹∂

$\mathcal{M}$ ayor Antonio Ceravolo was not happy. He sat at his ornate desk in his large corner office at Town Hall, running his thick fingers through his hair. After punishing his hair for some time, he started on his mustache. Pulling at the corners. First the right side, then the left. He had in front of him two pink message slips. The first was from his sister Patricia. The second was from Suzy Walker, the chairwoman of his reelection campaign. He knew that they both wanted to talk about the same thing. He knew that they were on opposite sides of the issue.

The politics here were very complicated. Patricia's organization, Stand Up for Life, had been a major contributor to his last campaign for mayor, through its PAC or Political Action Committee, and Patricia was very close to Father O'Malley. A lot of Antonio's support came from the members of St. Raymond's. Not to mention the personal contributions from Patricia and Salvatore. On the other hand, Suzy Walker had raised over $2 million for his last campaign, and she sat on the board of the Litchfield Women's Center. How could he find common ground here? These two important women were at opposite ends of the spectrum. That was why the mayor was literally pulling his hair out.

He got up from his desk and went to look out of the large windows into the park, searching for inspiration. He pulled back the heavy velvet drapes with hundreds of small gold tassels, wondering for a moment what Patricia was thinking when she helped him decorate his office. They always reminded him of Scarlett O'Hara's dress in *Gone with the Wind;* he quickly envisioned Patricia in the famous green dress. He tried to clear his mind. As he scanned the park, he noticed that the flowers were blooming. City workers were sitting on park benches eating their lunch. Young mothers were walking with their babies in strollers, and joggers were running along the path that went around the perimeter of the park. If he could only go for a walk. But as soon as he started to walk, people would stop him. Some just wanted to say hello, but others wanted to complain. About the pothole on their cul-de-sac. The fact that their kid had been redistricted, which he had nothing to do with. That their application for a zoning variance had been denied. No. He would come back from his walk with 12 new problems having had no time to dwell on his current problem.

So, first things first. Patricia, being his sister, could wait. He would figure out what to say to Suzy first. Suzy was a well-connected lawyer who lived and worked in town. She was a partner in the firm of Walker & Walker, with her dad, Herbert Walker. Suzy and Patricia were practically neighbors in Dorian Estates. While Patricia had just constructed her new palace, Suzy lived in the oldest and most exclusive enclave within Dorian Estates. Dorian Estates actually encircled Reade Way, a collection of six mansions tucked into the foothills of the Watchung Mountains.

Antonio had met Suzy through Salvatore, Patricia's husband. Salvatore and Harry, Suzy's husband, were partners together at Goldman Sachs. Suzy and Patricia knew that they were on opposing sides in the abortion debate, but years ago, no one could foresee this being a sticking point between them. Suzy knew that Antonio's public stance was pro-life, but since municipal governments do not fund medical services or make policy decisions regarding abortion rights, it did not occur to any of them that this would be a cause for concern.

He was sure that Suzy wanted him to stop this crazy demonstration that Patricia was planning. Actually, he had already asked Patricia to stop it. He had demanded that she have breakfast with him a week or so ago and told her to back off. She had told him that she would try, but that things were already in the works, and that Father O'Malley was pushing her. *"I just can't stop Thomas. He's so passionate about this cause,"* she said. Then, the next thing he knew, there she was on Channel 6 and now she was on the front page of *The Press*. The mayor took a deep breath, pulled down his expensive, pin-striped suit vest, and picked up the phone.

"Suzy Walker, please. Yes, it's the mayor."

"Antonio?" Suzy's crisp, northeastern-establishment voice came onto the phone.

"Suzy! How are you? How are Harry and the kids? I heard that Douglas got into Brown. Congratulations!"

"We wanted Yale, but what can you do? Antonio, I'll get right to the point. What the hell is Patricia doing? Are we really going over to the far right? Are we going to put women back in the kitchen and take away their shoes?"

"Now, Suzy..."

"Maybe we should ban birth control and each have ten kids. I mean, really! I understand that Patricia needs an outlet, but, Antonio, there needs to be a limit. Women in town, maybe someone you know, are going to be at the clinic that day. I mean, I hope no one shows up that day, which means they will have to postpone their appointment, but really. I just cannot understand how you let this get so far."

"Suzy, I hear what you're saying."

"Antonio, don't patronize me. I don't have to remind you that I sit on the board at the Women's Center, and I am outraged! First, it's not good for the town to be divided, and secondly, by a woman who is so close to Town Hall. It simply sends the wrong message. The wrong message, Antonio!"

"I have already met with Patricia and I give you my word that I will meet with her again."

"*The Press* has already called me for a comment. Helen Acker is writing a long piece for Sunday's edition. I would like to be able to tell her, this afternoon, that this demonstration has been canceled," Suzy said with authority.

"Canceled? Suzy, I don't think...I will call you back," said Antonio, closing his eyes and rubbing his temples.

"Before two," she snapped, and the phone went dead.

Antonio sat down, still holding the phone in his hand. "Damn you, Patricia," he swore under his breath. "I should have made you head of the Arts Commission." Maybe that was a solution. But, short-term, the demonstration had to be canceled. He dialed his sister's office number.

"Stand Up for Life." Simon answered the phone in his affected voice.

Jesus Christ. How does this gay guy reconcile working at a pro-life organization with his own life? All these people with their own agendas, Antonio thought. All looking to him to make the world right for them. Anger and resentment boiled up in his throat.

"Get me my sister," he commanded.

After two or three minutes, Patricia's silky voice purred into the phone, "Big brother, what's the matter?"

"I just got a call from Suzy Walker. She is demanding that we cancel this demonstration. Really, Patricia. I can't see you walking the picket line in your Jimmy Choo's. What the fuck were you thinking?" screamed Antonio into the phone.

"Do not curse at me, Antonio, or I will hang up this phone. If you want to talk like civilized people, fine, but one more curse and I will hang up," she said in a stern tone. The same tone he had heard her use with the twins.

The mayor tried to compose himself. "Patricia, darling, let me remind you that Suzy Walker raised $2 million for me in my last campaign. Let me also remind you that she sits on the board of the Litchfield Women's Center...."

"I really don't see what that has to do with me. I gave you $500,000 out of my own pocket, and then this organization raised another $800,000 through my connections with the parish of St. Raymond's. You ran as a pro-life candidate, for God's sake, and Suzy knew it," said Patricia.

"I did not run as a pro-life candidate. When I was asked my view that's what I said."

"What's the difference?"

Antonio knew he needed to find a way to get through to his sister. It was true. She had raised $1.3 million for his campaign. Less than Suzy, but still a lot of dough. Why did she have to attack the clinic in a public way? Why couldn't she just do what she did quietly?

"Patricia, honey, I need you to help me out here. You're my sister. Listen, I know you like the spotlight. Why don't we create a commission and you can chair it? Maybe for the arts? Something noncontroversial."

There was silence on the other end of the phone. Maybe, just maybe, there was hope. Antonio's palms were sweating. He couldn't believe that this was the little girl who had sat on his lap in family photos. How had she become so strong-willed?

"No, Antonio. I appreciate you trying to give me something *meaningful* to do with my time, but I have worked hard for five years to get this organization off the ground, and I actually believe in what it stands for. You'll just have to let the chips fall where they may. If it's any help, I won't actually be attending the demonstration. Father O'Malley is going to cover that for me."

Well, that was something he could report to Suzy.

"And the newspaper? Are we going to be treated to another front-page photo? And in front of Town Hall? Patricia! Maybe the whole family next time?"

"Really, Antonio. It was bottom of the fold. Don't you always say if you're not on top of the fold who cares?"

The Mayor knew he had to quit when he was ahead. He hoped that Suzy would be placated by the fact that Patricia wouldn't actually be at the demonstration. Maybe he would speak to Father O'Malley next. Maybe a discreet call to Salvatore. He hung up the phone, sat down in his big leather chair, and without thinking, started to pull on his mustache again.

NINETEEN

᷾

*B*y the time she was six years old, Linda Martinson knew that she was special. It was due to the way she looked. Petite body, yellow flaxen hair, cerulean blue eyes, a tiny snub nose, and big white teeth. All of her features were perfectly symmetrical. She was like a little porcelain doll. The entire Martinson family was blond and beautiful, but Linda had no physical flaws. Her sister, Cindy, was also a looker, but her hair was too thin. Arnold, her brother, was handsome, but he tended to gain weight.

Her parents were attractive people, but Linda was the perfect union of their good physical attributes and none of the bad. Living in a cocoon of praise and admiration for something she hadn't done—just inherited—made Linda both insecure and arrogant. She knew that she was prettier than the other girls, but she was smart enough to know that she didn't really deserve all of the constant attention.

The downside of her beauty was that men, not always with the best of intentions, were attracted to her by the time she was 10. That was also the year her father ran away with his yoga instructor and her mother was left to raise the three children. The good news was that Elsa Martinson was a wealthy woman in her own right and was not dependent on the child-support payments that came irregularly. But raising three children by herself was a burden, and one that Mrs. Martinson was not always up to. Unhappy about her plight, but not able to rebound and move on with her life, Elsa Martinson poured her energy into the church and various volunteer activities. Many times she left her own children to take care of themselves while she was feeding the homeless or planning a fundraiser.

Linda was the youngest of the three children and felt the most neglected. She learned two things early on. The first was that she could get Mrs. Martinson's attention if she was bad, and the second was that men could be manipulated very easily into giving her whatever she wanted. All of the Martinson kids attended St. Raymond's Parish Day School. In the second grade, Linda painted the chalk board in her schoolroom, and Mrs. Martinson was called in for a parent-teacher conference. In fourth grade she gave Sally Cullen a black eye, and again, Mrs. Martinson was called in. At camp, between seventh and eighth grade, she was caught playing doctor with Jimmy Silva in the locker room, and again Mrs. Martinson was called in. But then came the incident that Linda really didn't want Mrs. Martinson called in to hear about.

On her 15th birthday, in ninth grade, she lost her virginity to Mr. Edwards, her drama teacher. Mr. Edwards, fresh out of Rutgers University, was still 21 when he started teaching at St. Raymond's. He was smitten with Linda on the first day of class. He dreamed about her at night. He thought about her long, golden hair and her perfect eyes. He studied her face as she read the monologues that he assigned. He watched her walk down the hall in her plaid uniform, which she had expertly tucked up to expose most of her firm young thighs. He knew he was infatuated with her. She knew he was infatuated with her. He hoped no one else knew.

Linda had decided that it was time to lose her virginity to Mr. Edwards. He was older and would know what to do. She didn't want to deal with some teenage boy who knew less than she did. No, Mr. Edwards would be the one. She liked his straight sandy hair. It looked soft. And his large, doe-like eyes. He had a great smile and large feet. She had read in *Cosmopolitan* that large feet meant large other parts. She had tried out for the play, knowing that he was bound to cast her. He knew she was lazy, so he had given her a small but important part. They were doing *Peter Pan* and she would be Tinkerbell.

She planned to stay after practice on her birthday to tell Mr. Edwards that she needed help with her part. The day came, and she told him at the beginning of the rehearsal that she needed to see him afterward. Mr. Edwards was of average height, but when he looked down at Linda who was only 5'2" in her stocking feet, she made him feel big and powerful. She looked up at him with her large, innocent eyes and incredibly long lashes, and he began to feel dizzy with desire. He couldn't wait for the rehearsal to end. He snapped at the star, who kept fumbling his lines. His unusual behavior was not lost on Linda.

Finally, he could not stand the growing tension any longer, and he dismissed the cast 15 minutes early. Linda went to the girls' dressing room to get out of her costume. She took her time brushing her hair until it glistened and put on pale pink lip gloss. When she thought she had waited long enough for everyone to leave, she skipped down the back hallway to check the boys' dressing room and was happy to see it was empty. She found Mr. Edwards in his office. Entering the room noiselessly, she closed the door behind her, and sat on the leather couch across from his desk.

"What did you want to see me about, Linda?" he asked breathlessly.

"Sit on the couch with me, Mr. Edwards," Linda said, sticking her pointy little tongue out and running it over the curves in her bow lips.

Mindlessly, the man got up out of his chair and threw himself down next to her. She reached up and put her hand on the back of his neck, gently pulling his face down to hers. He kissed her passionately. When he turned his head to breathe, she started to suck on his earlobe. He fumbled with her white button-down shirt. She started to tear at his clothes, like she had seen women do in movies. Her short plaid uniform skirt flipped up, and he slid his hand into her white lace panties. She reached down and pulled her underwear off. Afterward, he couldn't fully remember the encounter. She laughed, putting her head back, displaying her teeth without cavities. Neither of them heard Father O'Malley knock on the door or enter the room.

"Mr. Edwards! My God, man. What is going on in here?" roared Father O'Malley.

"What?" Mr. Edwards scrambled to pull on his pants. "I don't know, Father, we were practicing Linda's lines..."

"Practicing her lines?" the priest screamed.

Mr. Edwards sat at the end of the couch with his head in his hands. His belt and fly open, exposing his tighty whities. Father O'Malley looked at Linda, still lying on the couch, now naked from the waist down. She did not rush to cover herself up.

"Linda! Fix yourself," Father O'Malley said sternly. "Mr. Edwards, you are dismissed. Get your things and get out."

Mr. Edwards stood up, swaying like a drunken man as he lurched toward the door, and grabbed it to steady himself. He turned to look at Linda, who was now gazing up at Father O'Malley. A guttural sound rose up in his throat as he turned his back on the scene and fled down the hall and out the door to the parking lot.

Linda slowly picked up her panties and turned them right side out. She stood up and pulled them on slowly. She sat down to put on her shoes, and Father O'Malley noticed that her silky hair was in a knot at the back of her head.

"Are you all right?" he asked, taking a seat beside her on the couch.

"Yes."

They sat in silence, each contemplating the turn of events.

"You'll have to comb your hair," said Father O'Malley.

"Loan me a brush, Father," she said with an enticing lilt in her voice.

"Now, Linda, you must..." but she cut him off.

"No, Father, you must not tell my mother," Linda instructed.

Father O'Malley knew that a scandal of this magnitude could bring down the school and him with it. Linda looked at the priest's curly hair and handsome face. She knew that news of one of his students being raped by the drama teacher would not have positive publicity value. She also knew that with a secret like this between them, she would be able to control Father O'Malley and make him do just about anything she wanted.

"I wouldn't want to cause a scandal," she added with mock innocence, politely folding her hands in her lap.

"No. We wouldn't want to ruin your young life with a scandal." With this, the priest and the girl slowly got up from the couch. Father O'Malley knew he had formed a dark bond with this young girl. He hoped it wouldn't destroy them both.

$\mathcal{T}$ W E N T Y

❧

$\mathcal{O}$he *Litchfield Press's* offices were located in a landmarked building one street north of St. Raymond's on Lincoln Road. The daily paper had been operating nonstop for 102 years, and Darius Greeley had been the editor and publisher for the last 44. *The Press's* motto, which appeared under the paper's name on the masthead, was "*Novus of Dies,*" or "News of the Day" in Latin.

Hung over and reeking of last night's gin, Greeley arrived at the newsroom around noon each day, but even in his most debilitated state, he was smarter than anyone else who worked at *The Press*—and most of the reporters had graduated from top-flight schools and were sharp themselves. He was an old-time newspaperman and wanted to know the who, what, when, where, why, and how from his reporters as they planned each day's edition of the paper. After fumbling around at his desk for a half-hour, he would meet with his reporters each day at 12:30 to see what the top stories were. Greeley wrote most of the editorials for the paper himself, from a decidedly conservative point of view.

It was Thursday. Helen Acker's eight-part series on women's reproductive rights would start this Sunday, leading up to the demonstration the following Saturday. Greeley had pulled Acker off her regular beat at Town Hall to write the series. He had replaced her with Bill Johnson, who usually covered school sports, but now that school was out and sports wouldn't start up again until August, Bill would cover the mayor. The Litchfield Town Council took July and August off.

The other three full-time reporters were Latitia Blackman, who covered education; Gary Milford, who covered statewide politics; and Fiona Rivington, who covered crime and women's issues. Rivington, the tall, auburn-haired recent graduate from Smith, thought that she had been the natural choice to write the series on women's reproductive rights, but Greeley had chosen Acker. Rivington was still making everyone uncomfortable at the daily meetings because she felt that she had been snubbed. Kit Stilton was one of *The Press's* two full-time photographers. Tom Wren, the other, stayed on-site at Town Hall. Loren Elliot, a freelancer, covered the arts; and Greeley had just signed on three college students as interns for coverage when the regular reporters went on summer vacation. Emily Elliot, Loren's daughter, was one of them.

With one word, Greeley called his reporters to the 12:30 daily meeting. As he ambled toward the conference room he would yell, "Time!" His large, gray form would slowly move itself from his office down the hall through the newsroom— a maze of cubicles, each overflowing with old editions of *The Press*, notes, magazines, phone books and clippings—into the large conference room. Greeley usually wore a gray button-down shirt with darker gray trousers. He had steel-gray, greasy, unkempt hair, and the very skin on his face had a light-gray sheen. He would yell the word only once, and all of the reporters would fall in line behind him.

Greeley sat at the head of the conference table in a large leather chair. After 44 years, even when he wasn't sitting in his chair, his imprint was. One of the first things that new staff members were told was to never, ever sit in Greeley's chair. Going around the table, each reporter had his or her place. Acker sat to Greeley's right, followed by Milford, Blackman, and Stilton. Johnson sat to Greeley's left, followed by Rivington and Elliot. Other freelancers and the interns chose random chairs at the other end of the table. Emily sat next to her mother.

As soon as they were assembled, Greeley said, "Acker. Give us a rundown of the series, and then we'll do ancillary articles." His gravelly voice started without pleasantries.

Acker pushed her glasses up on her nose and squinted at her notes. "Sunday will be the front-page piece that will feature the Litchfield Women's Center and Dr. Amy Friedberg, the chief doctor. I interviewed her, and she said some spicy things about when women should have children that I think will be controversial. On Monday, will be a background piece on Patricia Castellano and her organization, Stand Up for Life. I need art for both of these articles." By "art," everyone around the table knew she meant photographs. "On Tuesday, we'll run a feature on O'Malley. I'm hearing that he will be at the demonstration, and will be giving a sermon on Sunday on the issue. On Wednesday, we'll do side by side, 'History of the Pro-Life Movement,' which Latitia is writing, and 'History of the Pro-Choice Movement,' which Fiona is working on. Thursday is *Roe v. Wade*, and an article on the Supreme Court in the 1970s by Bill, and 'History of Abortion in New Jersey' by Gary— restrictions, etcetera. Friday, back to me, on the upcoming demonstration, which will, of course, be mentioned throughout the week. Saturday, I want to hold on to see what develops, and Sunday is coverage of the demonstration and reaction. We need someone to do 'Woman on the Street,' and somewhere I see an article about backroom abortion before 1973." Greeley had been writing feverishly.

"Where's the mayor in all this?" He threw the question to Bill Johnson, which annoyed Acker.

"I have not been able to get near him. We know that he said he was pro-life when he ran. Patricia Castellano is his sister, but Suzy Walker is his reelection campaign manager and sits on the Women's Center board. Seems old Antonio is caught between two powerhouses," said Johnson with a lazy smile.

"I called Suzy. No return call yet," said Acker. "I wish I coulda heard the conversation between her and the mayor when she got my phone message. Suzy is used to getting what she wants, but so is Patricia, so the mayor's in a bad spot." The entire table laughed. Loren and the interns didn't really know why they were laughing, but they laughed nonetheless.

"Get in to see him, Bill. We need something from the mayor," said Greeley. "Gary, what about those buffoons in Trenton? Senator Connors, and Assemblywomen Gold and Noonan? Have they weighed in?"

"I'm on it. I'm talking to Connors—he's their mouthpiece."

Greeley eyed Johnson suspiciously, seeming to doubt he could get a quote.

"Elliot. I want you to do 'Woman on the Street.' Bring your daughter and the blond," Greeley said, pointing to a studious-looking girl at the far end of the table. "Give them some experience interviewing random women. Get me ten opinions each, pro and con. With art. We'll run that on Sunday. Get out there today. We also need to get a hold of some demonstrators. Acker, get some names from Castellano. Give them to Rivington. Rivington, get it done for Friday." Acker and Rivington glared at each other across the table.

"I don't think we should just interview *women* on the street," said Blackman. "This is an issue that affects both men and women. And don't forget to interview black folks as well as white folks," she said, pursing her full lips.

"I had every intention of getting a diverse group of people," said Loren, her cheeks red with insult and hormones.

"Okay. Okay. No catfights," said Greeley. "Get men, too. Even though it *is* a women's issue. Even with all this equality, men still can't get pregnant. Let's move on." All the women at the table rolled their eyes.

"If they could, it wouldn't even be a debate," said Blackman.

"I said we're moving on," roared Greeley. Blackman pulled on one of her long hoop earrings, and raised her eyebrows.

"Okay. So, is there anything else going on in the city? Any good crime, Rivington?"

"Just the usual. Kids with pot. Outstanding warrants. Criminal mischief. There was a domestic disturbance over on Chester Road. Nothing serious. Just a lot of screaming and crying," said Rivington with a bored look.

"Elliot. Arts," said Greeley.

"The Litchfield Dramatic Club will be doing 'The Pajama Game' the weekend after the demonstration, and the Conservatory is doing 'Romeo and Juliet' the following weekend. I also wanted to do an interview with Sam Kennelworth, a local resident who will be appearing on Broadway in 'Jersey Boys.' We also have a Litchfield author who will be publishing her debut novel and a town artist who is showing his work in the Newark Museum." Loren was talking so fast by the end of her list that she was hyperventilating a little bit. Her colleagues were all staring at her when she looked up. Usually she only had one story to talk about.

Greeley eyed her over his glasses. "Okay. We'll hand some of these stories out to the interns, if any of them can string two sentences together. Nice initiative. Now. Get back to work." Greeley always finished the meeting with a command. As the reporters filed out, Loren hung back. She told Emily she had to talk to Mr. Greeley.

Once they were alone, she said, "Mr. Greeley?" He looked up at her but didn't say anything. "I wanted to talk to you about possibly…going full-time. There's a lot going on in town with

Arts and Entertainment, and I think I could find enough local stories to work a full week."

Greeley actually looked like he was thinking about it. Loren stood so still she could feel her heart beating. "Elliot, the thing is, if you go full-time, I'll have to offer you benefits, and it's just not in the cards." With that pronouncement, he got up, gathered his papers, and left her staring at his imprint in the chair.

TWENTY-ONE

❧

"Life must be protected with the utmost care from the moment of conception," wrote Father O'Malley. "The Catholic Bishops of the United States have said, 'Abortion and euthanasia have become preeminent threats to human dignity because they directly attack life itself. They are committed against those who are weakest and most defenseless. Sadly, they are practiced in those communities which ordinarily provide a safe haven for the weak—the family and the healing professions.'"

Father O'Malley sat trying to write his sermon for the coming Sunday but kept thinking of the demonstration instead. *Damn Patricia! How had this thing spun out of control?* He scrolled back up to the top of the page and read what he had written. Banishing Patricia from his thoughts, he forced himself to focus on his writing. Now for some history.

"Since the first century, the Catholic Church has affirmed the moral evil of every procured abortion. This teaching has not changed and remains unchangeable." Should he actually use the word abortion? How would the congregation react?

Maybe something less direct. He was having trouble focusing. He had two hours before he had to talk to that darn reporter, Helen Acker. And now the mayor had called. What did he want? Father O'Malley needed to clear his head. He would go for a run.

Once out in the park, he stayed clear of Town Hall. He didn't want to run into the mayor. He headed west to the far section, which was a forest with paths for jogging or walking. At night, the boys would play manhunt amongst the trees, falling over unseen logs and rejoicing in the call of the summer night. Father O'Malley remembered playing there himself, a long time ago, before Stephanie and all that had happened. It seemed like a lifetime ago. It seemed like someone else's life.

He had known her all his life, having been next-door neighbors. First, she was the skinny, annoying girl next door, and then, all of a sudden in 10th grade, she was the gorgeous, enticing girl next door. He remembered sitting out on his front steps shucking corn for his mom when Stephanie walked by on her way home. She looked like Angelina Jolie. All hair, lips, and boobs. He whistled at her and she turned and smiled. The next day he asked her to see a movie with him, and after that they were inseparable. For the next two years, they were the hot couple. Tall, gorgeous, popular. Everybody wanted to be them. The girls followed what Stephanie wore and the boys tried to walk like Thomas. They were the most popular couple in school. Until the senior prom and the night they got carried away.

Thomas came out of his reverie to greet two parishioners jogging in the other direction. "Good morning, Mrs. Peterson. Mrs. Reynolds," he nodded.

"Good morning, Father," they said, smiling.

He jogged up the path a quarter mile or so, his mind whirling—the sermon, Stephanie, Acker, Patricia, the demonstration. Maybe he should have tried to meditate instead of run. A mental image of his father rose up in his mind. *Oh great.*

Let's not think about him, Thomas tried to erase the image. His blue, buglike eyes popping out of his head the night he found out. His sharp tongue as he lashed out at Thomas, cursing and damning him. "You're no good. You've never been any good. You were a bad seed from the moment you were conceived," his father had said. Thomas realized his jog had turned into a sprint. He was breathing heavily, and a wave of dizziness washed over him. Slow down. Slow down, he thought. He willed himself to slow down.

He stopped running and bent over with his hands on his knees, his breath coming in loud gasps. He needed to get back to the rectory. He started to walk the way he had come. Slowly, his gasping slowed to normal breathing. Thank goodness it was too hot for most people to run. He forced himself to focus on his next task, which was to return Helen Acker's phone call. Such an unfortunate-looking woman, he thought as he exited the park.

$\mathcal{T}$ W E N T Y - $\mathcal{T}$ W O

᪥

$\mathcal{T}$he Sportsman was technically located in Litchfield, not in Freeport, the next town over, as some Litchfieldians liked to say. Technically, The Sportsman paid taxes to Litchfield and held a liquor license from Litchfield. Many of the mothers in town said The Sportsman was a bad influence and should be shut down. No one in authority took them seriously. Even the mayor had spent many a wild night there when he was young. No, the clients of The Sportsman had no reason to worry. Salvatore Castellano even owned a small share of the place.

Eduardo had been hanging out there for years. So, on Friday night when he found himself in a panic, he headed to The Sportsman. He had been calling Casandra all day to say he was sorry and that he wanted to make it up to her tonight. She had not picked up his calls on her cell or her landline. Not that he really cared about the girl, but she could make trouble for him. She could go to the cops or his house. She could go to the plant and make trouble with Jorge, Pia's father. All of this would be trouble he didn't need. He also didn't like the vision he had of her in a heap, unmoving, on the floor. What if he had really hurt her?

He had decided to go to The Sportsman first and then if she wasn't there, he would go to her apartment. The thought of going back there did not sit well in his gut, but if no one had seen her he had to go. The Sportsman didn't start to hop until 9 p.m., so when he got there at 7:30 it was nearly empty. That time after "Happy Hour," but before "Friday Night." He didn't want to go home and see Pia and her tired, sad eyes. So, he decided to hang out and wait to see who showed up. When he walked in, two or three guys were playing pool in the back. Jay was bartending.

"Jay, *que pasa?*" he asked, trying to sound normal.

"Eduardo! How's it hanging, my man? Get ya'a brew?" asked Jay, already reaching for a bottle of Corona, which he knew was Eduardo's drink.

"Sure, man. With a lime."

"You got it," said Jay, as he shoved the lime slice into the bottle. Eduardo put a $20 on the bar. He picked up the beer and tipped it at Jay.

"Hey Jay, you seen that girl Casandra?" He was trying to sound cool. Nonchalant. He didn't want to convey the urgency he was feeling. He figured he would ask Jay about Casandra before a crowd came in.

Jay thought for a minute. "No, I haven't seen her in a couple of days. She'll probably be here tonight. Why? You getting a little on the side?" Jay winked and smiled his crooked smile.

"No man," Eduardo said in a serious tone. Jay stopped smiling.

"I was just joking." Being a bartender, Jay knew about all the infidelities, and he knew that Eduardo was sleeping with Casandra, but he had violated the bartender code by actually teasing Eduardo about it.

A group of young girls wandered in around 8:15. Jay remembered them from a month or so ago. There was that sexy little blonde. Jay looked around for that other girl. The girl who had come looking for Michael. She didn't seem to be with the group tonight. Michael would be disappointed. Jay could tell Michael had a thing for that girl.

The little blonde gave Eduardo a seductive look as she approached the bar. Eduardo smiled in spite of himself. She was hot. Eduardo reminded himself that he already had enough trouble and went to sit at the other end of the bar.

Michael came in around 9 and saw the little blonde at the bar. He quickly scanned the bar looking for Clara. No luck. He walked over to Linda. "Hey, where's your friend?"

Linda looked him up and down. "What friend would that be?" she asked slowly, her incredibly blue eyes inspecting him.

"Clara."

Linda smiled. "How do you know Clara?"

"I met her the last time you guys were here. We played pinball together."

"You the guy who drove her home that night?" Linda lit a cigarette and blew the smoke to the side away from Michael.

Michael tried to gauge how much she knew. She looked at him directly. "Yeah. I gave her a lift," he said. "She here tonight?"

"No, she didn't come with us. Said she's feeling a little under the weather. I think she's at home. But I play pinball," she said suggestively.

"Maybe a little later. Jay," he called down the bar. As Jay walked toward him he asked Linda if she wanted a drink.

"Sure. A Tequila Sunrise. I think I know you from somewhere. You live in Litchfield?" she asked.

"Yeah."

"Wait a minute, do you go to St. Raymond's Church? Didn't you used to work there?"

"Yeah. I used to work with Father O'Malley as a carpenter." Michael looked at the girl again. Yes, she had been a little girl then, but he remembered her golden hair and pretty face. "Yeah. I think I remember you, too."

"Father O'Malley is a good friend of mine," said Linda. "You tell him you saw me the next time you talk to him."

Something in her tone made Michael uncomfortable. There was something akin to a threat in her words, but Michael couldn't understand it. Michael looked down at the girl. He felt that she wanted something from him, but he didn't know what.

"Anyway, I'm gonna play some pool. See you later." Michael walked toward the back of the bar. That girl was bad news, and he didn't want her going back to Clara and saying anything to upset her. The place was starting to fill up now. Music played from the jukebox, and groups of friends were laughing, couples were flirting, a dart game was in full swing, and people had lined up their quarters on the edge of the pool table for the next game. The newcomer challenged the winner of the last game.

Michael put a quarter down on the edge of the pool table. He went to get a pool cue and wait his turn. As he was watching the game, Eduardo came over and stood next to him.

They greeted each other and then Eduardo said, "Nice Mustang you got there. '67?"

"'69."

"Nice." Eduardo nodded his head.

"You get that job at Green Street?" Michael asked, alluding to the paint job.

"No. We didn't get it. Hey, you know that chick Casandra?"

"Yeah. Two doors down," said Michael, swigging his beer. "What about her?"

"Seen her tonight?" Eduardo watched the pool game. He didn't look at Michael.

"No...come to think about it, I ain't seen her for a couple days. I usually see her bopping around, but not in a few days. I'm up." Michael walked over to the pool table and started to rack up the pool balls. Linda and two of her friends came over to watch them. She made Michael nervous. He didn't know why. She sat on a bar stool, watching him, her shapely little legs crossed at the knee. She wore white shorts and gold gladiator sandals with three-inch heels. Her toenails were long and painted bright red. She smiled every time he sank a ball. Michael won the game and Eduardo was the challenger.

Michael and Eduardo played as the girls watched. Just as Michael won, Molly, Casandra's friend and Michael's ex, came walking down the center of the bar. The only thing missing from her body was a neon sign. Her small, compact frame had been decorated with 14 tattoos, rings on thumbs and toes, six earrings in each ear, and a large cubic zirconia stud in her exposed belly button. Three inches of skin could be seen between her low-rise jeans and her thin T-shirt. She took a seat at the end of the bar and stared at Eduardo, radiating a bad attitude. Eduardo shook Michael's hand and headed over to her.

"Hey," she said. "What have you done with my girlfriend?"

"What do you mean?" asked Eduardo.

"I mean I haven't seen Casandra in days. She doesn't answer her phone. The last I heard from her you were on your way over. She had to go so she could take a shower and get ready for you." Molly looked at Eduardo in an accusatory way with her small, light-brown eyes. Eduardo was distracted momentarily by the ring in her lip.

"I never saw her. I haven't seen her since last week," he lied. "When I got to her apartment there was no answer at the door."

"I'm thinking of calling the police. It's not like Casandra to go anywhere without telling me. I called her mother. She hasn't seen her. Jay says she hasn't been here. Now you're saying that you haven't seen her. I'm worried about her," said Molly.

"Did you go to her apartment?"

"Of course, I did! Just now. The light is on but she doesn't answer the door."

"She ever go out with Michael?" Eduardo asked.

"Who? Russo? No, Michael and me used to go out. Casandra never went with him," Molly said with a frown.

Eduardo could tell that he had planted a seed of doubt in Molly's mind. He looked at Molly, and saw her staring at Michael. Good, he thought to himself. If she was going to the police, it would be better if she mentioned both Eduardo and Michael.

Eduardo wanted to go over to Green Street to see for himself that Casandra wasn't there. "Hey, I gotta go," he said to Molly.

"Sure."

"See ya." Eduardo tipped his chin to Michael.

Once outside, he sprinted to his black truck and drove over to Green Street, parking far away from Casandra's apartment, and walked in the shadows to the stairs and then up to the second floor. He knew that the door had been unlocked when he left, so he tried it and the handle turned. After looking both ways down the outdoor hallway and seeing no one, he entered the apartment and saw Casandra on the floor. The air in the apartment smelled like rancid cheese and rotten eggs. He slowly approached her and his heart skipped a beat. His shirt was instantly drenched from sweat. There she lay in her striped underwear. Dead. Her face was bloated, her eyes open, staring at the ceiling like startled marbles, her tongue protruding from her mouth. Eduardo's hand went up to his mouth to stifle a scream. The room started to spin. He felt off-kilter, and started to slowly back out of the apartment, never taking his eyes off the corpse. When he felt the door behind him, he opened it a touch and peered out to see if anyone was coming. No one in sight. He left the apartment, closing the door quietly behind him.

He retraced his steps, trying to seem calm, and got back into his truck. Although he wanted to floor it, he drove slowly out of the parking lot. *What to do? Call in an anonymous tip? Wait until someone else finds her?* Molly obviously wasn't smart enough to try the door. Should he go back to the bar? He pulled over to assess his options. A Litchfield police car slowed down and stopped next to him. He powered down his window.

"Everything okay?" asked Officer James Quinn.

"Yeah. Everything's fine. I just pulled over to take a call," Eduardo answered calmly.

"Okay. You better move on."

"Thank you, officer."

Eduardo decided to go home. Too many people had seen him near the apartment building. He looked at the digital clock on the dashboard. 11:07. He hoped everyone would be asleep at home.

TWENTY-THREE

❧

Suzy Walker wore many hats. If she actually had a hat for every activity, she could fill a small closet. She was a wife and mother, a named partner at her law firm, chair of the mayor's reelection campaign, a member of the board of the Litchfield Women's Center and the Litchfield Dramatic Club. She was also active in her church, the Congregational Church of Litchfield, and the Litchfield Historical Society.

On Saturday morning she sat in her breakfast room, fuming. Her long-suffering husband, Harry, sat trying to read the morning's paper. He was tired of her constant involvement in everybody's business. He would have been happy if he could retire, move permanently to their eight-bedroom beach cottage in Spring Lake, and leave all of the politics and community business to other people. *Why did Suzy feel that she needed to run everything?*

"So, Antonio calls me back to tell me that Patricia won't be attending the demonstration. That Father O'Malley will lead the troops. And this is supposed to placate me. I told him that I want the demonstration canceled. *Canceled!* Are we living in the deep South, for Christ's sake? Have you spoken to Salvatore about this?" Suzy threw the question at Harry so unexpectedly that he choked on the sip of coffee he was swallowing.

"No, Suzy. I have not and will not speak to Salvatore about this. This is your affair. It's bad enough that I have to wear a tuxedo tonight and shake hands with a bunch of people I don't like at the Country Club. Really, don't get honored anymore! It's not a tribute. It's just a way for them to make money."

"Thank you, Harry. That was very touching. Thanks for your support. Patricia will be there tonight. Maybe I can get her alone," Suzy said, almost to herself. Then, addressing her husband, she said, "Harry, it doesn't bother you one bit that they are literally trying to shut down the Women's Center? What if Catherine got pregnant?"

At the mention of their 16-year-old daughter, Harry put down his paper and looked at his wife. "If Catherine got pregnant, we'd take her to Dr. DeVera and he would take care of it."

"You know, Harry, sixteen-year-olds don't always run to their parents when they get pregnant."

"Suzy, do you think Catherine is sexually active?" Suzy now had Harry's full attention for the first time that morning.

Suzy considered. "No. I don't think so, but it could happen anytime."

"I guess." The thought of some oaf fondling Catherine was really ruining his appetite. "What time is this thing tonight?" he said, to change the conversation.

"This thing, as you call it, starts with cocktails at 6:30 and dinner at 7:30. We'll be out of there by midnight..."

"Midnight!"

"I *am* the honoree. I can't leave early. Really, Harry. I'm late for the hairdresser." With that, she threw her napkin on the table and was gone. Harry shook his head and went back to his newspaper.

TWENTY-FOUR

ॐ

He got to the park at 9:30 a.m. Michael was rarely late, and this morning he was super early. Nerves, he told himself. He had actually thought about what he was wearing. This was a very rare occurrence. As he put on his nicest jeans and a new chambray shirt, he couldn't believe he had butterflies in his stomach. *Russo, man, get a hold of yourself. Nothing is going to happen between you and this girl. Fix the mess and move on.* He parked his car in the lot behind the tennis courts and got out, too nervous to sit. First, he leaned against the side of the car. Then he sat on the hood. Then he walked around to the back of the car and opened the trunk and started to straighten out the junk he had back there. He had his head buried in the trunk when she approached the car.

"Hi," she said. She surprised him and he bumped his head on the door of the trunk. "Oh, I'm sorry. I didn't mean to startle you."

He rubbed his head and laughed. "That's okay. I got a thick skull. Hi." He looked confused by her outfit. She was wearing a short pink tennis skirt with matching top and sneakers, and carrying her tennis racket.

"I told my mom I was going to the park to play tennis, so I had to wear this outfit. Do you think it's okay?" she said, looking worried.

"Yes, fine. It's fine. I was just going to say that I don't play." He smiled. "Maybe you could teach me." She looked scared that he would suggest they do anything together. "Only kidding," he said. "C'mon." He went to open the door for her.

"Thanks." *Today, and the day I have the abortion, and then I never have to see him again.* That was what she kept telling herself. *I'll never let him hurt me again.* She got in the car. He went around to his side and got in. When he had settled in and they were leaving the park, she said, "So, what exactly is this today? You said we had to go to mandatory counseling?"

"Yeah. You meet with the doctor or a psychologist and they talk about stuff." Michael realized he hadn't really thought this through. He had told her the counseling was mandatory because he wanted to spend time with her, but in reality it was voluntary.

"So, they're going to tell me to think about keeping...it?" Clara began to feel even worse than she already felt.

"Umm, maybe when we get there I should check to make sure that we have to go through this. I mean that's what the receptionist told me, but what does she know?"

Clara's head started to spin. Why did she keep getting in the car with this guy? Maybe there was another way. She tried to think about how to do this without him. A wave of nausea played in her throat. She coughed. "When we get there I will go in and talk to someone who knows what they are talking about. I am running out of time. I'm seven weeks pregnant. When is the actual appointment to do it?" Clara was working herself into a state. Her cheeks were red. She started to sweat. She looked like she was going to cry any minute.

This was going all wrong. Michael had pictured a quick chat with a nurse and then a long, intimate lunch where he and Clara got to know each other. After that, anything could happen. He realized he was living in a fantasy world. "You're right. I don't know what that woman told me. Let's go in and make an appointment."

"I want to do it this coming Friday. My mom will be out of town with my sister and I can go home and rest afterward without them. Can you do it on Friday?" she asked. He noticed that her bottom lip was shaking.

"Yes. Yes. I can do it whenever you want," said Michael.

They drove the rest of the way in silence. Out through town to Route 54. As Michael pulled into the parking lot on the side of the clinic, Clara noted the potholes, the overflowing dumpster, and the weeds. The building itself looked well maintained, but there weren't many other stores close by, only a small diner a few buildings down. Clara felt very out of place in her pink tennis suit. As they parked, she turned to Michael and said, "You wait here. I'll go in alone." She got out and slammed the door behind her.

Once outside the car, Clara felt like hidden eyes were watching her. She kept her head down and prayed that no cars drove by. *No one will see me. No one will see me.* She reached the door of the clinic and quickly went inside. Bright light and antibacterial spray stung her eyes and nose. The receptionist looked up, but Clara was stuck in place right by the door. She peered into the full waiting room and looked right into the eyes of Emma Greer, a girl in her biology class. Now, filled with terror, Clara turned on her heel and ran out of the clinic, back to the car where she pulled open the door and dove inside. "Go! Go! Just leave!" She screamed at Michael.

"What's the matter?" Michael asked, looking alarmed and slightly annoyed.

"I knew a girl in there. She saw me! She saw me!" Clara continued to scream as Michael started up the car and left the parking lot.

"Calm down, will ya? If she's there too, she's not going to tell anyone." Michael's eyes had turned a slightly darker shade of brown, and his jaw was set. "Did you make the appointment?"

"No," Clara mumbled through tears and loud sobs.

"Jesus Christ! I'll do it. I'll call them. Settle down," he said with an indulgent laugh.

"I can't fucking believe this is happening to me! Take me to the park," she demanded.

Clara was furious, but a little voice in her head warned her to be cool. He could drop her off and never come back. She would be all alone without him. The car suddenly felt like a cage. She couldn't breathe, her nosed was clogged, her head ached, and without warning, her throat started to contract and she knew she was going to vomit.

"Michael, pull over. I'm going to…" but Michael, seeing her hand fly up to her mouth and hearing the first retch, had already started to swerve to the curb. Before he even stopped the car, Clara opened the door and barfed into the street. Once Michael pulled over, Clara stumbled out, only to realize that they were on the outskirts of downtown on a Saturday morning. Putting her hands on her knees, she took a few deep breaths and got back in the car.

"Are you all right?" Michael asked.

"Just go," Clara said wiping her mouth on the back of her hand. "Let's get to the park." *So I can get away from you.*

Michael pulled back into the traffic. Clara slunk down in her seat and put her hand over her face. She felt like she was suffocating; whiffs of Michael's clean sweat and aftershave wafted over to her on the breeze of the air conditioning. Her pink skirt now had a scattergram of breakfast down the front, and the smell of vomit started to mix with the sweat and cologne. She opened the window for fresh air and tried to stick her nose out, while still covering her eyes.

"Why don't you just put a bag over your head?" Michael asked. "Then no one will see you. Do you really think that everyone is walking around town wondering what you're doing?"

"No, but people talk."

To fill the silence, Michael turned on the radio. He switched off Justin Beiber, Adele, and Katy Perry, and finally settled on Pink. They pulled into the park, made the wide loop around, and pulled into the parking lot near the tennis courts. Michael kept the car idling and half-turned in his seat to face Clara.

"Look, it's gonna be okay. We'll go on Friday and get it done and it'll be over. Just like it never happened."

"Maybe for you! But, Emma saw me!" Clara's voice was a whine.

"Don't get hysterical. Emma was at the clinic too. She's not going to go around saying you were there, because then, everyone knows she was there," said Michael, his eyes starting to darken with frustration.

"So, how are we making the appointment? Let's do it now. You call. Make it for next Friday at 9 o'clock." Clara tried to rid her mind of any thoughts not related to getting the appointment. "And, if they need a phone number or an address, give them yours."

Michael reached into his pocket for his phone and dialed 411. After the operator gave him the number, he hung up.

"What are you doing?" asked Clara, exasperation defining every word.

"What name should I use? Are you using your own name?"

Clara eyed Michael suspiciously, then stared out the windshield at the tennis players. Carefree people, playing tennis. Laughing. Talking. And she was in this disgusting man's car trying to decide whether she should use an alias when getting rid of her rapist's baby. All of a sudden, her anger turned to fear. She didn't know the right answer to his question.

"I don't know. What should I do? I've never done anything like this before." She was on the verge of tears.

"Well, I would say use a fake name, but if we get there and they ask for proof..."

"Proof?"

"Yeah, like a driver's license."

"I don't drive..."

Michael winced and wiped the sweat from his brow. "Then, your high school ID."

"Just use my name."

"What's your last name?"

For some reason, this question shocked Clara. She just assumed he knew, but how would he? "Mahoney," she said. "Clara Mahoney."

"They might ask how far along you are. Seven weeks, right?"

"Yes, that's what I think," said Clara.

Michael dialed 411 again and this time had the operator put him through. As he made the appointment, Clara started to bite her nails. She had never bitten her nails before. For some reason, it calmed her down. She liked the little clack sound they made as she bit through. She was down four nails by the time Michael hung up. "Okay. Next Friday," he said.

"Okay. Just pick me up outside my house at 8:30," she said, as she opened the door to escape. "I'll see you then." And she was gone.

TWENTY-FIVE

෧

ehind the beautifully painted public offices at Stand Up for Life, there was a space where no decorator had ever gone. This is where Sandra Stett, Patricia's fundraiser, had set up her picket-sign production area. Simon and Lee had been recruiting demonstrators through the website for weeks. One week out, they had a list of 58 people. Sandra, the mastermind of the demonstration, knew that she needed many more and had a plan to get them. She knew from the beginning that Patricia would not get involved with the details of planning the demonstration, recruiting demonstrators, renting staging, writing brochures, or securing permits. She knew Patricia would spend her time making sure her picture was in the paper and on the news, while Sandra did the real work.

Sandra Stett had moved to Litchfield from Peachtree Gables, South Carolina, six years earlier and had immediately set about the task of finding an organization that could do her work. Sandra, perky and blond, with a Southern accent that could melt caramel, was a skilled fundraiser, but she knew she didn't have the confidence to be the face of a movement. She also knew that Northerners would feel more comfortable following a fellow Northerner. She knew she needed to create a movement that would carry God's word to the people. She also knew that she was destined to play a role in the struggle to save babies' lives, but she needed a mouthpiece.

She believed that God had sent her Patricia Castellano to carry his words to the people. Sandra had been invited to join Stella Perez's book club, as a way to welcome Sandra to town. They had met through the mayor's Newcomers Club, which Stella chaired. After chatting, Stella had invited Sandra to read that month's book selection and come to her house for breakfast the next week for the book club meeting. As soon as Sandra walked into Stella's kitchen and saw Patricia holding court in Stella's breakfast nook, she knew she had found her woman, her mouthpiece.

For the next three book club meetings, Sandra watched Patricia. She was perfect. Beautiful, articulate, well-connected, and above all, vain. Patricia simply loved Patricia. She was a spokeswoman without a cause. Sandra just had to plant the idea, and she knew that Patricia would hear the calling. To raise the subject, Sandra suggested they read *The Doctor's Wife*, by Elizabeth Brundage, for the next month. She wanted to see Patricia's reaction to the book and the topic of abortion.

After Patricia let it be known that she was pro-life, Sandra moved in. She invited Patricia to have coffee with her the next day at the Litchfield Diner. She said that she had an idea that she wanted to run by her. Patricia agreed to meet. Patricia's twins had just turned 10 months old and had both begun to walk within minutes of each other. The Castellanos had added an *au pair* to their household, and Patricia was always looking for an excuse to leave the rambunctious boys with the help.

Even though Patricia was a New Jerseyan through and through, she had some of the attributes of a Southern woman. She was always impeccably dressed, coiffed, and accessorized.

She always had gracious manners, a generous smile, and a kind word. With her genteel way, she could cut her adversaries down and pierce them through the heart, and they would ask for more. One of her most charming characteristics was that she never told people what she really thought about them, and for this, people were always grateful. She made Sandra feel right at home. They understood each other in a way that Northern women, usually more forthright, sometimes even downright rude, could not.

And that was how the idea was planted in Patricia's brain that she had to start an organization that would stand up for life. By the time the lipstick was dry on the diner coffee mug, Patricia believed that it was her idea to form the organization. Sandra would help her, but Patricia would lead the charge, with her stunning face on brochures and billboards. With local TV news shows and a new website featuring her and her views on the sanctity of life. Who could object? It was a righteous cause. A noble cause. "Salvatore will be so proud of you, Patricia! His beautiful wife doing such good work," praised Sandra. "And your parents! You'll be doing work just as important, if not more so, than your brother's. He just fixes potholes, after all." Yes, this was brilliant.

In three months' time, they had rented the offices over the diner and Patricia had her first set of headshots taken. Patricia hired Sandra to work in the office as a fundraiser. She specialized in major gifts. In other words, she specialized in knowing who Patricia's friends were and then researching their net worth and giving Patricia the ammunition to ask them for "a gift." Many of these friends were members of the book club, and Sandra had targeted Stella as Patricia's first "ask," a fundraising term for asking for money. Peer-to-peer giving. That is what Sandra had taught her. Of course, Patricia ran in circles where people had disposable income and gave generously to their friends' causes. The Castellanos were out two or three times a week at various functions.

Sandra never pointed out to Patricia that she was a Baptist, not a Catholic. Patricia knew that she didn't go to St. Raymond's, but what other people did was very unimportant to Patricia. She never asked Sandra any personal information and Sandra volunteered little. She played the role of adoring sycophant so well that Patricia did not realize that she was being manipulated by a master. As time went on, Patricia needed someone in the office to answer phones and be on-site during the renovation. Sandra found Lee, lost in a sea of self-doubt. Sandra knew that she could manipulate Lee and get him to do just about anything she wanted.

After establishing the organization and after years of raising awareness through articles, brochures, and news interviews, Sandra knew it was time to make a bolder statement. Hence, the idea of the demonstration was born. Sandra had started to give Patricia information about the Litchfield Women's Center. Of course, Patricia knew it was there, out on the deserted county road where she never went. First, Sandra told her the story of a young girl who had gone there for an abortion, without her parent's knowledge, and ended up with an infection so deadly that she spent two weeks in St. Michael's Hospital. Second, she gave Patricia numbers. Hundreds of teenagers per year, thousands of women per year who went to the center for birth control and abortions. Patricia trusted Sandra to give her the facts. But a *demonstration?* That was another matter.

At first, Patricia had turned up her nose at such a white-trash idea. She was much more comfortable with distributing brochures and giving interviews. Until an article in an online blog suggested that her organization was a fraud. That it was created just to raise money for her brother, Antonio Ceravolo, and his political aspirations. After that, it was much easier for Sandra to get Patricia to go out on a limb. The last thing that Patricia wanted was for her organization to appear to be for the sole purpose of funding Antonio's campaign. How did that help her? Sure, it helped her that Antonio was the mayor, but she was not content to simply stand behind him at his swearing-in. She wanted to be a name in her own right. That was when they had set up her first meeting with Father O'Malley. It was only natural for Patricia to turn to her priest for support.

Sandra also loved the idea of the photograph of the tall, blond priest and the raven-haired socialite. That was a picture people would look at. No short, bald monks or society ladies with love handles and light-brown mustaches for her movement. No, Sandra knew what people wanted. They wanted their heroes to be better than they were, and by that, she meant better-looking. She had been trying to get a photo of the two of them together for some time, but Patricia didn't really see the need to have Father O'Malley in the photo. But that was before she had decided not to go to the demonstration. Now, the only way her photo would be in the paper was through the advance publicity and the distributed photo that she had finally agreed to take.

Sandra hired a photographer to take the photo on Sunday after the sermon. After Father O'Malley shook the hand of every member of his congregation, he and Patricia would go into the chapel and have a series of photos taken. Lee would handle the logistics. He was very good at orchestrating photo shoots and interviews. They expected that quite a few members of the local press would attend to hear Father O'Malley's sermon, and then Lee would herd them all into the chapel for photos.

As Sandra looked at the tables and the signs to be used next weekend, she couldn't believe she had gotten this far toward her goal. By next Saturday night, the Litchfield Women's Center would either be shut down or close to it. How could this nice, family community condone women killing their babies? Sandra knew that Patricia would take most of the credit, but maybe there would be a little left over for Sandra.

TWENTY-SIX

❧

"So, we just walk up to people and ask them a question?" asked Emily Elliot, as she and her mother Loren, Kit, and Mia, the blond intern, walked down Grant Avenue. The town was always crowded on Saturday morning. Young dads and their children were sent to town to give the moms a break. They would congregate at Litchfield Bagel & Bialy and then proceed to one of the town's two toy stores or Moe's Barber Shop. Packs of teenagers roamed the streets, and shoppers from Litchfield and surrounding towns went from store to store. The town was like an upscale shopping mall. Gap, Baby Gap, Victoria's Secret, Coach, Talbots, and Williams-Sonoma were interspersed in between mom-and-pop specialty stores catering to women or teenagers. GameStop was a popular hangout, as was Starbucks.

"Well, let's choose our people carefully," said Loren. "Let's go to the corner, where there's more room. We don't want to cause a traffic jam. I'll do the first interview, so you guys can see how it's done." The group moved to the corner of Grant and Maple, which was the center of town. Loren watched the pedestrians, looking for a woman who was alone to interview. People were more likely to give an honest opinion if they were alone.

A well-dressed, middle-aged woman approached. Loren had her tape recorder ready. "Excuse me, hi, my name is Loren Elliot and I am a reporter with *The Litchfield Press*. We're doing a feature article and asking residents' opinions on a certain topic. Do you have a minute?"

"Just a minute," said the woman.

"Thank you. Next Saturday there will be a demonstration in front of the Litchfield Women's Center out on Route 54. People will be protesting the fact that the center provides abortion services. How do you feel about a woman's right to choose?"

The woman collected her thoughts as the small group watched her intently. "I believe in a woman's right to choose. It's in the Constitution, or was decided by the Supreme Court, anyway. I find it unacceptable that residents of this town would line up outside a medical facility to slander their neighbors." The woman's voice gained conviction as she spoke, and ended with a defiant tone.

"Thank you. What is your name?"

The woman paused. "Josephine Nelson," she stated.

"May we take your picture?"

"Yes," she said, holding her head high.

After Kit took Josephine Nelson's picture, Loren turned to Emily. "Okay. You're up. Are you ready?"

Emily chose a kind, fatherly-looking man to interview. He was not as articulate as Josephine.

"I think…that women should be careful…, you know? They shouldn't get in that position."

Emily pressed him. "But what do you think about the protest?"

"I think…it's better to leave the whole thing alone."

Emily looked at her mother. Loren nodded.

"Thank you. What is your name?"

"My name?" the man became flustered. "I'm not giving you my name." And with that, he walked off, muttering.

"He looked so nice," said Emily with a frown.

The group took turns interviewing passersby for the next hour. They got five pro-choice and five pro-life comments. Greeley had asked for 10 of each. They decided to break for lunch and reconvene in an hour. Mia and Kit wanted to check out the sale at Gap. Loren, who was feeling very tired, wanted to sit down. Loren and Emily headed to the diner.

Emily looked at her mother when they were seated in the diner. She didn't look so good. She looked really tired, with bags under her eyes and a drained, haggard look on her face.

"Mom, are you feeling all right?" asked Emily, with a concerned look on her bright, young face.

"I'm just a little tired. I couldn't sleep well last night, what with dad's situation and all," said Loren. Loren debated whether or not to tell Emily the truth—tell her that she was pregnant and was actually going, herself, to the clinic next Friday to have an abortion. She wondered what Emily would say.

"Has Dad had any luck?"

"No, he's sending out resumes and calling people he knows in other districts, but no one's hiring. I don't think he'll be able to get another teaching position. I think he needs to consider alternatives, but you know your father, his passion is teaching. It's just so sad." Loren shook her head.

"He'll get something. Everybody loves Dad when they meet him." Emily smiled at her mom to lift the mood.

"So, what do you think about this protest?" asked Loren.

"Well, I'm definitely pro-choice. I also can't believe this is happening in Litchfield. It seems like something that might happen in Tennessee or some other Southern state, but not here. It's weird. Don't you think?"

"I do. You know how I feel about overly religious people trying to tell others what to do. I feel sorry for the women who will be there, at the clinic, that day."

"I wouldn't go that day. Would you?"

Loren knew her daughter didn't know what a real question that was for her. "No. I definitely wouldn't go that day."

TWENTY-SEVEN

᠅

What a mistake that had been, thought Michael, as he dropped Clara off in the park by the tennis courts. He had blown it. Why had he been so stupid and lied to her? She was a smart girl and had seen right through it. Damn. She had looked so perfect in her little pink outfit and she had smelled so good. He couldn't get her smell out of his mind. It was a mixture of fruit and soap and something more primal. It was driving him crazy. He felt bad that she didn't want to be seen with him, but he kind of understood it. Was it the fact that she was unattainable that fed the longing in his chest? Now he had to wait until next Friday to see her, and then that was it. He would never see her again. He knew that and still he wanted to take care of her. It didn't make any sense.

He left the parking lot and decided to just go home, take a cold shower, and maybe a nap. Or do some work on his car. Anything to forget about Clara. He drove through town and headed south, driving slowly back to Green Street. As he turned into the apartment house parking lot, he saw Molly sitting on the planter outside the stairwell leading up to his apartment. *Just what the doctor ordered.*

He got out of his car, thinking that to Molly, he would look all dressed up. She would be easy to seduce. "Hey babe," he said.

"Hey. Where ya been? You're looking fine, Michael," she said, smiling. The diamond stud in her belly button sparkled in the bright summer light.

"I've been out looking for you," he said in a gravelly voice, as he put his arms around her.

"Really? I thought you were over looking for me," she said, as she wrapped her legs around him. With one quick motion he picked her up and started to carry her up to his apartment.

"What the hell?" shrieked Molly, laughing. "Michael? What is going on?"

He put her down outside his door and pressed her up against the wall, kissing her hard, his tongue filling her mouth. With one hand he tried to get the key out of his pocket, and with the other he grabbed her ass hard. Always one to rise to the occasion, Molly started to tear at his belt buckle as he found the key and opened the door. He picked her up, still pressed to him, and walked the few steps into the vestibule, then kicked the door shut with his foot. She stepped back, tore her shirt off—she wasn't wearing a bra—and started to unbutton his shirt. He pushed her hand down to his pants instead. Then she pulled down her own shorts and panties and lay down on the tiny rug, spread-eagle, and waited for him to kick off his boots. She absent-mindedly played with the ring through her nipple. He jumped on her, with his pants still around his knees.

Afterward, as they lay panting on the tiny woven foot rug, Molly said, "So, ya missed me?" She made a sound like the yipping of a poodle.

"Yeah. I did miss you," said Michael, knowing that he wanted her to stay there all afternoon to take his mind off the girl in the pink tennis skirt.

"That's so sweet, Michael. I've missed you, too." They cuddled each other until their breathing steadied. "Michael? I really came here because I'm worried about Casandra. Michael, she's missing," said Molly, rising up on one elbow to look down at him. "I don't know where she is. Have you seen her?"

Thoughts of Clara started to make their way into his mind. He tried to focus. "No. I haven't seen her." He got up, pulled on his jeans, and went into the kitchen for a drink. Molly pulled on her clothes and went into the bathroom to clean herself up. When she came out, Michael was leaning on the kitchen counter, shirtless. "What do you mean she's missing?" he asked.

"I can't find her. I've called everyone I know who she might be with, but no one's seen her. Have you seen her?" Molly pulled herself up to sit on the opposite counter.

Michael tried to think back and realized that he hadn't seen Casandra for more than a few days. "Let's go over there," he said, and started to walk toward the front door, reaching down to grab his shirt on the way out. Molly jumped off the counter and followed him.

"That was nice, Michael," said Molly, hanging back.

"Yeah, nice." Michael went out of his apartment and walked two doors down to Casandra's apartment. That's when he smelled the sickly odor. It made him gag. Molly was coming up behind him. He put up his hand and looked her in the eye. "Let me go in. You stay here."

"Okay," she said, frowning, covering her nose.

Michael entered the apartment and knew immediately that Casandra was dead. He could see her bloated body, and the smell was overwhelming. He couldn't stand it. He covered his nose and mouth with one hand and turned around and went out. Molly looked at him questioningly. She looked scared.

"She's dead. We need to call 911." He groped in his pocket for his cell phone. *Shit, it must have fallen out.* He grabbed Molly's arm and pulled her back toward his apartment.

"No, I want to see her," wailed Molly.

"No, you don't." Michael tightened his grasp on Molly's arm. "You're hurting me," she cried.

Michael dragged her into his apartment and shut the door. He went over to the phone and dialed 911. Molly was crying and she threw her arms around his neck.

He hugged her and said, "It's okay," but he wasn't even convincing himself. When the operator picked up he said, "I'd like to report a dead body."

Molly really started to cry when she heard Michael call Casandra a "body."

TWENTY-EIGHT

❧

*H*adley and Ernest Hemingway swam in the lake behind the Great House, where swan couples had been swimming for 80 years, since the house was built. These two graceful swans had been named by the Swan Lake Country Club's caretaker because he had been reading *A Farewell to Arms* when he had been told to buy two new swans for the lake. The Swan Lake Country Club was the most elegant venue in Austin County. It had once been the country estate of Vladimir Sokolov, the famous dancer. Now, 50 years later, it had been turned into a country club, complete with an 18-hole golf course, tennis courts, gym, and indoor and outdoor pools. It was a favorite site for weddings and political and social fund-raising events. The house itself was a rambling faux chateau that had been designed to fit into the small hills of the land. Sokolov had put in two full theaters and a large dance studio that was now used for dinner parties. The club owners had left the wall of mirrors and the ballet barre where Sokolov and his troupe had practiced.

Tonight, everyone who was anyone in Litchfield would be at the Austin County Domestic Violence Law Initiative dinner to honor Suzy Walker and her firm, Walker & Walker, for their commitment to providing *pro bono* legal services for victims of domestic violence. The event would raise funds for the Safe Haven Shelter, a safe space for women who needed to run from an abusive spouse or partner and had nowhere to turn. Salvatore Castellano had recently agreed to sit on their board.

The mayor had called Salvatore that morning *mano-a-mano* to ask him to try to do something about his wife. Like two castrated roosters, they crowed and shook their plumage, both knowing that neither one of them was a match for Patricia. The mayor floated his idea of creating an arts commission for Patricia to chair, to distract her. Salvatore agreed, but neither had a good strategy to get Patricia to agree. They ranted and raved about Father O'Malley's involvement in the demonstration, but neither was going to condemn him publicly. In fact, Salvatore had agreed to make a sizable contribution to St. Raymond's capital campaign in exchange for Father O'Malley leading the rally without Patricia.

After calling Salvatore, the mayor had called Nina Adler, the executive director of the Safe Haven Shelter, to make sure that they were not sitting anywhere near the Walkers at the dinner. Since Suzy would be at the head table, and usually everyone important wanted to sit at the head table, Salvatore made up this convoluted story about how he and Patricia wanted to make the night be about Suzy and not about them, so they wanted to take a back table. Nina knew immediately why Salvatore was calling and why the Castellanos and the Walkers should not sit near each other, but told Salvatore how gracious he and Patricia were and that she would accommodate the request.

The one person who would not understand why they were not seated at the head table would be Patricia. Salvatore knew that Patricia could sit right next to Suzy all night and not bat an eyelash. His wife's conviction that she was the most important person in every room never ceased to amaze him. Of course, it also made her very desirable, and Salvatore was completely under her spell when he was with her. When they were apart he had a little more clarity, and he could allow himself to feel the usual range of emotions, but in her presence it was sad for him to admit that he was not in her league.

As he watched her get ready for the evening, he mulled it over in his mind. Should he tell her about the seating arrangements? Bella, Patricia's personal maid, was fixing her hair in an updo with an intricate pattern of pearl bobby pins, forming a design in her black hair. He loved the way her hair grew on the back of her neck. As Bella worked, he watched Patricia try on an emerald ring from her enormous free-standing jewelry case, which held scores of necklaces, bracelets, rings, and earrings. There was something so fascinating about watching a woman adorn herself. All the great painters had been entranced by women half-dressed, combing their hair or toweling themselves after the bath. It was truly erotic to watch. Salvatore knew that Patricia would not allow herself to be touched after getting ready, so he took a deep breath, decided not to ruin the tranquility of the moment, and went into their palatial bathroom to take a cold shower.

Only a mile away on Reade Way, Suzy Walker and her husband, Harry, were also getting ready for the big night. Instead of a personal maid, Suzy was working with her personal assistant, Ginny, putting the final touches on her speech. Suzy's simple yet elegant taupe silk gown hung from a hanger over the door to her closet.

Harry wore a frown as he tried to choose which of his tuxedos to wear. Suzy saw him holding one and then the other in front of himself as he stood in his briefs, socks, and unbuttoned shirt in front of the mirror.

"Wear the Ralph Lauren," she stated.

"Do you really think so? The lapels are kind of flashy," said Harry in a monotone.

"Yes, you'll look handsome. Give you a little pizzazz," said Suzy, turning back to her desk.

"No one will be looking at me, darling," he said, clearly showing his annoyance with the evening.

"Harry, I supported you wholeheartedly when you were honored by the United Way and we had to go and sit with those ghastly football players they always drag out. Please, try to be a bit more supportive," said Suzy.

"That was Michael Strahan we were sitting with."

"Who, dear?"

"The football-player-turned-talk-show-host. That was Michael Strahan."

"Okay, dear." Suzy turned to Ginny. "I want to say very clearly that I feel we must support *all* of the organizations that support women. Write that in. I want Patricia to hear that in a public setting. Of course, she's never stepped foot in either Safe Haven or the Women's Center. Maybe that's what I should suggest to her. Not publicly, of course, but if I have a chance to speak to her alone."

"I think you should avoid her like the plague," said Harry. "The last thing we need is the two of you going at it while all our friends and neighbors look on."

"Really, Harry. We're both civilized women. We'd never make a scene in public," said Suzy, as she put on her pear-shaped diamond earrings.

TWENTY-NINE

❧

Two squad cars responded to Michael's call and arrived at the Green Street Apartments in under six minutes. The Litchfield police dispatcher was not used to hearing a young man's panicked voice talking about a dead body. Michael was waiting at the top of the stairwell as the officers got quickly out of their cars. An ambulance pulled in right behind them.

Officers Quinn and Rea ran up the stairs. Michael and Molly both started talking at once.

"We couldn't find her...." said Molly

"I tried the door...." said Michael.

Officer Quinn put up his hands. "I can't listen to both of you at the same time. Where's the body?"

They walked down the hallway toward Casandra's apartment, four doors down, and the stench became unmistakable. The officers took out face masks and put them on.

"Stay out here," said Officer Rea to Michael and Molly.

The paramedics from the ambulance followed the officers into the apartment carrying their equipment. Two more police cars pulled up. Detective Samuel Bickford arrived with the second group and gave Michael and Molly a long, penetrating look before he walked down to the apartment. Molly had been hanging onto Michael for support ever since they had made the discovery. Other police cars arrived. Equipment was brought up. Yellow police tape was hung. The superintendent was summoned.

Detective Bickford came out of the apartment, took off his mask, and gulped in a deep breath. He breathed in the fresh outdoor air and shook his head as if to get the bad air out.

"Can I ask you guys a couple of questions?" he asked, moving down the hallway away from the crime scene. Michael and Molly nodded "yes."

"So, do you know who the victim is?" Molly looked at Michael to see if she should answer. He nodded.

"Casandra Keller," said Molly, wiping her forefinger under her running nose.

"And what is your name?" Detective Bickford had a small pad and was making notes.

"Molly Dolan."

"And yours?" He tipped his chin toward Michael.

"Michael Russo. We've been wondering where she was for a few days now. Then today we decided to go in her apartment and see if she was in there. And she...was."

"Do either of you have a key to the place?"

"No, the door was unlocked," said Michael. Detective Bickford gave him another long, hard look before he made a note.

"Which girl is your girlfriend?"

"Neither. I mean, me and Molly here, we used to go out, but not anymore."

Molly pouted at this piece of information. She had thought that after today's developments there might be hope for her relationship with Michael. As they talked, Police Chief Leonard Chodor arrived with the Homicide Task Force. The chief was an intimidating man with thick black hair, hooded brown eyes, and a large, fleshy nose that headed down his face in a straight line, taking a sharp turn to the left midway down, where it had been broken several times.

"Hello. I'm Chief Chodor. What's the situation, Bick?" he asked Detective Bickford.

"These two found the deceased girl in her apartment. Looks to me like she's been in there for a few days. When did you last see Casandra?" Bickford asked Molly.

"A few days ago. We went to Victoria's Secret to buy panties." Molly wailed and buried her face in Michael's chest.

"Does she have family?" asked the chief, looking at Michael.

"Just her mom. Do you want her number?" answered Molly.

"Do you have her address?"

Molly pulled her face away from Michael's shirt and said, "1214 Tuttle Street in Freeport."

Bickford made a note.

"We'll need both of you to come to headquarters so you can fill us in. Detective Bickford will take you down. You two live here?" said the chief.

"I do," said Michael.

"Okay. I'll go see the girl's mom. Bick, you take these two downtown. Quinn, Rea, you finish up here," commanded the Chief. "How old is she?" he asked Molly.

"Twenty-two."

"Got siblings?"

"No."

"Shit," said the chief.

$\mathcal{T}$HIRTY

❦

iona Rivington sat at her desk at *The Press* offices, buried in books, articles, and notes on her story on the history of the pro-choice movement. She had taken her sandals off and had her feet with the dark-maroon nail polish up on a chair. Her long, auburn hair was pulled back in a bun, and she wore a short, white sundress and thick black-rimmed glasses.

She was trying to decide between two quotes to start her article. The first was a quote from Joycelyn Elders, who was the U.S. Surgeon General under President Bill Clinton. Elders said: "We really need to get over this love affair with the fetus and start worrying about children." Fiona liked this quote a lot. The other quote was from Katha Pollitt, the columnist for *The Nation,* who wrote: "Young women need to know that abortion rights and abortion access are not presents bestowed or retracted by powerful men (or women)—Presidents, Supreme Court justices, legislators, lobbyists—but freedoms won, as freedom always is, by people struggling on their own behalf."

She decided to go with the Elders quote. It was shorter and more powerful. As she sat up and started to pound away on her laptop, Greeley came ambling down the aisle between the cubicles. He looked excited and was holding a small piece of paper in his hand.

"Rivington! Get your shoes on. There's been a murder. A murder in Litchfield! This is great," Greeley said, with a sinister-looking grin. Rivington turned around, slipping her sandals on.

"Greeley, it's 'great' there's been a murder?"

Greeley looked perplexed.

Rivington frowned, shook her head, and asked, "Who's been murdered?" as she picked up her slim reporter's pad and pen.

"Casandra Keller, twenty-two, found at the Green Street Apartments. Body's been lying there for days. Go over there. Take Blackman with you. Stilton will meet you there. I almost want to go myself." Greeley couldn't contain himself. A murder *and* the demonstration! This was a great week for news. He looked at Rivington, who wasn't moving real fast.

"Rivington. Get going," he ordered.

"I think I know her. I think she was in my class in high school. I can't believe it. She's my age," Fiona said, looking dazed.

"Well, get over there and find out everything you can. She was found by two locals. Molly Dolan and Michael Russo. They've been taken down to headquarters."

"I know both of them, too. She was in my class. Michael was a year ahead. Maybe I should go to headquarters and talk to them, instead of going over to the apartment."

"Fine. You go to headquarters, and Blackman will go to the apartment. I'll get Wren to meet you there. See if you can get a shot of the two of them. Now go!"

Helen Acker, who was revising her front-page story for to-morrow on the Litchfield Women's Center, and was just about to send it to Greeley for a final edit, listened to the conversation between Greeley and Rivington. She couldn't believe that he was pulling the whole staff off of the series, *her* series, to run around town chasing a news story. Of course, murders did not happen every day in Litchfield, and so she had to admit that the story had news value, but she had worked too hard. Would he bump her front-page story? He had said the girl's name was Casandra Keller. Acker Googled her and found one mention of her being arrested for possession of a small amount of marijuana. She breathed a sigh of relief as she silently thanked God that Keller wasn't a well-connected person with important parents, or the demonstration would have become a small article on page 4.

Acker went back to her editing, but she couldn't concentrate. She was nervous about having to go to the Swan Club that evening for the Suzy Walker event, but it couldn't be helped. *All those stick-thin society ladies in their designer dresses.* She had even toyed with the idea of buying a new dress, but the thought of going to the mall and having to try anything on was too awful. No, they would just have to accept her in her work clothes. She knew everyone involved with the Women's Center would be there, and she wanted to see if there was any interaction between Suzy Walker and Patricia Castellano. Also, Bill Johnson had not been able to get a quote from the mayor, and Acker knew she would be able to corner him.

She finished editing the piece and went over to see the layout editor. As she walked up behind him, she could see the image of Dr. Amy Friedberg's gentle face on his screen. Rachel Horowitz, president of the center's board, had put some pressure on Friedberg to have her photo taken for tomorrow's edition. It would run in the upper-right-hand corner of page 1, alongside Acker's bylined story, "Local Doctor Believes Women Should Have Right to Choose." She was proud of this piece. She was proud of the series. She had tried to be objective. She was sure that this was her ticket to the big time. As she sat there staring at the computer screen, she thought that with these clips, *The New York Times* would beg her to work for them. She allowed herself a smile, which instantly turned into a frown as she thought about Casandra Keller, who was now threatening all of Helen's hard work from the mortuary.

THIRTY-ONE

❦

The crowd in the foyer of the Swan Club was making it hard for Patricia to make a grand entrance. She usually liked to arrive late enough to have people notice her, but tonight there were just too many people to be able to see her. As the doorman held the door for her, she caught a glimpse of herself in a mirror placed to the right of the door. She smiled. She looked stunning in her strapless, emerald-green vintage gown with impressive emeralds both around her neck and hanging from her ears. Bright-red lips and heavily made-up eyes finished her look. She quickly peeked at Salvatore, who looked so handsome in his tux. His thick, salt-and-pepper hair—still more pepper than salt—was shiny with gel, and his face was lit up with a broad grin.

Although her arrival was not as impressive as she had hoped, the throng of partygoers did part for her and Salvatore to get to the center of the room. She spied her brother, the mayor, over to the left and purposely went to the right side of the crowd. She and Salvatore knew everybody, so they inched their way into the gathering, stopping every foot or so to air-kiss another couple. She saw Elsa Martinson and Father O'Malley talking, and headed in their direction. Elsa was good-looking, with her porcelain skin and big blue eyes, Patricia thought to herself, as she noted Elsa's bold fuchsia gown.

As they continued to make their way over to Mrs. Martinson and Father O'Malley, she saw that Stella and George Perez were there. Stella was wearing that lavender Prada gown that Patricia had tried on but didn't buy. Thank goodness. She would have had to leave if they were both wearing it. It didn't even look like a designer dress. More like Target. She smiled and continued to thread her way over to O'Malley. Wow! Look at that. Who was wearing that slinky, gold-mesh gown? Really, it was a tad too much. The young woman turned to face Patricia, two cameras dangling from her thin neck. Oh heavens, when did photographers start to wear designer dresses and look like runway models?

Finally, they had made their way through enough designer gowns and tuxedos to fill a small boutique. The room was swirling in color, perfume, and jewels. Patricia loved nothing better than a black-tie event.

"Don't you look fabulous, Elsa? Father O'Malley," Patricia dazzled them with her naturally beautiful smile and unnaturally white teeth.

"Patricia, darling, emerald is your color. Not everybody can wear it," said Elsa. "And Salvatore, aren't you looking handsome?" Elsa reached up to kiss the air in Salvatore's general direction.

"Father," said Salvatore, shaking O'Malley's hand.

"Isn't it wonderful when people come out for a good cause," said Father O'Malley.

At this point, the fabulous-looking photographer walked toward the group. Patricia watched Salvatore watch her approach. She was a thing of beauty. Honey-blond hair, big brown eyes, and a small, pointed chin. She must have weighed 110 pounds, but was much taller than Patricia.

The photographer held out her hand to Patricia as she approached. "Hi, Mrs. Castellano, I'm Kit Stilton with *The Press*. May I get a photograph of the four of you? It may take me two shots. I'm still a little shaky from this afternoon."

"Well, I guess that would be all right. Father? Elsa? Is it okay with you?"

"Why are you still shaky from this afternoon?" asked Salvatore.

"Well, I had to go shoot the scene of the murder. I've never done a murder before and it freaked me out," said Kit, as she tried to push the group closer together so that she could get them all in one photo.

"What murder?" Patricia blurted out.

"So sad," lamented Father O'Malley. "So young. I saw an early report on *watch.com*."

"Yeah, a girl was murdered in the Green Street Apartments. I didn't see the body. It was gone, thank God, by the time I got there, but the blood was still on the floor and the place smelled really bad…." Kit scrunched up her adorable little nose.

"Do you know the name of the girl?" asked Elsa Martinson.

"Casandra. Casandra Keller. Twenty-two years old. Been dead for days. Okay? Ready? Smile," instructed Kit. Patricia was the only one who could rise to the occasion and give a megawatt smile. The others were still pondering the poor dead girl in the Green Street Apartments.

"Okay. Thanks," said Kit, as she looked around to see who else she needed to photograph.

Over on the other side of the room, Mayor Ceravolo and his wife, Sophia, were telling the same set of facts to Suzy Walker. Suzy always looked like a lawyer, whatever she wore. Even in a gown and dangly diamond earrings, she still looked as if she should have been carrying a briefcase. That was fine with her. She didn't need to be done up like a princess. But the news of this girl who had been murdered was certainly going to put a damper on her evening. She had wanted this

night to be about the Safe Haven Shelter, and now she stood
there wondering if the girl could have used the services of
the shelter. Had she been killed by a jealous husband or boyfriend? The mayor said she was unmarried. He said they had
no leads at this time. He said the body had not been discovered for days.

How horrific, thought Suzy, as she saw Rachel and Manny
Horowitz arrive with Dr. Amy Friedberg. Rachel, president of
the Litchfield Women's Center Board of Directors, was one
of Suzy's closest friends. Suzy signaled to them to come over.
In the background, a five-piece orchestra played show tunes,
and waitresses circulated with champagne and mini-quiche.
Two full bars were at either end of the room. It was almost too
crowded to get to either of them. Suzy saw that the press was all
here. Helen Acker, Gary Milford, and Darius Greeley himself
were here from *The Press*. DeShawn Fletcher from Channel 6
was set up in the corner, with lights and camera. Jamie Ross
from the new online newspaper, *watch.com*, was here, as well as
many photographers, a radio reporter and a reporter from the
New Jersey Chronicle. Ginny, Suzy's assistant, was setting up times
for them to interview Suzy.

Suzy looked around for Nina Adler, the executive director of Safe Haven, when a noise came up from the crowd, and
Suzy knew that the state politicians had arrived. State Senator
Kevin Connors and Assemblywomen Lori Gold and Angela
Noonan always arrived at these functions together. They had
a system. They would stand in a circle, back to back, and move
through the crowd like a three-headed monster with six arms.
Like waltzing, in one smooth motion their right hands shook a
voter's hand, while their left grabbed the person's elbow. Hold
for eye contact. Three seconds and release. Then the monster
would rotate and move forward. This way they only had to greet
and shake hands with a third of the room. It took them about
20 minutes to make their way over to Suzy and the mayor.

While she waited for the three-headed monster, Suzy scanned the room for Patricia. There she was, surrounded by people, talking to Father O'Malley. Suzy imagined that they were plotting right now. Better to forget about her. She turned to see Nina Adler coming toward her. Her hair was prematurely gray and hung straight to her chin and then was cut in a severe angle, longer in the front and shorter in the back.

"Suzy! You look radiant. Look Suzy! Look at the size of the crowd that has come out to honor you! How can I ever thank you?" The ladies very gingerly hugged, so as not to disturb either's hair or makeup.

"Nina. It's not me we're here for. It's you and the good work you do. Don't forget that. Watch out, here they come." As she spoke, the three-headed monster had made its way to the feet of the honoree to pay homage.

Connors, Gold, and Noonan took turns congratulating Suzy and getting the facts about the murder from the mayor. Suzy and Harry were huge political fundraisers and had a great deal to say about who was elected. They could literally derail a campaign if they wanted to. Suzy had money and clout. Harry just had money, so first they adored Suzy and then Harry. Again, working as a team, the three-headed monster became a purring, stroking, obsequious animal, rubbing the hands and purses of those who fed it.

The cocktail party had reached critical mass. A tinkling bell rang to signal that the guests should move into the dining room. Suzy excused herself to visit the ladies' room.

As the mayor guided his wife toward the dining room, Helen Acker, wearing her best beige formless frock, fell in step beside him. "Mayor Ceravolo, can I get a comment on the upcoming demonstration?"

Mayor Ceravolo looked down at Helen Acker as if she were a fly on his Armani tux. "Helen, we are here tonight to honor Suzy Walker who has given tirelessly to the cause of legal representation for abused spouses. Let's enjoy the moment." He pursed his lips together in annoyance.

"Isn't it true that Suzy Walker raised over $2 million for your last campaign? And that she sits on the Women's Center board?"

The mayor stopped walking. "Yes, Helen, those are both true statements."

Helen, realizing that the mayor was not going to bite, changed topics. "Mayor, what do we know about the murder of Casandra Keller? Do you have any suspects?" By this time, the rest of the reporters in the room had noticed Helen and the mayor and headed over. Realizing he was not going to make a quick getaway, the mayor decided it was easier to give a brief statement and then be allowed to go to his seat.

"Here are the facts about the Casandra Keller case. At midday today, two friends of the victim found her dead in her apartment. The coroner has not released a report yet, but early evidence indicates that she was dead for two to three days before she was found. It looks as though she was beat up and left to die. We have no suspects at this time. Chief Chodor and Detective Bickford are hard at work, right now, looking for the assailant. And mark my words, he or she will be caught." Here the mayor paused for effect. "If any of your readers or viewers have any information about this heinous crime, I would ask that they contact the police department. Thank you." And with that, the mayor boldly took his wife's arm and escorted her into the dining room.

Meanwhile, Suzy stepped out of the bathroom stall and saw Patricia reapplying her lipstick in the powder room next door. Only one other woman was in the room. Suzy waited for her to leave and then entered the powder room and stood behind Patricia until Patricia noticed that she was there.

Patricia paused mid-lip when she realized who was there. Without saying a word, she finished applying the other side of her lip and turned to face Suzy. For a minute, the women stood, boldly staring at each other, gathering their thoughts.

"I'm glad you're here tonight supporting an organization that helps women," Suzy said, with a challenging edge to her voice.

"I always support women and their families," Patricia countered.

"Don't give me a sound bite, Patricia. I am a direct person, and as such, I want to tell you that you are making a huge mistake going after the Women's Center. The center provides a range of health services to a lot of women, not just abortions." Suzy knew her voice was growing louder.

"Do you know that your daughter could walk in there tomorrow and have an abortion and you wouldn't even know it?"

"Don't make this personal, Patricia. Do you know that the Supreme Court decided that abortion is a constitutionally protected right?"

"Don't give me legal advice. I'm talking about babies, Suzy...."

"No, we're not...!" At this point, the two women were shrieking. Their red faces and blazing eyes were all Salvatore saw when he entered the bathroom to stop the fighting.

"Patricia! Suzy! Get a hold of yourselves. Do you want the press in here taking photographs of the two of you? Now stop it!" he hissed.

Both women had taken a step toward the other and were standing with clenched fists. Salvatore took Patricia by the arm and dragged her out of the bathroom. It took her 30 seconds to compose herself before she walked into the reception area on their way to the dining room. Everyone was seated at the round tables with the rose-colored clothes. The only person standing was Harry, his eyes searching the room for Suzy.

"She's coming," was all Salvatore said to Harry as he and Patricia walked past on the way to their table. Harry noticed the tight grip Salvatore had on Patricia's arm.

THIRTY-TWO

⟨❧⟩

"This is DeShawn Fletcher, Channel 6, bringing you an update on today's breaking news of the grisly murder of twenty-two-year-old Casandra Keller in the Green Street Apartments." Eduardo and Pia watched the handsome young reporter on the 11 O'clock News. "I am here now with Michael Russo, a friend of Casandra's, who went looking for her today and found her dead in her apartment. Two doors down from his own. Michael, can you describe the scene when you went to Casandra's apartment today?"

The image on the screen went from the handsome black reporter looking fresh and excited to the image of an Italian young man who looked troubled. His large black eyes radiating sadness and confusion over the day's events.

"Well, I was with another friend of Casandra's, and we were wondering where she's been. She'd been missing a few days, and we finally went to her apartment and I tried the door and it was unlocked. She was on the floor. She'd been badly beaten and there was a dried pool of blood around her head. I left and called the police."

Back to DeShawn: "The police are asking anyone with information that may lead to the capture of Casandra's killer to contact them at 1-888-555-1000. Police Chief Chodor is also asking Litchfield residents to be extra careful. Lock your doors and don't walk alone at night. Again, this is DeShawn Fletcher, Channel 6 News. Back to you, Angie, in the studio."

The girls had gone to bed and Pia was surprised that Eduardo had not gone out drinking. She actually wished that he would leave so she could relax.

"Isn't that terrible? Only twenty-two! I'll pray for her tomorrow at church," said Pia.

"You don't know what happened," Eduardo said with a furious sneer.

Pia knew from his tone that he would start a fight with her now. There was nothing she could do or say to avoid it. He wanted to start a fight. Any words she said would give him the opportunity to scream at her and lose control. Staring at the television, she remained silent, wanting to go into the kitchen and get away from him, but not daring to get up. She could feel the anger welling up inside of him, filling the room. His cheeks were red and his eyes bloodshot. Trembling now, she knew if she made a move he would lash out.

He wanted her to get up so he could smack her for leaving. Visions of Casandra floated in front of his eyes. Her open, lifeless eyes. Blood seeping out from the fan of her hair on the floor. His chest felt tight. He looked down and caught sight of Pia's foot and ankle. He noticed that she had not shaved her legs. Thick, black hairs grew on the top of her foot. It disgusted him. While he waited for her to move, his anger grew and swirled in his head.

Pia thought about running for the front door, but then she would have to leave her babies asleep upstairs. If she bounded up the stairs, she would draw him to them. If she ran into the kitchen, she could grab a knife, but if he killed her, then her babies would be alone. Her mind was racing. He cracked his knuckles. She looked straight ahead.

He reached out to get the remote, and she thought he was reaching out to grab her, and she flinched. That was all he needed. He grabbed her arm and twisted it until she rolled off the couch.

"Eduardo, don't," she pleaded. His answer was a slap to her face. He hadn't intended to draw blood, but he had broken her nose, and blood streamed down her face. She looked up at him and saw a madman. He picked her up and threw her down. He fell on her, trying to hold her down. She struggled, and his rage exploded. Blinded by anger, he pummeled her with his fists.

Maria had heard her mother's voice. She quietly crept out of bed and hurried to the top of the stairs. When she looked down, she saw her father bent over her mother, repeatedly punching her with his fists. She saw the blood on her mother's face. He started to strangle her. Maria silently went to the upstairs phone and dialed 911. She whispered to the person who answered that her father was killing her mother and they must come immediately. She gave them the address. Then she went and woke Carmen and took her to hide in the closet in their parents' room. She thought he would go to their bedrooms first. Next, she looked for something to hit her father with. She remembered that he kept a baseball bat next to his bed in case an intruder came into the house at night. She went to get it. As she did, she heard the sirens. She knew they were coming for him. As she left the room with the bat, she heard the urgent knock on the front door.

Downstairs, Eduardo heard the banging, but it didn't penetrate into his brain. As Maria ran down the stairs and through the living room, Eduardo looked up at her and then down at Pia, who was bloody and crying. He looked at his hands, and there was blood all over them. He looked up as Maria opened the door and two police officers with billy clubs ran into the room. Eduardo saw them approaching him as if they were moving in slow motion. He stood up and started to turn toward the back of the house, away from the police. As he did, the first officer reached out and hit him hard on the back of his neck. The second officer hit the back of his thigh, forcing him down on his knees. The three men wrestled together until Eduardo lay on his belly, chest heaving, sweating, grunting. Officer Quinn pulled out his handcuffs and put them on Eduardo, purposely cutting into his skin as he clasped them together. He squatted down, holding his billy club so Eduardo could see it as Officer Rea called for an ambulance. They heard a second squad car pull up outside.

Maria had gone to the kitchen and grabbed a towel to sop up the blood oozing from Pia's bleeding nose. She sat next to her mother on the floor and hugged her. She tried to stop the bleeding.

"Where is Carmen?" whispered Pia. She was still too frightened to speak.

"Don't worry, Mommy. She's safe, upstairs," Maria said, wiping Pia's face. She wondered how her sister was holding up in the closet. She must be very frightened. "When they take him, I'll go and get her."

Pia was shocked that Maria was so in charge of the situation. Maria had said the police would take Eduardo before Pia even thought about it. Pia realized that Maria must have been the one who called the police. She looked at her daughter with awe and fear. She was afraid to tell the cops to take Eduardo, but Maria had no such fear.

"Maria, go and call Stella. Tell her to come. Then go upstairs and comfort your sister." She looked at Maria, and Maria understood that Pia needed to know if the younger girl was all right.

"Let me help you up." Officer Rea reached down and helped Pia to her feet and then to the couch. "Are you okay? We're taking your husband in. You need to go to the hospital. Is there someone who can come to be with your daughter?" asked Officer Rea.

"I have two daughters. Maria, my oldest, just went to call my sister. She'll come and we'll all go down to the hospital," said Pia.

"Okay. We'll wait until she comes." Officer Rea sat with Pia on the couch.

The two officers from the second squad car came in and conferred with Officer Quinn, and then they approached Eduardo, one on each side, pulled him to his feet, and hauled him out the door. Pia closed her eyes as he left.

"Bitch," he muttered, as he was dragged past her.

Officer Rea looked at Pia's bleeding nose. He pinched the top of her nose and the blood slowed. "You'll be okay now," he said comfortingly.

Maria came back downstairs. "Aunt Stella's coming, Mommy." Maria sat down on the floor at Pia's feet. "She was at the Country Club at a party."

Pia remembered that Stella had told her she was going to a fancy event at the Swan Club. She wondered if George would come with her. Tonight was a turning point. She would not live with Eduardo again. Tonight she would ask Stella to take her in. She felt scared and alone.

"Maria, go and get your sister," she said.

When Maria had gone upstairs, Officer Rea took out a little pad and asked Pia her name and her age, then Eduardo's name and age, and the children's names and ages. As she answered these mundane questions, she started to feel a little better. They heard the ambulance's siren in the distance.

Suddenly, Carmen ran down the stairs and burst into tears when she saw her mother's swollen and bleeding face. Large black-and-blue marks had started to form on Pia's arms. Now that the immediate danger had passed, Maria started to cry. Officer Rea got up off the couch to let the girls be close to their mother. They sat down on either side of Pia and huddled close, both to protect and be protected by her.

The ambulance medics arrived at the same time as Stella and George. Stella gasped when she saw her sister's face bloody and swollen. One eye had started to blacken and swell shut. Blood had sprayed all over her shirt. The girls were crying, and Stella, still wearing the lavender gown, joined the group on the couch.

THIRTY-THREE

❦

The clock struck midnight as Father O'Malley entered the rectory. He was tired from the evening's festivities. Patricia had made him very nervous, and it had taken more than a few glasses of cabernet to calm him down. And now he had at least an hour's worth of work to do on his sermon. As he walked into his office and put on the light, his cell phone rang. He looked down at the number on the screen and shuddered. Not now, he thought. He knew she would just keep calling until he answered. And if she couldn't get him, she would come to the rectory.

"Hello."

Pause.

"It's late and I have mass in the morning."

Pause.

"Yes, I know we have to talk."

Father O'Malley winced at whatever was said on the other end.

"Come tomorrow night."

Pause.

"Yes, at dusk."

$\mathcal{T}$HIRTY-$\mathcal{F}$OUR

❧

$\mathcal{B}$y the time they got to The Sportsman, Michael had remembered something that he hadn't before. He remembered that he had seen Eduardo Fernandez at the apartments. What day was that? It seemed like a long time ago, but so much had happened. He tried to get his tired brain to remember.

Earlier, he and Molly had left police headquarters, where they were separately questioned for about an hour. "Don't leave town," Detective Bickford said as they were leaving. Michael and Molly gave each other a look. They hadn't done anything wrong. They were the heroes. Casandra would still be rotting in the apartment if they hadn't gone to look for her. No good deed…, Michael thought.

As they walked out of police headquarters, a swarm of reporters had descended upon them. Channel 6 had interviewed Michael. Then Molly had wanted to go to see Casandra's mother and had asked Michael to take her. After seeing Mrs. Keller, Molly was so upset that Michael felt he had no choice but to take her home to his apartment. He also felt kind of protective of Molly after all they had been through today. He had already decided to let her sleep at his place tonight.

They had driven over to Freeport, which technically was leaving town, but Michael didn't think the cops would object to a sympathy call. Mrs. Keller and Molly had cried together for a good hour, but when Mrs. Keller got out the photo albums, Michael couldn't take it anymore and said he was leaving. By that time, other relatives had arrived, and Molly agreed to go.

They went back to his apartment and tried to eat a sandwich, but the stench of the body and the grayness of her flesh kept repeating in his mind and he couldn't swallow the rare roast beef that Molly knew he loved. Michael got in the shower and made the water as hot as his skin could bear. He wanted to wash the image of Casandra out of his brain, but every time he closed his eyes, there she was, worse than any horror movie. He got out of the shower and lay in bed. Molly came over and crawled in beside him. They made an attempt to fool around, but Molly kept crying and Michael felt numb.

"Hey, you know what?" Michael asked. "Let's just go over to The Sportsman and get a couple beers." Michael looked down at Molly's swollen eyes and her red nose and wondered if this week could get any worse. He had the pregnant girl, the dead girl, and the girl he knew it was going to be hard to get rid of. He rolled over and went to the dresser for some clean underwear.

"Michael?"

"Yeah..."

"Who do you think killed her? She was supposed to see Eduardo that night..."

"Was she screwing him? I saw him at the apartments."

Molly, of course, knew that Casandra had been sleeping with Eduardo Fernandez, but she was afraid to tell the cops, so she wasn't sure she wanted to tell Michael. Eduardo had a bad temper and he was married. Molly didn't think Eduardo had killed Casandra, but maybe he did—and she didn't want Eduardo to be mad at her after the cops went to his house. "I don't know, maybe," she said, as she got up and pulled on her jeans.

Michael decided not to press her. He wasn't sure he wanted to know. They finished getting dressed and headed out to the bar. Michael had been all over the news at both 6 and 11 o'clock, and the gang at The Sportsman had watched him and had been waiting for him to arrive. Girls were crying and being consoled by the young men. Truth be told, Casandra and Molly didn't have a big group of close girlfriends, but the news of the young woman's death had made everyone nervous.

They arrived at The Sportsman when the night was in full swing. Lady Gaga was singing on the jukebox, but as they walked in, there was a hush. As Michael and Molly walked the length of the bar, people treated them with the respect due to someone who has just appeared on the news. Molly was hugged by all the women and the men shook Michael's hand. Jay gave them their first drink on the house. They found bar stools at the far end of the bar and held court from there. Michael was tired of the whole mess and really just wanted to drink his beer and play a game of pool, but there was a constant line of people who wanted to hear firsthand what had happened.

Just as he thought he had personally updated each person in the bar, the doors flew open and Detective Bickford stood in the doorway, surveying the scene. Michael and Molly had both told the police that they hung out with Casandra at The Sportsman, and now the detective was here to check it out. Jay's first thought was how lucky he was that he didn't have anyone underage in the bar. He quickly scanned the room. He was safe.

Detective Bickford was a tall, impressive-looking man with small eyes, a big basset- hound nose, pock-marked skin, and grayish lips. His beady eyes missed nothing. He noted Michael and Molly at the end of the bar, but he wanted to talk to the bartender. Bartenders knew a lot. Sometimes they had to be persuaded to tell, but they knew. He walked up to the bar, and Jay went over to him.

"You got a guy here who can take over for a few minutes? I want to talk to you outside," said Detective Bickford.

"Oh…yeah…." Jay scanned the crowd. Keith was there. He worked the bar Tuesday and Wednesday nights. Jay called him over and asked him to cover for a few minutes. Keith took over and Jay and Detective Bickford went outside.

"So, what do you know about this girl Casandra?" Bickford started right in without pleasantries as they walked over to the side of the bar away from the parking lot. He lit a cigarette.

"She comes here a lot. Or I guess I should say, she came here a lot. I can't believe she's…gone. She and Molly were really tight," said Jay.

"What about boyfriends? She date Michael Russo?"

"No, Molly used to date Michael."

Detective Bickford could tell by the look on Jay's face that he was thinking something through. "What is it? Spit it out."

"I think Casandra was sleeping with an older guy."

"Gotta name?"

"He's married."

"The plot thickens. Gotta name?"

"Eduardo. Eduardo Fernandez. Comes in here sometimes."

"He here tonight?"

"No, actually, he was here last night looking for Casandra. She wasn't here."

"Know where he lives?"

"No, like I said, he's married."

"Got it." Bickford took a long drag on his cigarette. "Anything else I should know?"

Jay thought for a minute. "No, that's it. I'm gonna head back in."

"Yeah. Okay." Bickford headed to his unmarked car. Jay headed toward the bar. Bickford turned around as Jay opened the bar door. "Hey Jay!" Jay turned. "Thanks." Jay nodded and entered through the door into the music and sounds of life.

$\mathcal{T}$ HIRTY-$\mathcal{F}$ IVE

చ్

here he was on the 64" flat-panel television screen in her basement. Larger than life, Michael Russo's black eyes stared at Clara from outside of Police Headquarters. Apparently, he had found one of his friends dead inside her apartment. He was also hugging a woman with a large ring in her nose. Clara had never considered the possibility that Michael had a wife or a girlfriend. She had never asked him anything about himself. Seeing him on the screen terrified her.

Before she saw him on the television, he wasn't really real. She couldn't imagine him ever walking into her house or talking to anyone she knew. He belonged in another world. She never wanted him to enter her world. Now here he was in her basement. Clara was relieved that she could hear Agnes screaming and jumping up and down overhead. That meant that her mother would not be watching the news right now. Not that her mother would ever make a connection between this man, who looked like a gang member, and Clara. Clara shut off the television and lay down on the great big semi-circular couch.

She reached out and grabbed an ancient teddy bear. Hugging it felt good.

Clara had taken to wearing baggy shorts and extra-large T-shirts. It wasn't that she was getting fat, because she threw up just about every meal she ate. No, it was that her boobs were the size of small cantaloupes, whereas before, they had been the size of ripe peaches. Less than a week to go until it was over. But now that Michael had been on the television in her basement, she suddenly realized that he would not disappear after Friday. He would still live in that dingy apartment. She hated to think of that place—and now a poor girl had been found dead a few doors down. Clara felt like she was going to cry. Had Michael killed the girl? No, she didn't think so. That was crazy.

She hugged the teddy bear and thought about her situation. She had no one to turn to except the very person who had hurt her in the first place. She wished she could go to her mother. But, with the screams and the commotion upstairs, she put that thought out of her head immediately. How could she go to her overburdened mother with a problem? Her mother called her "a breath of fresh air." Clara knew that she was her mother's strength. She knew that she could never cause a problem for her. She had always brought a smile to her mother's lips. She was the only person who truly made her laugh. She could not stand to be the person who made her mother cry.

Maybe she should tell Linda, and the two of them could go to the clinic on Friday. Linda had just gotten her driver's license. But even with a ride, where would she get the money? $600. She had $230 from her Sweet Sixteen party, which now seemed like a lifetime ago, but her mom had already asked her how she was going to spend it. Also, did she really trust Linda? As soon as she told Linda, all the girls would know. Then one of them would tell her mother, and the telephone chain would begin. No. She would follow the plan. A feeling of unease started to form in her brain. Michael had been annoyed with her when he left the park. She had insulted him by not wanting to be seen with him. *What if he didn't show up? What if he thinks I'm a snooty little bitch? What if the woman on the television is his girlfriend? What if he tells her?* Clara's head was swimming with what-ifs. She started to cry, but not many tears were left.

Friday would be Clara's one chance to get rid of the problem. Her mother was taking Agnes to a three-day program for autistic teenagers. They were leaving on Thursday evening. Mr. Mahoney would go to work as usual on Friday morning at 7:30, and then Michael would pick Clara up at 8:30. She didn't want him in her house or even at her front door. But now here he was on the news. Would he be able to come for her? She didn't even have his telephone number. She did know where he lived, but she never wanted to go back to that apartment. Sighing, she decided she just had to believe that he would come.

THIRTY-SIX

⚜

The first responder insisted that Pia ride to the hospital in the ambulance when Pia wanted to go in the car with her girls. George finally told Stella to go in the ambulance with Pia, and he would meet them in the emergency room with the girls. Pia's splitting headache and dizziness made it impossible for her to argue. The technician had her breathing oxygen into her mouth through a clear plastic tube, because her nose was broken in so many places.

Once away from the girls, both women started to cry. Stella just couldn't believe that Eduardo had done this to her sister. She realized now that she had doubted Pia's story that Eduardo beat her. Surely Pia had exaggerated Eduardo's temper she had said to herself; the reality was so far removed from Stella's own circumstances that she couldn't imagine that Pia had been in danger in her own home. Holding Pia's hand in the back of the ambulance, she tried to be strong and stop crying, but when she looked at Pia and saw the blood and the bruises, the sobs kept coming.

"Pia, I'm sorry. I didn't believe that he would hurt you like this. You'll stay with me and George. You can never go back to him. Never," proclaimed Stella. "I hope he rots in jail. George will get you a good attorney. It's over, Pia. And Maria seeing that? How terrible." She knew she was saying too much. "You rest now. Everything will be fine." She took Pia's hand in hers.

It was a 15-minute ride to High Ridge Hospital. Pia had fallen into a light sleep by the time they arrived. She was taken into a stall in the emergency room, and Stella went looking for George and the girls. They were already there in the uncomfortable waiting-room chairs, looking tired and worried. She couldn't help but notice, as she walked toward them, that the girls were both carbon copies of Pia. The way Pia used to look before the bruises.

When the girls spotted Stella, they ran to her and threw their arms around her. She tried to comfort them. "Your mother will be fine," Stella said. Carmen seemed reassured; Maria looked at her with questioning eyes. Stella told them they would wait to hear what the doctor said, and then she would take them home to her house. Carmen was hungry, so George agreed to take her to the cafeteria. After they left, Stella sat with Maria, holding her hand.

"Maria, what you did tonight was very brave. Your mother will recover because you took action. Not every girl your age could have done what you did. I'm very proud of you." She looked at Maria's young face and saw a strength there that she had not noticed before.

"I knew he was hitting her." The girl looked at her aunt with fear, defiance, and regret. "I've known for a year now, but she pretended that everything was okay." Maria started to sob. "I never want to see him again. He would make me do things and watch me when I did them. He would make me bend over to pick things up for him or burst into my room when he thought I was getting dressed." Stella listened with growing horror.

"I started to push my dresser in front of my door when I got changed on weekends and he was home."

"I had no idea...but that's behind you now. You and your mother and Carmen will live with us. I don't want you to worry. You will never be alone with him again. Maybe we can work it out so that you will never have to see him again...."

"I'll testify against him. I'm not afraid of him. I want him to go to jail, but..." Maria looked like she wanted to say something else.

"But what?"

"I'm afraid my mother will take him back."

"Together we will make sure that she doesn't," said Stella with conviction. Inwardly, she feared the same thing.

THIRTY-SEVEN

❦

"I don't like men who beat up women," Detective Bickford said to Eduardo Fernandez. "They're cowards." The detective was in an upbeat mood. He couldn't believe his good fortune. After leaving The Sportsman, he headed back to the station house, where the desk sergeant told him that Eduardo Fernandez had just been brought in for beating up his wife. Now Bickford didn't have to go looking for him. He was questioning Eduardo in one of the station's interrogation rooms with a one-way mirror. Officers Rea and Quinn and Chief Chodor watched from the other side of the glass.

Eduardo sized up his interrogator. Overweight, ugly big nose, pockmarked skin. He was the type who had to beg for it. Eduardo knew that Pia would never press charges and that he would be out of jail as soon as this pig asked him a few questions.

"Women wouldn't take it from *you* if you hit them," snarled Eduardo. "I hit them and they come back for more," he bragged.

This guy is a real psychopath, thought Bickford. "So, where do you want to start? You wanna talk about your wife… or your mistress first?" Eduardo's blue eyes squinted up slightly, and his bravado eased up a bit. He didn't answer.

Detective Bickford had been on the Litchfield Police Force for 28 years. He had been a detective for the last ten. He had seen every kind of liar. The innocent liar. The forceful liar. The committed liar. The transparent liar. The crying liar. The crafty liar. He knew techniques to break them all. One technique was to wait them out. He had put a question on the table, and now he would wait until Eduardo decided to answer it. He wouldn't let him off the hook by answering for him. He watched a thin film of sweat start to bead up on Eduardo's upper lip.

Dried blood was sprayed all over Eduardo's T-shirt, and splotches of it were dried on his face. As the sweat started to roll down from his hairline, the blood began to streak his cheeks. It looked like he was crying blood. Detective Bickford got out his nail clipper and started to clean under his nails. He had all night. They could hear the ticking of the clock. Bickford knew that the chief and the other officers watching from behind the one-way mirror were getting impatient. He didn't care. Waiting it out was the first technique he would use to break Eduardo down. Ten minutes passed. Bickford took a small notebook out of his back pocket and started to make notes. He was actually making a grocery shopping list, but he would look at Eduardo once in awhile before making a note. He knew that Eduardo thought he was making notes about him.

Finally, Eduardo laughed and said, "So, that's it. You have to beg the ugliest bitches for a lay?"

Bickford thought to himself, "The best defense is a good offense." Crafty. Maybe Eduardo was smarter than he looked. But he hadn't answered the question posed to him, so Bickford smiled and went back to his notebook. Another 10 minutes went by. Eduardo's right leg began to bounce up and down. Bickford stood up and stretched. He went and sat next to Eduardo on the table, looking down on him.

"My wife is a whore. I caught her with the electrician, and so I beat the shit out of her. Okay? Happy now? She'll never press charges on me. You're wasting your time. I'll be out of here in the morning." Eduardo looked up at Bickford.

"Now we're getting somewhere. So, you want to talk about your wife first. I think we're talking about attempted murder. Your two young daughters were in the house, so we'll slap you with attempted murder in the presence of a minor. Juries hate people who threaten kids. Your wife's in the hospital now. Last I heard, it was touch and go. We have two eyewitnesses who are cops, so that's pretty solid right there. You're looking at ten to fifteen." Bickford's tone was confident. "Now, let's talk about your mistress. Casandra Keller, who was found dead today in her apartment."

"Never heard of her."

"That's not what they're saying down at The Sportsman. I was there earlier, having a beer with the regulars. Word is that you were banging Casandra." When Bickford said the word "banging," he banged his fist as hard as he could on the table right in front of Eduardo's face.

Eduardo stood his ground. "Never heard of her," he said defiantly.

"Well, we dusted for prints all over the apartment today. The doorknob is always a good source of prints. Of course, so are the bathroom and the bed. Girl was found in her panties. You're right. Maybe she was with someone else." Eduardo glared at Bickford. Like a rat in a trap, he sat locked to the chair.

"Nice-looking guy, that Michael Russo. He lives in the Green Street Apartments, too. He found her, ya know? I'm sure he was banging her, too."

"Is that who told you I was with that girl?" Eduardo screamed. "Russo? Russo? Yeah, he was banging her. Definitely. He probably killed her. Italians are jealous men."

"But *you* were jealous. You said earlier, you were jealous about your wife's alleged lover. Are Hispanic men jealous, too?"

Eduardo laughed. His handsome face was disfigured by a horrible grin and deranged- looking eyes.

"Did you kill her, Eduardo? I'm asking you straight out."

The only answer was laughter.

THIRTY-EIGHT

❧

The old Neo-Gothic church sat 800 people, and on the morning of Father O'Malley's sermon on the sanctity of life, every pew was full. Even the side chapels were packed. Inside the nave of St. Raymond's, parishioners were filing in for the ten o'clock mass. It was a gorgeous morning, and the sunlight streamed in through the vibrant blue, red, and gold stained-glass windows over the altar at the front of the cathedral. As soon as Linda Martinson went through the massive doors into the main entrance with her mother and siblings, she saw the bronze statue of St. Raymond to her left and the marble statue of the Madonna to her right. She remembered running circles around these two life-size statues when she was a little girl in knee socks, the ribbons in her hair floating out behind her as she fluttered in a figure-eight from statue to statue.

Linda followed her family up the aisle past the crossing to the empty pew that was roped off for the church's most important volunteers, like Linda's mom, Mrs. Martinson. Linda looked up at the marble altar and then up at the pulpit, where she knew Father O'Malley would stand to give his sermon. Her

mother had said that he would be giving a very important sermon this morning. Linda was very interested in hearing what
he had to say. She looked to her right and saw her mother's
face in profile as she knelt in prayer with her eyes closed and
wondered what her mother was praying for.

She heard the voices behind her get louder and turned
around to see the mayor, his wife and children, and his sister,
Patricia Castellano, with her husband and children arriving.
Litchfield's royalty. Her own mother spent a great deal of time
raising money for the mayor as well as the church. Linda always
liked to see what Mrs. Castellano was wearing. She had style.
Linda would give her that. She looked great in her white linen
suit and three-inch, white patent- leather pumps. Her black
hair was thick and wavy. Of course, Linda felt that she, Linda,
was actually more beautiful than Patricia Castellano, but she
had to admit that the woman knew how to wear clothes. As the
mayor's entourage passed by, they stopped to greet her mother,
and Linda was forced to smile and say hello.

She didn't like to say hello to the mayor. He always looked
at her a little too long and held her little hand in his big hairy
paw as if he wouldn't let go. Last year, when her mother had
taken her to Town Hall to drop off a check, she had been left
alone with him in his office. He had sat down next to her on
the couch and put his hand under her chin and looked into her
eyes. Linda remembered that he smelled like cigarettes and lavender soap, and there was a faint smell of liquor on his breath.
He gave Linda the creeps. But, here he was. She had no choice
but to stand up and shake his hand. And, there it was. The lin-
ger. The look. With his wife not two feet away! Linda did not
understand adults.

Politely, she took her hand back and looked behind her to
see who was there. As she did, the mayor and his pride moved
on to the first pew, which was always unofficially reserved
for them. All the usuals were in attendance. The Murphys.
Connollys. MacCreadys. Venezias. Gagliotis. Who was that way

in the back? Michael Russo. Why was he here? She had seen him on the news last night. He had found a girl dead in her apartment. Linda thought she knew the dead girl. She had seen her at The Sportsman with the girl with all the ink and rings in her head. Now, *she* was a looker, Linda thought to herself sarcastically.

The mayor and Patricia and their brood settled into their pew. They always sat in the same place. Patricia was happy that the church was full, because everyone would hear the sermon. She knew the church held 800, and every seat was occupied. She was nervous for Father O'Malley. She had woken early and went downstairs to get the newspapers and was furious when she saw that Helen Acker had the nerve to start her series with an article featuring Dr. Amy Friedberg. Patricia had specifically asked Helen to start the series with an article on Stand Up for Life. *Why couldn't people follow directions?* And, she noted that the doctor's photo ran *top of the fold*—in the position of honor. The top left-hand corner. Dr. Friedberg looked angelic. Not like a baby-killer at all. More modern-day Florence Nightingale than Lizzy Borden. *The Press* had given her a huge pull-quote in a box. It said: "Obviously, the goal is to reduce the number of unintended pregnancies, but at the same time women must have access to safe, legal abortion services without interference from government or church."

On page 2 there had been a short article about the upcoming demonstration. Patricia decided to call Greeley and sweet-talk him a little so her article tomorrow was as prominently placed as Dr. Friedberg's article. The entire bottom half of the front page had been dedicated to the girl who had been found dead. Patricia seriously hoped the killer was not found today. That would push her article and photograph, slated to run tomorrow, farther back in the paper.

Patricia knew that by adding the church to her quote, the doctor was throwing it in the face of all those gathered here this morning. How could Dr. Friedberg insult all of these people?

That would be Patricia's quote when she was interviewed later. Needing an excuse to look around and see if the press was here, Patricia turned around in her seat and greeted the Murphy's, who were seated right behind her. As Mrs. Murphy droned on about the family's plans to go to Europe, Patricia scanned the crowd. Yes, there they were in the back. The herd. Helen Acker. Fiona Rivington. DeShawn Fletcher. Jamie Ross. The blond model-photographer from last night. A few other reporters. Good. Now they would have the other side of the story. She looked back and saw Lee busily scheduling the reporters for interviews and photographs of her and Father O'Malley right after the service.

When the parishioners had taken their seats, the organist began to play the processional hymn, "We Adore You, O Christ," and the entire congregation rose to their feet to sing and watch as Father O'Malley entered from the back of the church and made his way up the center aisle. When he arrived at the altar, he kissed its cold gray marble and called the people to prayer. Then the congregation began the synchronized dance of standing and sitting, listening and responding, praying and reading. Like a conductor, Father O'Malley led his flock through the rituals of the introductory rites.

Just when the men were getting tired of sitting and standing, it was time for Father O'Malley's homily. The congregation settled in and tried to get comfortable on the hard wooden benches as they watched the priest climb the spiral staircase to the ornate wooden pulpit. When he was ready, he stretched out his long arms draped in satiny fabric, and stood with closed eyes, drawing his followers to worship. The congregation felt his passion. Like a brilliant actor, he made them wait. Finally, he said softly, "Friends, Jesus is the giver of life. Jesus said, Do unto others as you would have others do unto you. This, the 'Golden Rule,' is written in the Book of Matthew. The Bible teaches that the son shall not die for the sins of the father! This means that no one can justly compel one to suffer or die for the sins of the other, especially without his or her consent. It is written in Psalm 139 that God creates us in the womb. *In the womb.*" Father O'Malley's voice had risen and he let the word "womb" hang in the air like a celestial cloud over the worshippers' heads.

He continued, "The pro-choice ethic is radical utilitarian individualism. This ethic worships the me, myself, and I instead of Jesus and God, our father. People, things, or events are acceptable if and when they benefit the me. This is antithetical to Jesus's Golden Rule. The Golden Rule is what Christian living is all about. That is what the prophets have taught us."

Father O'Malley spoke for 30 minutes and no one moved. They hung on his every word. Pregnant women placed their hands on their bellies in an instinctual, protective way. Little children, who had no idea what he was talking about, were spellbound. Wives took their husband's hand. Men admired his oratory skill. The reporters in the back were furiously taking notes. Helen Acker wondered if Father O'Malley would make hard copies of the sermon available. Patricia Castellano had to tame her lips into submission and not allow them to smile. *Damn, Thomas! You are brilliant!*

In the last pew, sitting at attention, was Sandra Stett. The skin on her upper arms had goose bumps, and the short hairs on the back of her neck were standing up. She knew that God was truly speaking through Father O'Malley. She felt his divine presence in the vaulted ceiling of the cathedral. As soon as the sermon was over, she slid out of her seat and was gone.

THIRTY-NINE

The kitchen table was strewn with papers, forms and applications as Loren and Peter Elliot tried to figure out how to keep Marshall and Emily in college come September. Marshall had one more year at NYU, and Emily was a sophomore at The College of New Jersey.

"They could both live at home and commute," said Peter, his round, bald head resting in one hand. "That would save us a bundle. Marshall could take the train into the city, and Emily has her car—which she has to start paying for. They also both need to get jobs to pay for their books and clothes and anything else they might need."

Loren frowned. Marshall loved living in the city and Emily loved being in the dorm. They would both be so disappointed.

"Loren, don't look like that. This is real life. Sometimes things get rough," exploded Peter.

"I know. I know. Calm down," soothed Loren. Peter had been sending out resumes, answering ads, and calling his contacts in other school districts, but so far, no luck. As the days passed, his patience wore thinner and thinner, and his stomach grew larger and larger. Peter ate when he was upset, and since Loren was pregnant, she was hungry all day and all night. The snack cabinet overflowed with chips and soda and cookies.

"I think we should try to take a second mortgage," ventured Loren.

This suggestion set Peter off. "Loren, who is going to give us a second mortgage? We have no income, for Christ's sake," he yelled.

"Stop yelling," she yelled. "We'll apply for financial aid. We'll take loans. I have an interview on Monday for that secretarial position at Weichert Realty. Maybe I can train to be a real-estate agent."

"Maybe Emily has to take a year off and work…." said Peter.

"Why Emily?" Loren snapped.

"Because Marshall only has one more year. Then he can get a job and be on his own or live here and help us out."

"Look, we have a little savings. Let's try to keep them both in school. That's been our goal since they were born," said Loren.

"Loren, don't you get it? We might need that savings to keep a roof over our heads!" he was yelling again.

Loren started to cry. Her hormones were raging and she cried all the time. Peter looked at her and felt bad. He knew she was also upset about the baby. The baby. How could she be pregnant *now*? He felt as if his life was spiraling out of control. No job. No prospects. Two kids in college looking to him to keep it all together. No money. And now, a baby!

He picked up the paper to try to divert himself. There on the front page was a long article on the Litchfield Women's Center. The doctor looked like a nice lady.

"Will Dr. Friedberg be your doctor on Friday?" he asked.

"Yes," Loren sniffled.

"She looks nice," said Peter, holding up the paper.

"I saw it," said Loren, nodding and wiping her nose. "They're picketing the center the day after I go. I can't believe they're doing that in Litchfield. Usually it's done down South or in the Midwest, but here?"

"Patricia Castellano and Father O'Malley are behind this," said Peter. "Catholics use the clinic's services just as much as any other religious group."

"Tomorrow there will be a big article on Castellano's organization Stand Up for Life, and Father O'Malley's involvement with the demonstration. You're right. They are behind all of this," said Loren.

"And what's O'Malley's story? He certainly wasn't a monk in high school. He and his girlfriend were the most popular couple in the school. I remember. I wonder what happened to change his mind about women?" asked Peter.

"I have no idea." Loren got up and went to the refrigerator. "I'm hungry again," she said. Peter just sat and stared at the wall. He looked as helpless as he felt.

$\mathcal{F}$ O R T Y

᠅

$\mathcal{I}$t was better not to be pretty when you were in jail. Eduardo had found that out when he was thrown into a holding cell with 20 or so other lowlifes. After Detective Bickford had taken a distinct dislike to him, Eduardo was moved to the county jail, instead of the sleepy little cell in the basement of Litchfield Town Hall, which was usually empty. Now, he was bunking in the big-time with drug dealers and prostitutes. During the first night he had to endure the touches and flirtations of a number of fellow inmates. He hadn't slept a wink. Every time he had started to nod off, he had woken with a start to find some demented hoodlum circling him.

To his surprise, he had been arrested, and he was being held pending arraignment on Monday morning. Eduardo was wrong in thinking that Pia needed to press charges. The police were eyewitnesses to his brutality, and therefore, she did not have to do anything. Bail—his only hope was to get out on bail—and to do that he needed Pia to testify for him. Stella and that little bitch Maria—*his own daughter*—would tell Pia not to help him, but he knew if he could only talk to Pia she would. Surely, once she got out of the hospital she would come to him. And now Bickford, that bastard, was trying to link him to Casandra. He thought he had thrown him off the track by saying that Michael was sleeping with her, but if Bickford asked around, no one would back that up.

Eduardo reflected on all of his mistakes. He had really fucked up. He needed to get out on bail and flee the country. Yes, he needed to get the fuck out of here. Shit. Here comes that big, fat, black queen. This guy just won't take no for an answer. Eduardo knew he had to start a full-out brawl so that the guards would take him out of the holding cell. He put his head down and ran full-force at the black queen, hitting him in the stomach and sending him flying into two sleeping drug addicts. Then, screaming and cursing, he started to lash out. Kicking. Punching. He had started an uprising. The anger of the inmates lit up the cell. It was on fire, with years of anger streaming out of these men like lava erupting from a volcano. All 20 guys were punching, kicking, biting, throwing each other against the walls, choking each other. It took the guards a half hour to come to the holding cell. Half the guys were bloody and broken by that time. The guards came in with billy clubs and Mace. Eduardo got hit over the head and sprayed in the face. Then he put on a show. He started holding his face and screaming and crying. They took him and threw him in a small cell, where he couldn't get in trouble. He sat down on the cot, relishing the pain. He sank into the pain until it was all he knew. He smiled. He had achieved his goal. He was alone.

FORTY-ONE

ee and Simon both hated to go to church. It reminded them of their childhoods when their mothers would drag them to church every Sunday. They were both lonely and awkward teens. Both had struggled with the reality of being gay in a homophobic world, and where was homophobia worse than in the Catholic Church? However, today they were in church to work, not worship. First, the professional photographer they had hired would take a formal photo of Patricia, the mayor, and Father O'Malley, and then they were responsible for setting up post-sermon interviews, which would be held after the recessional and the receiving line. They anticipated that it would take an hour and a half for 800 people to file out.

The mayor had not agreed to this photo yet, but Lee and Simon were hopeful that he couldn't refuse to have a photo taken with a very popular priest after his well-attended sermon. And, after all, blood was blood, and Patricia was his sister.

Simon, although gay through and through, liked to flirt with good-looking women. He had made a beeline for Kit Stilton the minute she had walked in the door. *Kit, sweetie! You do know how to accessorize!!* Much to Lee's chagrin, they had been flirting all morning. Lee could hear them laughing in the chapel. Kit had already gotten a good photo of Father O'Malley preaching, so she and Simon had gone into the chapel to scout out the best spot for the post-sermon photo shoot. Lee knew that it was harmless, that Simon and Kit were like fish with bicycles, but all the same, he felt like Simon was cheating on him.

Lee checked his list. First, they would do a press conference, and then a few reporters had asked for private interviews. Helen Acker, of course, would be first with Patricia. Then, Jamie Ross from *watch.com*. Jamie had the advantage because his story would be posted this afternoon online. He didn't have to wait for tomorrow's paper. Then, DeShawn Fletcher, and then two or three weeklies. They wouldn't get out of there before two o'clock.

The congregation began to clap. Lee knew Father O'Malley must have finished his sermon. It was unusual for Catholics to clap. Patricia would be in a good mood. He took a peek in the chapel and saw Simon telling Kit a story. She was doubled over, laughing. Lee realized he had his hands on his waist and was tapping his foot when Simon looked over toward the door. Lee spun around quickly, flipping his hair in a sharp rebuke, and went back to his herd of reporters. He felt like a frigging shepherd. It was nice to have them stuck in the pews, where they couldn't move around.

Kit came out of the chapel with a smile on her dazzling face, her brown pixie eyes twinkling and her hips swishing. She went outside to set up for an outdoor shot.

"Having fun?" Lee asked Simon, with his mouth all bunched up.

"Oh, stop it," said Simon, and put his hand on Lee's behind and gave it a squeeze.

"Really, in church!" said Lee, smiling again.

The service had ended, and the parishioners had started to file out of the church. Father O'Malley, Patricia, and Mayor

Ceravolo had taken their places just outside the church doors. The entire congregation had been moved. Swept up in Father O'Malley's rhetoric, they felt sure of their belief in the sanctity of all life. Michael, not as moved as the rest of the congregation, hung back in the shadows of the vestibule, hoping to catch Father O'Malley alone.

Linda walked out slowly with her mother. She was wearing a blue-and-white striped shirt with a chambray bustier, a white skirt, and leather gladiator sandals with four-inch heels. As she walked down the aisle on her way out of the church, there was not a man who didn't look at her with longing. Her hair, which hung heavily down her back, shone gold in the sunlight that streamed in through the glass, and the expression on her perfect face was blank as she watched Father O'Malley take his place outside the doors of the church.

Though Father O'Malley was usually relaxed after mass, Linda could tell that he was nervous today. It was something about his furrowed forehead and his lack of eye contact with his parishioners. She knew from her mother that his sermon today was important because of the demonstration next Saturday. She had also seen the photographers hanging around, and assumed they were waiting for the priest. His anxiety made her chuckle, a low, throaty sound, as she watched him smiling and accepting the praise of the hundreds of people streaming out of the church. Most of the people were hungry now, it being close to lunchtime, and moved on quickly, but there were always a few who wanted to tell him a story or news of a sick relative on the way out. Patricia and the mayor had left the receiving line about 15 minutes ago to go back to the chapel, but it was Father O'Malley's job to greet every parishioner.

It took an hour and a half for his flock to wade by. While shaking hands and exchanging pleasantries, Father O'Malley was aware of Linda watching him, presumably waiting for her mother. She had not greeted him, but exited the line to avoid him. Michael was also standing in the shadows, waiting to talk to him. Near the end of the line, Father O'Malley made a mental note that the Fernandez and Perez families were not there this morning. It was very unusual for their whole clan not to show up.

Old Mrs. Hutchinson was the last person to leave the church. She used a walker and didn't like to be rushed or pushed. "That was a beautiful sermon, Father," she said, as she slowly exited the grand doorway. "Abortion has always been around, Father. In my day, the young women would go to butchers out in the old Howard Johnson's Motel. I'm not sure it was better that way. I think it might be better to keep it legal." Old people always spoke their mind, Father O'Malley thought to himself.

"We need to reach the young women and let them know there are options, Mrs. Hutchinson. I certainly don't want young women to use back-alley doctors. I want them to consider adoption if they really can't care for their child," said Father O'Malley.

"Back-room butchers. No anesthetic," she mumbled, as she continued to move her walker forward a few inches and then propel herself to follow it.

Father O'Malley held his breath until she was past him physically. He saw movement and knew that Michael was approaching him.

"Father, got a minute?" Michael asked, still partially hidden behind the church doors that stood open. Father O'Malley walked to him and the two men receded into the shadows.

"Michael. How are you?"

"I'm okay."

"I saw you on the news. That must have been a terrible thing to find that young girl. Do you want to talk about it?"

"Well, the thing is...I...might know something about her that I didn't tell the police. I know she was seeing this guy. You know him, but he wasn't here this morning...."

"Do you want to tell me who it is?"

"Eduardo Fernandez. And the thing is..."

"Eduardo Fernandez? Pia's husband?"

"Yeah. I saw him at the apartments that day. When the police were questioning me, I just didn't make the connection, but then last night I did. Do you think I should call the detective?"

"Yes, Michael. I do. If you know something, you must tell them, and Michael…regarding your other situation…you need to know that there will be a demonstration at the Women's Center on Saturday. I don't know what arrangements you've made…?"

Michael cut the priest off. "Yeah, I understand. I'm taking care of it." Michael cursed himself as he walked across the church lawn and into the parking lot. *Michael, man, why the hell do you keep going back to O'Malley? Enough. He doesn't need to know any more.*

Quickly, he opened his car door, got in, and closed his eyes. Visions of Clara popped into his head. Her smiling. Her crying. Her smooth skin. How soft. How he wanted to go and spend the afternoon with her. He pictured her in her pink tennis outfit. So sweet. Her firm thighs all sun-tanned. Then he thought of Molly. What would Molly look like in that outfit, with all of her tats and studs? He smiled.

He wanted to go home and call Detective Bickford and tell him about Eduardo snooping around the apartments that day. He didn't know if it was the day Casandra was killed, but it might have been. He drove home from the church and was amazed to see Detective Bickford leaning on his unmarked car in the parking lot, chewing a toothpick. Now Michael felt nervous. Why was the detective here? He wished he had called the detective sooner, instead of wasting time listening to that long-winded sermon. *Why does Father O'Malley say all that nonsense?* He parked his car and went over to the detective.

"Hey, Detective Bickford. You won't believe this, but I was just coming home to call you. I just came from St. Raymond's, and I was talking to Father O'Malley, and I told him I thought of something after I left the police station, and he told me to call you right away. What are you doing here?" said Michael, talking very fast and hardly pausing to breath.

"Hello Michael. Going to church, huh? You usually a church-going guy?" asked Bickford real slow.

"Well, no. But Father O'Malley and me, we're kinda friends, and I wanted to talk to him." Michael had the distinct feeling that this was not going well. "Anyway, here's what I wanted to tell you. A few days ago, this guy called Eduardo Fernandez came here and he told me he was seeing about a painting job with the super, but, you know, and I should'a told you this the other day, but I didn't think to, he was, like, seeing Casandra. You know what I mean? They met at The Sportsman." Michael now felt that he had told the detective everything that he knew.

Detective Bickford made a few notes. He seemed to be thinking over what Michael said. "So, what day was Eduardo Fernandez here?"

Michael tried to think. "I think it was Friday, but it might'a been Thursday. I really don't remember."

"How do you know Eduardo?"

"He comes down to The Sportsman sometimes."

"It just so happens that I spoke to Eduardo Fernandez last night, and he said that you and Casandra were an item. He said that Italian men are very jealous." Michael's face turned white when he realized what the detective was saying.

"Detective Bickford, I'm telling you that I never slept with Casandra. I never touched her. I've always been with Molly when I was with those two. You ask Molly."

"Somehow, I don't think you'd confide in Molly if you were sleeping with Casandra," said Detective Bickford.

"Well, that's probably true, but Casandra and me, we was just friends. Just friends." Now Michael was starting to get annoyed. "You ask down at The Sportsman if anyone ever saw me with Casandra, and they'll tell you no. Ask Jay. He knows who's sleeping with who."

Detective Bickford started to laugh. "I've already spoken with Jay, and he confirms your story that Eduardo was sleeping with Casandra. Settle down, Michael."

"Well, you know, I feel like I did a good thing by finding her and all, and I don't need anyone saying I killed her."

"So, you say Eduardo was here about a painting job?"

"Yeah, that's what he said. Talk to the super. I gotta go." Michael went upstairs taking two steps at a time. Detective Bickford watched him until he turned down the hallway and moved out of sight.

FORTY-TWO

r. Amy Friedberg lived on the outskirts of Sunken Meadow. The heart of Sunken Meadow was full of six- and eight-bedroom homes, but on the outer ring of the area were smaller homes. Dr. Friedberg's was a brick center-hall colonial, painted white. The bottom floor in the front had two large picture windows on either side of the front door, one in the living room and one in the dining room.

On Sunday morning, Dr. Friedberg sat on her couch in her breakfast nook, looking at her own image in the morning's paper. Rachel Horowitz, the president of the Litchfield Women's Center Board of Directors, had called her and pressured her to have the photo taken. *"You look like a caring doctor, not a monster. We need to demystify the procedure—and you,"* Rachel had said. It was a good likeness. Dr. Friedberg felt that she looked like she was doing good works. However, she was happier toiling away in obscurity. She didn't want to be in the spotlight or make a political statement. She just wanted to do her job and now here she was on the front page of the paper. Helen Acker had quoted her honestly and accurately. She would have to write her a note. Is that what one did? When a reporter did her job accurately? *Dear Helen, thanks so much for being accurate. It's a rarity these days.* She had no idea. She got up, walked over to the counter, poured herself another cup of coffee, and took it back to the couch.

Her mind kept racing forward to Saturday morning and whether she should shut the center. Why would she give appointments to women and let them show up to a picket line? But some women could only come on Saturdays, and she didn't want to deny them services. Flip, she argued one side. Flop, the other. She went back to the paper and read the story about the poor girl who had been found dead. Probably a victim of domestic violence, thought Dr. Friedberg. What a terrible thing. Now, the police were out looking for the killer. She looked at the photograph of the two friends who had found the girl. Michael Russo and Molly Dolan.

As Dr. Friedberg sat finishing her coffee, the phone rang. It was Jamie Ross from *watch.com,* looking for a reaction to Father O'Malley's sermon this morning. "No comment," said Dr. Friedberg, and hung up quickly. This was going to go on all week. She tried to ready herself, and decided to start by taking a shower. As she walked through the living room on her way to the stairs, the phone rang again. This time, she answered it from the end table in the living room, by the big picture window. There was no one on the line. Dr. Friedberg was still standing in front of the window when the first brick flew through it, nearly missing her. Glass shards, like small missiles, sprayed out into the air as the heavy brick fell by her feet. Larger pieces of glass fell straight down onto the window ledge, bursting into thousands of sharp, glistening fragments as they hit the floor. She turned, as if in slow motion, and started to run toward the hallway, as the next brick soared into the room. Feeling the adrenaline flow through her veins, she ran to the kitchen. Alert to every sound, every movement, she picked up the phone and called 911.

"Send the police. Someone is throwing bricks through my window. Hurry!"

Crouching down, under attack in her own home, she hugged the wall, moving to the stairwell, like a cat, silent and guarded. She ran upstairs. Dressing quickly, she looked around for anything she could use as a weapon. Remembering the sharp scissors in her sewing basket, she went to the closet, pulled the basket off the shelf, found the scissors and put them firmly in her fist. She peeked out the upstairs window and saw no one. Then she heard noises in the backyard. Movement. Footsteps. She calmed herself by silently chanting: *The police are coming. The police are coming.* She could hear people on the side of the house now, whispering, moving toward the front. The front, which was now open from the broken window. Sounds of heavy boots on the front porch. She sank down on the floor and wedged herself behind the rocking chair in the corner.

Finally, she heard sirens. Slowly, she got up and went to the top of the stairs. She could see the front door from where she stood. Through the door's three little windows, she thought she saw movement. Minutes seemed like hours as she waited for the police to arrive. She could hear the sirens getting closer and she sat down on the stairs hugging her shoulders for comfort. The sirens stopped, car doors slammed shut, a knock sounded on the door. She flew down the stairs and opened the door for the police, and when she did, she saw that it had been spray painted. In big, bold red letters, it said, "Baby Killer."

FORTY-THREE

After church, Linda and Clara had made plans to go to the Far Hills Mall. There were four malls within driving distance of Litchfield, but the Far Hills Mall was the nicest and had all the stores the girls loved. Coach. Tiffany & Co. Abercrombie & Fitch. American Apparel. Lucky Brand Jeans. Linda and Clara liked to go there, walk around, get ice cream from Cold Stone, and buy clothes. They each had their own credit card which they were given on their 16th birthday. This was a rite of passage for the upper-middle-class girls in Litchfield. Linda had a Visa card and Clara had American Express. The bills were sent to their homes, and unless they bought something very expensive, the bill was paid with the other household bills.

Linda, who had just turned 17, pulled up in front of Clara's house in her tiny Honda Civic and beeped the horn. Clara came out quickly, wearing a pair of black gym shorts and a big black T-shirt. Linda watched her approach the car with a look of disapproval on her face.

"Are you into the grunge look now?" Linda greeted Clara, as she opened the door. "Really! Where did you get those hideous clothes? From Agnes?"

"Does it look that bad?" asked Clara, looking hurt. She hated when Linda insulted Agnes.

"Yeah. You look like crap," she snorted. "What is wrong with you? The first thing we'll do is buy you something new, so I don't have to be embarrassed. Good, now we have a mission," said Linda, never one to spare her friend's feelings.

Clara knew that Linda would pick out something tight and sexy. She didn't want Linda to have a good look at her boobs, which were growing bigger by the hour. "I really want to buy a new iPod. I want to go to the Apple store." Clara didn't need a new iPod, but she didn't want to buy a new shirt.

"Why? What happened to your iPod?"

"I can't find it," she lied. Linda drove out of Sunken Meadow to Main Street, which led to the highway.

"Okay. So, we're in church this morning—you are so lucky that your mother doesn't believe in all this God crap—and the mayor comes in and he starts practically drooling when he's shaking my hand. He is *so* gross. His wife is standing right there. Like three feet away. Men are so disgusting," declared Linda.

"It's not that my mom doesn't believe in God, she just can't take Agnes to church, and she won't leave her at home."

"Always Agnes. Isn't there an institution to stick her in? I mean, life is short," said Linda.

"Lin, stop. At least Agnes keeps me out of church," said Clara, trying to make a joke to disguise the fact that Linda was hurting her feelings.

"Anyway, it was so boring. Father O'Malley was blabbing on about how abortion is murder. Everyone in the church is getting all swept up in his preaching, and I'm looking around at the girls I know sitting there who have all used the services of the clinic, and they're all nodding and agreeing with him. I mean, half the people there were such hypocrites. I asked my mother on the way home, and she said she believes in abortion," said Linda.

"Yeah, my mom said the same."

They got on the highway and Linda drove as fast she could toward the mall. "Yeah, and then he starts talking about 'do unto others as you would have others do unto you,' and he's trying to say that you shouldn't kill an unborn baby, but it's just a bunch of cells, it's not really a baby. Don't ya think?" asked Linda.

"I don't think it's a baby," Clara said, wanting to change the subject. "After Apple, let's go to Tiffany's. I want to look at the Elsa Peretti jewelry."

"I am *not* walking around with you in that outfit. After Apple, we're going to Abercrombie. We're talking about my reputation here. You look like shit."

"Linda, you can really be a bitch sometimes."

"Maybe, but really..." Linda shook her head in disapproval. She turned off the highway and into the parking lot of the mall. She parked behind Bloomingdale's, and the two girls got out of the car. They headed into the store and entered the shoe department, taking a few minutes to look at the sandals. As they walked out of the store, Linda went on in her staccato way, "Hey. You know that guy from The Sportsman? Michael? With the mustache? The one who took you home that night you got drunk?" Clara felt her stomach lurch. "I saw him on the cover of *The Press*. He found one of those skanky girls dead in her apartment. Did you hear about that? He was asking for you one night when me and Joyce went back there. I think he likes you."

"Great." Clara rolled her eyes. "I know. I saw him on the news. That's really scary that a girl was murdered in Litchfield. I overheard someone in the bagel store this morning say she was naked when he found her. Linda, what do you think of that guy? Michael?"

Linda looked at Clara with her bright-blue eyes. Clara could see Linda's brain clicking.

"Why? Did you screw him?" she asked, so loud that two old ladies who were passing by turned around.

"Linda. Shut up! No, I did *not* screw him," Clara whispered, taking Linda by the arm and moving away from the old ladies. Linda kept glancing at Clara. Clara's face started to get red.

"You did. You screwed that guy." Linda stopped and pulled Clara around to face her. Clara couldn't lie anymore.

"If you tell anyone, I'll kill you. I fell asleep in his car and when I woke up I was in his apartment. He was on top of me."

"He raped you?"

Clara's face crumpled when Linda said the word "rape." "I guess. I don't know."

"Did you say he could?"

"I was passed out. I didn't say anything…."

"Sounds like rape to me…."

"Linda, I'm not telling anyone about this. I'm not telling anyone he raped me. I don't want my mom to know. Under any circumstances. Okay?" Clara pleaded, shaking Linda's shoulder for emphasis.

"I'd put his ass in jail…." stated Linda tapping her foot. "What an asshole."

"And Linda, that's not all…" Clara stopped here and bit her bottom lip.

"Clara, you should go to the cops. Turn that bastard in. What do you mean, that's not all? What else did he do to you?" A look of actual concern crossed Linda's face—an unusual occurrence. Clara started to cry. "What?" Linda's brain was clicking again. She looked at Clara's ugly T-shirt, and suddenly she knew. "You're pregnant! That's why you're wearing this hideous outfit. That's why you haven't been going out."

"Linda, I'm serious, if you tell anyone I will kill you. I do *not* want my mom to find out. Do you hear me?" Clara was squeezing Linda's arm, desperate for Linda to reassure her.

"Calm down. I'm not going to tell anyone. What are you doing about it?"

"Going to the Women's Center, and now there's this crazy demonstration and all this press attention. I'm going on Friday. He's taking me." Clara felt weak in the knees and walked over to a bench and sat down. Linda followed her. They sat on the bench, watching the shoppers walk by. There were a lot of young mothers with their babies. Clara didn't want to look at them, but she didn't feel like shopping either.

"You're going with him? Why? I'll take you," Linda said.

"Lin, I have to get the money from him."

"Hmm. How much is it?" asked Linda.

"$600. Where would I get $600?" Clara watched Linda storing that information. Her face got this blank expression when her brain was working. It was like she couldn't take in information and store it at the same time. "And Linda, now I'm afraid that he won't show up because he's all over the news," sobbed Clara.

"Oh, that will be old news by Friday. He was at church this morning. Probably praying for divine forgiveness. I saw him sitting there, all by himself. He used to work at St. Raymond's and he's friends with Father O'Malley, but I've never seen him at mass before," volunteered Linda.

"What do you think that means? That he's changing his mind about taking me?"

"How would I know what he's thinking? I don't know if it had anything to do with you. I'm just telling you he was there. I'm hungry." Linda stared at Clara's stomach. "You don't look fat, but who could tell under those revolting garments. Don't pregnant women eat all the time?" Linda stood up and looked down at her distraught friend. "Look Clara, don't worry. I told you, I think he likes you. He'll come. He doesn't seem like such a bad guy. I'm sure he was just horny that night. Not that he should have raped you, but..."

"I never want to see him again afterward," Clara declared. Linda reached down and pulled Clara to a standing position.

"And you won't have to. Now, c'mon. I'm starving. Subway or Au Bon Pain?" Linda looked at Clara, who was clearly miserable. "We can hit the maternity department on our way out of Bloomingdale's," Linda suggested with a snicker.

"Linda, this is serious," reprimanded Clara.

"Your clothing situation is serious," smirked Linda.

"You are impossible," said Clara, but she had to admit it felt good to tell her secret to someone.

$\mathcal{F}$ O R T Y - $\mathcal{F}$ O U R

❧

$\mathcal{U}$sually the whole staff of *The Press* didn't work on Sundays, but Greeley was willing to pay overtime this weekend because the papers were flying off the stands. Demonstrations. Murder. Right-wing sermons. Now his contact at police headquarters said that Dr. Friedberg's house had been vandalized. He had already sent Gary Milford and Tom Wren over there to get a quote and a photo. He hadn't felt this level of excitement since he'd been in the press corps in Vietnam. Darius Greeley was the happiest man in Litchfield!

Tomorrow's front page would be packed. Patricia Castellano had already called him to remind him that her picture needed to be *top of the fold* and as big as Dr. Friedberg's picture. At first he had been annoyed with her call, but she was the reason that the town was in a swirl and also the reason his newspaper was selling better than it had in years, so he didn't mind accommodating her. Kit had gotten a great shot of Patricia, Mayor Ceravolo, and Father O'Malley after the sermon today, and that would run over two columns. The headline, "Local Socialite Stands Up for Life," would run over four columns.

There would be a second shot of Patricia with her boys on page 7 with the continuation of the article. She looked as fabulous as ever in both shots. Greeley thought she would be pleased.

Also on the front page would be a story on Father O'Malley's sermon and the 800 parishioners who had turned out to hear it, and a story on Casandra Keller's murder, with her high-school yearbook picture. Now, where should the article on the doctor's house go? Greeley decided to wait and see what the photo looked like.

The reporters started to trickle into the newsroom around two o'clock. Here was Acker, looking dour as usual. She came in with Kit and Fiona. They sat down around the conference table and took out their laptops to check their email.

"Damn. I hate *watch.com*," exclaimed Kit. "Look. Jamie already has a photo and caption from the church online. He'll have his story written in an hour or two. How are we supposed to compete with that?"

Greeley heard her complaints as he walked in the room, but nothing was going to spoil his day. "Quit your complaining. We did a double run last night, and stores are calling for more. This is the best sales day we've had in years. Nothing is going to bother me today. How did it go at St. Raymond's?" he asked no one in particular.

"It was like God himself had come down to preach," said Acker with a sneer. "They hung on his every idiotic word."

"It was worse than that. It was like he was overturning the Supreme Court," said Rivington.

"I wasn't really listening, but I got great art. I emailed the best one to you," Kit said to Greeley.

"I love it. I already gave it to layout." As Greeley looked at his watch, Latitia Blackman hurried in. She was assigned to the Keller murder. "Acker, Rivington, you need to be objective with these articles. I know you're both femi-nazis, but let's do some real reporting here. Father O'Malley is entitled to be treated fairly. Don't give me one-sided feminist propaganda."

"Settle down, Greeley," said Acker. "We're just talking. And I take it as an insult when someone calls me a femi-nazi. Just for future reference."

"What'a ya got, Blackman?" asked Greeley, ignoring Acker.

"My contact at police headquarters says they brought some guy in on a domestic violence charge, the wife's in the hospital, and somehow he's connected to Casandra Keller," said Blackman. "I couldn't get a name or anything, but I thought I'd go over to the hospital after this and snoop around. If she was beaten up as bad as I heard, she might still be there. Greeley, your contacts say anything?" Blackman looked up from her notes and caught Greeley staring at her thick lips with the gooey maroon lip gloss.

Greeley, realizing he had been caught staring, cleared his throat, "What's the connection? Angry guy, beat up his girlfriend, then went home and beat up his wife?" asked Greeley.

"Don't know. Maybe someone saw him with the girl."

"Good idea. Go to the hospital. I'll call downtown. I'll see if I can get anything. Who's going to go interview the murder victim's mother, so she can tell us what a good girl she really was?" asked Greeley. "Where's Johnson? Nothing's going on at Town Hall."

"He's not working today," said Kit. "Why don't you call Loren?"

"Okay. I will," Greeley yelled and slammed his hand on the table. "Now get going. We're gonna have the best week ever," he said with a smirk.

FORTY-FIVE

❧

She had the black outfit ready. Black jeans. Black long-sleeve T-shirt, sweatshirt, and boots. Sandra Stett pulled the black hood over her head, covering her short blond hair. Her wide-set, light-blue eyes were determined. The hood caught on her sterling-silver earrings as she pulled it down over her face. *Damn.* She parked a block behind the Litchfield Women's Center past Route 54 where acres of protected forest started. Feeling her knapsack, she made sure that she had the can of red spray paint. The two teenagers she had hired to do the doctor's house had done a great job, but she wanted to deface the abortion clinic herself.

There were no cars on the highway as she walked down the side road and onto Route 54. No headlights. She hugged the storefronts as she walked the half block between the street where she had parked and the front of the clinic. It was an unremarkable-looking building with an inconspicuous sign. On the far side of the building was a parking lot. The wooden front door was her target. She shook the can, scrunching her nose at the sound the metal balls made. Her eyes darting right and left to make sure no one was around. Quickly, she did her dirty work, admired it for a half a minute, and then slowly slunk her way back down Route 54 and up into the trees.

Safely back in her car, she pulled off the hood and the black shirt. She still had on the simple pale-pink shirt and pearls she had worn to church that morning. She thought about the boys she had hired to help her when she went to Smithtown the week before. The boys jumped at the chance to earn $100 for less than an hour's work. Smithtown was three miles west of Litchfield, but it might as well have been on another planet. Once out of Litchfield, as Sandra had driven west, it was like slowly watching the economy fade into a recession. The stores changed from the fancy clothing stores and bistros of downtown Litchfield to strip malls to vacant lots and fast-food restaurants. She knew she was finally in Smithtown when the discount liquor stores and check-cashing shops outnumbered every other kind of store. Smithtown was truly the armpit of Austin County.

She knew all about Smithtown, because that was where most of the demonstrators would come from. For a small stipend and lunch, she had been able to recruit 300 demonstrators through the Baptist African Methodist Episcopal Church, otherwise known as the Baptist A.M.E. Church. To get the pastor's help, Sandra had made him a sizable payment, ostensibly for the church, but Sandra knew it would go straight into his pocket. Since Patricia rarely looked at the books of Stand Up for Life, Sandra didn't think the expenditure would be questioned.

Now that her work at the clinic was done, she had an itch to go and drive by the doctor's house to revel in the mischief that she was causing for Dr. Friedberg. What would be the harm if she took the long way home and drove out to Sunken Meadow? She plugged the doctor's address into her GPS, made a K turn, and headed south through town. Sandra thought of all the nice people living in all these beautiful homes and what a good thing she was doing for them by ridding the town of that clinic.

She turned onto Stone Way and looked for the house that should be boarded up. "Destination is ahead on your right," said the GPS. Sandra slowed down and saw the workmen at the house. They were fitting a board into the open space where the window had been. The front light was on and another work-man was already painting the door. *Damn!* She wished she had come earlier to see the actual words. The boys had been told to get a photograph to feed to the papers. They had been told to email it to her. She started to drive home to see if they had.

FORTY-SIX

❧

*P*ia knew it was wrong, but she prayed that she would miscarry. *Dear God, please don't bring another child of his into this world.* The damage to her nose was so severe that she would need plastic surgery, her eye was swollen shut, and her lip was split and had needed 12 stitches to keep it closed. But, despite the pain, she longed to feel some sign that she would lose the baby. All day Sunday and through the night, she had prayed that God would take the baby. That He would see that a child born of this union at this time was a mistake. But, no such luck. She had finally told the nurse she was pregnant and asked for a sonogram. A healthy heartbeat was her answer. She would still have to go to the Women's Center on Friday. She needed to talk to Stella alone. To make a plan. What would she do without Stella? She knew that the girls were safe with her and George, but when they came today to visit her, she had to talk to Stella without them.

On Saturday night, when the nurse had told them that Pia would be admitted, the girls had been reluctant to leave her, but finally, teary-eyed and exhausted, they had agreed to go home with Stella and George. Stella, wearing her wrinkled gown, now stained with blood and dirt, and George in his tuxedo, tie gone and top buttons open, had whisked the girls away to safety. Pia thought of Maria and Carmen, probably huddled together for comfort, asleep in each other's arms. The thought of them, protected, calmed her.

She must have drifted off. For a minute she didn't know where she was, and then she remembered. All of a sudden she was in a panic, mind racing, fear and confusion welling up. What if Eduardo got out of jail and went looking for the girls? For Maria, who had called the police on him? Pia knew that Eduardo would never forgive Maria. Never. Then she remembered that the girls were safe with George and Stella. Eduardo would never dare to break into George's home. She wished her girls were with her, but she knew that was selfish. They were sleeping in Stella's beautiful house, in soft sheets smelling of fabric softener. She could see their long hair splayed out on the pillow. Yes, think of them. That was good. She couldn't wait until they came to see her. She hoped the doctor would let her go home to Stella's.

Pia raised her hand to her face. She felt the bandages. She could only see out of one eye. The other was too swollen to open. Her arms ached from trying to stop Eduardo and from receiving his punishing blows. Her back hurt and her breasts ached. She wondered what she looked like. She thought of her mother seeing her yesterday, lying in a hospital bed. Beaten and swollen. The older woman had started to cry as she entered the room, but Pia's father had inspected his daughter with a hard, distant look.

Pia had been with her doctor, a young Indian woman who looked to be about 25, when they all burst into the room. Her parents, the girls and Stella, George and little Juan. Even though she was young, the doctor recognized the look on the father's face and said, "Five minutes, everybody."

"Where is he?" Mr. Munoz asked Pia, after the doctor left the room.

"I don't know. In jail. The police took him away." Pia started to cry.

"Who cares where he is?" yelled Maria. "He tried to kill her. Don't you see?"

"I do see," said Mr. Munoz, and everyone in the room stood still, waiting to see whose side he would come down on. Finally, he reached out his hand and stroked Pia's brow. Some of the tension in the air dissipated. Maria took one of her mother's hands and Stella took the other. The family surrounded Pia; the women wept. Mr. Munoz and George stood silently, while little Juan scrambled onto the bed.

Unseen by Pia's family, a young, black woman with very short hair and glossy maroon lips, paused outside the room. She looked at the scene in the room and knew instinctively that she had found the woman who had been beaten by her husband. *Damn, girl! He did a number on you!* Latitia turned her face away, cursing that it was an awkward time for her to burst in and ask for a quote.

She slowed down slightly, long enough to note the name on the door. Pia Fernandez.

ℱ O R T Y - ℐ E V E N

When it was time to get up, Dr. Friedberg had already been awake for hours, tossing from side to side, looking for comfort. She dragged her tired bones out of bed and headed for the shower. The hot water felt good, but somehow she felt vulnerable. *Was that a thump? Dry leaves crackling under boots?* She turned the water off, quickly dried herself, dressed, and went downstairs for coffee. She didn't even want to see the morning papers. She felt fragile. Jagged, like the broken glass from her window. She didn't want to read anything that was going to upset her. She decided to just go to work and do her job and get through the day. The sight of the boarded window stopped her in her tracks. She felt violated. She had vacuumed up the broken glass, but made a mental note to do it again when she got home. She was sure that shards were hidden under the chairs and in the carpet. The workmen had said they would come while she was at work and replace the glass.

She poured her coffee into a disposable cup and left the house at 6:45 for the 15-minute commute across town to the clinic. She arrived at 7 on the dot to see that her house had not been the only building to be defaced. She pulled up in front of the clinic and saw that the words "Dr. Friedberg is a Baby Killer" had been spray-painted on the clinic door. Again, in red paint. She knew she had one hour before her first patient arrived. She went inside quickly and made three calls in rapid succession. The police, the handyman, and Suzy.

"Suzy? It's Amy. It's happened again. They spray-painted the clinic. Suzy, I have an eight o'clock appointment. Some woman is going to arrive here and see this. All of this has to end. Is there anything we can do legally?" All of her frustration came pouring out.

Suzy, in her car on her way to work, exclaimed, "Jesus Christ! I feel like the whole world is turning upside down. I'm in my car. I'm coming over. I'll call Rachel."

The police, the handyman, Suzy, and Rachel, all pulled into the parking lot at the clinic within minutes of each other. Officers Quinn and Rea came out of the squad car slowly. They were tired. They had worked harder in the last few days than they had worked in years. After a few hours of shut-eye at the station, they were back at work. They longed for their sleepy town to go back to sleep.

Before they even made it over to the front door, Dr. Friedberg said, "I want the door painted over before eight o'clock. I have a woman coming in for an appointment, and I don't want her to see this."

Officer Rea looked at Officer Quinn with a frown before he said, "This is now a crime scene, Dr. Friedberg. You can't paint over the evidence."

"What?" exclaimed Dr. Friedberg, silently cursing herself for calling the police. "This is terrible. I will not have her walk past this, this—I don't even know what to call it."

"Okay. Let's try to be creative here. Can we take the door off the hinges?" asked Rachel. The handyman went to inspect the door.

"Officers, surely you understand that we need to get this cleaned up as soon as possible. This vandalism, this harassment, has got to be stopped," declared Suzy.

"Well, Ms. Walker, you can't paint over the evidence and then expect us to solve the crime," said Officer Quinn, sounding a little on edge.

"I think I can take it off," said Hank, the handyman. Suzy, Rachel, and Dr. Friedberg searched the faces of Officers Rea and Quinn. The officers looked at each other. They walked away from the women and huddled.

"Okay, we'll take the door off and move it around back, but once your patient gets here, we're putting it back on and doing our job," said Officer Quinn.

"Okay, but please try to work quickly. I have other patients coming. Thank you," said Dr. Friedberg, breathing a sigh of relief. "Let Hank get to work. I need this moved by 7:50," Dr. Friedberg said to the group. "Suzy, Rachel, let's go inside. I only have forty-five minutes before I need to be in surgery," she said, leading the group into the clinic. The policemen, who hadn't been invited in, decided to watch the door being removed. Dr. Friedberg ushered Suzy and Rachel into the conference room and closed the door.

All three women sat down, shaking their heads. Dr. Friedberg had a dazed look on her face. Suzy knew she had to take control of the situation. "On the way here, I was thinking that until the demonstration is over, we're going to have to hire security guards to be posted at Amy's house, and here, at the clinic. Around the clock. And we need beefed-up patrolling at both spots. Rachel, we need to call an emergency meeting of the board tonight to discuss the situation."

"Yes, I agree. I'll have my secretary draft an email to the board. We'll meet here tonight at eight. I think the security is a good idea. Amy, what do you think?" asked Rachel. Besides being president of the Women's Center board, Rachel

Horowitz was a hedge-fund manager. She had graduated top of her class at Stanford and then top of her class at Yale. She was 55 years old, short, wide, and wore her straight-brown hair with thick bangs. She was always the smartest person in the room.

Dr. Friedberg struggled out of her daze. The only thing she wanted to think about was her patient, Ms. Zimmer, who would be here momentarily, but she tried to follow the conversation. "Okay. I don't really like the idea of having security guards at my home, but I guess it's necessary."

"Rachel, you have to call the mayor and ask him to make a statement. I can't. I quit as his campaign chair yesterday and I don't think we're on speaking terms," said Suzy, in her clipped, rapid-fire way.

"You quit as his chair?" Dr. Friedberg and Rachel both exclaimed at the same time.

"It got ugly. I screamed. He screamed. But seriously, how can I support Antonio when he's supporting the demonstration? He should have stopped Patricia weeks ago, before this thing got out of hand."

"These things take on a life of their own. I'm not sure she can stop it. It's a rotten shame," said Rachel.

"I have to go," said Dr. Friedberg, who stood up to go meet her patient.

"Amy, don't worry. We're here and we'll be with you every step of the way," said Rachel, reaching over to hug the doctor.

"Thanks. To both of you. We'll talk later." Dr. Friedberg left, closing the door behind her.

As soon as the door was closed, Suzy said, "Antonio Ceravolo has got to go. We need to find another candidate for mayor."

"You're right. You are *so* right." Rachel leaned into the table, pushed up the sleeves of her tan sweater set, and took a notepad out of her enormous purse.

"Who can we get?" Suzy leaned in as well, adjusted her Rolex to note the time, and started to mentally go over her contact lists.

"Do you think we can get a cup of coffee around here while we jot down a short list?" asked Rachel, as she picked up the conference-room phone and dialed the front desk.

$\mathcal{F}$ORTY-$\mathcal{E}$IGHT

$\mathcal{A}$t eight o'clock on Monday morning, Eduardo was handcuffed and taken, along with 20 other guys, out of the jail into a secure elevator, which took them down to an underground tunnel, then into another secure elevator, to go up into the courthouse across the street to be arraigned. In an unjust world, it was beautiful symmetry that now Eduardo's face was as beaten in and battered as Pia's. He had two black eyes and a slash down his right cheek, which the infirmary doctor had hastily stitched up to stop the bleeding. He had spent the rest of the night in solitary confinement. Detective Bickford's face exploded into a delighted grin when Eduardo came slowly up the hallway.

"This is justice if I ever saw it," he laughed, slapping Eduardo on the back, hard, making him lurch out of line. He continued to laugh as Eduardo was led into the holding room to the left of the courtroom. Like a dangerous tiger caught in a trap, Eduardo glared at Bickford out of slitted eyes. Hatred flowed through the air from Eduardo to Bickford, making Bickford howl with mirth. He hadn't had such fun in a long time.

Eduardo, the other male detainees, and two women from the women's prison sat in the holding room, waiting for the Superior Court judge to appear in the courtroom, so that the proceedings could begin. It was an old building and was in need of some repair. The beige paint in the holding room was peeling in one corner where water had dripped in during the last heavy rain. The prisoners sat in orange plastic chairs. Most of them had been picked up the previous evening for disorderly conduct or resisting arrest and would be out of the courthouse in a few hours. Eduardo was the only one charged with a first-degree crime. Officers Quinn and Rea had made a formal complaint against Eduardo.

Judge Charlene Davidson was an efficient and deliberate Superior Court judge. She was known for sizing up a defendant with a look or two and pronouncing judgment without further delay. The assistant district attorney and the defense counsel knew to be brief and to the point when in front of her. It was said that she merely had to look at a defendant to decide whether he was a piece of shit or worth saving in some fashion. Detective Bickford took delight in the fact that he knew that Judge Davidson would see Eduardo as the piece of shit he was before the assistant district attorney rose from his chair. He had bought himself an extra-large latte to watch the show.

As soon as the judge stood in the doorway to the courtroom, all of the various clerks, the sheriff's sergeant, police officers, and lawyers went to their places. The defendants were all brought in and sat on wooden benches in a box to the left of the judge. As their case was called they stood to face their fate.

In the press section of the courtroom, Latitia Blackman had her own large caramel latte with smeared maroon lipstick all over the edge. She was furiously assaulting her iPhone as the parade of drunks was dispensed with by Judge Davidson. She was happy to see that Jamie Ross was not there. This was her scoop. She could feel it. She was waiting for anyone with the last name of Fernandez. She was waiting for Pia's husband

and Casandra Keller's lover to appear. Greeley's contacts at police headquarters had said that a guy named Fernandez had been Keller's lover.

Eduardo was the last case on the docket. Judge Davidson had released every other lowlife to their own recognizance, except one, who had pleaded guilty. She had tried to inform him of his rights, but he still wanted to plead guilty. Must be a gang member who was safer in jail than on the street. The judge shook her head. Frankly, at this point, she was getting hungry. The clerk called the *State of New Jersey v. Eduardo Fernandez.* Judge Davidson glanced up, having been bored to death by 22 stupid people who had wasted her time, and locked eyes with Eduardo. Eduardo stood up. Now here was someone to contemplate. She sat up a little straighter. Her mouth, heretofore relaxed, tightened. Latitia Blackman put her iPhone in her purse.

Judge Davidson read the charge. She swiveled her chair and looked directly at Eduardo. Obviously, his cellmates had taken a liking to him, and he had tried to fight them off. "Do you speak English?" she asked him.

"Yes."

"Are you a citizen of the United States?"

"Yes."

"You know that you have the right to remain silent and that anything you do or say can be held against you in a court of law?"

"Yes."

Judge Davidson paused. She noted that Eduardo now looked straight ahead. *Here's a proud asshole. Tries to kill his wife and shows no remorse whatsoever.* "You know that the complaint against you is sworn by two police officers?"

"I do now," he said smugly.

"Do not ever have an attitude when you are in my courtroom. Do you understand?" asked Judge Davidson, pointing a long finger at Eduardo.

Eduardo looked straight ahead.

"Do you understand me, Mr. Fernandez?" Judge Davidson asked again. She waited. Her stomach growled. "Look at me when I'm talking to you." Eduardo continued to stare straight ahead. "Bail is set at $1 million. Prisoner is remanded to the county jail. Defendant will appear before a Grand Jury on, let me see…" Judge Davidson looked to the clerk and whispered, "Give me a date in September." The clerk whispered back.

"The defendant will appear before the Grand Jury on September 30."

A guffaw was heard from the gallery. Judge Davidson looked startled. Detective Bickford bowed his head like a schoolboy who had been reprimanded by the teacher.

$\mathcal{F}$ORTY-$\mathcal{N}$INE

⚓

$\mathcal{P}$atricia's kitchen was larger than many small homes. It was really three rooms, painted a pale yellow, which wove around a large, circular table that sat 10. Audubon prints of brightly colored birds were displayed on the walls. Toucans and pelicans watched visitors as they walked by. In the first room were an overstuffed couch and two huge chairs in coordinating yellow and green fabrics. The second room had the table, a desk, and two computers, and the third room was the actual kitchen: Two Bosch refrigerators, an eight-burner stove, four ovens, two sinks and a wet bar, countless appliances, and a wall of floor-to-ceiling glass cabinets where ceramic dishes, bowls, and cups were displayed.

This is where Father O'Malley was summoned on Monday morning and where he found Patricia overseeing the preparations for the twins' birthday party. Thirty little monsters would be descending on the house at noon for lunch and then swimming in the pool. Individualized pizzas that had been preordered for each boy by his mother or nanny were being made on the long white marble island. Two cooks were working on the pizzas and another one was decorating 60 cupcakes. Fourteen of the kids coming had nut allergies, six had diabetes, four were lactose intolerant, and one was allergic to wheat. Patricia did not believe in allergies, so the twins, Sammy and Tony, ate anything they wanted and showed no signs of allergic reaction to anything.

"Good morning, Thomas," said Patricia, when she saw the priest enter the far corner of the kitchen some 50 feet away. Father O'Malley, not wanting to yell, waved and continued to walk toward her. He looked at the assortment of birds on the wall as he approached. No finer collection had ever hung in a gallery he was sure.

"Good morning, Patricia," he said, at the end of his journey. "What's going on here?"

"It's the twins' birthday. They're turning six. I can't believe it." Patricia and Father O'Malley looked out the back window just in time to see Sammy push Tony to the ground and get him in a headlock. Tony elbowed Sammy in the groin, and both boys started to howl.

"Mmm," was all Patricia said. "Carry on here, Carmelita. I'll be back in a little while. We'll be in the study. And find Ilsa and tell her to mind the boys." Ilsa was the boys' Swedish *au pair,* but she was much more interested in the gardeners and her suntan than watching the twins.

They walked out of the kitchen through the black-and-white foyer and into Patricia's study. The maid had laid out a thermos of coffee, cups, sugar, and milk. "Coffee, Father?" asked Patricia.

"Yes, please." They both sat on the brown leather couch in front of the coffee table. Patricia poured them both a cup.

"Father, I am deeply troubled by the defacing of both Dr. Friedberg's house and the clinic. I never foresaw something like this. What if Dr. Friedberg had been hurt? I would feel terrible. I want to figure out if there is something we can do to prevent...," here Patricia paused.

"I am also very upset by these outrageous acts. Do you have any idea who would do anything like this?"

"I haven't a clue. No one on my staff would ever dream of doing anything like this, but we don't really know who the demonstrators are...."

The priest and the socialite sat sipping their coffee. They sat staring straight ahead. They were the perfect contrast to each other. Patricia's black hair fell in soft waves, outlining her beautiful face with the gold in her large brown eyes glinting, and her pointed nose and her full red lips set just so. She sat with her shapely legs crossed demurely at the knee. On the other hand, Thomas's blond curly hair was streaked honey and gold, his eyes were as blue as lapis lazuli, his masculine features were sunburned, and his lean body had the look of a born athlete.

They sat side by side, pondering their inability to control what was happening, for quite some time. Both realized that they had shown a surprising lack of forethought when they had jumped into this exercise. Both felt secure in their lives of privilege. He, protected by the cloth, and she by the cash, had not been forced into thinking about the meaning of their cause to ordinary, desperate people.

After searching her soul and coming up empty, a smile appeared on Patricia's face. "We'll issue a statement," she said.

"Yes, a statement condemning these acts of violence. We never wanted to have a violent demonstration," said Father O'Malley. "I just wanted to spread God's word."

Patricia gave him a look, raising one arched eyebrow a bit. "Let's draft something. I'll call Greeley. Should we call DeShawn Fletcher and read it on the six o'clock news?"

"I don't have the media savvy that you do, Patricia," said Father O'Malley. "I think I'd rather see my words in print than my face on TV."

Patricia looked at Father O'Malley with a knitted brow and a questioning look. Why someone would want to read their words in a box in the newspaper, instead of see their image on television, was a mystery to her. As for Father O'Malley, he felt he wanted to hang back and not take center stage.

FIFTY

❧

Freeport was the working-class town next to Litchfield. There was a running joke among Litchfield wives that when they threw their husbands out of the house for an indiscretion, the men landed in Freeport. Still wanting to be near their kids, but not being able to afford two houses in Litchfield, the estranged husbands and fathers were banished to apartments in Freeport. Another group of folks in Freeport were divorced wives whose kids were grown, so there was no longer any need for them to keep their houses in Litchfield. Out on their own, many times trying to pick up the pieces of their careers that had been derailed by child-rearing, these were sad women. Veronica Keller was one of them.

Greeley had called Loren and told her to go out and interview Veronica Keller, the mother of the girl who had been murdered. Loren, eager for work, had agreed to go, but now that she was heading over to the Gladwell Garden Apartments, she was nervous. How do you interview a woman who has just lost her daughter? Images of Emily floated through Loren's mind as she drove east on Grant Avenue through Litchfield into Freeport. If anything happened to Emily, Loren wouldn't even be able to talk, let alone give an interview. Loren had seen Casandra's picture in the paper, and Marshall had said he knew her when they were in high school. She was a pretty girl in a tough kind of way. Too much eye makeup, hair bleached blond, a stud in her nose. Still, if you washed all of that away, she was just a young woman with her whole life ahead of her.

At the traffic light, Loren undid the button of her jeans. She was only five weeks pregnant, but her stomach was already swollen. *Third child, stretched muscles.* A few more days to go, and at least she could take care of this problem. She felt bad. She loved babies, little soft cheeks, that amazing baby smell. But, she was in no position to have one now. *You have to think of Emily and Marshall. You can't put any more pressure on Peter.* Of course, her "babies" were adults, but they still depended on her. The kids had taken it well when she and Peter had told them they would have to commute to school, but Loren knew that they were upset. They had both volunteered to get jobs to help out.

She made a turn into the apartment complex and pulled over to the curb. She wanted to collect her thoughts. Jot down a few questions. How to begin? "Mrs. Keller, I'm so sorry for your loss. My name is Loren Elliot, I'm with *The Press*, and I'm here to report on the worst day of your life. Can I come in?" No, probably not a good start. How about: "My name is Loren Elliot, and *The Press* wants to help you find the murderer of your only daughter. May I come in?" Seriously, how did you do this? At last, completely paralyzed, she dialed Helen's number.

"Acker," Helen's nasal voice quacked after only one ring.

"Hey, Helen. It's Loren. Yeah. I'm out in front of Veronica Keller's apartment and I have no idea what to say to this woman. Can you help me out? What should I ask her?"

"Start off by saying that you are deeply sorry for her loss. You're probably about the same age. Throw in some line about having a 20-year-old daughter yourself and then ask her if she has any idea who did this to her sweet daughter. Then just listen. That's all you need. Can you do it, Loren?"

"Yeah. I can do it. Just never did it before. Thanks, Helen. Anything going on?"

"Just a lot of follow-up on Friedberg's house, the clinic, the murder investigation. Another ordinary day in Litchfield," joked Helen. Helen was feeling good, because so far, Greeley hadn't bumped her series for any of these other stories.

"Yeah, just an ordinary day," mimicked Loren.

"Anyway, gotta go."

"Thanks, Helen."

"Don't mention it."

Loren looked up at the apartments and wondered how much the rent was. She looked down at her swollen belly. What would it be like for her and Peter to live here and raise the baby? They could sell the house and move into a two-bedroom apartment. But, where would Marshall and Emily stay when they visited? How would they all be together? She slowly moved the car into an empty parking space and then looked down at the paper in her hand. Apartment 2G. By the time Loren found the apartment, she had her speech down pat. She rang the bell, and a tired-looking woman answered the door. She said nothing.

Loren started her spiel. The woman held up her hand. Loren stopped.

"I'm not Veronica," said the woman. Loren noticed that the woman had no bottom teeth. "I'm her mother. Veronica's down at the funeral parlor." She shut the door in Loren's face.

Loren turned around on the stoop. She felt like she shouldn't be there. She was beginning to doubt that she had the right stuff to be an investigative journalist, when she saw a car drive up and a young woman get out. The first thing that she noticed was the tattoos and rings in the girl's face and ears. Loren realized she was still standing on the stoop when the young woman approached.

"Hi," said Loren.

"Hi," said Molly. "Do you know Casandra?"

"No. I'm...I'm with *The Press*."

"The newspaper?"

"Yes. I was assigned to do an article on Casandra's mother and how she's holding up. But she's not home."

The girl bit her fingernail and looked at Loren as if she was trying to make a decision. "I want to talk to the press. My name's Molly Dolan and I was with Michael Russo when he found the body, and I know something that I've been trying to tell someone since this all started, and I don't know who to call or what to do." The girl was starting to cry now, and Loren felt more like a mother than a reporter.

"Do you want to go and get some coffee? Are you hungry?" Loren walked down the steps of the porch and put her arm around Molly's shoulder.

"I am hungry. I haven't really eaten since we found her," said Molly.

"That was some time ago. Let's go to the diner," said Loren, guiding Molly down the path to her car.

FIFTY-ONE

On Monday, Pia's doctor decided that Pia needed to stay in the hospital a little longer, so a surgeon could re-break her nose and insert small plastic tubes to keep her airways open. This would be a temporary fix until the swelling subsided and a diagnosis could be made on how to restore the look of her natural nose. Keeping the airways open was functional, as opposed to cosmetic. Pia could elect to do a cosmetic procedure in the future, or not.

Pia and the girls were devastated that Pia couldn't go home yet. Her nerves were frayed. They all just wanted to go to Stella's, where there were no visiting hours, just endless hours together. The girls climbed into bed with their mother and cuddled to try to forget what had happened. Carmen had made an origami swan that morning at Stella's house and gave it to her mother now. They were all complimenting her and looking at the swan when Detective Bickford walked in. The laughing and *ohhing* and *ahhing* turned to silence as Detective Bickford stood in the doorway.

"Yes?" said Stella, moving over to the doorway to block the man from entering the room. "Can I help you?"

"My name's Detective Bickford with the Litchfield Police. I want to take Mrs. Fernandez's statement."

"Can you come back later?" asked Stella.

Detective Bickford looked at his watch. "No, this is important."

Stella looked at Pia, who was happily resting, with Maria and Carmen lying on either side of her in the bed. Stella hated to break up this beautiful moment, but she also wanted to help the police in their investigation. She wanted Eduardo to stay in jail. She quickly made a decision and ushered the girls out of the room and took them to the cafeteria. Detective Bickford approached Pia's bed slowly. He liked to drink in details of the people he interviewed. The way this woman was lying in the bed, the way she had allowed her sister to make decisions for her and then take away her children, told the Detective that she was a repeat victim. This was not the first time Eduardo Fernandez had taken out his anger on his wife. She looked up at him with her one good eye. The other was completely black-and-blue and swollen shut. The telltale ring of bruises around her throat told him that Eduardo had tried to choke her.

"Good afternoon, Mrs. Fernandez. I'm Detective Bickford, and the first thing I want to assure you of is that your husband will be locked up until his case goes to the Grand Jury on September 30th. He was arraigned this morning and the Judge saw him for who he is. She purposely set the trial date as far away as she could. That's good for you. Gives you time. Time to heal."

Pia had a rush of emotions. She wanted Eduardo to stay in jail, so that he couldn't come after Maria, but it frightened her to know that he was angry. She had spent so many years worrying about Eduardo's mood, that even now when he was locked up, because of what he had done, her first instinct was to do everything in her power to calm him. To appease him. To alleviate his rage. Even as Detective Bickford started to speak to her, all she could think about was Eduardo's face when he was striking her and how his wrath must be growing. She feared that a prison cell could not hold his hatred.

"The District Attorney is charging him with attempted murder in the presence of a minor. He could get up to twenty years in jail. I'm not saying he'll get twenty years, but he could. We have an airtight case against him, seeing that Officers Quinn and Rea saw him...ah, with you, and Maria opened the door for the police, but I do need to take a statement from you. Do you want to tell me what happened?"

Pia hesitated. She didn't know where to begin. How could he understand that she had just been sitting on the couch, and when she flinched, Eduardo had gone crazy? "I don't really know what happened. We were watching the news and he got mad. It was a story about the girl who was found dead."

"Casandra Keller?"

"Yes. I think that was her name. I'm not really sure. Anyway, I could feel his anger growing, like it does. I made a comment that I felt sorry for the girl and he threw me to the ground. Punching, slapping, banging my head on the floor, choking me." Pia started to tremble.

"It's okay. It won't happen again. He's in jail and we're gonna make sure he stays there. Ah, you don't know the girl? The girl on the news? Do you, Mrs. Fernandez?"

"No."

"Does Eduardo know the girl?"

"I don't think so. I wouldn't know."

"Mrs. Fernandez, is this the first time your husband hit you?" Pia's mouth started to quiver. Tears fell from her swollen eyes. She shook her head. Detective Bickford looked down at Pia's bowed head. *How do people go from loving each other to this?* He pulled a chair over toward the bed, sat down, and reached out to pat Pia's hand. "It's okay. You're safe now. Do you have somewhere to go when you're released?"

"Yes, I'll be staying with my sister."

"I'm gonna write up this report and then come back for you to sign it. You need to have your sister take some pictures of your bruises. I'll talk to her about it. Sometime when your girls aren't here. I might have to get a statement from your daughter, but let's see if we can get by without it."

"Yes, let's not upset her any more than she is. Please."

"I'll see what I can do. I'm going to leave these papers here for you. They explain your legal rights."

"Okay. And...thank you," she said.

"Here's my card. Call me if you need anything." The tall detective stood up beside the bed, his fingers brushing the felt of his hat. He searched his brain for a few good words to say to this woman, but none came to mind.

FIFTY-TWO

⤸

Loren and Molly had decided that they didn't want to go to the Litchfield Diner. Too many ears. Instead, they went to the Freeport Subway, which was new and frequented by teenage boys eating huge quantities of meat and bread. None of them cared what two women were talking about at the last table in the back. Loren had told Molly to go and sit down and she would get them a sandwich. In the back of her mind, she knew she shouldn't spend the extra money on Molly's sandwich, but she would try to get Greeley to reimburse her. Loren purchased two meatball subs, two cokes, a bag of potato chips, and two chocolate-chip cookies. She was starving! She brought the tray back to the table, where Molly was waiting.

"Wow!" said Molly with a smile, looking at the tray full of goodies.

"Let's eat. Then talk," said Loren, sliding into the booth. The two women dug into their subs and ate like people who have real hunger, as opposed to eating just because it's mealtime. Without speaking a word, they consumed every last morsel on the tray. When Loren finished eating, she rolled the wrapping from the sub into a ball, took a breath, and gave the girl across from her a good look. Her long hair could use a wash, her white T-shirt was yellow around the armpits, and the ring in her nose was slightly askew.

Loren's belly was now literally bursting over the top of her pants. She tried to open the button without Molly noticing. Once she had accomplished it, she felt the zipper sliding down and it felt good. She knew she would have a problem standing up at the end of the interview, but she decided not to worry about it now. She reached into her purse and pulled out her reporter's notebook and her pen.

"So, you're a friend of Casandra's?" she started.

Molly was still wiping her mouth with a paper napkin. She seemed to be thinking. What was it that she wanted to say? "She was my best friend. Kind of…my only friend," she began. "We met in second grade. That's a long time ago now. We hung out ever since. The thing I wanted to tell someone is…" here Molly stopped. She pushed her limp hair behind her left ear. She straightened the bone that pierced her eyebrow. Loren winced.

"What did you need to tell someone, Molly? You can tell me. I don't have to report it. I'm like your mom. I have a daughter, Emily. She's twenty. How old are you?" asked Loren, putting her pen down.

"I'm twenty-two."

"My son is twenty-two. Marshall Elliot. Do you know him?"

"I know who he is. He was super smart. He wouldn't know me," said Molly, shaking her head.

"I bet he would. If he didn't know you it would be because he was always studying so hard. Marshall was a very serious student." Loren felt sorry for this young woman, who, behind the tattoos and rings, was just a frightened little girl. "Molly, tell me what it is."

"Casandra was sleeping with this guy. I think he hurt her." Molly covered her face.

"Are you afraid of this guy? Is that it, Molly?" Loren had not written a word in her notebook.

"I guess. I'm not sure what I'm afraid of, but I'm afraid of something."

"Do you want to tell me his name?"

"Yes…Eduardo…Eduardo Fernandez. He's married and I think he has kids. I never liked him. He would come into The Sportsman, that's where we hang out, and Casandra would leave with him. Leave me at the bar. I know everybody, so it was okay, but still, she would leave me and go home with him. When she was going to see him, she didn't want me around. The day she died…I know he was coming over to her apartment. We had gone to Victoria's Secret that afternoon and she had bought new panties. She thought he would like them.…" Molly looked up at Loren. "Listen, I know you're a reporter, but you seem real nice. Please don't print all I just said. I want to tell the police but I'm afraid when I'm with them."

Loren took Molly's hand. She sat, comforting her, for a half hour. "Listen, Molly, I'm not going to write this up for the newspaper, but you have to tell the police, because they need to catch this man. You have to help them. You need to do it for Casandra. You need to do it for yourself."

"You're right. I have Detective Bickford's card. Can I call him in your car?"

"Sure. I have to go to the ladies' room, but I'll be right back, and we'll call." Loren got up, hiding her open pants with the tray, ditched the tray, grabbed her pants, and went into the ladies' room. Once behind the door, she sucked in her belly and closed the snap. *Tomorrow, sweatpants.*

As they walked out to Loren's car, Molly turned to her and said, "Listen, I know you're a reporter, so you can use what I told you, but just say it's from an anonymous source. Can you do that?"

"Thanks, Molly. Now let's call this Detective Bickford," she said, as she opened the car door.

FIFTY-THREE

⚜

They had started using a large whiteboard with colored markers after Chief Leonard Chodor saw one on a television crime show. Officer Rea, who had been an art major at college until his father had insisted he switch to criminal justice, liked to use the different-colored markers. He was very proud of his graphs and charts and lists of key witnesses. The other officers and detectives felt foolish standing up in front of the room writing on the board and were happy to let him play this role.

Chief Chodor had called Officers Quinn and Rea and Detective Bickford into a meeting to see where they were with the Casandra Keller case. They sat around a long, brown, rectangular table that was scarred by cigarette burns and rings from coffee cups. They were no longer allowed to smoke in the room, so they broke every hour to go outside and have a cigarette. A picture of Mayor Antonio Ceravolo stared down at them from the gray wall.

"It's been one helluva week. I can't remember another week like this in the last twenty years," started Chief Chodor, running one of his hands over his tired eyes. Everything about Chief Chodor was big. He stood 6'6" in his socks and weighed 250. He wore a size 13 shoe, and his neck looked like a telephone pole. No one wanted to mess with Chief Chodor. As excited as Darius Greeley was by all the goings-on in town that sold newspapers, Chief Chodor felt an equal amount of anxiety. It was his responsibility to find out who had committed murder in his peaceful little town. Unlike for Greeley, there was no benefit for him or the police department from any of the things going on—the murder, the vandalism, the demonstration.

"Rea, get one of your markers and go up to the board," instructed the chief in a gruff tone. Rea looked at Quinn, Quinn looked at Bickford. Rea reluctantly went up to the board and picked up a green marker, then turned and looked at the Chief.

"Now, I want you to write the word 'Knuckleheads' in all caps," the chief's voice was getting louder with every word, "and under it, I want you to write your name and your partner's name." When Rea didn't move, the chief slammed his fist on the table. "Whose brilliant idea was it to let the handyman at the clinic take the door—that had been defaced—off the hinges and take it around back? Which one of my officers thinks it's okay to tamper with evidence? Or is it both of you who think it's okay?" Here, the chief looked hard at one officer and then the other.

Officer Rea stood at the front of the room, holding the green marker. Finally, he stammered, "Dr. Friedberg was adamant...," his voice trailing off.

"*Doctor Friedberg was adamant!?!*" yelled Chief Chodor. "Is Dr. Friedberg now running the police department?"

"We put it back," offered Quinn. "We waited for the woman to arrive at the clinic, the woman who Dr. Friedberg was worried about, and then we put it back and took our photos. Dusted for prints..."

"Gentlemen, I understand that we are under a lot of pressure this week, but I want you to know that I will not tolerate any deviation from standard procedure. Do you understand me?"

"Yes, sir," said Officer Rea.

"Yes, sir," said Officer Quinn.

The chief took a full minute to stare down both officers before he moved on. "And you can thank Suzy Walker for calling me to thank me for your consideration. I had to hear it from her that my procedures were so easily sidestepped." The chief let that sink in a moment and then continued. "So, where are we? Bick? What have you got on the Keller case? Do we have a suspect?" asked the chief, looking at Detective Bickford through bloodshot eyes.

The detective loved to be called "Bick" by the chief. It meant that the chief saw him as a friend. An equal. Someone he depended on. "I'll tell you what I think, and then we'll figure out how to prove it," said Detective Bickford, opening his small notebook. "Jay, the bartender at The Sportsman, told me that Casandra was sleeping with an older, married guy, named Eduardo Fernandez. Turns out that Fernandez is the same Fernandez you guys brought in Saturday night for beating the shit out of his wife. Both of the people who found the deceased have now told me that Keller was sleeping with one Eduardo Fernandez. That's Michael Russo and Molly Dolan…." said Bickford.

"Hey…," Quinn broke in, "I just thought'a something. One night last week I asked a guy to move along. He had pulled over by the side of the road near the Green Street Apartments. Thinking back, I think it was him. Fernandez," said Officer Quinn.

"What are you talking about, Quinn?" said Chief Chodor with an annoyed tone.

"When we brought Fernandez in on Saturday night, I didn't make the connection. I saw him on Friday night, I think, stopped on the side of the road on Green Street. Near the apartments. He was driving a black truck. He said he just pulled over to take a call," said Quinn.

"Check to see what kind of car Fernandez drives," demanded Chief Chodor. "Now get out of here and don't move any doors."

$\mathcal{F}$ I F T Y - $\mathcal{F}$ O U R

❧

$\mathcal{T}$here were five members of the Litchfield Women's
Center Board of Directors: President Rachel Horowitz,
Vice President Dr. Norman Rubin, Recording Secretary Suzy
Walker, Corresponding Secretary Nina Adler—who was also
executive director of the Safe Haven Shelter—and Treasurer
Felix Johns, who was a retired banker. Dr. Friedberg attend-
ed all board meetings, but was not a voting member of the
board. Darla, Dr. Friedberg's secretary, took the minutes. That
Monday night, all five directors had rearranged plans to at-
tend the emergency board meeting that had been called in
response to yesterday's vandalism at both the center and Dr.
Friedberg's house.

None of them really liked to go out to the center at night.
Route 54 was dark and lonely, and they all felt a little vulnerable in the parking lot, getting into their Porsches, Jaguars,
and Mercedes. Dr. Friedberg had never before felt nervous at
any time of the day or night at the clinic, but after the bricks
and the graffiti, even she was feeling a little uneasy. Suzy had
called and offered to pick her up, and she had agreed. Usually

the board tried to have its meetings on Saturday mornings, but Rachel and Suzy had felt some urgency in bringing the board together tonight. The two women had hired the security firm of Young Semple without the entire board approving the expenditure, and they had never done that before.

When the board members had all gathered and helped themselves to the coffee and cookies that Darla had set out for them, Rachel brought the meeting to order.

"Thank you all for coming on such short notice." Rachel slowly looked around the table, making eye contact with each director in turn. "I thought that we needed to have a conversation about the extraordinary recent events in Litchfield that involve the center. As you all know, Patricia Castellano and Father O'Malley have been planning a demonstration in front of the center for next Saturday. One of the things we need to discuss is closing the center for just that day. Next on the agenda is the vandalism, both at Dr. Friedberg's home and here at the center. Suzy and I were here this morning, after Dr. Friedberg arrived and found that the front door had been spray-painted, and we decided to hire security for both sites until the demonstration is over, but we need board approval to issue a check, and so we need to discuss that, too." Rachel looked around the table at her fellow board members.

Everyone was nodding, so she carried on. "Sources at *The Press* tell me that somewhere in the neighborhood of four hundred demonstrators will be here Saturday morning. The center is usually open from eight to noon on Saturday. I recommended to Dr. Friedberg that we close the center for one day, but she informs me that there is one young woman who has a nine o'clock appointment, who can only come on Saturday. Dr. Friedberg, please tell us about this patient." Every head that had been listening intently to Rachel now turned toward Dr. Friedberg. They all noted that she did not look like her normal self. She was usually calm and neat, but tonight she kept rolling her pen between her hands, and her hair had been pulled back hastily in a disheveled bun. She hadn't slept the night before, after the attack, and today she had been stressed, as she continued to see patients and deal with the vandalism and the police.

"Yes. Thank you, Rachel. We got a call this afternoon from a young girl who is pregnant and who can only come on Saturday. I want to be here for her. I haven't seen her, so I don't know how far along she is," said Dr. Friedberg. "I'm thinking of asking her to come before the clinic officially opens or in the afternoon. To miss the crowd. The bottom line is, I don't want to turn her away. I did speak to her, and she feels alone. She has no one to help her. In cases like these, if we turn her away, there could be risks."

"What kind of risks?" asked Rachel.

"Well, the worst risk would be that she could harm herself," said Dr. Friedberg.

"I don't know if we should keep the center open for one girl," said Felix Johns, who was 82 years old and had taken part in many pro-choice demonstrations in Washington. "We won't be able to control the crowd, and she could be in danger."

"I can't believe that anyone would attack a young girl," said Dr. Rubin, who had joined the board of the Litchfield Women's Center just to have the position on his resume when he ran for a New Jersey State Senate seat in the upcoming election.

"Norman, they threw bricks through Amy's window yesterday. In broad daylight!" said Suzy. "Anyway, I do think this girl needs to have access to services. Can we help her at another location?"

"We can try," said Dr. Friedberg. "But she sounded scared, and if she balks at going somewhere else, I want to open for her," Dr. Friedberg said decisively. She looked around the table at her board. "That's what we're here for. We need to be here for this girl."

"Okay, so what I'm hearing is that we will try to find services elsewhere. If we cannot, or the girl won't go, we will try to work with her to come early or arrive late," said Rachel. "If all else fails, we will proceed. Are we all in agreement? Say aye."

A chorus of "Ayes" sounded around the table.

"Okay, so, moving on. Suzy and I signed a contract today with Young Semple for them to provide security at Amy's house and here, at the center, from this morning through to next Sunday morning. If we feel that protection is still warranted after Sunday, we will reassess. Are there any questions?" asked Rachel.

"How much?" asked Felix Johns.

"We will have two officers at Amy's house and the two you saw on your way in here at the center, for $65 per hour around the clock. On Saturday we will increase to ten guards at the center, with a chauffeured car to bring Amy here—if we open—and home. The total cost will be somewhere around $30K. I know it's a lot of money, but we don't want anyone to get hurt," said Rachel.

"What about my staff? Can we offer them transportation on Saturday? They might not even want to come. These are young women with children at home." Dr. Friedberg put her head in her hands. "I can't believe this is happening."

Suzy, who was sitting beside her, reached out and squeezed her shoulder. "I can't believe it either."

"I don't think we should shut down. Screw them. Who are they to shut us down?" Nina Adler had been sitting quietly at the far end of the table. "I think we open for business as usual. What kind of a message will we be sending if we shut our doors when we're threatened? I think we hire guards to bring this girl, and any other girl, woman, or family who needs our help that day, safely into the clinic. We have money in the bank. I, for one, will not fold when threatened by this Stand Up for Life group," Nina's black eyes were on fire by the time she was through. Her hands were curled into fists, which she used now to pound on the table.

Felix Johns, who had been nodding off slightly until Nina started to speak, slammed his hand down on the table. "Who the hell does Patricia Castellano think she is? And where is her brother, the mayor? I'll never vote for him again."

"Did you see her on the news tonight? Issuing her statement? Denouncing the physical violence of the attacks?" asked Dr. Norman Rubin.

"Yes, I did. Patricia loves to see herself on television," said Suzy. "And, you all should know that I have stepped down as Antonio's reelection campaign chair." Suzy looked around the table, sizing up the people here with her. Her steely blue eyes were hard and unforgiving, her small mouth was a short, straight line drawn in pink, her honey-blond hair was crisp. "We're looking for a new mayoral candidate." She drew out the word *can-di-date* into three syllables, her eyes resting on Dr. Norman Rubin.

Norman's eyes met her gaze with new enthusiasm. He knew that she knew his aspirations. He had been thinking of running for the State Senate, but when opportunity knocks…

Rachel Horowitz sensed that she had lost control of her meeting. Nina was on a crusade. Suzy and Norman were mentally planning his election. Felix Johns was fighting fatigue. Dr. Friedberg was worrying about her patient. Only Darla seemed content with her role of simply taking notes.

"Okay, okay, everybody. Let's go back to the cost of the security firm. Amy, we'll add transportation for your staff on Saturday, if we open. Can I get a motion? Felix, as treasurer, make the motion," instructed Rachel.

Felix Johns sat up straighter and cleared his throat. "Yes, I hereby make a motion to hire the firm of Young, uh, Rachel, what is the name of the firm?"

"Young Semple," said Rachel.

"Yes, yes, Young Semple to provide security for the clinic and Dr. Friedberg's home at an approximate cost of $30,000. May I have a second?"

"Second," said Suzy.

"All in favor say aye," said Rachel.

"Aye," said the board.

FIFTY-FIVE

❦

*D*ooley's Funeral Parlor was just a few blocks from St. Raymond's, so Father O'Malley had walked over before the services and was now walking back. The night was cool and he was glad that he had been able to get away from the mourners when he did. As a priest, he sometimes found it difficult to feel extreme sorrow for the dead, when he was expected to feel sorrow so often. He was glad that the funeral had been for an elderly person who had lived a happy and productive life. The funeral services for the very young were the hardest, and those for the unfortunate were equally hard, but when the deceased had lived a long and fruitful life, it was just easier for all concerned.

As he approached the church and started to walk up the stairs that cut through the hill, his cell phone rang. He looked down. A weight descended on his shoulders. He answered.

"Yes?"

Pause.

"You're where?"

Pause.

"Come in the back." He proceeded up the hill to the church.

FIFTY-SIX

*L*atitia Blackman did not have all the legal constraints that the police did when it came to writing her story. *The Press* could always issue a correction or a retraction the next day. After her visit to the hospital, and her appearance in court to see the two halves of the Fernandez family, and the aftermath of their Saturday TV night together, she was convinced that Eduardo Fernandez had not only beaten his wife silly, but that he was also the killer being sought in the Casandra Keller murder case.

Still editing her piece in *The Press's* offices late on Monday night, long after everyone else had headed home, Latitia was bleary-eyed from sitting in front of her laptop for hours. She got up, stretched, and went to the kitchen to get herself a cup of tea. On her way back to her cubicle, she saw Loren Elliot slouched in her chair, looking depressed. She decided to stop and see what was wrong. "Hey Loren, are you all right? I assumed everyone else had gone home."

Loren looked up at Latitia and tried to focus. After taking Molly home, she had come back to the office in hopes of catching Greeley, who must have headed out to the Grant Tavern next door. Loren had no idea what to do with the information that Molly had given her. Being an Arts & Entertainment reporter, she had never used an anonymous source before. She was feeling very nauseous, and now Peter was stressing her out by telling her she should find a different clinic to go to. He was concerned with all the talk of the demonstration. She had mentally prepared herself to go to the Women's Center, and that was where she wanted to go. The demonstration would be on Saturday, and her appointment was for Friday. Her mind was swirling back and forth between her story and her situation, as Latitia pulled up a chair next to her. She decided to ask for the young reporter's help. "Yes, I'm fine. I'm just having trouble with my story. Can I ask you a question?"

"Sure, what's up?"

"Well, Greeley sent me over to Freeport to talk to Casandra Keller's mother, and she wasn't at home, but I met someone who told me some things about Casandra, but then said that I couldn't use their name. They said they wanted to be an 'anonymous source,' and, frankly, I've never quoted an anonymous source," said Loren.

"It's easy. Instead of giving the person's name, you just say, 'said an anonymous source,' or 'the source asked that their name be withheld.'" Latitia paused, then added, "What did they say? Why don't they want to be quoted by name?"

Loren hesitated. Somehow, it was scary to be talking about a man who might have murdered someone. She looked at Latitia, who was staring at her with penetrating brown eyes.

"They said that Casandra Keller was sleeping with this married guy. Eduardo Fernandez..."

"I knew it!" screamed Latitia, hitting the top of Loren's desk with her palm, a big smile forming on her gooey maroon lips.

"What?" asked Loren, taken aback by Latitia's outburst.

"Well, a guy named Eduardo Fernandez was arraigned this morning for beating up his wife so bad that he put her in the hospital, and he's also being held for questioning in the Keller case. I went to the arraignment, and I went to the hospital to get a look at his wife. She looks like she was beaten by a pack of guys, but according to a nurse, it was only her husband. The cops actually saw him do it." Here, she paused. "Listen, your source is giving us proof that he was sleeping with Casandra. Maybe we can do a double byline."

"Yes!" Loren was only too happy to follow Latitia's lead on this story. "Let's do that." Loren felt so relieved that she smiled for the first time in a week.

$\mathcal{F}$ I F T Y - $\mathcal{S}$ E V E N

᳇

$\mathcal{S}$ kinny jeans. They were the rage that summer. Skinny jeans and little ruffled skirts that barely covered the butt. Everything was tight and small. It was getting harder and harder for Clara to get dressed each day. After getting lunch at the mall, Clara and Linda had gone to H&M, Abercrombie & Fitch, and Diesel, looking for something that Clara could wear to hide her swollen boobs. They had found a peasant blouse that was kind of formless, and Clara had bought one in turquoise and one in lilac. It was already Tuesday. Three more days, she told herself.

As she cut the tags off the lilac shirt, she worried about confiding in Linda. She didn't have to worry about Linda telling her mother, Mrs. Martinson. Linda and Clara's mother were not that close. No, but she might tell the other girls. Lois or Peggy or Joyce. She slipped the shirt over her head and started rummaging through her dresser for a large pair of shorts. Usually she wore a size 2. Maybe something of Agnes's? Maybe not. Her mom would wonder why she was borrowing Agnes's clothes—she never had before. She found a pair of old gym shorts and cut them down so they would be short, short but she could loosen the drawstring to accommodate her slightly bloated belly. She couldn't believe how nauseous she was all the time, and anything tight made her feel worse.

When she thought she looked all right, she realized that she was hungry again. She just had a big breakfast an hour ago, but now she needed a snack. She threw the clothes back in her drawers and opened her bedroom door. Agnes was pacing in the hall between Clara's room and the hall bathroom. The hall was wide, with a brightly colored runner down the center, and Agnes liked to walk back and forth while her mother showered.

"Mom's showering?" Clara asked rhetorically. "She'll be out in a minute," she said, to reassure Agnes.

"I know she will. I know she will," Agnes said nervously.

"Do you want to come to the kitchen with me and get a snack?"

"No. It's not snack time."

"Well, I'm hungry," said Clara, and turned toward the stairs.

"It's *not* snack time," Agnes said emphatically.

Oh, no. Here we go. Agnes was still getting used to Clara being home all day in the summer. When Clara went to school, there was a definite schedule that the household followed, but now that it was summer, Clara came and went whenever she wanted, ate when she wanted, slept when she wanted, and Agnes was struggling with the lack of routine in the house.

"She'll be out in a minute, Agnes," Clara said, starting to move past her sister to get to the stairs. As she did, Agnes started to flap her hands and groan. "Do you want me to stay here with you?" No answer. Suddenly, Clara felt very nauseous. She knew that she was going to throw up. She covered her mouth with her hand and started to run down the hall toward the stairs.

Agnes started to shriek, throwing herself down on all fours and banging her head on the ground. Clara knew that she couldn't just leave Agnes pounding her head on the floor, so she stopped running and went back to Agnes. As she reached down to grab Agnes's shoulders to prevent her from hurting herself, Agnes arched her back, and her head hit Clara in the stomach causing Clara to throw up all over Agnes's back. Agnes felt the hot vomit seep through her thin T-shirt and started to howl. Clara retched again, this time missing Agnes and staining the carpet and spraying the wall.

Mrs. Mahoney, wearing only a towel, opened the door to the bathroom to see her two girls writhing and dripping with vomit.

"Oh my God! What is going on here?" she screamed at Clara.

"I'm sick and Agnes is acting out!" croaked Clara. "Take her so I can take care of myself," Clara said, choking on stray pieces of the eggs and sausage that had been her breakfast. Mrs. Mahoney grabbed her bathrobe and quickly put it on. She tried to calm Agnes and moved her into the bathroom to clean her up.

Clara went into her bathroom, closed the door, and locked it. Turning on the faucet, she went to the sink, threw cold water on her face, and rinsed out her mouth. She looked down at her new shirt that was now covered with puke, and started to cry. Her mother would be mad and somehow blame this on her. She started to run the water in the tub to drown out Agnes's howling. If Agnes were only normal, Clara thought, I would be able to go to my mother for help. Clara sat on the edge of the tub and gave in to the fear she had been feeling for weeks now. Her thin, young shoulders hunched over, and she covered her face with her hands. She let the tears come. It felt good to cry.

$\mathcal{F}$ I F T Y - $\mathcal{E}$ I G H T

❦

After the doctor had rebroken her nose and inserted tubes so she could breathe, Pia had gone home to Stella's house. She had walked in the front door, gone straight to the sunny back room with the big windows, and curled up on the couch. She wanted to be helpful. She wanted to go in the kitchen and peel carrots and bake and wash dishes, but she just couldn't get up. Her body ached, and she was exhausted. Exhausted in a way that she had never felt before. It was Tuesday, and she knew she had to get herself together before her appointment at the Women's Center on Friday.

The girls were very happy to have their mother out of the hospital, and they played nurse all afternoon. "I want you to rest now," said Carmen, pretending to take Pia's pulse.

"I'm making a chart for your medications," said Maria. They fought over who would refill their mom's water glass. Who would get her ice cream. Who would brush her hair.

Stella prepared the large guest room for Pia. It had a king-size bed, and she suspected that the girls might want to sleep in it with their mother. Stella was glad that her four older boys were at camp. It made the house so much quieter. By the time they got back, she and Pia would have a plan. While she was getting out the extra pillows, Pia came into the room. Every time Stella looked at her, a shock ran through her body. The bruises on Pia's face were hideous. Blue and black, with touches of red and green. Stella had never seen anything like it.

Pia quietly closed the door. "Stella, how am I going to get out of the house on Friday? What will I tell the girls?" she asked, sinking into a cozy chair in the corner of the large bedroom.

"Pia, let's not worry about it today. Friday is a lifetime away. You need to rest and feel better. Don't think about it now. Maybe you'll change your mind...about doing it," ventured Stella.

The expression in Pia's one open eye grew hard. "I will not. I will not have his child. Stella...I think...he murdered that girl on the news. I knew he had a woman...I was glad. That detective who came to the hospital thinks he killed her. I can tell."

"Did he say that?" Stella stopped fluffing the pillows and waited for her sister's answer.

"No, he just asked me if Eduardo knew her. But Stella, when Eduardo got so angry...before he went crazy...we were watching the news and it was the story of that girl. The detective said he would be in jail until September. Thank God." Pia closed her eye and sat, without moving, in the chair. Stella went to her, pulled up a footrest and sat on it. She took Pia's hand.

"Pia, we're going to get through this. Do you hear me? Everything is going to be okay. I'll be with you. George said you could stay here as long you needed."

Pia did not move. Stella watched a large, lone tear develop in the corner of her sister's eye and slowly make its way down the swollen hills and valleys of her face.

$\mathcal{F}$ I F T Y - $\mathcal{N}$ I N E

❧

$\mathcal{T}$uesday morning was the mayor's weekly press conference. It was an open format, held in the Red Room at Town Hall, where first the mayor made announcements about his accomplishments, and then reporters asked questions about his mistakes. Even though Bill Johnson had been assigned to Town Hall, Helen wanted to hammer the mayor about the demonstration. She had also gotten an anonymous tip that Suzy Walker had pulled out on Antonio as his reelection campaign chair. That would be a huge hit to his fundraising efforts.

Helen was in a good mood as she showed her press identification to the cop guarding the door. A few years back, people had come and gone from Town Hall as they pleased, but now, after 9/11, there was a cop stationed full-time at the door. Helen thought this measure of security was a waste of taxpayer money. There was just no way Al-Qaeda was going to order an attack on the Litchfield, New Jersey Town Hall. She pushed this minor annoyance to the back of her mind and focused on her story that had run today.

The Press had run a piece yesterday on Father O'Malley's sermon, along with a Q&A of parishioners and an entire page of photos, and now, today, 900 words on the priest, with two photos. Helen had to hand it to Kit, she could even make a priest look lascivious. There he was in his black clerical garments with the white collar tab, positively leering at the photographer. The other photo was of him preaching from the ornate pulpit at St. Raymond's, which was decorated with winged figures of a man, a lion, a bull, and an eagle, representing the Gospel writers Matthew, Mark, Luke, and John. The pull quote for the story read, "Since the first century the church has affirmed the moral evil of every procured abortion. This teaching has not changed and remains unchangeable." – *Father Thomas O'Malley.*

Helen lumbered into Town Hall, her large feet with huge big toes sticking over the tops of her sandals never actually leaving the floor, and trudged down to Room 6, where the reporters hung out. Should she share the news of Suzy pulling out of the mayor's campaign with her fellow reporters? They would know soon enough when she asked the question. She decided to keep it to herself as she shuffled down the hall, dragging her feet over the royal-blue carpet with the official Litchfield City crest. Hard wooden benches that looked like church pews lined the walls, reminding every citizen not to get too comfortable in Town Hall. Large portraits of past mayors hung in gold frames on every wall.

Room 6 did not have the same feel as the other official rooms of Town Hall. The carpet was a brown-and-gray herringbone weave circa 1970, and the desks that were stuffed into the small room looked like they had been obtained from the Salvation Army. The blinds on the windows were dirty and had ceased working in the 1980s. None of the chairs matched. A thick layer of dust lay over the piles of old newspapers that covered every surface. *The Press*, Channel 6, *watch.com*, and the local radio station all had assigned desks.

DeShawn Fletcher and his cameraman were the only other reporters in the room when Helen entered. When he saw her, DeShawn's face broke into a grin. "So, you heard?" he started.

Damn, thought Helen, he knew. "Heard what?" she said in a flat tone.

"Oh. Oh! You wanta play it that way?" cajoled DeShawn.

"I have work to do, DeShawn," Helen said, sitting down at her desk and getting her laptop out of its bag.

DeShawn started to dance around behind Helen's back. Wriggling and shaking himself at her back. Stan, the cameraman, started to crack up. Helen turned quickly and caught DeShawn thrusting himself in her direction.

"You disgust me," she hissed. She looked at her watch and decided to go to the Red Room and get a front-row seat. She grabbed her laptop and the bag and brusquely stomped out of the room. She nearly pushed down Jamie Ross as she did. Jamie and Helen were perfect opposites. Helen looked like an unmade bed, with her uncombed hair and her oversize tan T-shirt and brown skirt, in contrast to Jamie's perfectly slicked-back hair and his stylish clothes. Even his laptop bag looked brand new, as if human hands had never touched it.

"Well, excuse me," Jamie declared, as Helen blew past him. "What's got her panties in a bunch?" he asked DeShawn.

"Who knows?" said DeShawn rolling his big brown eyes. "I don't even want to think about her panties! I guess she's frustrated because I get to air my story tonight, and you'll post yours today, and she has to wait until tomorrow. Probably not the only thing she's frustrated about. You know what I mean?"

"I guess," said Jamie, who was already reading his email.

Paul Minetta, the mayor's press secretary, stuck his head in the room. "Mayor'll be ready in five," he proclaimed, holding his hand up with five fingers extended. DeShawn, Stan, and Jamie grabbed their gear and headed out to the Red Room.

The Red Room was one of three ceremonial rooms in Town Hall. It was a medium-size room with folding chairs set up theater style and a podium at the front with the Litchfield crest emblazoned on it. The Litchfield flag hung on a pole to the right, and the American flag to the left. Behind each flag was a large window with lush, red velvet drapes tied back by black-velvet sashes. The walls were painted a deep red and the carpet matched. Hence, the Red Room. Next door was the Green Room, and upstairs was a larger room for receptions called the Gold Room. General Washington gave a speech there in 1774, and so it was alternately called the Washington Room.

There were two doors in the Red Room, one for the public and the press in the back, and the other for the mayor in the front. He could enter the room and was able to walk directly to the podium. A wide aisle was kept down the middle of the room so that the cameras in the back could get a clear shot of the mayor as he spoke. Mayor Antonio Ceravolo, like his sister, used the camera to his advantage. A tall, muscular man of 43, he had thick black hair with just a touch of gray at the temples, an infectious grin, fleshy features, and a youthful twinkle in his eyes. He knew he had to get out in front of the demonstration and the girl's murder before the press asked him about them. He had brought Chief Chodor with him to give a report.

Seated in the chairs at the press conference were a mélange of people—press, police, good government types, or "goo-goo's" as they were called by the staff, concerned citizens, and mayoral staffers. They were all dressed casually, except the mayor, who wore an expensive gray suit, a lavender tie with little flowers, and a matching pocket handkerchief. He strode into the room followed by the chief.

"Good morning everyone," he started, and then, seeing Carl Walden, the head of Citizens for Patrol Reform, pointed at him and said, "Congratulations, Carl, on the birth of your new daughter." A murmur of congratulations was heard throughout the room. Always the politician. Always working the crowd. The mayor had a gift for remembering faces, names, and relationships. Policy bored him to tears but give him a room of nobodies and they suddenly felt like superstars.

"We will start by having Chief Chodor give us an update on the Casandra Keller murder investigation," the mayor began. "I want to say, once again publicly, to the Keller family, how sorry we are for their loss and to reiterate that we are moving forward as expeditiously as we can in apprehending the killer. Chief?"

Chief Chodor stepped to the podium and took out his notes. "Good morning, we have an announcement to make. We are currently holding a suspect, one Eduardo Fernandez, who we hope to indict as soon as we have forensic evidence. He was known to be having an extramarital affair with the deceased. If anyone has evidence or knowledge of Fernandez's activities on the night in question, please contact me at police headquarters. Any questions?"

Five hands shot up from members of the press.

"Jamie?"

"How was Fernandez arrested?"

"We brought him in on a domestic-violence call. Saturday night."

"Bill?"

"How are you holding him without forensic evidence?" "We're holding him on the domestic-violence charge. Two officers saw him strangling his wife."

At that point, Paul Minetta stepped in front of the chief, "We'll be moving on now. All reporters who have more questions about this matter, please see me after. Mayor?"

"Thank you, Paul. The next topic is the upcoming demonstration at the Litchfield Women's Center on Saturday. We will be closing Route 54 between Saratoga Boulevard and Southbend from six a.m. to one p.m. We will be policing the area, but we are expecting a peaceful demonstration with no violence." Here the mayor paused and looked directly into the cameras at the back of the room. "I want to ask for the cooperation of the demonstrators. We are standing by your right of free speech, but I will not hesitate to arrest anyone disturbing the peace that day. We will shut down the demonstration if there is one act of violence between now and then or during the event. Do not come early. Do not stay late. I thank you for your cooperation."

Helen's hand shot up.

"Yes, Helen," the mayor said with annoyance.

"Is it true that Suzy Walker has stepped down as your reelection campaign chair, and is it because of the demonstration?" A buzz went up from the floor.

Paul Minetta quickly stepped between the podium and the mayor and started to call the press conference to a close. But Mayor Ceravolo knew that he had to take the high road and meet this one head on. He gently but sternly pushed his press secretary out of the way, "Helen, my great friend Suzy Walker has been the most generous and dedicated supporter of this town, and I will continue to count on her for advice and guidance. She is truly an inspiration. Thank you for asking." With his non-answer answer complete, he smiled for the cameras, gave a wave, and was gone. He exited out the door leading to his office. Police Chief Chodor shut the door behind him and stood, as if on guard, in front of it. The press briefing was over.

S I X T Y

❧

$\mathcal{T}$he sermon had been great for fundraising. Elsa Martinson, chairwoman of St. Raymond's capital campaign, had 400 copies run off and sent to the families and members of the church, with a cover letter from her. Her mailing had been ready to go on Monday morning. From the collection plate alone, the church had raised over $8,000 and the Castellanos had come through with a $250,000 matching grant. Mrs. Martinson would be happy to tell Father O'Malley that the capital campaign had already raised $48,000. They were on their way to achieving their $1 million goal.

In her letter, Mrs. Martinson had purposely positioned the sermon as a talk about the wonders of life. She had never used the word abortion, as she knew that half of the women in the congregation were pro-choice and that 90 percent of the men were. No, she had highlighted Father O'Malley's words about the Golden Rule, but not his conclusions about the fetus. She had highlighted his words about Jesus being the giver of life, but not his words about radical utilitarian individualism. Words that didn't sound holy. Words that you had to think about to understand. No, she highlighted love and Jesus and birth. Basically, if parishioner's had not been at the sermon, and had only read the highlighted portions of the mailing, they would have absolutely no idea what the sermon was really about.

That wasn't important, thought Mrs. Martinson to herself, as she sat in the rectory office that Father O'Malley had given her to run the capital campaign. She had a desk and a file cabinet to keep all of the campaign records. On her desk sat an old office telephone, one of those big, black heavy phones that had been popular in the 1950s. Mrs. Martinson liked the feel of the phone in her hand, instead of her light Android with its tiny buttons. Her office was next to Father O'Malley's office, and she had noted that he was not there as she came in. She knew he had been helping the Antonellis, who had lost their mother to lung cancer. Mrs. Antonelli was only 59, and the diagnosis had come as a shock. Mrs. Martinson thought that the funeral was today, Wednesday.

She had come to the office to look at the mail and count any checks the church had received. She would log the amounts and the donors into her ledger and then she would take the checks to the bank. She was also working on a fundraising brochure for the campaign, which Father O'Malley had not wanted to spend money on, but that Mrs. Martinson felt was necessary. It just seemed more official to have something to leave behind when you were making a call, or if someone requested more information, there was something to send them.

As Mrs. Martinson sat, up to her elbows in papers and letters and checks, Kit Stilton stuck her impish little pixie face into the office. Mrs. Martinson looked up and stared at the beautiful young woman, who had two cameras slung around her neck. She was wearing three T-shirts layered over each other, with the largest one on the bottom of the stack. First there was the tangerine v-neck, then a white tank, and on top of that, a red batik-print smock. On the bottom, she was wearing black leggings that fell to her rounded calves, and a short, ruffled miniskirt that was plaid and black. Even though Mrs. Martinson was used to the fashion efforts of her own two teenage daughters, she was impressed with the time and money it must have taken this young woman to put that outfit together.

"Good morning!" sang Kit, looking at Mrs. Martinson with her twinkly eyes.

"Good morning!" said Mrs. Martinson. "May I help you?"

"I was just looking for Father O'Malley. Have you seen him?" she twinkled.

"I think he's at the Antonelli funeral. Is there anything I can do for you? Do you want to leave a message?" asked Mrs. Martinson.

The young woman smiled but didn't say anything. She clearly just wanted to see Father O'Malley. Mrs. Martinson felt like reminding this young girl that it was a priest they were talking about, and not an eligible bachelor.

"I took his photo for the paper. Did you see it?"

"I did. Are you the photographer for *The Press*?"

"Yes, I'm Kit Stilton."

"You did a good job," lied Mrs. Martinson. She had actually thought that the photograph made Father O'Malley look too handsome, too friendly, not pious enough. "Er…I really need to tend to this business. Why don't you come back later?"

"Yes. I will. Thank you." Kit walked away down the hall.

Mrs. Martinson went back to her books and her letters. There were checks for over $5,000 and pledges for an additional $10,000. She smiled. Her lips felt dry and she reached into her purse and pulled out her lipstick and her compact and applied a fresh coat of color. When she started to collect her things, she heard laughter coming from Father O'Malley's office. Pulling her bag up on her shoulder, she picked up the envelope of checks for the bank and headed out of the office.

As she passed Father O'Malley's office, she looked in and saw Kit Stilton sitting on the priest's desk, with Father O'Malley standing in front of her. They were both laughing. Kit had one foot up on his chair. Elsa pushed the door open and stood in the doorway. Father O'Malley looked surprised to see her.

"Mrs. Martinson! How are you? How's the campaign going?" he asked naturally.

Mrs. Martinson took a step into the room and he walked toward her. Kit still sat on the desk. Turning to watch Father O'Malley and the older woman, she used her thin, graceful arm to hold herself up. Mrs. Martinson was tongue-tied. Clearly, there was something wrong going on here, but what could she say? *Stop talking to that young girl! It looks like you're flirting. Be careful.* As she stood looking from one to the other, she noticed that a familiar jacket was thrown over one of the chairs in front of Father O'Malley's desk.

Now, instead of staring at Father O'Malley and his guest, she pondered the jacket. Why was it so familiar? Father O'Malley's eyes followed Mrs. Martinson's eyes to the jacket. Kit saw him tense up.

"My jacket! Father O'Malley! There it is!" Kit exclaimed.

Father O'Malley looked at Kit. "Yes, Kit, there it is!"

"That's what I came to get," said Kit, grabbing the jacket and heading toward the door. "Thanks again."

Kit was gone, and with her, the jacket. Still puzzled, still feeling that there was something she was missing, Mrs. Martinson turned and left the rectory.

S I X T Y - O N E

&

$\mathcal{M}$ ichael woke up and looked over to see Molly curled up beside him. She had been slowly worming her way into his apartment since the day they found Casandra. He had to tell her today that she had to go home. The only problem was that tonight was Casandra's wake, and Molly would be upset. He went into the bathroom, and there was all her stuff. Pink toothbrush, Dove deodorant, hairbrushes, gels, mousse, makeup. Jesus Christ, all this crap! He couldn't even find his own toothbrush. He took a quick shower, got dressed, and checked his phone for messages. Then, he couldn't help himself, he clicked to the photo he had taken of Clara.

Her slim form walking away from the camera conjured up all kinds of images in his mind. Her long legs, her delicate graceful arms, her long, thick curly hair pulled back in a ponytail. That stupid dog. He wanted to be with Clara, but she was unattainable. He knew that. She was like a flower that he had defiled. He knew she was dependent on him for a few more days and then she would never speak to him again. Still, he decided to go over to the park and see if she was playing tennis.

He was working on a construction site and he wasn't due there until 1 p.m.

Leaving Molly asleep, he drove over to the park and left his Mustang in the lot behind the tennis courts. He walked through the playground full of young mothers, nannies, babies, and toddlers swinging on the swings and climbing on the wooden jungle gyms. A row of boxwoods separated the playground from the tennis courts. He walked to the end of the hedge and surveyed the courts. Middle-aged moms trying to stay in shape dominated every court. It was probably some kind of league having a tournament. He headed back through the playground. Two black nannies sitting on a bench gave him a suspicious look. He realized he did look a little out of place with his black jeans and combat boots.

He climbed back into the Mustang, drove out of the parking lot, and started the slow drive out of the park. Then he spotted the dog. He was on a very long leash, and sitting on a bench, all by herself, was Clara. She looked deep in thought. Her pretty face was pensive. She wore large sunglasses with white frames. Her full lips pulled slightly downward at the corners. He slowed down, took out his phone, and took another photo of her. She was wearing a turquoise peasant blouse and white leggings. The road in the park was a gigantic circle around the entire park. The speed limit was 5 mph. Since he had already driven past the parking lot, he had to drive around the entire perimeter of the park again. He drove as fast as he could around the park, swearing at cyclists and Rollerbladers who got in his way. He pulled back into the parking lot by the playground, parked, and jogged over to the bench. She was gone. Scanning the walking path, he spotted her and the dog, and trotted up to her.

"Hey," he said. He startled her. "I'm sorry. Did I scare ya?"

Clara looked straight ahead like a cornered animal. "Hi," she said woodenly, then closed her eyes briefly to gather her patience. *Be nice. Don't say anything to offend him. Stay centered.*

Spiro Agnew was much friendlier. He started to dance around Michael's feet. Michael had to dance around too, in order not to trip over the leash. "Stop it, Spiro," she reprimanded.

"Listen, I was wondering…do you want to get some lunch?"

He watched her body tense up. "Um, I, have the dog."

"Well, you could take him home."

They walked on in silence. "I'm not really eating well these days."

"Are you sick?"

"All the time." It was an accusation. "Listen, I can't really… I can't really walk with you." *Why does he keep coming to see me? I don't want him to get the idea that we might be friends—or more.* He stopped walking. She stopped a few feet ahead and turned back. "Someone might tell my mom. I'm sorry. I'll see you Friday. Okay?" Spiro pulled on her arm and she started to walk off. As she looked back at him, she saw his mouth clench in disappointment. Or was it anger?

$\mathcal{S}$ IXTY-$\mathcal{T}$ WO

❧

$\mathcal{M}$ aria and Carmen had not left Stella's house since they went there on Saturday night, except to go to visit Pia. It was now Wednesday, and with Pia home from the hospital, they hadn't asked to see their friends. They didn't answer their cell phones or text messages. Maria refused to go back to theatre camp which she had started the week after school ended. Pia was afraid for them to be out of her sight and she didn't want to impose on Stella even more and ask her to host playdates. She knew Stella would, but she didn't have the emotional energy to ask her. Maria and Carmen had similar interests, so they amused each other, but Pia knew they shouldn't stay stuck in the house. She also wanted them to be busy on Friday when she had to go to the Women's Center. She didn't want them asking a lot of questions about where she was going.

She wandered down to the kitchen, where Stella and the kids were setting up for breakfast. The smell of freshly baked blueberry muffins wafted down the hall to meet her. Pia stopped in the doorway and took in the Norman Rockwell scene: little Juan, standing on a chair, stirring the frozen orange juice in a pitcher, Carmen setting the table, and Maria reading the newspaper, while Stella fried ham. It almost made Pia cry to think how lucky she was that Stella had taken her in. Carmen ran over to her mother when she entered the room and hugged her.

"Good morning, sleepyhead," said Stella, smiling.

"Good morning. It smells fantastic in here." The swelling of Pia's eyes was better, but she still couldn't fully open the right one, and now both were black and blue from the procedure.

"Auntie, look, we made juice," said Juan, beckoning Pia to come to the island in the middle of the kitchen to see.

"You're doing a great job. I can't wait to have some," Pia said, as she took extra time to study Juan's juice. When she had given it as good a look as she could with her swollen eyes, she turned to Maria, who had not stopped reading the newspaper. "What are you reading, Maria?"

Maria looked up as if just realizing that her mother had come into the room. "What? Mommy! I didn't see you come in."

"Well, good morning," said Pia, walking over to the table. Maria folded the paper over and put it on the chair next to her. It was clear that she didn't want Pia to see what she had been reading.

"Sit down, Mommy. Can I get you some coffee?" Maria asked.

"No, I'm going to have orange juice," she said, sitting down next to Maria. She looked at her daughter. Maria's long, straight hair was parted in the middle and neatly combed back into a ponytail. She wore a dark-green tank top with a leather necklace. What was going on in that head? Maria had saved her life. Pia thought Maria was different somehow—no longer a little girl. She had seen too much violence. She knew too much.

"Mommy, we're going to swim in the pool today," said Carmen, seemingly oblivious, as most nine-year-olds would be, to the dramatic changes going on in her life. "Aunt Stella said we could. Can we, Mommy?"

"Of course, honey. Did Uncle George pack your bathing suits? We'll have to check after breakfast. Where's my orange juice?" Pia called over to Juan. Stella brought the pitcher over to the table and poured a small glass for everyone. Pia tasted it. "Um. This is the best orange juice I've ever had."

Juan smiled. "Carmen can wear one of my bathing suits," said Juan. Everyone besides Juan laughed.

"That's very nice of you to offer, honey," said Pia.

They ate the warm muffins and ham and drank juice. After, the girls went upstairs to see if their bathing suits had been packed. The phone rang and Stella went to answer it. Pia picked up the paper that Maria had been reading. "Domestic Violence Incidents Hard to Count." The article was an interview with Nina Adler, executive director of the Safe Haven Shelter, which helped women in all of Austin County. The shelter was a safe place where a woman and her children could go when they initially left an abusive situation. The location of the shelter was a secret. There was a hotline for women to call. Adler was quoted as saying, "Several studies have shown that in 60 to 75 percent of families in which the mother is battered, the children are also battered." Later in the article, Adler commented that "the prevalence of domestic violence is hard to gauge because, first and foremost, it often goes unreported."

Pia knew she needed to talk to her children about what had happened. She needed to talk to them about their father. She tried to think through what she was going to say to them. It was a very fine line she had to walk. The girls needed to know that they were safe from Eduardo, but he was also their father. She needed to tell them what the plan was going to be for their future. Where were they going to live? They couldn't stay with Stella forever. But, before she could put all the pieces together, she needed to get through Friday's appointment. She got up and finished clearing the table and washed the dishes as best she could.

$\mathcal{S}$ I X T Y - $\mathcal{T}$ H R E E

$\mathcal{P}$ eter Elliot had been waiting to hear from the head of human resources at the high school in Waterbury all day. He had gone on a promising interview the day before, and he had a good feeling about getting hired. Marshall and Emily had been troopers about living at home the next year and getting jobs to help out, but Peter knew even those measures were not going to get them through the year. He had been sending out resumes, calling contacts, surfing the web, but things were bad all over the state and no one was hiring. Miraculously, Waterbury wanted to continue its world languages program, and the school's Mandarin teacher had announced she was going out on maternity leave and would not return.

He had rushed over to Waterbury yesterday and met with the head of human resources and the principal of the high school. He felt good when he left and was expecting an offer today. He had gotten up, mowed the lawn, eaten a bowl of Special K, and sent out two resumes to prove to the hiring gods that he was still trying. He wasn't taking anything for granted.

The other thing that he wanted to do today was to see if he could find a clinic other than the Litchfield Women's Center for Loren to go to on Friday. He didn't like all the news about the demonstration and the priest at St. Raymond's denouncing abortion. He and Loren were not Catholic. They really weren't religious. They had been born Protestant, he Lutheran, she Methodist, but neither believed or ever went to church. No, he was afraid some fanatic would try to shoot the doctor and hit Loren instead or try to burn down the building and Loren would be unconscious inside. These people were making him feel like a criminal, and he resented it. He hoped he could find another facility that could take her before their insurance ran out.

As he was Googling abortion clinics in Austin County, the phone rang. Maybe he and Loren could even have a conversation about not needing to go to a clinic, was his last thought before he got up and went to answer the phone on the table by the couch.

"Yes, Ms. Cantor. How are you?" It was the human resources lady. Peter crossed his fingers and shut his eyes. As he listened, his shoulders went weak. He slid down onto the couch. His free hand went up to his head. Finally, he said, "Thank you."

Loren found him sitting on the couch when she got home. She had been riding high all day from her front-page double byline with Latitia Blackman on the Casandra Keller/Eduardo Fernandez piece. She had never had a story anywhere near page one before. It was exhilarating to walk by the newspaper machines downtown and glance over and see her name in the window of the box. She felt important. She felt like a star. Things were looking up. Her story and then Peter's interview. But when she opened the front door and saw him sitting on the couch with one hand on his head, she knew their short lucky streak was over.

Throwing her purse down on the chair in the tiny foyer, she went right over to Peter and sat down beside him. She took his hand and looked into his eyes. They teared up. "Peter, what happened?"

"They decided to cancel Mandarin. Loren, I'm never going to get another job," he cried.

"Yes, you will. Maybe not as a Mandarin teacher, but maybe as a translator or in the library…"

"Loren, just stop talking," Peter said with a desperate tone that Loren had rarely heard before. She ran her hand through her thick red hair. Her eyes welled up. She got up and walked over to the computer. She saw that Peter had been looking at other clinics. "I'm going to the clinic in Litchfield. Nothing's going to happen there on Friday."

Without opening his eyes, Peter asked, "How do you know that?"

"Because this is New Jersey. I'll be fine."

"Let's call the one in Silway."

"Peter, I'm not calling another clinic. It's already Wednesday," she raised her voice.

"Fine," he said, feeling totally defeated.

S IXTY-$\mathcal{F}$ OUR

ॐ

$\mathcal{D}$ *amn these socialites, picking their causes without regard for the trouble they make.* Dr. Friedberg cursed Patricia as she picked up the phone to call the girl with the Saturday appointment. The women she helped were victims, for the most part, in one way or another. Take this girl, for instance. She sounded like a teenager who obviously had no one to turn to for help. Now, she was turning to Dr. Friedberg, and Dr. Friedberg was determined to be there for her. She dialed the girl's cell number. It was Wednesday morning at 10 a.m.

A drowsy female voice answered. "Hey."

"Hello, this is Dr. Friedberg from the Women's Center. Can we talk for a few minutes?"

"Um. Okay," said the girl.

"Do you know that there is going to be a demonstration here at the center on Saturday morning?"

"Yes."

"Do you know how far along you are?"

"No."

"I met with the center's Board of Directors last night—they're my bosses—and they would prefer that you come a different day. They think it might be better for you not to have to deal with all the protesters. Can you come on Monday?"

"No, I have to come on Saturday. It's the only day I can come."

"Maybe we can book an appointment for you at another center."

"No, I live in Litchfield. I don't want to go anywhere else."

"Okay. The protesters are starting to arrive at 8:30. Can you come at 7:30 to avoid them?"

"No, I have to come at 9."

"Can you come after 11:30?"

"No, I have to come at 9. I have to come when my parents won't be home."

The more the doctor tried to direct the girl away from the center on Saturday, the more the girl dug in her heels.

"Is there another reason why you don't want me to come to the center?" the girl asked.

"No. I want you to come. I want to help you, it's just…"

"I have to go." The phone went dead.

Damn. Dr. Friedberg looked at her watch. She had an hour before her next appointment. She picked up the schedule for the week. Busy this afternoon. Busy Thursday. Very busy Friday. Fridays were always busy because the women then had three days to recover before they had to go back to work or school.

Pia Fernandez. Why was that name so familiar? Dr. Friedberg couldn't figure out why that name was ringing a bell. She thought back to that morning's papers. Yes, there had been a story about a domestic-violence case, and now the husband was a suspect in the killing of that girl. Casandra Keller. Where was that newspaper? She shuffled papers around on her desk. There it was. On the conference table. She got up and went over to it. Yes, *The Press* had a story about this man, Eduardo

Fernandez, who was being held because he had put his wife, Pia Fernandez, in the hospital. Could it be the same woman?

She picked up her phone and buzzed Darla. "Darla? Has Pia Fernandez called about her appointment on Friday?" Dr. Friedberg listened. "Well, if she does, let me know." No cancellation. Dr. Friedberg thought back to what Nina Adler had said that night at the Swan Club. "In the United States, a woman is more likely to be assaulted, injured, raped, or killed by her male partner than by any other type of assailant." Pia was an unusual name. She switched around a conference call, so that she would have more time to spend with Pia.

SIXTY-FIVE

⟜

Reverend Atlee Turnipseed pulled his 1972 Cadillac into the parking lot of his favorite check-cashing joint in Smithtown. He wanted to cash this check as soon as he could. On the way into the storefront he had to laugh. *Crazy-ass white woman!* Looking sweet as Grandma's rhubarb-and-strawberry pie in her pink sweater and little perky hairdo. Handing him a check for $5,000. Made out to him, not the church. She knew where that check was going. No doubt about that. And then they had worked out a fee for each demonstrator, plus lunch. Twenty dollars for each demonstrator, of which he would take $5 per head. Boy, it had been his lucky day when Miss Sandra Stett had pulled into the lot at the Baptist A.M.E. Church, where he was the pastor.

He had been sure she was lost and was stopping to ask directions at the church, but she had jumped out of her car with a big ole' smile on her disingenuous face and had used her gracious manners to walk him into his office and cut a deal without ever batting an eyelash. She was all business once they got right down to it. She had it all worked out. Now, Reverend

Turnipseed was old enough to believe in abortion. Back in the '60s, down in Georgia, he had seen too many girls taken in by men who called themselves doctors, but who had never seen the inside of a classroom after they were kicked out of high school. Young girls, married women, unmarried women, older women—the stories of backroom abortions were enough to make any person vote twice for *Roe v. Wade*.

The thing was, though, now that abortion was a constitutional right, and his parishioners went to the clinic when they needed to and nobody was ever the wiser, the church had to preach against it. It was a conundrum. In a way, it was safe now to take the high road. He knew it didn't make any sense, but it made the old ladies happy—the old ladies who came to church and decided not to remember when they might have needed those services. Sometimes his whole church was filled with women over 50 and their grandchildren, and that's what they wanted to hear, so that's what he gave them.

After cashing his check, he headed back to the church to meet with two guys who Miss Stett was sending over to finish planning this event. He couldn't wait until Sunday, when life could go back to normal. He drove down Main Street and pulled into the parking lot at his church. Sam and Joshua, the two homeless drunks who lived in the parking lot, were asleep beside the dumpster. Reverend Turnipseed always allowed them to sleep it off in the basement, and it annoyed him to no end when they slept outside. They made the church look poor and undignified, thought the reverend. He pulled up in front of them and beeped the horn to wake them up.

"Go downstairs, damn you," he called, as he got out of his car.

"Wha?" stammered Sam.

"Why?" stammered Joshua.

"Damn fools. Just damn fools," muttered Reverend Turnipseed, as he turned around to go into the church. A car had just pulled into the lot. A cute little silver car. In the front seat were two of the gayest young men Reverend Turnipseed had ever seen. Reverend Turnipseed shook his mangy head. *These must be the two she done sent me. Shit. What am I supposed to do with them?* Maybe they weren't there for him. He could only pray. He walked up to the church doors and went in. Fifteen minutes later, his secretary buzzed and announced that Mr. Lee Laquess and Mr. Simon Wong from Stand Up for Life had arrived.

Reverend Turnipseed stood to greet his visitors. He was tall and lanky with long coarse hair and brown teeth. A polka-dotted line of black freckles marched across his flat, choco-late-color nose. Simon and Lee both cowered a little as they approached his desk. In his long, black robe he appeared even bigger and blacker. They sat in the two wooden chairs in front of the Reverend's desk as directed.

"Good morning, boys," said Reverend Turnipseed, drawing out the word "boys." "How can I help you?"

"Sandra sent us over with the plan for Saturday morning, and we wanted to go over it with you," volunteered Simon, who looked up at the reverend and crossed his slim legs at the knees.

"Yes." Reverend Turnipseed didn't want to make it too easy for these boys and took his time moving behind his desk and sitting down.

"The buses will arrive here at your church at 8 a.m. There will be six buses. The demonstrators should board quickly. We want them on site at 8:30 a.m., but not prior to 8:30. The dem-onstration is to be a peaceful demonstration. We're just looking for folks to walk with the signs we will provide for three hours. Lunch will be served back here in your parking lot at noon. In and out. That's the plan." Simon stopped talking and frowned.

"Will there be bathroom facilities for the demonstrators?" asked Reverend Turnipseed.

Simon looked at Lee. Lee looked at Simon.

"Porta-Potties. We need Porta-Potties. Yes, we'll have them," said Lee, making a note.

"How will the stipends be distributed?" asked the reverend.

Lee looked at Simon. "Each demonstrator will receive an envelope when they get off the bus back here."

"Why don't you let me handle that part of the proceedings...," suggested the reverend.

The silence hung in the air over the reverend's desk. It was a thick silence. The three men stared at each other. Simon and Lee had their orders from Sandra. It was a standoff.

"We'll get back to you on that." Simon made a note in his notebook. "Lunch will be sandwiches, chips, soda, and a special treat—chocolate," he laughed.

Reverend Turnipseed couldn't decide whether or not that had been a racist remark. He raised his shaggy eyebrows.

"Do you have a list of names for us?" asked Lee. "Names of the actual people who will be demonstrating?"

Reverend Turnipseed took his time answering. "We'll get back to you on that."

"So, to recap, we'll get back to you re the distribution, and you'll get back to us re the names," said Simon, looking up from his notebook. "We'll talk to Sandra and give you a holler," he pouted, looked at Lee, and got up to leave.

"Gentlemen," said Reverend Turnipseed without getting up.

Once outside, Simon and Lee walked across the parking lot toward the car. Although it was still early, the sun was hot. A burst of warm air hit them as they opened the car doors. "I wish we could just go to the beach, instead of back to that stuffy office," said Lee.

"I've been thinking," said Simon, as he got in the car and pressed the buttons to open all the windows and let the hot air out. "I think we should have breakfast with our favorite reporter, Helen Acker, and let her know where the demonstrators are coming from. What'a'ya think?" he asked with a grin.

"I love it! I'm so disgusted with this whole operation," Lee said conspiratorially.

Simon gave Helen a quick call, and she agreed to meet them for breakfast at the IHOP on the outskirts of town so that they could talk, and hopefully, not be overheard by anyone important. Upon entering the IHOP, Simon surveyed the tables. There she was, at a booth in the back—looking more unkempt than usual. The woman was an oily monochrome, thought Simon, as he walked toward her. If ever a woman needed a makeover, it was Helen Acker. Her hair, skin, and eye color were almost identical. He tried to imagine her with blue eye shadow, mascara, coral blush, and a light-pink lipstick. Maybe he would send her a basket of cosmetics.

"Helen!" Simon sang, bending down to try to give her European air kisses, one near each cheek. She backed away like a cat and eyed him severely. "No? Okay," he said, and slid into the booth. Lee put out his limp-wristed hand and Helen gave it one shake.

"Are we eating? I'm hungry," Helen declared flatly. "I haven't even had my coffee. I can't think without my coffee."

"I know what you mean," nodded Lee.

The waitress came over and they ordered. Helen had the special—two eggs, bacon, hash browns, rye toast, and coffee. Simon ordered half a grapefruit and water, and Lee had whole-wheat toast, dry, and coffee. The waitress immediately filled their cups.

After fixing her coffee with cream and lots of sugar, Helen took a loud sip and made an attempt to push her stringy hair out of her eyes. She looked at Simon. "Okay. You got me here. Better be good." She rummaged through her purse and took out her reporter's notebook and pen. She used her short, stout middle finger with the bitten nail to push her glasses up on her nose.

"We want to talk off the record," said Simon.

"Off the record," repeated Lee.

Helen looked from one small man to the other. "Okay," she finally said, knowing that she would circle back and try to get something on the record.

Simon moved in closer to the table. "Stand Up for Life is paying the demonstrators a stipend and busing them in from Smithtown." He sat back, giving a furtive glance around to see if anyone he knew was at a nearby table. Lee was nodding, with his eyes large and serious.

"All of them?" Helen was making notes.

"Let's say, most of them. Litchfield does have a few crazies," said Simon. The waitress brought the food, putting most of it down in front of Helen.

"Who are you working with in Smithtown?" Helen asked, digging into her eggs and bacon.

"Well, it's not really us," said Lee.

Helen was sopping up egg yolk with her toast. "Who, then?"

"Sandra," said Simon, who was working on perfectly extracting a triangle of grapefruit from his grapefruit half.

"Sandra?"

"Sandra Stett," volunteered Lee. "Our fundraiser. Stett with two t's." Helen wrote down the name.

"Who's she working with?" A trickle of yellow goo was running down from the corner of Helen's mouth. The food and the information were exciting all of her senses.

Simon and Lee looked at each other. Simon nodded his head. Lee shrugged his shoulders.

"Reverend Turnipseed at the Baptist church in Smithtown," said Simon.

"Does Patricia Castellano know about this?" Helen asked, mercifully wiping the goo from her face.

"We don't think so," said Simon and Lee in unison.

"She's hardly been in the office. Sandra has been running the show," said Simon. "We're just getting a paycheck. It's not our cause."

"Fascinating," said Helen, looking from Simon to Lee and back again. She now realized that they were gay lovers. "Just a job for you two? So, where's our crusader? Sandra Stett? In the office?"

"Probably," said Lee.

"And Mrs. Castellano?" asked Helen.

"She never gets in before eleven, sometimes noon," said Simon. "Anyway, we wanted someone to know the truth about the protesters. Of course, when you see them you will know, but we just wanted to give you a heads-up."

"Did you call DeShawn?" Helen asked, suddenly annoyed.

"Not yet," said Lee.

"What will it take for you to give this to me as an exclusive?" asked Helen.

Simon looked at Lee, Lee at Simon. They hadn't discussed that possibility. "Well, you definitely can't use either of our names. An anonymous source. That's what you'll have to say," said Simon.

"So, you won't give this to anyone else today?" asked Helen.

"Can you get it on the front page?" asked Simon.

"I have to do some investigating, but I think I can."

"Patricia wants her picture in the paper one more time. She told me so yesterday," interjected Lee.

"I think this might be the perfect article," said Simon with a grin. "Do you need art?"

S I X T Y-S I X

❦

$\mathscr{O}$he forensic team had no hard evidence to tie Eduardo Fernandez to Casandra Keller's murder. They could prove that Eduardo had been in the apartment at some time, but the fingerprints on the doorknob had been smeared by Michael, Molly, and the various police officers, and by Detective Bickford himself. The prints on Casandra's body couldn't be retrieved, because her body had started to turn to mush by the time she was found. She hadn't been wearing any clothes, except panties. There was no evidence of sexual contact. The attack must have been swift, because she hadn't fought back. There was no skin under her nails to show she tried to scratch her attacker. The actual cause of death was a deep gash to the back of the head that was caused by hitting the wrought-iron leg of the coffee table. The bleeding from the wound had at first knocked her out and then had slowly made her bleed to death.

The police had many people telling them that Eduardo was Casandra's lover. Officer Quinn had seen Eduardo in his truck, pulled over to the side of the road near the Green Street Apartments, on or around the day Casandra was killed, and had told him to move on. Michael Russo would testify that Eduardo had come to the apartments the day of the murder to allegedly see about a painting job. But there was no murder weapon. There were no eyewitnesses. Everyone in the police department knew that Eduardo was guilty, but what did they have to convict him? Only circumstantial evidence.

Detective Bickford had obtained a warrant to search the Fernandez's house because Eduardo could be placed near the apartment on the day of the murder. In addition, they were going to charge him with attempted murder and endangering the welfare of a minor in their case against him for beating Pia. Two police officers were eyewitnesses in that case and the police felt certain that the Grand Jury would send the case to trial. Eduardo would be held in jail until the Grand Jury would meet in September, and then it could easily be a year before the case went to trial. They had time.

Bickford, Quinn, and Rea rode over to the Fernandez's house with the search warrant. George Perez, Pia's brother-in-law, had agreed to meet them at the house so they didn't have to break the lock.

"I really want to get this bastard," said Bickford, who was uncomfortable in the back of the squad car. The backseat of a squad car was intentionally claustrophobic and uncomfortable. There was no legroom, because the police officers usually had the front seat pushed back as far as it could go. "He's a psycho if I ever met one."

George had the Fernandez's front door open and was going through the mail at the kitchen table when the police walked in. "Good morning officers, detective," he said. "I would like to request that the least amount of damage be done to the premises. Pia's in no shape to deal with a house full of broken furniture and everything spilled out on the floor. Okay, guys?"

"You got it. Thanks for letting us in." Bickford nodded. "How's she doin'?"

"She looks a little better." George shrugged his shoulders and shook his head.

"We'll go easy on the house," Bickford finally said.

"Thanks."

"I'll go upstairs," said Officer Quinn.

"I'll start with his desk," said Officer Rea, pointing to a desk in the living room.

"I'll poke around," said Detective Bickford, who followed George out to his car. "Hey, Mr. Perez, you know anything about Fernandez's extracurricular activities? If you know what I mean?"

George looked at the detective with a beleaguered look. "We don't see each other socially. We're family. He's always there on holidays, but I don't go drinking with him or anything like that. I know he hangs out at The Sportsman. I know he has other women, but I don't know who they are or where they live," said George. "I don't know anything about that girl they're trying to link him to in the newspapers."

"Thanks, George. If you learn anything, give me a call." Detective Bickford walked back into the house. George watched the burly detective walk away. He shook his head and hoped that they didn't find any evidence linking Eduardo to Casandra. How could he bring his family to church if his brother-in-law was a murderer?

They spent about two hours going through drawers, laundry bins, and closets. The only space they tore apart completely was Eduardo's closet. The master bedroom had two small closets. They literally took everything out of his and threw it on the floor. In the back of the closet was a small strongbox. It was locked. Officer Quinn took the box out to the garage, where he found a hammer and banged on the lock three times until it broke. As he opened the lid, the strongbox turned into a treasure chest. It was filled with nude photos of Casandra Keller, a videotape, and a key.

Finally, they were getting somewhere.

SIXTY-SEVEN

❧

This was the worst summer for crime on record in Litchfield. "How could this happen on my watch?" Mayor Ceravolo asked himself. He sat in his wood-paneled office at home, with the door closed, and poured himself a scotch. *One to settle the nerves.* Tonight was Casandra Keller's wake, and the mayor had to make an appearance. He took a big gulp, feeling the harsh liquor burn his throat. It felt good. His leather chair felt good. Ahh, if only he could stay home tonight. Stay in his chair. That was the downside of being an elected official. There was an event almost every night. He rang the intercom button to the kitchen. "Cecilia, wake me in half an hour," he instructed the maid.

Across town, Michael and Molly were also getting ready to go to the wake. They both wore all black. He was wearing a pair of black trousers he had worn to a wedding once, a black man-tailored shirt, and black boots, and she was wearing a black dress, black stockings, a short black bolero jacket, and black pumps. She had taken a few of the rings out of her face and ears out of respect for Mrs. Keller.

"I'm scared, Michael," said Molly. "I've never been to a wake before. Have you?"

Michael tucked in his shirt. He was still thinking about how Clara had blown him off today. "What?"

"I said I've never been to a wake before. I'm scared." She came up behind him and put her arms around his waist. "You look sexy all in black."

Michael ignored her. "There's nothing to be scared about. The casket's going to be closed. She was too far gone when we found her. It's just a box at the front of the room, and you talk to Mrs. Keller, and I guess her father will be there, and then you get down on your knees and say good-bye to Casandra."

"What'a ya mean? Get down on my knees?" Molly's small, almond-shape eyes got as round as they could.

"In front of the casket. You pray or say good-bye or just stay there for a minute. Just follow me. Don't worry." She touched his belt provocatively. He pushed her away. "Could we just get through this?" he asked with a tone of annoyance. He walked into the living room.

Molly thought she looked good enough to be going into New York City to a club. She didn't want to think about Casandra. She liked to think of her as alive and at The Sportsman right now, waiting for her. Although if Casandra were alive, Molly wouldn't be here right now with Michael. In that way, Casandra's death had been good for her. It had given her and Michael a second chance. Not that he was acting like he was in love with her or anything, but she was staying at his place, having sex with him, eating dinner with him, waking up with him, going to the wake with him. Yes, in that way Casandra's death had been good, but in all other ways it had been bad. She and Casandra had been best friends since elementary school. When Michael finally kicked her out, who was she going to turn to? Who was she going to hang out with?

"Let's go," Michael called from the next room.

They drove to Dooley's Funeral Home and pulled into the parking lot. It was only half full, but they were early. They got out and entered the building. It smelled like Glade. As they entered the room marked "Casandra Keller" they heard some-one call "Michael." It was Jay. Molly threw her arms around his neck. She was already crying.

"Hey, it's okay." Jay looked at Michael over Molly's shoulder. Michael rolled his eyes. As they stood in the vestibule, other guys from The Sportsman started to come in. They all looked uncomfortable in long-sleeve shirts with collars.

"Should we go in?" asked Michael. It was more of a statement than a question.

The small group filed into the room. Mrs. Keller sat in the front row on the right side of the casket. Her two sisters sat on either side of her. Her head was bent over and she was crying. Mr. Keller sat alone on the left side, looking bewildered. A few neighbors and other people who had known Casandra from work sat dispersed throughout the chairs. Michael, Molly, and the guys from The Sportsman made their way up to the front of the room. Michael bent down and kissed Mrs. Keller on the cheek and then stepped back, letting Molly hug and cry with her friend's mother. The other young men waited and felt un-comfortable. After awhile, Michael decided to go over to Mr. Keller, and all the young men went with him. They offered con-dolences. No one was crying on this side of the room, and the young men felt better. Mr. Keller was relieved to have someone to talk to.

Paul Minetta, the mayor's press secretary, arrived 10 min-utes later. Dressed in an appropriate blue suit and tie, he sur-veyed the scene. Friends, family, no press, piece of cake, in and out. As he turned to go back outside to call the mayor, he bumped right into Fiona Rivington, the reporter from *The Press*.

"Fiona. Did Greeley send you here to write a story about the grieving mother?" Minetta asked with disgust.

Fiona glared at the press secretary. "I knew Casandra in high school. I also know Michael and Molly, so if you'll excuse me, please. Is the mayor coming to win a few votes?" she sneered.

"Touche," smiled Minetta.

Fiona stuck her nose in the air as if she were far superior to anyone who might stoop to go to a funeral for anything other than genuine concern for the family of the deceased. As she headed in, Jamie Ross from *watch.com* arrived. He nodded to Minetta, entered Casandra's room and quietly sat in the back.

The mayor's black car arrived out front, escorted by a squad car. Detective Bickford and Officers Quinn and Rea fell in line behind him as he walked up the front steps of the funeral parlor. The mayor met Minetta at the top of the stairs to be briefed on the scene inside. Mother and two aunts to the right. Father to the left. Michael and Molly, the two who found the deceased, were dressed in black from head to toe in the front. The mayor would know them from the newspaper, and Minetta would be by his side to introduce. Fiona Rivington and Jamie Ross were there. Looked like a 15-minute stop, tops.

"Minetta, where's the photo op?" asked Mayor Ceravolo.

"The what?" asked Minetta.

"Are we setting up a photo of me and the grieving mother? The heroes who found her? If not, what the fuck am I doing here? This is an election year, Minetta. You didn't call the press and set this up? You know what? You're fired. I will make it happen myself," said the mayor, pushing Paul Minetta to the side of the stairs. Bickford, Rea, and Quinn filed into the funeral home behind the mayor. None of them even looked at Minetta.

Mayor Ceravolo entered the funeral home. Checking the small announcement board, he headed toward Casandra's room. He stopped in the doorway and spotted Jamie Ross. They looked at each other, and the mayor nodded his chin the slightest bit. Then he approached the mother. Jamie Ross made a large circle around the guests and ended up in the aisle to the side of the mayor as he hugged Mrs. Keller. The photo, on *watch.com* that night, showed the mayor with his eyes closed, comforting the grieving Mrs. Keller. Jamie gave the photo to the mayor who sent it out to the papers with a statement. Jamie Ross enjoyed unlimited access to the mayor that summer.

SIXTY-EIGHT

❧

The Mahoney house was like a minefield. Clara never knew what to expect when she woke up or when she got home, or what fight would break out while she was in the shower, taking out the garbage, watching television. Mealtime was the worst. Especially dinner. Agnes was tired and cranky by then and couldn't hold it together any longer.

Because of constantly being on high alert, Clara had an overdeveloped sense of how others were feeling. From a look or a gesture, she could discern the inner workings of those around her. It was a curse. The burden of children who grow up with alcoholics, schizophrenics, drug addicts, autistic siblings, or just assholes. Any illness that carries with it huge mood swings.

This Wednesday morning, just like every morning, Clara woke up wondering, what will be the crisis of the day? Her family had made it, miraculously, through the night, but what awaited them? What should she worry about first? Before getting up, she would run through the events of the day, to calculate how bad her day would be.

Her talent for reading other people did not just pertain to her immediate family. Clara picked up on the emotions of everyone she interacted with. This morning, she was worried about Michael. She knew that he had been insulted by her comments the day before and that he was angry with her. Because of this, she had slept fitfully. Why should he help her? Why was he helping her? If she never wanted to see him again, why in the world *would* he help her? And now she had made him mad. Just when she needed him to come through for her on Friday. She thought about going to The Sportsman tonight and hanging out with him. She needed to reassure him. To be nice to him. She knew that Linda would go with her. But how could she hang out with Michael and not go back to his apartment? Now that Linda knew the truth, could she trust her not to say anything to him at the bar?

She decided that she had to see him. She had to know that he was going to help her. She called Linda to ask her to go to The Sportsman. She had endured Linda's cruel wit: *"Going to see Daddy? I'd love to go."* They made plans. Clara would go to Linda's house after dinner and then Linda would drive to the bar. Mrs. Martinson was going to a church meeting, so the girls could hang out at Linda's house before they went. Before this mess, they used to do this all the time. They used to put on their makeup together. Swap clothes. Drink a beer. But now, Clara didn't want to wear a lot of makeup. She didn't want to attract anybody's attention. She just didn't want Michael to be mad at her and blow her off. He could. She knew that. He really had nothing to fear from her. If she told people now what he had done, they wouldn't believe her. She had waited too long.

What would she say to Michael? She didn't know. Reaching for the lilac peasant blouse, Clara wondered if her mother was getting suspicious about her wearing the same two blouses all week. But her mother was preoccupied with packing for her trip with Agnes, so Clara didn't think she'd notice. By the time her mother and Agnes got home on Sunday, this would all be a bad dream—a nightmare—that was in the past. She loved the thought of Saturday. Saturday morning she would wake up and she would be free.

After dinner, she walked over to Linda's house and rang the bell. When Linda opened the door, she was all dressed up. She had on a tight, light-blue cami with lace and a short skirt with ruffles. She was wearing white sandals with a wedged, four-inch heel, and three necklaces of varying lengths hung around her neck.

"We are going to The Sportsman, aren't we, and not the Waldorf Astoria? Remember? The shitty little dive?" asked Clara as she walked into the foyer.

"Well, we *are* going out to have a good time. I know you can only fit into a few things, but let's see if we can't make you more presentable," Linda snarled. "At least put on some makeup!"

"Linda, I don't want any trouble tonight. I just want to be sure that he's coming on Friday. I don't want him to get any ideas. Like, I like him, or want to be with him," said Clara.

"Honey, the best way to get any man to do anything for you is to make him think he wants you," said Linda, looking at herself in the hall mirror. "I am gorgeous," she said matter-of-factly.

"Linda," Clara laughed. "You certainly are conceited."

"Just honest. C'mon." Linda led Clara upstairs to her room. Linda's room was a textile merchant's dream. The decorator had taken the color purple and used it in every hue to create a teenage girl's paradise. The walls were hung with purple silk. The cover for the double bed was made from at least six different purple and gold fabrics of flowers, toile, stripes, solids, and checks. All designer colors, all matching and blending. Next to the bed was a vanity with a lighted mirror and a skirt of fabric that matched the bedspread. A small, comfortable couch and chair were in one corner, audio equipment in the other. On one wall was a huge mural of Linda done in an Andy Warhol style, painted, and repeated in different colors.

Linda brought Clara into her walk-in closet. "Mmm. This might be a challenge, since you're already a size bigger than me in your natural state, and now you border on behemoth."

"Linda, really, I just want to be comfortable. I'll put on a little mascara if you insist."

"Go sit at the vanity," commanded Linda, as she left the room. Five minutes later, she came back with a white silk blouse with a scooped neck and three-quarter sleeves with a ruffle at the end. "This would look fabulous on you and it's not tight."

"Whose is it?"

"My mom's, but it's been in her closet for a long time. Look, it still has the price tag on it. She's never going to wear it." Linda ripped off the tag and threw it on the bed.

Clara picked up the tag and looked at it. "$225! Linda, I can't wear that!"

"I'm telling you. She bought it years ago," insisted Linda.

"Really? It is pretty...." Clara reached up to feel the creamy silk.

By the time they left Linda's house, Clara was as dressed up as Linda. Linda had insisted she put on eye shadow, mascara and liner, blush, and this gold shimmer powder. She wore light-pink lipstick and dangly silver earrings. Linda drank a beer in the kitchen on the way out. Clara tried a sip, but it made her stomach feel sick. Next weekend, she could have all the beer she wanted. She promised herself.

The Sportsman was crowded for a Wednesday night. No one asked the girls for identification as they tried to find a seat at the bar. Clara looked around to see if Michael was there. At first, she didn't see him, but after a few minutes, she saw him in the back leaning on the bar with his back to the front door. Clara was too shy to go back there and talk to him. She decided to wait until he turned around and spotted her. As they were settling in, two guys came over.

"Hey, haven't seen you girls here before," said an all-American jock type, smiling at Linda.

"Hey," said the other one, tipping his chin to Clara. He was tall, with curly brown hair and a gentle smile. The young men bought the girls a drink—Linda decided to try a Cosmo, Clara got a Coke—and tried to have a conversation over the music. Jay, working the other end of the bar, spotted Clara and didn't know whether to tell Michael or not. He knew that Molly had been trying hard to pretend they were a couple, and Jay knew that Molly could get very nasty if she thought this little girl was trying to worm her way between them. He didn't need a catfight in his bar. He decided not to say anything as he went down to say hello.

"Hey, gorgeous. I mean the gorgeous sisters. I don't know which one of you is finer," Jay said to Linda and Clara, giving them one of his endearing lopsided smiles. "How ya been?"

"Great," said Linda, with a witchy smile.

"Okay," said Clara, with a pout.

"Well, I see these two gentlemen have already set you up. The next one's on me." As he turned to look down the bar to see if anyone needed a drink, Jay saw that Michael was staring at him talking to Clara. Jay smiled. Michael did not. He looked like a trapped dog. Jay could see that Molly's arm was around Michael's waist. Jay looked at Clara, who was also looking at Michael and the arm.

Michael turned around and continued talking to his friends. Linda was flirting with the muscular jock, and Clara wished she had stayed home. *Now I've made it worse. He's not even coming over to me, and he has that girl with him.* Clara wished she could magically teleport out of the bar and into her bed. Suddenly, she realized someone was talking to her. "Do you want to play?" asked the voice.

Clara looked up at the curly-haired guy. "I'm sorry, what did you say?" Clara raised her voice over the blaring song pulsating from the jukebox.

"Pinball. Do you want to play?" he screamed into her ear. Clara didn't know what else to do. If he left, she would be sitting here all alone. She got up and started to walk over to the pinball machine, the young man followed her. As she reached the pinball machine, Michael stormed by her, dragging Molly by the hand. He looked right past Clara and did not acknowledge her. The young man put two quarters in the machine and moved aside to give Clara the first ball. Clara realized she recognized the girl Michael was dragging behind him from the newspaper and the TV news. She had been with Michael when he found the dead girl.

Preoccupied, Clara lost the first ball in 30 seconds. She smiled meekly and stepped down from the platform that the machine was on, and the young man took his turn. As she stood there waiting for her turn, Michael came hurriedly back into the bar, alone. He walked over to her and handed her a bar napkin with a phone number scribbled on it. "Call me tomorrow," was all he said before he rushed out, giving the tall young man a dangerous look.

Clara stood in the bar. Music and laughter swirled around her, and she thought she was going to cry. Now she had made her situation worse than it was this morning. Now Michael thought she was in the bar picking up other guys. That was the last thing she wanted him to think.

SIXTY-NINE

ate Wednesday afternoon, Mayor Ceravolo had decided that it was worth one last shot. He would pay Father O'Malley a visit on his way home tonight after the wake. He knew it was too late to prevent the demonstration from taking place at all, but he wanted to impress upon the priest how important it was that the protesters remain calm and that no one get hurt. This was a controversial, emotional issue, and people could get swept up in the moment. He told his driver to take him to St. Raymond's and to wait in the car.

There were no lights on in the church itself when the car pulled into the back parking lot. There was a light on in the first floor of the rectory, and the mayor was headed toward it when he heard banging. It was coming from a work shed behind the rectory. It sounded like someone was hammering. The mayor swung around and headed toward the sound. As he got closer to the shed, he could hear rock music under the slow, steady pounding of a hammer hitting wood. He knocked on the door, but whoever was inside couldn't hear him. He tried the doorknob and pushed the door open to find Father

O'Malley, sweaty and naked from the waist up, building what looked like a chair.

"Hello, Mayor," said a sultry voice from the back of the shed. The mayor looked confused. "Look Father, we have company," purred Kit, as she got up from a chair behind the workbench, holding her forever-present Cannon, and walked toward the mayor. Father O'Malley stopped hammering and wiped the sweat from his brow with a towel.

"Mayor Ceravolo! Is everything all right?" started Father O'Malley, looking around for his shirt. As he did, he looked at Kit. "Kit was taking some photos for her portfolio. I think we're done. Right, Kit?"

Kit looked at Father O'Malley just a little longer than she should have. "I guess I've got just about everything I'm going to get tonight," she said. The mayor felt himself start to sweat.

"Okay. We'll talk tomorrow, then," Father O'Malley said to Kit. She walked to the door and turned back to look at the two men.

"Mayor. Father." She paused for effect. Her perky brown eyes glistened, and her face broke into a grin. She slipped out the door.

Father O'Malley found his black shirt and put it on. "Have you ever done any woodworking?" he asked, running his hand over the freshly carved wood. "It's very therapeutic. When I have these tools in my hands, all the problems of the world seem far away. It's so simple. You hammer the nail into the wood and you make something. No words. No politics. Just the nail and the wood."

Mayor Ceravolo had lost his thunder. "I don't have time for a hobby in my line of work. Thomas…" he started.

"Antonio, you need to take the time. The time to reflect. The time to rest. I know that you are concerned about the demonstration. I would be lying if I told you that I wasn't, but it is an important message—that life shouldn't be taken for granted.

That's what I am going to talk about on Saturday. The sanctity of life." He smiled at the mayor.

It all seemed so rational. A priest, talking to people about the sanctity of life. Telling them that life shouldn't be taken for granted. Who could argue? Who, indeed? The mayor's funders, that's who.

"You make it sound so simple and you know it isn't," said the mayor. "This is a political issue that has already cost me dearly. Hundreds of 'caring' people can whip themselves into a mob in a matter of minutes, and that's what I wanted to talk to you about. You need to control the crowd. Your words will either whip them up or calm them down. It's all up to you, Father. It's all up to you." The mayor was tired, his shoulders suddenly drooped. He wanted to go home. "What time are you going to speak?"

"Well, I will be speaking to the people all morning, but to the crowd…around ten o'clock. I will only speak for fifteen minutes, and then the marchers will walk and carry signs. I will do everything I can to make sure it's peaceful."

"I'm counting on you," said Mayor Ceravolo, fixing his dark-brown eyes on Father O'Malley's face.

"Antonio, we are so alike, you and I. We try to do our job. But we're practical. We bow to the pressures of others in order to achieve our own goals. Don't we? We have both chosen very public professions. We stand in front of others and tell them what they want to hear so that we can achieve a few of our own goals. I have funders. You have funders. My office has rules. Your office has rules. This whole thing is outside of where we want to be, but here we are." As he spoke, he had been moving closer and closer to the mayor. By the time he was finished, he was very close to the mayor. Their faces were a few inches apart.

"It's in your hands," said Mayor Ceravolo. "It's in your hands."

SEVENTY

❧

Sandra Stett had gotten to the office at 6 a.m. on Wednesday and left at 8 p.m. She couldn't even remember if she had eaten dinner. She recalled taking a bite of a piece of pizza, but then being called away, and when she tried to find it again, it was gone. Sandra was bone tired, but she still had one more task to do tonight. It was her present to herself. She had worn black pants, and now she pulled a black long-sleeved T-shirt over her head. She got in her car and headed out to Route 54. When she was halfway there, her cell rang. She pressed the button on the steering wheel to connect to hands-free calling.

"Hello?"

"Miss Stett?" It was Reverend Turnipseed.

"Reverend. What can I do for you?"

"About the stipends…"

"Yes? What about them? We're not going any higher than twenty. We agreed on twenty each, Reverend," Sandra said firmly.

"It's not the amount, Miss Stett. It's the distribution."

"What about it?"

"I think it would go smoother if I handled the distribution."

Sandra was getting close to Route 54 now. "Simon told me he was waiting on the list to determine the actual distribution. Have you sent us the list? We need to know that we are going to have real demonstrators."

"It's in the fax machine."

"Fine. We'll leave the distribution to you." Sandra clicked the disconnect button. As she crossed over Route 54 to park her car beyond the clinic, up in the forest, as she had the last time, she saw the large body of the guard standing beside the center door. *What? They actually hired security!* She made a k-turn and drove by the front of the center. Outside, standing guard, there were two extra-large men. She couldn't believe it. How was she supposed to spray-paint the door? She drove up Route 54 and pulled over a half mile down the road.

Sandra Stett was pissed. This threw a big dent in her plan of defacing the center tonight and on Friday night before the demonstration. She wondered if the doctor's house was guarded as well. As she sat there stewing in her frustration, her brain was twirling and swirling. Where could she go? Rachel Horowitz's house? The president of the Litchfield Women's Center board? No, security system for sure. Town Hall? Too public. She wondered if it was guarded all night. Probably. She decided to drive back to Dr. Friedberg's house to see if the baby killer was guarded. As she drove, she thought: *God calls each of us to defend the innocent.* That is what her pastor back home had always said. Wasn't that what she was doing? Why was God putting all these obstacles in her way?

She took back roads through town to Stone Way. As she drove by Dr. Friedberg's house, she could just make out through the bushes, a tall man standing outside the house. And so, they were guarding the doctor, too. *These sinners knew no shame.* Preoccupied, Sandra sailed through the stop sign at the corner. The next thing she knew, she heard sirens and saw flashing lights in her rear-view mirror. *Damn!* She pulled over. The cop car pulled up behind her.

Officer Thompson got out of the squad car and took his flashlight out of the leather clip that held it on his belt. The streets in this part of town were very dark. He walked slowly over to Sandra's car. He shone the light in and saw a young blond woman with a big smile. "License and registration," he said.

"I am sooo sorry, Officer. I was thinking about getting home to my little boy, and I sailed right through that stop sign. I know I deserve a ticket and you should give me one. I am so sorry. It's just that Dickie is sick with one of these summer colds, and you know how bad you feel when you're little and you're sick and your momma has to work late." Sandra poured every ounce of southern charm that she could muster into her little monologue as she handed her documents to the officer.

"I'll be back," said Officer Thompson. He went to his squad car to run Sandra's license through his computer. The computer came back with a clean record in two minutes, but there was something bothering Officer Thompson. Call it police-officer's intuition. He decided to ask her to step out of the car.

"Where do you work, Ms. Stett?" asked Officer Thompson.

This question threw Sandra. She had expected the officer to let her go. "I work..."

"Please step out of the car." Officer Thompson took a step away from the car.

Sandra looked up at Officer Thompson, making her strange square-shape eyes as big as she could. "Officer, I work downtown. I was just driving my friend home. What is the problem? I told you to go ahead and give me a ticket."

"Please step out of the car." Officer Thompson reached down and opened the car door. As he did, a can of red spray paint fell on the pavement and rolled under the car. "What the...? What was that?"

"I think it was my hair spray," Sandra lied.

"Get out of the car." Officer Thompson's tone was now stern. Sandra got out of the car. The first thing he noticed was that she was dressed all in black. "Why are you dressed all in black?"

"I was cold in the air conditioning at work and so I pulled on this long-sleeve T-shirt."

"Where does your friend live and what's her name?"

Sandra knew she had now woven a web of lies that she couldn't substantiate. There was not a woman in town who would pretend to be her friend.

"Officer, I don't understand. I just went through the stop sign. Please give me a ticket and I'll be on my way."

"I asked you a question. Who is your friend and where did you just drop her off?"

Sandra said the first name that popped into her head, "Patricia Castellano." Of course, the officer knew who the mayor's sister was and he knew that she didn't live in this neighborhood. He also knew that she ran the pro-life organization that would cause him to miss his son's baseball game on Saturday morning.

"Get in your car and pull it up," said Officer Thompson. Sandra got in the car. The urge to floor it and drive away was overwhelming. She moved the car up, and Officer Thompson went and picked up the spray paint. He walked back to Sandra's car.

"Ms. Stett, you have the right to remain silent…." As he finished reading Sandra her Miranda rights, she felt like she was going to pass out. She was being arrested. But her work was not yet done.

SEVENTY-ONE

❦

"Stop whining," said Michael, as he drove Molly back to his apartment. "You are the biggest whiner I know."

"I'm not whining, baby. I just wanna know why we had to leave the bar in such a hurry." Molly was quite drunk, and her words slurred together. She reached over and ran her finger around the curve of Michael's ear. He ignored her and looked straight ahead. She undid her seatbelt and turned toward Michael, leaning over to lick his ear.

"Cut it out! I'm driving," he said, pushing her away with one hand and driving with the other. However, he had to admit to himself that his resolve to break up with Molly and take her and her stuff home tonight began to wear thin. The sight of Clara had made him want to have sex, and he knew that even if he dumped Molly and went back to The Sportsman to find Clara, his chances of having sex with her were slim to none. Why had she come to The Sportsman? Had she come to see him? He thought she had, but then she was playing pinball with that jerk, Tony. A real pretty boy, that one, with his soft curls. Michael had always wondered if he was gay, but the way he was looking at Clara, now he didn't think so.

"I'm hungry, baby. Let's go to McDonald's," Molly said in her whiny way.

"No, we're going back to the apartment," Michael said sourly. The thought of Clara and Tony was pissing him off. Maybe that little slut went to bars all the time and picked guys up. Maybe this baby wasn't even his. By the time they pulled into the Green Street Apartments, Michael was in a foul mood. He got out of the Mustang, slammed his door, went around to Molly's side of the car, opened the door, and pulled her out. Pushing her against the car, he kissed her roughly. Then he started pulling her through the parking lot and up the stairs.

When they got to the landing, he fumbled for his keys as Molly fumbled with his belt buckle. One thing he did love about Molly was that she was just as horny as he was. He opened the door, picked her up over his shoulder, and carried her to the bedroom where he threw her roughly on the bed. She pulled down her pants. No longer able to control himself, he opened his pants, got on top of her, and entered her as quickly as he could. He crushed her with his weight and stuck his tongue deep in her mouth. They climaxed quickly and lay panting without moving. For a moment, he forgot about Clara and let himself feel the extraordinary physical pleasure. He rolled off Molly and they lay side by side, spent. His last thought before he fell asleep was that he would tell her in the morning that she had to move out. Throughout the night, he woke up thinking about Clara. Each time, Molly gave him the distraction he needed. By morning, he was clear headed and knew what he had to do.

SEVENTY-TWO

Eduardo lay on his cot in his cell. He lay there, hating Pia, hating Maria, hating Stella. He hated all these women. But he also hated George and his father-in-law, and that bastard, Bickford. Bickford brought out his anger, his rage. Imagining that he had Bickford alone and handcuffed to a chair, Eduardo punched the air, again and again, until Bickford's face was raw—if only in Eduardo's mind. Twist his neck. Ah, that felt good. As for that little bitch, Casandra, he was glad she was dead. They were all against him.

Sleep—if only sleep would come. Stanley, his cellmate, snored above him. Eduardo could smell his sweat. It was disgusting. He closed his eyes and started to nod off, but a vision of his mother's face, with her twisted mouth and angry eyes came floating up into his mind. *You little bastard! I could be happy, but for you.* She was always screaming at him. In his dream he saw her hand coming at him, but he was never quick enough to avoid the slap on his little cheek. He had never known his father, but he had known the string of men that his mother brought home. She was a whore, his mother, all women were whores. Thoughts of his mother were always with him. He was born in Puerto Rico. His mother was 17 at the time. When he was 15, he followed some friends to New York, but the memories of her went with him. Fifteen years of pain she had caused him, and then a lifetime of anger.

Now, he would rot in jail. His attorney, the public defender who had been appointed to his case, had told him today that the police had found his box. His secret box with the photos and the key to Casandra's apartment. It was still circumstantial evidence, but the videotape was concrete proof that they were lovers. He hoped they showed it in court. It would be a real show for the court clerks.

Eduardo never planned to get married and have a family. It just happened. After working odd jobs, he met Jorge Salinas, Pia's father, in New York City on a construction site. Jorge owned a paint plant in New Jersey, but he worked on jobs all over the tri-state area. He was a strict, old-world type of guy and he had taken Eduardo under his wing. Eduardo had never had the friendship of an older man—a father-figure—and he tried to form a bond with Jorge. He was 20 at the time. Under Jorge's guidance, Eduardo started as a painter, but rose through the ranks, and was now the assistant manager of the plant. He had been on his way to owning that plant. Damn, he regretted that part of this mess.

He still thought Pia loved him and might help him. They had met at a family picnic day that Jorge had thrown for all the guys at the plant. She was cute and fresh. Jorge had encouraged Eduardo to take Pia out on a date. He took her to Applebee's, and they ate chicken tenders and drank beer. Eduardo knew that Jorge wanted him to date Pia, and she was easy to be with. She was undemanding, uncomplicated. He had also looked at Stella, but she was more willful. There would be passion with that one, but also violence. For a short time, he had tried to be someone else. He had tried to be a good guy. But then the demons would surface. After an evening with Pia, his mother's image would come to him while he slept. He would wake up in a sweat. Angry, frustrated, hurt. It was fine when they lived apart, but when they got married, Pia was there when he woke up angry, and he confused the two in his rage.

Then, the babies. Girl babies. He hated when they cried. He hated her tending to them. Kissing them. Stroking them. Rocking them to sleep. Spending her time with them. How he hated that. How he resented it. Finally, he had someone who cared about him, and then Maria was born, siphoning off Pia's time, pitting Eduardo up against his own child. Because Maria was born first, he hated her more than Carmen. Maria had ruined the little time he might have been happy. After she was born, the only time Pia was completely his was when they were having sex. Then, when Carmen was born, it was just too much. There was no space for all of them and his rage. He had to let it out. He started beating Pia because she deserved it for neglecting him.

It was always their fault. His mother's fault. Pia's fault. Maria's fault. Casandra's fault. He lay on his cot soaked in sweat. The thoughts were coming too fast now. He got up and went to the front of the cell and started to scream. The inmates woke up. The guards rushed over to see what was going on. Eduardo was in a frenzy. He was screaming and shaking the door to his cell, and then he started to bang his head on the bars. The guards charged into the cell. He punched the first guard in the face, breaking his nose. The second guard ran at Eduardo and hit him in the temple. Eduardo fell to his knees. The guard punched him on the back of his head with all his force. Eduardo hit the ground. He was out cold. The guards had given him just what he wanted.

$\mathcal{S}$ E V E N T Y - $\mathcal{T}$ H R E E

❧

$\mathcal{I}$n New Jersey, for a first offense, vandalism is a crime punishable by a fine, restitution to the victim, and community service. When Officer Thompson brought Sandra Stett into the Litchfield police headquarters, he wanted to get some information out of her. He led her into the interrogation room and let her sit there, stewing in her thoughts. He made a few notes about what she had already said. He knew he had to tread carefully, if she really was a friend of Patricia Castellano's. He went looking for the sergeant on duty.

Sergeant Gregory Staler was sitting at his desk, sipping his Starbucks coffee, when Officer Thompson walked into his office. The entire police department was in a bad mood. They had never worked so hard, or been as busy, as they had for the last week. At first, all of the action had been exciting, but now it was just tiring. They missed their uneventful rides around town, only stopping to hassle a few teenagers now and then, maybe write out a few parking tickets. Now, they were dealing with violations that required them to review procedure, and that damn demonstration was hanging over their heads.

"Thompson. What's up?" asked the Sergeant.

"Hey. I just picked up a woman. Sandra Stett. Went through a stop sign over on Stone Way, by the doctor's house. Said she was rushing home to her sick son. When I pulled her over, a can fell out of her car. She told me it was hair spray, but Sarge, it was red spray paint. I think we found our vandal. She's throwing around Patricia Castellano's name. I have her in interrogation room two," Thompson reported.

"How did the can fall out of her car?" Sergeant Staler looked at Officer Thompson over his reading glasses.

"I just felt like she was hiding something, and I asked her to step out of the car. When I opened the door, it fell out."

"Let's go talk to her." The two men walked down the corridor toward interrogation room 2, making a stop into the room beside the interrogation room, which had a one-way window into interrogation room 2 on the shared wall. They watched Sandra biting a hangnail, eyes bulging as she stared into space. "Let me take it," said Sergeant Staler.

Officer Thompson stayed behind in the viewing room. He watched Sergeant Staler enter the room. Sandra Stett looked up and stopped biting her hangnail. She studied the Sergeant's face. Sergeant Staler circled the table, sizing up Sandra Stett. She had taken off the black T-shirt and was wearing a sleeveless, lemon-yellow, knit top with a single strand of pearls. He noticed that she had pockmarked skin under her makeup. Her hair looked greasy.

"Ms. Stett, I'm Sergeant Staler. What were you doing out on Stone Way?"

"I was driving a friend home. Really, all of this over a stop sign? I told the other officer to give me a ticket. I admit that I ran the stop sign, and I'm sorry," Sandra looked up at the sergeant.

"What is your friend's name and address, Ms. Stett?" commanded Sergeant Staler.

Sandra Stett decided to go for it. "Patricia Castellano." She let the name hang in the air.

Sergeant Staler smiled a crooked smile. He turned the chair in front of him around and straddled it. "Now, Ms. Stett, if you do, indeed, know Patricia Castellano, you know that she doesn't live anywhere near Stone Way. So, the question remains, what were you doing on Stone Way?"

"Of course I know she lives in Dorian Estates, but it's faster for me to get home on the back roads."

"So, you drove Mrs. Castellano home? How do you know her?"

"I work for her."

Interesting, thought Sergeant Staler. Castellano runs that organization staging the demonstration, the organization rallying against the doctor living on Stone Way.

"Why did you have red spray paint in your car?"

"Well, you know the demonstration on Saturday?" The sergeant nodded. "We were making signs, and I guess one of the cans of paint must have fallen out of the bag. We're a small organization and I went to the store myself for supplies."

Sergeant Slater pondered what to do. There was definitely something about this woman that didn't add up. He decided to call Patricia Castellano and check out her story. On his way out the door, he turned to her and asked, "Who's with your son, Ms. Stett?"

"My son?" *Gotcha*, thought Sergeant Slater. Sandra's face and neck went red.

"Do you have a son, Ms. Stett? Is it Ms. or Mrs.?" Slater had come back into the room and closed the door.

Sandra's face was scarlet, and she had started to sweat. She had told so many little lies that she had spun a web around herself. One little white lie on top of another little white lie, and now she was smothering under the pile.

"No, I don't have a son," she stammered.

"But you told Officer Thompson that you were rushing home to your son." Sergeant Slater raised his voice to claim his superior position.

"I told him that because I felt bad about running the stop sign. This is all a misunderstanding. It's just a stop sign." Sandra put her face in her hands and started to cry.

"Well, if your story checks out with Mrs. Castellano, I guess…"

"Do you really need to bother Patricia? It's so late, I mean…"

"Is there anything you want to tell me about the spray paint and Dr. Friedberg's house?" asked Sergeant Slater, sitting back down in the chair across from Sandra. "I know you know who she is if you work for Mrs. Castellano."

Sandra shot her head up tall. "Is that what you think? That I spray-painted Dr. Friedberg's house? I can assure you that I did not! That happened during the day, and there are a number of witnesses who will swear that I was at work all day. We had a very busy day that day."

"I'm sure you did. I'll be back after I call Mrs. Castellano." Without waiting for a response, Sergeant Slater left the room.

SEVENTY-FOUR

⌇

How to stay in the story…hmmm…how to get one more photo out of this? It was Thursday morning and Patricia sat in a lounge chair on her terrace, sipping coffee and scheming. The demonstration was happening anyway, so Patricia might as well take advantage. She knew she wouldn't have this opportunity again. Antonio and Salvatore would see to it that she was kept busy with other things—she knew how they worked. Even Father O'Malley was holding his breath, wishing the demonstration was over. But, certainly, there would be press opportunities after the fact. Follow-up interviews. Talk shows. Maybe even in New York. Why does it have to be local? Antonio probably wouldn't mind so much if she were on the New York stations. As Patricia pondered the possibilities, the phone rang. She picked up the remote phone and saw her brother's number. She winced and debated letting it go to voice mail, but she knew she would end up speaking to him at some point. What was she supposed to do to placate Suzy Walker? Even if she shut down Stand Up for Life tomorrow,

Suzy wouldn't be happy. She clicked the green button. "Good morning," she answered cheerily.

"It is *not* a good morning, Patricia," Antonio said coldly into the phone. "I am up to my balls in phone messages from supporters who are unhappy that the Women's Center is coming under attack. And did you see Helen Acker's piece in *The Press* this morning? You're busing people in from Smithtown? Smithtown! Patricia, what are you thinking?"

Although it was already 9:30, Patricia was still wearing her yellow silk bathrobe. She played with the belt as she walked up and down on the terrace listening to Antonio's tirade. Her two-inch stiletto slippers went *click clack click clack* on the slate. "Calm down, Antonio. We are not busing anyone in from Smithtown," she laughed.

"Patricia, where are the people coming from who are protesting? Do you really think that 300 Litchfieldians are going up to Route 54 to march on the clinic that they all use? Patricia, sometimes you are so wrapped up in your own little world that you have no idea what's going on! Even in your own organization!" screamed Antonio.

"Father O'Malley is..." Patricia started.

"Oh, and let me tell you a thing or two about your precious Father O'Malley! I go over to St. Raymond's last night to talk some sense into him, and he's half naked with that blond photographer!" Antonio was now pacing in his office on his side of the conversation, and Patricia was pacing on her side.

"Thomas? Half naked? Antonio, seriously. You need to settle down. It'll all be over in a few days. It'll all be forgotten by the election. Antonio, you've got to forget about politics for a minute and think about what I'm really saying. Don't you remember when we were small and Mommy would tell us that the purpose of life was to raise our children? That was the most important thing. That's what this is about. It's about the children."

"Oh, my God. You sound like you really believe this. Patricia, it's fine to think about the children when your husband's a wealthy stockbroker and you live in Dorian Estates, but what about the desperate women? That's what this about. Everyone does not live in your idyllic little world!" The mayor ran his chunky hand through his thick hair, closed his eyes, and counted to ten. He could hear Patricia's voice blabbing on but he couldn't really focus on the words. He was trying to figure out what he wanted her to do. While he was thinking, her phone buzzed.

"Antonio, I'm getting another call. It's the pediatrician. I've got to go." She hung up and clicked the button for call-waiting.

"Hello, Thomas," she said. "We need to talk. Antonio is like a man possessed...."

"That's why I'm calling. He came to see me last night. He asked me to control the crowd on Saturday. Patricia, where are these protesters coming from?" asked Father O'Malley. "According to Helen Acker's article this morning, they're coming from Smithtown."

"I assumed that they were coming from Litchfield. I'll have to check with Lee when I get to work. Where is this article?" Patricia had kicked off her slippers and was marching through her perfect, emerald-green lawn toward the pool. She went through the wrought-iron fence and over to the lounge chair, where she had left the paper, unopened.

"The article says that you have hired buses and are paying protesters to come to Litchfield. Patricia, is that true?" Father O'Malley sat in his office in his jogging suit, drinking an orange Gatorade.

Patricia's phone buzzed. She took a quick look at the screen. The police department. "Thomas, I need to take this call. Talk later." She hit the flash button on the phone.

"Good morning...Yes, this is she." It was Sergeant Slater. He reiterated the story of the night before, which ended with Sandra Stett being held in the Litchfield jail. The sergeant and Officer Thompson had decided it was best to keep Sandra overnight and call Patricia Castellano in the morning. They had decided not to take the chance of getting the mayor involved late at night.

Sergeant Slater had come to the end of his monologue. "So, Mrs. Castellano, did Sandra Stett drive you home last night?" Patricia paused to think. Her mind quickly ran through different scenarios. *Yes, Sandra did drive me home.* Sandra would go free and run the demonstration. *No, Sandra did not drive me home.* Even Patricia felt shy about lying to the police. And, besides, Kenny, her driver, would be questioned. He had brought her home at 5 p.m. "Mrs. Castellano, are you still there?" asked the sergeant.

"Yes, I'm sorry. It's just that I've been so busy. I was just trying to…recall last night. No, Sandra Stett did not drive me home. Kenny, my driver, brought me home as usual." Patricia was now sprinting toward the house. She needed to get to her office and see what the hell was going on.

"Thank you, Mrs. Castellano." The phone went dead.

SEVENTY-FIVE

᪣

*T*he chocolate was like a buried treasure deep in the flaky croissant. Helen had decided to start her diet next Monday, but now on Friday, after a long week, she was indulging with not one, but two, chocolate croissants. As penance, she had gotten skim milk in her coffee. It was awful. *Hardly worth drinking.* Maybe there was some half-and-half in the kitchen. She sat in her cubicle, savoring every bite of the sweet, greasy pastry. When she was done, she wiped the flakes of crust off her chin with a recycled napkin, pushed her glasses up on her skinny nose, and went back to the sidebar she was writing for Saturday's paper. It was a roundup of the four most important Supreme Court cases dealing with contraception and abortion: *Griswold v. Connecticut, Roe v. Wade, Webster v. Reproductive Health Services,* and *Planned Parenthood v. Casey.*

Helen thought about the women in the first two cases, who had gone all the way to the Supreme Court to argue their beliefs. Estelle Griswold, the executive director of the Planned Parenthood League of Connecticut in 1965, was convicted of giving married women contraceptives, which were illegal at the time, and Norma McCorvey, the real "Jane Roe," was a poor, unmarried, pregnant 23-year-old woman from Texas, who became the plaintiff in the most famous lawsuit after *Brown v. Board of Education*. In 1973, she allowed two young attorneys, Linda Coffee and Sarah Weddington, to use her case to file a lawsuit that would challenge the Texas anti-abortion laws and change history.

Helen read excerpts from the decisions online to find a pull quote for her article. She was looking for something that summed it all up. After an hour of trolling Wikipedia she found a quote from *Planned Parenthood v. Casey*. "At the heart of liberty is the right to define one's own concept of existence, of meaning, of the universe, and of the mystery of human life." She copied the quote down as a possibility.

As she researched the legal cases, her eyelids became heavy. She closed her eyes and rolled her head around on her chubby neck. It was difficult to read all this legalese and try to figure out what the authors were really talking about. Privacy, preambles, penumbra, it was like a foreign language. She leaned her cheek on her palm and her elbow on her desk and closed her eyes. Ah, so nice to rest. As she dozed off, she heard the familiar rasp of Greeley's voice.

"Time!" he croaked, as he walked through the newsroom to the conference room. Like little chickens following the mother hen, Fiona, Latitia, Kit, Bill, Gary, and Emily fell in line behind him. Helen sat up, stretched, and followed at her own pace. Helen was riding high now. Her series had produced the largest sales in *Press* history. Advertisers were calling the newspaper—that hadn't happened in five years. Each morning edition was literally too hot to keep on the shelf. They were doing double press runs and even then couldn't keep the newsstands stocked. Subscriptions were up. Like gold stars on her resume, she kept track of *The Press's* stats so she could use them in cover letters to better employers.

Greeley was happy for the first time in 30 years. He figured he had the rest of this week, and a few days into next, to capitalize on the town's misfortune. He was planning a huge Sunday issue after the demonstration on Saturday, with full in-depth coverage and a two-page photo spread. People liked photos. He wanted interviews with key demonstrators. Of course, Father O'Malley would have good placement. He was the most photogenic priest ever. Greeley's mind was brimming with ideas.

"Everybody here?" Greeley's eye ran down the right side of the table. "Acker. Milford. Blackman. Stilton." His head turned to the left. "Johnson. Rivington. Wren. Elliot. Elliot."

"Okay. Acker. Where are we? By the way, great scoop with the Smithtown story. Who are your sources?" asked Greeley in his gruff tone.

"Greeley, if I spread their name around town, they'll never talk to me again." She eyed him over her glasses with a look of profound disgust on her face. "As far as the series is concerned, tomorrow we have *Roe v. Wade* by Fiona, the Supreme Court in the '70s by Bill, a history of abortion in New Jersey by Gary, an update on the upcoming demonstration by me, Latitia is covering the Keller case, I'm trying to get a one-on-one with Suzy Walker...."

"I've already started a piece on Suzy's move from Ceravolo to Rubin for mayor," Bill Johnson said with a sneer. "I spoke to Suzy not minutes ago."

Helen eyed him with suspicion. "Minutes ago?"

"*Min-utes* ago," taunted Johnson, drawing out the word and pointing his chin smugly at Helen.

"Helen, you have enough to do. Let Johnson take it," Greeley interjected. "Milford, where are we with Senator Connors, Gold and Noonan?"

Milford opened his iPad. "I got a quote. You're gonna love it. Right. Here it is...speaking for all of them, Gold said, 'We believe in women's rights, but we also uphold the First Amendment.' It's like these guys take a course in political speaking."

"Well, at least it shows we spoke to them," sighed Greeley. "Let's talk about Saturday. Who is actually going to be on site?"

All hands went up except Loren Elliot's. Emily looked at her mother quizzically. All eyes turned to Loren. "I'm sorry. I'm busy this weekend, starting Friday," she said.

"This is the busiest weekend we've ever had, Elliot!" roared Greeley.

"I'm sorry, sir," she winced.

"Little Elliot, you'll have to fill in for your mother. Blackman, what's new with the Keller case? Have those bumbling idiots down at police headquarters found any shred of evidence to link anyone to the one and only murder in Litchfield? What's going on with that sleazebag Fernandez?" Greeley was back to his feisty self.

"I think there's been a development, but no one's talking. I know they got a search warrant for the Fernandez house, but they're not saying what they found. I've been hanging around at the station but no leaks. The creep's being held on the domestic violence case. They moved him to the county jail and he's not going anywhere. They have time," reported Latitia. "I have contacts. If they found something, I'll find out."

"Well, find it out before *watch.com*. Key-rist! I hate that Internet. It's going to finish us. Rivington, did you go to the funeral?"

Fiona Rivington looked uneasy. "I did, but not as a reporter."

"You're always a reporter, Rivington! You can cry in mourning with one eye and report with the other!" he hollered. "Ross had a photo on *watch* within the hour."

"I'm not a photographer!" Rivington's face was red and she was hyperventilating slightly. She did not like to be yelled at. "There really wasn't any news, except the mayor trying to get a few votes."

Greeley and Rivington sneered at each other. "Johnson, what's the word with Rubin? That arrogant piece of shit! Has Suzy Walker lost her mind backing him for mayor?"

Johnson took out his reporter's pad and flipped through the pages. "Suzy's holding a mayoral campaign kick-off news conference for Rubin on Saturday morning at the Swan Club at 10:30. It's a brilliant move on her part, cutting right into the demonstration's coverage."

"I love Suzy! She can sell a newspaper. All the WASPs will be there for her and all the Jews for Rubin. God love her! Now we really have a photographer shortage. Kit, how many photographers do you need to cover the demo?" "I think Wren and I can cover it." Kit was the only one in the room who sat back in her chair as if she didn't have a care in the world. All of the reporters were sitting at attention, trembling in fear that Greeley might explode at them next. But Kit sat back in her chair with her long legs crossed, looking like she had never sweated a drop of perspiration in her life. As usual, she was dressed in many layers of skimpy clothing. Her ever-present cameras sat on the table before her.

"Then who the hell will cover this press conference now?"

"I can do it," Emily Elliot said meekly.

Greeley turned his head to see who had the audacity to speak in such a meek fashion in his presence. He ran his hand through his greasy hair and then wiped it across his mouth. He didn't want to crush this stupid girl in front of her mother. For some reason he liked Loren Elliot. Her red hair reminded him of his mother.

"*You* are going to cover a press conference?" Greeley asked repressing a snort.

Bill Johnson didn't look very impressed. He wanted good art to attract readers to his story.

"I think I can do it," said Emily. Loren smiled. Greeley scowled and pondered. Everyone in the room watched him.

"Kit, you take Little Elliot with you to the demonstration and Wren will photograph the press conference," Greeley pronounced. "Now get to work!" He stood, pulled up his baggy, gray pants, and walked out of the conference room.

After work, as Loren and Emily were driving home, Emily looked glum. Loren knew that she felt bad because Greeley

THE RECOVERY ROOM

wouldn't let her cover the press conference. "Maybe next time," she said encouragingly.

"Yeah. Maybe," said Loren pulling at a loose string on her jean skirt.

"I was proud of you for speaking up and believing in yourself. I know your pictures will be great. Take some good shots at the demonstration and Greeley will see how talented you are." Loren smiled at her daughter.

"Why aren't you going to be there, Mom? Where are you going?"

"I have to go to the doctor on Friday for an outpatient procedure. It's nothing, really. I might be a little tired over the weekend. That's all." Her tone told Emily not to ask any more questions.

SEVENTY-SIX

Greeley shuffled back to his office and shut the door. Time to call Bickford and see what he had on the Keller murder. He sat down at his overflowing desk and pushed some papers away to get at his Rolodex. Darius Greeley did not keep his contacts in his cell phone like modern editors did. He liked to do things the way he had been doing them for the last 40 or so years. He rolled the ancient Rolodex wheel, its white cards yellowed with age, until the Bs came up. He flicked through until he found Detective Bickford's card.

Greeley liked "Bick," as he called him. They were cut of the same cloth. Many nights they could be found at the same gin mill having a few before they went home to their wives. Hundreds of secrets were buried between the two of them. They probably knew more about the people in Litchfield than anyone else. Greeley was an old-time newspaperman, and Bickford was an old time cop. He and Bick went way back. They trusted each other. They helped each other. If Greeley needed details for a story, Bick filled him in. If Bick needed to get a story out, Greeley printed it. It was a symbiotic relationship.

They needed each other to get their jobs done. So, Greeley picked up the heavy black earpiece to his 1940s phone, and dialed Bick's number.

"Bickford."

"Bick, Greeley."

"I've been waiting for this call."

"My reporter says you found something in the search of Fernandez's house. Something to link him to the Keller murder."

"Can't say now. Ears all around. Call you later."

"I'll be waiting." Greeley hung up and knew that he would have his scoop. He needed to make room in tomorrow's paper. He leaned back in his big, comfortable chair and smiled. What a week!

SEVENTY-SEVEN

❧

Clara could hear the screaming and pounding as she typed the security code into the panel that opened her garage door. She had ended up spending the night at Linda's house and wanted to get home to say good-bye to her mother and Agnes before they left for their weekend retreat. It had been a team effort to get Linda and her car home from the bar the night before. Since Clara couldn't drive, she had convinced Jay to help her carry a very drunk Linda out to her car, drive Linda's car home, and get his friend to follow them in Jay's car. It had taken all of Clara's charm to maneuver Linda and the young men. She swore to herself that it was her last trip to The Sportsman.

Already nervous about the procedure the next day, she wanted to hug her mother and tell her she loved her. She wanted to feel her mother's arms around her and see her familiar face. Even though Mrs. Mahoney had no idea where Clara was going in the morning, it would give Clara courage to know her mother loved her. She slipped into the garage door, up the steps, walked through the kitchen, and was on her way to the stairs, as the yelling and thrashing got louder and louder.

Packing was always a problem. Agnes hated for her things to be moved and didn't really understand the concept of taking things with you, hidden in a suitcase. She depended on order. She thrived on routine. Clara really had to question the wisdom of taking these autistic kids to a retreat. They hated to go anywhere. What was the goal? But the timing was great. With her mother away, Clara could do what she needed to do without worrying too much about her mother finding out. Reluctantly, she headed upstairs.

As she opened the door to Agnes' room, she saw Agnes pick up the packed, but still open, suitcase and hurl it at Mrs. Mahoney. "Take out!" Agnes screamed, as the suitcase hit Mrs. Mahoney in the shoulder, causing her to fall sideways onto the bed.

"Agnes! Calm down," said Clara in an even tone. "Mom's taking your things to the car. To go in the car you need to put them in a suitcase. That's all."

Agnes started to spin when Clara entered the room. Her hands were flapping by her sides and she was spinning around faster and faster. Mrs. Mahoney sat on the bed, rubbing her shoulder, with a distraught look on her face.

"Agnes. It's okay." Clara stood between her mother and her sister and motioned her mother to repack the suitcase which Mrs. Mahoney did without getting up from the bed. "Agnes, I'll bet they have pudding at the hotel. Remember last year? When you came home you told me about the pudding. Remember?" Agnes reached out and pushed Clara toward the bed.

"Shut up!" Agnes shrieked. "Get out of here!"

"No, Agnes. I want to help you," said Clara.

Agnes stopped spinning. She was out of breath. She started to jump up and down. When she saw that her mother had repacked the suitcase, she ran over and dumped the contents out. "Clara, I think you should go," said Mrs. Mahoney.

"I'm trying to help."

"I know, but it's…"

Clara looked at Agnes, who wouldn't look at her. "Fine," said Clara, and left the room. She went across the hall to her own room and threw herself down on her bed. She was hungry. She was nauseous. She was frightened. She could still hear the chaos coming from Agnes' room. Why had she bothered to come home at all? Resentment swelled up in her chest, and she started to cry. She thought about Michael the night before. "Call me," he had said. She knew she had to call him today and make sure he was still taking her. She must have nodded off, because the next thing she knew, her mother was standing by her bed. She looked tired and disheveled. Her hair, which had been tied back in a ponytail at some point today, had come mostly undone, and stray curls stuck out wildly from both sides of her head. She had black circles under her eyes and a scratch on her left cheek.

"Clara, I need your help. I'm giving Agnes some Benadryl to calm her down, and I need you to sit with her in the car while I finish getting ready," said Mrs. Mahoney. She had been giving Agnes a little Benadryl for years, to take the edge off or put her to sleep while she drove alone with her.

"Okay," said Clara, wishing that her mother would say something kind to her, anything.

Mrs. Mahoney turned to leave the room. "And Clara, don't get into trouble while I'm gone."

Clara sprang up in bed. Her mother did this sometimes when she was stressed out. She lashed out at Clara. But not today. Clara couldn't let it go today. "Do I ever give you any trouble? Would you even notice if I did?" Clara's large blue eyes glared at her mother. She got up, pushed past her mother, and stormed out the door. "I'll be in the car," she said, in a deep, raw, furious voice that her mother had never heard before.

"Clara! Come back here!" yelled her mother, but Clara just kept walking down the hall. "Clara!"

Clara finally turned at the top of the stairs and said, "You know, Mom, you think that you're such a great mother, because you insist on taking care of Agnes by yourself without nurses, but what about me? Are you the best mother to me? Do you even know what's going on in my life? Think about that while you're driving. Think about all the times I needed you and you didn't even know it." Clara started to go down the stairs. "I'll be in the car."

"Clara, wait. I didn't mean it that way...." stammered Mrs. Mahoney.

Clara looked up at her mother from the stairwell. "Really, Mom? What way did you mean it? What trouble do you think I might get into? You don't know my friends, because they're not allowed to come here. They might witness a scene. You don't even know who I'm hanging out with. You just assume that I'll take care of myself because I always do. And you know what, Mom? I will take care of myself, because there's no one else who cares. So, go. Get Agnes ready. Dote on Agnes. She might be killing herself right now for all we know. She's pretty quiet. You better go," fumed Clara.

Mrs. Mahoney's hand went up to her face. She felt the heat flow into her cheeks as if Clara had slapped her. Clara, who never challenged her. Clara, who never gave her a problem. Why had she said that to her? As she stood there in the hallway, she could hear Agnes emptying the suitcase again.

SEVENTY-EIGHT

*he Litchfield Women's Center Board of Directors put out a statement late on Thursday afternoon. It appeared on *watch.com* within the hour. It read: "The Litchfield Women's Center will remain open to serve our patients on Saturday. Our dedicated staff will not be deterred from providing quality health care in the face of extremist, anti-choice advocates who would attempt to sway the public's perception of the center. Here are a few facts: Last year the center provided more than 2,000 women with gynecological exams, over 1,800 women with birth control, gave more than 500 women referrals for life-saving mammograms, administered over 1,500 free pregnancy tests, supplied over 1,000 cervical-cancer screenings, and provided more than 1,200 hours of counseling. Access to abortion is legal, constitutionally protected, and consistently supported by a majority of Americans, yet anti-choice organizations interfere with these rights. On Monday, we will again open our doors for business as usual and women and their families will be welcome." The names of all of the members of the board of directors were signed below the statement.

The statement had been written by Suzy Walker and Rachel Horowitz and sent around by email to all the board members for editing and comment. Rachel had stopped by Suzy's office after talking to Dr. Friedberg about keeping the clinic open for this one girl who insisted upon coming at nine o'clock on Saturday morning. She would have to walk right through the demonstration. Rachel felt that by closing the clinic on Saturday morning, they would avoid photographs of distraught women entering the clinic or being forced to turn away due to the anger of the mob. There was only one girl who had actually made an appointment, but on any given Saturday, 15 to 20 women often just showed up.

Suzy and Rachel had drafted the statement together, bouncing thoughts and words off each other for reaction. Suzy had come up with the term "anti-choice." The movement was always described as pro-life, and who could argue with that? But "anti-choice"—that was a good counter-description. Suzy was glad that Rachel had taken the initiative to drop in at her office. The center had been on her mind all week, but she had been in court on various matters and hadn't been able to focus on it. She had spent what little time she had, informing the mayor that she would not support him in the next election and telling Norman Rubin that she would. There was a year before the primary, so she had time to raise money.

It was good that Rachel had suggested releasing a statement and had come to her to help put it together. As feminists in the early '70s, she and Rachel had gotten an overdose of the "we are woman, hear me roar," philosophy. After growing up with smart mothers who had used their talents to cook well-balanced meals all of their adult life and never pursue any of their own passions, Suzy and Rachel had taken the other road and pursued all of their career passions, leaving their children with nannies and never cooking one full meal their entire adult life. Meal preparation was blamed for keeping women down in the '70s and '80s and didn't have a comeback until the late '90s, when it suddenly became chic to be a lawyer or doctor who could also prepare *coq au vin*.

Suzy looked down on women like Patricia Castellano who went to fancy schools only to achieve the degree of MRS. Patricia, 10 or so years younger, had made peace with the idea of being dependent on a man. She didn't want to rise with the sun and be at the office by 8:00, she just didn't feel the need to prove herself in that way. Suzy and Rachel could never sleep at night without a paycheck. Suzy knew the pendulum had swung and younger women wanted to stay home to spend time with their children—that she could understand—but what she couldn't understand was why an educated woman would not believe that women needed to make their own decisions about their bodies. Why couldn't Patricia have chosen something less important to meddle with?

After Suzy and Rachel had issued the statement that the clinic would remain open on Saturday, they sat chatting in Suzy's well-appointed office. "I spoke to Chief Chodor, and he assures me that his officers will be at the demonstration in full force," said Rachel. "I still think we should close the center on Saturday and reopen on Monday."

"But Rachel, that would be like letting Patricia and her position win. They would have been successful in shutting us down. No, I'm with Amy on this one. If we give in to them once, they would claim a victory. No, we have to show them that we're not backing down," said Suzy with conviction. "I'm going to Norman's press conference that morning. Will you be at the clinic? To support Amy? I mean inside. Just to make sure everything is okay?"

"I guess you're right about staying open," Rachel agreed reluctantly. "Yes, I'll be at the clinic. I'll arrive early and be there for Amy."

SEVENTY-NINE

Worrying. What was the point? It didn't help anything. It didn't change anything. It was the opposite of proactive. But still, Pia needed to worry. Sometimes she felt that if she worried enough, it would ward off bad things. She knew that this made no sense, but still, she was afraid not to worry. She hadn't felt contentment for so long that she had almost forgotten what it felt like. Each night, before Eduardo had gone to jail, she lay down and waited for the worrying to begin. Sometimes she was so tired that she fell asleep immediately, but the worry always woke her. She never made it through the night. She never knew what she would wake up worrying about. It was like while her body slept, her mind went into overdrive. Poring over conversations, gestures, looks, and actions, until finally, she woke, having discovered why something had happened or why something might happen tomorrow. She worried about things that she had said to Eduardo. She worried about things he said to the kids. She worried about things he had done. She worried about things that he would do.

It was usually around three o'clock in the morning when she was suddenly wide awake, her eyes open, her brain churning. She had to lie very still not to wake Eduardo. She would wake with some bad thought about the girls. That they were unhappy or that they were going to be hurt. Everything seemed worse in the middle of the night. She would use this time to fantasize about how to get away from him. She spent hours being angry at herself for being so weak. She would finally fall back to sleep after a few hours. When the alarm went off, she was exhausted.

Now, with everything that had happened, she was in a constant state of worry and fear. It was not only at night. Even when she was awake, she worried about how they were going to live. Where they were going to live. Where she would get a job to support them. She tried to focus on the girls. They were so sweet and kind to her. But Maria was silent about what had happened, and Pia knew that inside her daughter must be confused and angry and scared. Pia knew she had to talk to Maria, but not yet. First, Pia had to focus her strength on getting through tomorrow. She and Stella had decided to tell the girls that she had to go back to see the doctor. Pia had no idea how she would feel afterward. The nurse on the phone had said she would have to rest for a day or two, and that was before Eduardo had beaten her up. She was still recovering from the beating, and now she had to find the strength to have the abortion.

She couldn't see the end of her suffering in sight. Detective Bickford had called Stella's house that afternoon, wanting to speak with Pia. He said that he wanted to warn her before the news was formally released. Eduardo was going to be charged with the murder of Casandra Keller. During the search of Pia's house, the police had found evidence linking Eduardo to Casandra. Detective Bickford said there were photographs and a videotape. He wanted Pia to know so that she could prepare herself and her children for the publicity that was bound to come. She didn't have to ask what kind of photographs or videotape. There was only one kind that the detective would feel the need to warn her about. It was thoughtful of him to call.

She hadn't even allowed herself to think about Eduardo killing that poor girl. *The girl whose mother is still alive.* She had read that the mother lived in Freeport. Her heart went out to that woman. Pia knew Eduardo was capable of killing. If Maria hadn't called the police, Pia, too, might be dead. How awful for that poor young girl. How had Eduardo met her? She had no idea. She shuddered to think that the girls would know that their father was a murderer. Maybe she should move away from Litchfield, but where would she go? She could hear the girls coming up the stairs. They were giggling and joking. Thank God for her girls. They were her strength.

EIGHTY

'❧'

*A*fter her unpleasant morning on the phone, Patricia dressed quickly, and hurried to her office. Dressing quickly is relative. Some people can shower, dress, and be ready to go in 25 minutes. Others take a respectable hour. But for Patricia, showering, dressing, blow-drying her hair, putting on her makeup, and instructing her house staff usually took no less than an hour and a half. And that was with the maid doing the ironing.

This morning, Patricia was wearing a sunflower-yellow St. John's suit and Jimmy Choo pumps. The way she was dolled up, she looked like she was going to have lunch with the queen, not going to confront her office staff about details of their upcoming event. After speaking with Carmelita and Ilsa at length about the children's schedule for the day, she called Kenny, her driver, and told him to pick her up. Kenny had been out in the backyard watching Ilsa, the *au pair*, in the pool with the twins, and so it only took him a few minutes to get in the car and drive to the front door.

While they were driving to town, Kenny looked in the rearview mirror and saw the telltale signs of his mistress's bad mood. The blazing brown eyes slightly squinted, the tight-set mouth, the ramrod-straight posture. *Uh oh, someone's in for a bad time. Thank you, lord, that it's not me.*

When Patricia arrived at the office, Lee, Simon, and five volunteers whom Sandra had recruited somewhere were working in the back room, putting together hundreds of signs with varying slogans. The majority of them simply said "Stand Up for Life," but there were many that proclaimed "Don't Kill Your Baby," some that shouted "Abortion is Murder," and a smattering of "Abortion is Forever." Patricia winced as she looked around the room and saw the word "Abortion" everywhere. She closed her eyes to compose herself.

"Simon. I'd like to speak with you in my office." Before waiting for a reply, she turned on her pointy heel and headed through the door.

Simon and Lee exchanged a look of dread. Lee felt helpless. He knew if he tried to go with Simon, Patricia would order him out of her office. Simon shrugged his shoulders, smoothed down his black hair, stuck his chin out defiantly, and followed Patricia down the hall. Patricia waited in the doorway until Simon was in the room, and then closed the door soundly.

"Simon, are we recruiting demonstrators from Smithtown?" Patricia's delivery was clipped and edgy.

"Sandra said..." Simon started.

"*Sandra said?*" roared Patricia. "Since when do you take direction from Sandra?"

"I...well..." Simon's head was swirling. When *had* he started taking direction from Sandra? It was certainly true that Sandra had been coordinating all of the plans for the demonstration. "I thought she was...planning the demonstration...." Simon's voice trailed off.

"This is *my* organization. Do you understand that? No one makes decisions without my authority, ever again. I want a full report by the end of the day on every penny that has been spent on this event, whom it went to, and what it was for. I want a list of every demonstrator who has signed up. Do you understand me?" Patricia was now towering over Simon and shouting down at him. Little droplets of her saliva were spraying over his face. He took a step backward.

"I'm not really sure I can put a full report together without Sandra, and she hasn't shown up today or called in. I'll try." He took another step back. Patricia closed her eyes and tried to pull herself together.

"That will be all," she whispered through clenched teeth, as she turned and strode to her desk. Simon pivoted on one foot and was out of the office and down the hall to the restroom before she could change her mind. Once inside, shaking with rage, he washed Patricia's spittle from his face.

Lee had been listening on the other side of the door, but had run back to his desk when he heard Patricia say "that will be all." He wanted to go to Simon in the restroom, but just then the office front door opened and Father O'Malley swooped in, with his blond curls all wind-tossed and a worried look on his handsome face. He almost took Lee's breath away.

"Father O'Malley," Lee stammered. The tall priest looked down at Lee sitting at his desk as if he hadn't noticed Lee was there.

"Lee, how are you? Is Mrs. Castellano in?"

"Yes, she's in her office. Please have a seat and..." As Lee reached for the phone to buzz Patricia, the priest held up his hand.

"Don't bother. She's expecting me." With that, he strode across the waiting room and down the hall.

Lee breathed in deeply through his nose. So much commotion this morning, he thought. They rarely had a visitor. He wondered how Simon was doing in the restroom. He was trying to decide whether or not to go to him when the door opened again, and Sandra slunk in. The first thing Lee noticed was that she was still wearing the same yellow shell that she had been wearing the day before. Her hair looked dark and greasy, and her mascara was smudged under her bloodshot eyes. Without foundation, her skin was pockmarked and mottled. She looked like she had slept in an alley the night before.

"Is Patricia here?" she whispered to Lee, holding one finger in front of her lips to signal to Lee to be quiet.

"Damn, girl. You look like shit. Where have you been?" asked Lee, looking up at her with his nose squished up like he was smelling rotten eggs.

Sandra looked down at Lee, and then she looked down at her shirt. A brown coffee stain was dried between her breasts. Her hand went to it as if she was noticing it for the first time. Her hand went up to her hair and she pulled on the matted bangs that stood in clumps on her forehead.

"Now, I'm not telling you your business, but if Patricia sees you like this she's gonna fire your ass. Go home. Take a shower and come back. I'll tell her you called in sick, but that you're feeling better and will be in later. And Sandra, Patricia knows about the demonstrators. That they're coming from Smithtown. She is *not* happy." Lee shook his head from side to side. "No, she is *not* happy. Now go. Hurry."

Without a word, Sandra turned and left the office, just as Simon slipped out of the restroom, trying to look as if nothing happened. He came into the waiting room and sat in the visitor's chair beside Lee's desk. "Where is she?" he whispered.

"In her office with the sexy priest," said Lee, lifting one eyebrow.

"O'Malley?"

Lee nodded. "Sandra just dropped in looking like a greasy mess. Still wearing that yellow shell that washes out her color. Obviously never made it home last night. Didn't see *her* as a player. I told her to go home and have a shower, then come back."

Simon was wondering if he had miscalculated telling Helen about the demonstrators coming from Smithtown. Maybe he had just made trouble and extra work for himself. And where had Sandra been? He couldn't believe that she had hooked up with anyone. She was the abstinence queen. And why was O'Malley here? He looked at Lee. "Patricia wants a full report by the end of the day. She wants to know where every penny was spent, whom it went to, and what it was for, and she wants a list of every demonstrator who has signed up. How are we going to pull that together without Sandra? And now you sent her home?" he hissed.

Lee's cheeks had become red and hot. He turned his back on Simon and started to check his email. He clicked on *watch. com*'s daily update, and there on his screen was a story about Sandra being released from jail. "Oh my God," he exclaimed. "Simon, look at this!" Simon had started to walk away, but hearing the amazement in Lee's tone, he came back and looked over his shoulder.

"Holy shit! It's Sandra—detained overnight for questioning! Red spray paint?" Simon exchanged a knowing look with Lee. "She was stopped near the doctor's house. Do you think? Our little Sandra. So pure. 'Only doing God's work.'" He mimicked her southern accent. "Wow." Simon started thinking about Sandra in a new light. She had been manipulating them all along. Even Patricia. When Simon had moved out to Litchfield from the city, he had assumed that nothing ever happened in this idyllic suburban town. Boy, had he been wrong.

EIGHTY-ONE

❧

*L*oren Elliot tried to hold back the tears, but they just kept coming. Whether she was at home or at work, the topic of conversation was abortion. At home, Peter was continually talking about the demonstration and wanting her to find a different clinic. At the paper, all the reporters were working on stories having to do with abortion. Whether they were researching the Supreme Court, the history of the pro-life movement, or *Roe v. Wade*, they were constantly comparing notes and debating the issues. She couldn't take her mind off her situation. Even Emily, when they were driving to work or coming home, talked nonstop about the topic.

She sat at her desk in her cubicle with the gray dividers and thought of Emily when she was a baby. Strawberry-blond curls, wide blue eyes, sweet little round nose. She was a happy baby, always smiling and gurgling with excitement. What would this new baby look like? Loren's hand went instinctively to her belly. *Don't think about it as a baby. Try not to think about it at all.* But, here she was. Fixated. Was it a boy or a girl? Would it look like Emily or Marshall? Marshall had Peter's black hair and dark eyes. She wiped her nose on the last tissue she had and decided to go to the ladies' room to hide in one of the stalls until she felt more in control. She peered around the divider into the empty hallway. Putting her head down, she quickly walked to the ladies' room.

Once inside the swinging door, she locked herself in one of the stalls and sat on the toilet, wiping her nose with inadequate pieces of toilet paper. She just wanted the procedure to be over. The pregnancy was making her very emotional—her hormones were toying with her rationality. *Stay focused on finding a full-time job, one with health benefits.* She couldn't even fit into her one good suit. She had to think of her whole family, about paying the mortgage, saving their home, keeping Emily and Marshall in school. Making sure that the kids got a good education had been their goal for more than 20 years. She just couldn't take on a new baby. She let out a loud sob, just as Emily swung open the bathroom door and marched in. Emily stopped in her tracks and stared at the tan metal door. Loren stared at the same door from the other side. A minute passed while Emily debated whether to say anything. Then she recognized her mother's sneakers.

"Mom? Are you okay?" Emily asked.

"Yes, I'm fine," choked Loren, but when she spoke she started to cry again. Waves of wrenching sobs filled the bathroom.

Emily continued to stare at the door. "Mom, what's wrong?"

Loren tried to control her heaving sobs. She started to collect toilet paper from the roll, but it kept breaking off in small pieces. She dropped the little slips of paper on the floor and they started to pile up at her feet. The more frantically she pulled, the smaller the pieces. "Dammit," she said under her breath.

"There's a whole roll out here," offered Emily, who was watching the toilet tissue float to the ground like flakes of light, dried snow.

Loren wiped her face as best she could, stood up, and opened the stall door. Her eyes were red and swollen, her nose was running, and pieces of toilet tissue were stuck to the bottom of her sneakers. Emily held out the roll of toilet paper. Loren took the roll and went to sit on the couch.

"Is it Dad's job? Or...is there something else?" asked Emily.

"I'm sorry, Emily. I don't want you to see me like this. I'm fine. Really..." Her thought trailed off, and she started sobbing again.

Emily sat next to her mother on the couch and hugged her. Loren cried harder. "He'll get another job," Emily said confidently.

Loren looked up at her daughter. Emily had recently had her hair cut in a stylish bob and looked very grown-up. Loren couldn't help but reach out and touch Emily's soft cheek.

"Mom, are you sure you're all right? Because I really have to go," Emily stammered. "Greeley's letting me write a small piece on older women who have abortions, and...Mom, what's the matter?"

Loren's face had turned bright scarlet, and her eyes bulged out of her face. She started to choke. Emily patted her on the back. "Mom! Mom!" Loren got up and walked over to the sink, where she threw cold water on her face. "God, Mom, you're scaring me."

Loren said, "Go. I'll be fine. Write your piece. It's a good opportunity for you."

"Are you sure?" Emily stood awkwardly in the middle of the bathroom, turning one ankle toward the door.

"Yes, I'll see you later." Loren looked up and tried to smile.

Emily hesitated, her eyes thick with concern. Loren nodded her head. "Okay," agreed Emily, and left the bathroom.

Loren turned back to the sink and let the cold water run on her wrists. She took a few deep breaths and decided that she was going home for the day. Let Greeley fire her. She didn't care.

$\mathcal{E}$IGHTY-$\mathcal{T}$WO

᪥

$\mathcal{A}$gnes' head was getting heavy in Clara's lap as she sat in the backseat of the car waiting for her mother to repack the suitcases. She looked down and pushed the hair out of Agnes's face, so peaceful, so serene. Like a volcano after the eruption. Clara just wanted her mother to get going at this point. She was sorry that she had lost her temper, but sometimes her mother had tunnel vision. Her mother was tuned to one channel, the Agnes channel. Clara tried to tell herself that it didn't matter. *More pressing things need to take priority. Urgent things. Like my appointment tomorrow morning.* There would be another time to talk to her mother about how she felt, but today she needed to focus on Michael and make sure he would be there for her. She would have to call him and try to see him tonight. She sensed that if she was just nice to him, he would do anything for her. She decided she would smile and be pleasant. Maybe suggest a movie, anything to stay away from his apartment.

Her mother had put on the air conditioning when she had started the car for the girls, and now Clara was getting cold.

Goose bumps sprang up on her arms, but her legs were sweating under Agnes's thick hair. Clara reached out toward the controls on the dashboard, but her arms weren't long enough. Just as she decided to move Agnes onto the seat, the back door of the house swung open, and her mother emerged, pushing one suitcase out the door in front of her and pulling another behind. Clara held Agnes's head as she slipped her legs out from under her, opened the back door of the car, and went to grab one of the suitcases. Her mother and she avoided looking at each other as they put the suitcases in the trunk.

"Dad should be home by six-thirty. I left lasagna. I'll have my cell on all the time. Clara, I'm..."

"Don't worry, Mom. It's okay." Clara reached out to hug her mother, and when she pulled back, there were tears in both of their eyes.

"I love you," said Mrs. Mahoney.

"I love you too, Mom," said Clara.

ℰIGHTY-𝒯HREE

෧

𝒯rust. Patricia realized now that she had allowed herself to trust Sandra Stett. Why in the world, on God's green earth, had she allowed herself to do that? She wasn't usually a trusting person. Had she really been vulnerable to Sandra's southern charm? Patricia didn't think of herself as naïve or easily manipulated. No, she just had not been paying attention. She had been negligent, she admitted to herself. She wasn't planning on admitting it to anyone else, especially Salvatore, but she had to admit it to herself. Who was this woman, Sandra Stett, who lied to the police, possibly vandalized property, and recruited the poor to act as pawns in her pageant?

Patricia also had to admit to herself that this whole demonstration was Sandra's brainchild. Patricia had thought, up to this minute, that it was her idea, but she realized now that Sandra had put the idea in her head and then had made it easy for Patricia to think that it was her idea. Patricia wondered if Sandra had been let out of jail, or if they had locked her up when Patricia wouldn't confirm her alibi. As she sat at her computer trying to call up the organization's checking account online, the door burst open, and Father O'Malley bounded in unannounced.

"Patricia, have you been able to get to the bottom of this news about the demonstrators being bused in from Smithtown? Do I have to tell you that our reputations are on the line? In particular, my reputation, because let me remind you, you have conveniently worked it out so that *you* will not be at this demonstration. And now, I will be standing amidst a sea of people who have been bused in for a photo op. Patricia, I am beside myself...." Here, Father O'Malley petered out and put his hands over his eyes and pressed down on his temples.

Patricia was sitting in her antique chair behind her immaculate antique desk. She looked up at Father O'Malley with a truly distraught look on her face. She listened and knew that she had to buy time to find out what was going on in her own organization. She didn't want to own up to the fact that she had virtually no idea about the details of the demonstration.

"Thomas," she started. Her voice was soothing and full of concern. "Thomas, I only just got into the office. My event organizer isn't here. She must be out taking care of last-minute details. I have asked for a full report on all aspects of Saturday's event. I'm sure you're busy...."

"Patricia, don't give me your slick treatment. This is serious. What the hell is going on?" Father O'Malley's voice was raised, and he leaned over Patricia's desk, steadying his weight on both of his hands. He leaned so far over that his face was not far from Patricia's face. She recoiled and sat back in her seat.

"Thomas, do *not* raise your voice at me," she warned.

"I'm past caring about what you want...."

"How dare you?" Patricia's eyes were like daggers.

"Patricia, it's *my* face that is going to be all over the newspapers and Channel Six. It's my reputation that will go down to the depths of hell. I could lose my parish. What will you lose? You'll just move on to the next distraction...."

"Distraction?" Patricia was now standing on her side of the desk, roaring back. "Is that what you think this is for me? A distraction?" she shrieked.

"Yes. That's what everyone thinks," Father O'Malley yelled, nostrils flaring.

Patricia's hand went up to her chest. She looked aghast. Her breath was coming fast.

"You'll just go back to your protected life with your army of servants, but where will I go? You'll go back to your family, your husband, your children, but what parish will take me in?"

"Thomas, you're overreacting. You're not preaching against the church. What you're doing is totally in line with…"

"You know it's not that simple. Nominating committees don't want troublemakers."

Outside, in the hall, a clean and composed Sandra Stett listened to their argument, wondering how she could turn this moment to her advantage. Should she burst in, or wait until he left? Sandra thought Patricia and the priest both might turn against her, united in their anger and self-interest, but she looked to heaven, and God told her this was her moment. She threw open the door and stepped inside the room, shutting the door behind her.

Her voice was calm and soothing as she started, "When the people protest in Washington, D.C. or New York City, do they all come from Washington and New York?" she asked in an even voice. "Luke says, 'Jesus traveled about from one town and village to another, proclaiming the good news of the Kingdom of God.' He goes on to talk about the people who traveled with him. It doesn't matter where a person lives if he believes in God's word. Father O'Malley, you certainly know this to be true."

Patricia and Father O'Malley were so shocked by Sandra's unexpected entrance into the room that they stood staring at her, speechless. Patricia was the first to recover.

"So, they let you out of jail? Come in. You have a lot of explaining to do," commanded Patricia. Sandra took another step toward the center of the office. Father O'Malley fell into one of the leather chairs in front of Patricia's desk, looking spent and pale. Patricia smoothed her skirt and sat down, taking a deep breath through her nose.

"I ran a stop sign," stated Sandra, looking earnest.

"What?" asked Patricia sharply.

"I ran a stop sign and the police pulled me over. I got flustered and I told the cop I had driven you home. I thought if I mentioned your name they would let me go, but the cop went nuts and tried to get me to step out of the car. I was afraid, so I didn't, and he yanked open the door and a can of spray paint fell out. I had bought it for the signs for the protest. It was all a misunderstanding." Patricia stared at Sandra, and Sandra boldly met her gaze.

"I don't know what the two of you are talking about, but are the protesters coming from Smithtown?" asked Father O'Malley in a tired voice.

"Some of them," said Sandra, calm and confident. "It doesn't matter where they come from."

"But it does, you stupid girl," said Patricia. "We're not in Galilee. This is Litchfield. Why didn't you consult me on this? And how much is it costing me?" Patricia had come around from behind her desk to confront Sandra.

"You weren't here. I needed to move forward...."

"So, it's going to be me preaching to poor black folks?" said Father O'Malley to no one in particular.

"Reverend Turnipseed..." started Sandra.

"Reverend Turnipseed!" exploded Father O'Malley. "That poor excuse for a man of God! Is that who is bringing the protesters?"

"Who's Reverend Turnipseed?" asked Patricia.

"He's the minister at the Baptist A.M.E. Church in Smithtown. He was just brought up on charges of bilking old ladies out of their life's savings..." Father O'Malley blurted out.

"Enough," shouted Patricia. "I have heard enough. Now, the three of us are in this together, whether we like it or not. The demonstration is less than forty-eight hours away. We've got to pull ourselves together and get our heads in the game. Let's think. We have to strategize. What is our game plan...?"

Sandra smiled inwardly. Patricia was not going to cancel the demonstration. Everything was working out. Sandra's plan would be implemented. They all moved over to sit at the table and go over the details.

&IGHTY-&FOUR

⤚

olly Dolan was never naked. Even without clothes, her body was adorned. Michael came out of the shower and stood looking at her as she slept. Her most shocking tattoo was a snake whose head started in the middle of her stomach, his long skinny tongue darting out right above her belly button, and then his colorful body swirled its way down in a huge S, slithering through her pubic hair and ending, ostensibly, in her vagina. Its scales were green and red and yellow, and one of its eyes was winking. Around her right ankle was a daisy chain and on her left breast was a heart with an M. She had gotten the heart tattoo when she and Michael were dating, but she had pointed out to him that it could stand for Michael *or* Molly.

Besides the ink, she had an assortment of rings, jewels, and silver rods stuck in her ears, nose, eyebrow, tongue, one nipple, and her belly button. She also wore silver rings on most of her fingers and a few of her toes. As he stood there looking down at her, he thought, she was more like a piece of art than a sleeping woman. She looked exotic now at 22, but Michael hated to think of what she would look like at 52 and beyond. He walked over to his dresser and grabbed a pair of boxers. The sound of the drawer woke her up.

"You all showered already, baby?" she purred.

"I think you took some skin off my pecker with that thing in your tongue," he replied, and continued to get dressed. "Go take a shower. I gotta go to work. First, I want to take all your crap back to your apartment."

Molly was now wide awake. She sat up in bed, pulling the soiled sheet around her. "What the hell, Michael? What's going on? I'm confused. Last night you couldn't get enough of me, and now you're throwing me out?" She got up, walked over to where he stood, and confronted him, stark naked.

"I'm not throwing you out. It's just that…I don't want to hurt you. You know you're only here because Casandra died and we were pushed together. We shouldn't let it go on. It'll be worse for you the longer you stay here." Michael looked down at her and knew she was going to start crying. He hated that. Women always resorted to crying when they didn't get their way. "You know I'm right," he said defensively.

"You're not right. We're good together." She reached out to touch his arm and he pulled it away from her.

"I'm going to get us some breakfast. When I get back, I want you to be dressed and packing." He walked toward the door without looking at her again. *Just keep walking. You're almost at the door.* He heard some movement behind him, but kept walking, until the beer bottle hit him in the back of the head.

He stopped in his tracks, gathered his wits, scrunched his hands into fists, and continued out the door, slamming it behind him. Once outside, he rubbed his head and cursed her. He didn't care. He wanted to stay focused. He had to have her out of the apartment, so he could talk to Clara on the phone, and he hoped, see her tonight. He glanced at his phone. Two missed calls, neither from Clara. He got in the Mustang, pulled out of the parking lot, and the phone rang. It was her.

"Hello?" he answered.

"Michael?"

He felt tongue-tied. He was starting to sweat. "Yeah. Hi. How are you?"

"Okay. Michael, I went to The Sportsman last night to see you…." Her voice sent ripples down his spine.

"You did?"

"Yes, I was wondering if I could see you tonight? If you're not busy…"

"No. I'm not busy. Where should I pick you up?"

Clara paused, then said, "I'll meet you in the park again. At eight-thirty. Near the tennis courts."

"I'll see you there."

"See you there."

Michael pressed the disconnect button on his phone. He smiled. *Wow! Just like a fantasy.* He wondered why she wanted to see him. Maybe she no longer needed him tomorrow. Maybe she had told her parents. He doubted that, because why would she want to meet him then? If she had told them, the cops would be coming to see him. Maybe she liked him. He was a good-looking guy. The ladies always went for him. Somehow that seemed too good to be true. He felt like he had won the lottery, been handed a gift. A devious thought started in the back of his brain. It started out fuzzy, and then there it was, clearly formed in his frontal lobe. She was pregnant already. There was no reason for them not to be together again.

$\mathcal{E}$IGHTY-$\mathcal{F}$IVE

&

$\mathcal{T}$he fresh air felt good on Father O'Malley's face as he walked back to St. Raymond's after his confrontation with Patricia. The late afternoon sun was bright and he put on his black sunglasses as he hurried back to the rectory to meet with a couple who wanted to set their wedding date. A priest with a scowl would surely frighten them off. He wanted to shake off his anger and frustration before he reached the church, but his mind wouldn't let go of the facts. It was already Thursday. In two days, he would be standing in front of hundreds of protesters, mostly bused in from Smithtown, who were only there for a photo op. He had never envisioned his involvement with the demonstration turning out this way. Originally, he thought he would stand next to Patricia at the podium and listen to her talk about the evils of abortion and the work of her organization. Now, he was the one that would be standing at the podium—alone. He had only agreed to be a part of it because Patricia and Salvatore were such large donors to St. Raymond's. *Money is truly the root of all evil.*

As he rounded the turn in the road and started to climb the stairs to the church, his cell phone rang. He looked down at the number. Now what? He grimaced as he answered the call.

"Yes."

Pause.

"Things are very busy for me now, with the demonstration on Saturday. Could we meet…"

Pause.

"Tonight is not the best time for me."

Pause.

"No. No. Of course, I know you feel all alone."

Pause.

"Okay. Okay. Come in the back. Come as late as possible."

Could this day possibly get any worse? He opened the rectory door and saw her standing in the shadows. He just caught a hint of her shiny, gold hair in the light streaming in from the stained-glass window at the end of the hall. She had called him from his office.

ΕIGHTY-ΣIX

୶

Sandra needed white demonstrators. She had to make sure that there were some white people in the crowd when Father O'Malley spoke, and she hoped that Reverend Turnipseed could help her. It just wouldn't look like a Litchfield event if everyone were black. Patricia was right about that.

After Father O'Malley had stormed out of Patricia's office, the real interrogation had begun. Patricia was not really mad that Sandra had recruited protesters from out of town, she was just mad that the mayor and Father O'Malley had read about it in the paper first. Actually, she was mad that it had run in the paper at all. Sandra had a few ideas about who Helen Acker's source was but she would straighten that out later. Patricia wasn't thrilled with the $5,000 payment to Reverend Turnipseed, but she understood that business had its costs. Sandra had also confessed that she was paying the demonstrators for showing up. Now it would be easier for Sandra to prepare the money for the stipends without having to hide it from Patricia.

As for Sandra's arrest, Patricia had told her that they would talk about it at length after Saturday. For now, Patricia had made it clear that Sandra was never to utter her name again when she was trying to get herself out of trouble. But Sandra knew that Patricia needed her to get through Saturday, and Patricia wasn't going to let a little suspected mischief get in her way. She had told Sandra to work something out with the Baptist preacher to make sure the demonstration didn't look like a prayer meeting at his church. "Find some white people" were Patricia's parting words before she kicked Sandra out of her office.

Sandra sat in her own small office, praying that Reverend Turnipseed would pick up his phone. This was her third attempt to get him in 10 minutes. She didn't want to leave a message and she didn't really want to drive over to Smithtown, but she would if she had to. Finally, after the ninth ring, she heard the reverend clearing his throat before he drawled, prolonging each vowel, "Was just reading *watch.com*. Have you seen your article? Really, Miss Sandra..."

"Look, I don't have time for this, Reverend Turnipseed. We need to have a frank discussion and meeting of the minds about how the demonstration is going to look on Saturday."

"How do you mean, gonna 'look'?" asked the reverend, nice and slow, like he was discussing the weather.

"I mean...it can't just be Father O'Malley and a bunch of..."

"Spit it out, Miss Sandra. You're talkin' to a friend. Are you trying to say black folk? Is that what you're trying to say, Miss Sandra?" he poured on a thick, black southern accent.

"There's been some discussion here about bringing in protesters from another town. We were wondering if...there are any..."

"C'mon, Miss Sandra," encouraged the reverend.

"Fine! Can you get us any white folks?" Sandra blurted out.

Sandra heard the reverend start to laugh. It was a deep, dark, melodious sound that started somewhere in the reverend's chest and rose up slowly to emerge as part song, part cough, from the smile on his face. "Well, let's see now. I think the white folks that I gotta get will charge a little bit more than the black folks I already got."

Sandra bared her teeth at the phone. "How much more, and can you get them?"

"See, here's the problem. I'm gonna have ta pay the black folks I already got, and then I gotta pay the new white folks. But I think I can get a hundred for fifty dollars a head."

"Fifty!" exploded Sandra. "That's outrageous. Twenty-five." Sandra again heard the deep laugh that was even jollier than it was a few moments ago. She knew that she had to pay. "Okay. Forty."

"Fifty and that's final. I gotta go. My next meeting's here, Miss Sandra. Yes or no?"

"Damn you, all right!" Sandra slammed down the phone. She did a quick calculation. $5,000. Well, it was done. She had to move on.

EIGHTY-SEVEN

❧

After dinner, Pia had to lie down. She wanted to clean up the post-dinner mess, but she just couldn't. Every inch of her body was in pain, and she was nauseous. She didn't think the spaghetti dinner had agreed with her. Stella told her not to be ridiculous about the dishes. She told her to go and take a rest. Reluctantly, Pia climbed the stairs as Maria, Carmen, and Stella cleared the table. George had taken Juan out for ice cream. As they scrubbed pots and put leftovers in the refrigerator, Carmen's cell phone started to ring. It was Sylvia, a friend from school.

"Take your call, honey," said Stella. "Your sister and I will do the rest." When Carmen looked at her guiltily, Stella said, "Go, shoo. Talk to your friend." Carmen smiled and ran downstairs to the basement, where there was a comfy couch.

Maria stood at the sink, rinsing the dishes and putting them in the dishwasher. She looked over at her aunt, who was pouring sauce from a pan into a Tupperware container. Stella had lightened her jet-black hair to a rich, chestnut brown with a few golden highlights. Maria thought it looked chic. Aunt Stella looked like her mother, but prettier. Her features were more delicate, and her eyes were hazel, not black like Pia's. Although Stella had five children, she was very slim, with long legs and large breasts. Maria looked down at her own growing bustline and secretly hoped that hers would never be as big as Stella's. She didn't want any men looking at her. Her father had looked at her, and it scared and repulsed her. She wanted to stay with Stella forever, never wanting to go back to her father's house, never wanting to see him again. He was dead, as far she was concerned.

Stella looked over at Maria and saw a ferocious look on her young face. "Maria? Are you all right?" Maria looked at Stella as if she were surprised that she was there. She had been so absorbed in her own thoughts that Stella's voice seemed to come from another world.

"Yes, I'm all right," she said, unconvincingly.

"Maria, I know that you have been through a lot. But, you're going to be okay. Your mother's going to be okay. She's going back to the doctor tomorrow. I'm taking her in the morning."

"I'll go with her."

"No, I need you to stay here to look after Juan and Carmen. Okay?" Neither Pia nor Stella would ever involve Maria in Pia's visit to the clinic the next day. They had agreed that Maria would be told she had to look after the younger children.

"I hate him, you know. I wish he were dead. I really do," she said, with hatred streaming out of her dark eyes. She felt light-headed with the force of her hatred.

"I know. I know." Stella went over to Maria at the sink and wrapped her arms around her. "If it's any consolation, I think he will be in jail for a long time. You don't have to see him. You and Carmen and your mother can stay here, with me, for as long as you want."

"Will I have to testify? Will I have to tell them what happened? Will he be there? Watching me? In the same room? I couldn't bear it, Auntie Stella. I just couldn't bear it." She shuddered and buried her face in Stella's neck.

Stella hesitated because she truly did not know the answer to those questions. Maria might have to testify. "Let's not think about it now. I'm not sure exactly what will happen. I'll try to find out from Detective Bickford. He seems very nice. Listen, Maria, I want you to call a friend, have some fun. You need to get your mind off of all of this. Try to make a plan for tomorrow." She leaned away from Maria to look her in the eyes, but Maria put her head down on Stella's shoulder. "Do you think you could do that? Your friends are welcome here."

"But you said I had to watch the children."

"Well, tomorrow night, then. Go out tomorrow night or invite someone here. Will you do that?"

"I'll think about it. I don't want to answer their questions. Both of my parents have been in the paper all week. All of my friends must know what happened. And I don't want them to see my mother." Maria walked over to the huge Viking stove and started to wash down the burners.

"Then we'll get some movies and have movie night. How does that sound?"

Maria looked at her aunt and tried to smile. "Better."

EIGHTY-EIGHT

❧

A little after 8:00 on Thursday night, Michael drove to the park to meet Clara. He couldn't get Molly's screaming out of his head. *She can curse dirtier than any of the guys at The Sportsman.* She came up with combinations of religious figures, animals, and indecent acts that just weren't right. His hand went to the scratches on his cheek. They really hurt. He had used every ounce of self-restraint not to smack her back. He knew if he started, it would be hard to stop. So, instead, he just grabbed her by the wrists and dragged her into her apartment, threw her on the couch, and then went and emptied her stuff in the parking lot and drove away. He knew he had not seen the last of her, but he hoped she wouldn't bother him tonight.

Tonight. He had been thinking about tonight all day. After he dumped Molly off and went to work for a few hours, he had gone to Target and bought new sheets for his bed. All the ones he had were stained and torn, and if he could get Clara back to the apartment, he wanted it to be nice for her. He had chosen sheets with a blue-and-gold stripe which looked very expensive but were actually on sale. Then he had sprung for a new navy-blue down comforter. He had opened a Target credit-card account to get the bedding, because after he paid for the abortion tomorrow, he would pretty much be broke.

He really hoped the baby was his, because he was a dumb fuck if it wasn't. Then the joke would be on him. He didn't want to think of sweet, innocent Clara being with another guy, so he decided to believe that it was his. She just didn't look like the kind of girl who fooled around that much. She wasn't a virgin. He knew that. But still, she wasn't flirtatious, like that blond friend of hers. Now, that one, you couldn't trust that one. She was sexy, but she was sexy trouble. If you had sex with her you were in trouble. No, Michael preferred Clara's vulnerable smile, her dimples, and her dark, unruly hair.

He was almost at the park, so he took out a pack of Juicy Fruit gum and put a stick in his mouth. He was nervous. How crazy was that? Since he was a teenager he had had so many girls, but this one was different. After turning the Mustang into the park, Michael started to drive around the outer loop to the tennis courts. It was 8:15 when he parked the car and decided to sit outside on the hood. It was the end of June, one of those delicious summer nights. The ice cream truck played "Happy Days Are Here Again." He spotted her walking toward him through the soccer field. She looked so feminine in her loose turquoise shirt and jeans, her long hair dancing around her face on the cool evening breeze. Michael felt excited. First-day-of-school excited. Good, yet nervous. Anything could happen.

Suddenly, Clara looked up and smiled at him and he felt the tension drain from his body. He decided to let her come to him. It seemed to take forever for her to walk over to his car. He stared at her, memorizing her every movement, so that he could think about it later. The way her hips swayed, the way she pushed a stray wisp of hair from her eye, the way her long, delicate arms moved, her profile when she turned her grace-ful neck to the side. Then, he started to feel too excited and couldn't look at her anymore. He looked down at his muscular arms and flat stomach. He was wearing a white v-neck T-shirt, faded jeans, and a black leather belt. His black, wavy hair was parted on the side and neatly combed.

"Hi," she said when she finally reached him. He fought the urge to take her in his arms and kiss her on the mouth. He took a deep breath.

"Hey, long walk." He pointed his chin toward the soccer field.

"Yeah." She smiled and laughed. Her cheeks broke into dimples, and her eyes twinkled.

Michael laughed. *She's flirting with me.* "So, where do you want to go?" he asked.

"I don't know. The movies?" All of a sudden, she looked upset. "What happened to your face?" Michael's hand went to the scratches on his face.

"I got in a little scuffle. It's nothing," Michael said dismissively. "Is there something you want to see? At the movies?"

"Let's just drive out to the Cineplex and see whatever comes on next," she suggested, tilting her face to look at him. He jumped lightly off the hood of the car and walked over to the passenger door, which he opened for her.

"Your chariot awaits, m'lady," he said, smiling. Clara got in the car. Michael ran around to his side, got in, and they drove to the large movie theater out on Route 63. Inside were 12 theaters, all showing different movies. "Iron Man 2" was the next show to start. He bought her candy, popcorn, and soda, and then watched her eat it all. He ate a Kit Kat. The movie stunk. As Michael pretended to watch Robert Downey, Jr. cavort around in his iron suit, he was tempted to put his arm around Clara. He watched her out of the corner of his eye, in the flickering light of the dark theater, and had to resist the urge to touch her. He spent half of the time trying to decide how to get Clara to go back to his apartment, and the other half worrying that Molly would be there if he did.

Clara was feeling a little less anxious. Now she felt confident that he would come tomorrow morning and pick her up. She just had to get through the movie and figure out some way to get him to take her home without pissing him off. He was being very nice. He was funny and seemed to be genuinely concerned about her. She decided to wait and see what happened. Maybe he would just take her home. That was probably too good to hope for.

The movie ended, and they waded out to his car through the mob of people hurrying into the parking lot. Michael and Clara were both tense about what would happen next. The easy conversation that they had shared going into the movie theater was gone. Clara was quiet, and Michael tried to lighten up the mood by cracking stupid jokes, which even he didn't think were funny.

They got in the car, but Michael didn't turn it on. Young men and women walked between the cars, holding hands, laughing, yelling to each other. Sitting in the car, Clara felt like she was underwater in a glass boat, watching the people, like fish, swim by, talking, changing direction, moving away, but she couldn't hear what they were saying.

"Well, thank you. I should go home," she said tentatively.

"Why'd you want to see me?" he asked suddenly. He had adjusted himself in his seat and was half-turned to her. His big, black eyes looked sad.

She looked at him and felt this was not going to be easy. "I… just…wanted to make sure about tomorrow." As the words left her mouth, she wished she had said something more complimentary. She wished she had said she just wanted to see him.

"Oh."

"I mean, I wanted to see how you were and talk about tomorrow." He suddenly reached out his hand and ran his finger down the side of her face.

"I missed you," he said softly. Clara looked down, feeling embarrassed and a little frightened. She didn't really feel that she could say she missed him too. She wasn't a good liar, and since she had spent the last few weeks hating him, she wasn't sure how it would come out. She finally just looked up at him with her deep-blue eyes and long black lashes, with such an earnest face that without thinking, he moved in and kissed her gently on the lips. He ran his fingers through her soft hair and pulled her to him. She felt his energy coursing through his body. It was like electricity. He kissed her deeply. She felt lost and wanted to push him away, but knew that she couldn't. When he pulled away, his eyes were still closed. He sucked in air through his nose, put the key in the ignition, and started the car. The parking lot had emptied out, and he wound his way back onto the highway.

"You'll come for me tomorrow morning at eight-thirty?" she asked hesitantly.

"Let's not talk about it yet." He reached over and put his hand possessively on her thigh and kept it there. She looked down at his big hand on her little leg. Her eyes moved up from his hand to his tanned, muscular forearm, and then up to his bulging bicep. She was both intimidated by and intrigued with this muscular arm. She knew he could hurt her with it. She knew he could use it to hold her down. He squeezed her thigh when they got to a red light, and she saw the muscle tighten and relax. She felt a little weak, scared. They drove silently through town, and she knew he was taking her to his apartment. She didn't know how to stop him. She couldn't fight with him and expect him to pay $600 tomorrow to get rid of her problem. Whatever happened, she had to get rid of the problem.

They got to the Green Street Apartments and Michael slowed down. He scanned the lot for Molly's car, but didn't see it. After parking in his space, he got out of the car and went and opened her door. Clara looked up at him. Extending his hand, he helped her out of the car. They walked upstairs and he let them in. The apartment was bigger than she remembered it and cleaner. What she didn't know was that Molly had been cleaning it for the past week. Clara walked to the middle of the living room and didn't know what to do or say. It was obvious to her that they were there to have sex and that conversation was unimportant. While she was lost in her thoughts, he came up behind her and put his arms around her, sticking his nose in her apple-scented hair. He felt the hard swelling of her stomach with both his hands and then started to travel up to her swollen breasts. When he gently squeezed them, she gasped and arched her back slightly. The pain felt good in a way she didn't understand. He kissed the side of her neck, and she closed her eyes.

"Michael, don't." Clara took a step forward and turned to look at him.

"You're already pregnant, Clara, and I want you so bad," he said, putting his forefinger under her chin and lifting her face to his. "You're so beautiful. I can't stop thinking about you. I can smell your shampoo when I close my eyes."

"I..." But before she could protest further, he pulled her to him and kissed her, long and deep. She felt weak. All her strength left her, and her knees started to fold under her. Then he picked her up in his arms and carried her to the bedroom and put her down gently on the new dark-blue comforter.

She knew she would do anything to make sure he was there for her tomorrow.

EIGHTY-NINE

❧

*I*t was Friday morning, and Dr. Friedberg noticed that the knot of tension in her stomach grew tighter with each passing day. She kept revisiting her decision not to close the clinic on Saturday. Her gut was telling her that she was doing the right thing, but still, she had her doubts. The girl who insisted on coming during the demonstration was going to be all over the television and the newspapers and there was nothing that Dr. Friedberg could do about it. She kept reminding herself that because the clinic provided a host of services, the press could not be certain that the girl was having an abortion that morning. Still, Dr. Friedberg wished she had been successful in convincing the girl to come on another day.

Dr. Friedberg shook her head and looked down at the growing pile of mail on her desk. She picked up a bunch of envelopes and started to leaf through them. One was an invitation to be the keynote speaker at the National Abortion Federation Annual Dinner. The topic was the IUD, or the intrauterine device. Dr. Friedberg thought that the IUD was one of the most effective forms of birth control, because once inserted, it stayed in place and human error was taken out of the picture. She liked to recommend it to teenage girls, because they don't ordinarily have sex in the same place each time, and they don't want their parents to find their birth control pills or diaphragm. Insert it and forget about it and it's 99 percent effective. Dr. Friedberg had decided to talk to the 16-year-old who was coming in today about this form of birth control.

She flipped through a pamphlet that had been stuck in the invitation. Her eye ran down some of the quick bullets on the inside cover:

- *1.2 million abortions are safely performed each year;*
- *abortion is the most common surgical procedure performed on American women; and*
- *one in three women will have had an abortion by the time she is 45 years old.*

Dr. Friedberg put the invitation down and rubbed her eyes. She thought back to her days at medical school when she had joined Medical Students for Choice, a group started in California by med students who wanted abortion training taught in their schools and in their residency programs. She had formed a chapter of the group at UPenn and had convinced the administration to include lectures about abortion in the medical-school curriculum. She still kept abreast of what was going on in the medical schools, because what the students were taught was the key to the future.

Enough reverie. She picked up her schedule for the day. Her first patient, Pia Fernandez, had to be the same woman whose husband was all over the news today. Now here was a woman in crisis. Married to an alleged murderer. Just out of the hospital. Physically beaten. Worried about her children. Dr. Friedberg's heart went out to this unknown woman, and she wanted to help her. She hoped that Pia was strong enough emotionally for the procedure today. Although it would put her schedule behind, the doctor wanted to spend some extra time with Pia.

Dr. Friedberg took a sip of coffee, a bite of bagel, and sat back in her chair. Slipping her glasses off her nose, she rubbed her eyes. When she opened them, she glanced at the photo of her mother on her desk and realized that she was beginning to look more and more like the woman in the photograph. She remembered her own crisis with her stepfather, and felt grateful that her mother had supported her through her abortion. She hoped that Pia had someone she could turn to for support.

$\mathcal{N}$ I N E T Y

❧

$\mathcal{J}$amie Ross got out of bed and groggily made his way to Fiona's apartment door early Friday morning. He opened the door, and still half asleep, picked up *The Press*. Although this was his first morning in her apartment, he knew that Fiona would have her paper delivered to her door, as all reporters do. He tucked it under his arm and went into the kitchen, where the automatically timed coffee pot had finished brewing. He poured a large mug and sat down on one of the stools at the counter. Fiona didn't believe in air conditioning, so Jamie wore only his tight purple Hanes. He took a sip of coffee while he scanned the front page. When he read the most prominent headline, he spit the coffee all over the paper and started to choke.

He heard, "Are you awright?" coming sleepily from down the hall.

"God dammit! I've been scooped!"

"By who?" asked Fiona, walking half-asleep into the kitchen in a leopard-skin cami and matching thong. As if by remote control, she poured herself a cup of coffee and went over to Jamie.

"By you. By *The Press*! 'Search Reveals Nude Photos, Video-tape and Key to Dead Girl's Apt. at Fernandez House,' Jamie read out loud. "'An anonymous source detailed...'"

"Who wrote it? Helen?" asked Fiona, trying to look over Jamie's shoulder.

"No, Latitia. That bitch. Who's her source?" he growled.

"Settle down. You're getting your Hanes all in a bunch. You might hurt something," Fiona kneaded Jamie's neck. "You've gotta calm down."

"Cut it out." Jamie pushed Fiona away. "I've never been scooped before. This sucks. Look here. The mayor's holding a press conference at ten. Let's go? I need to take a shower first." Jamie headed down the hall. Fiona sat down on the stool and started to read the article.

Jamie came back and grabbed her by the arm, and without saying anything, pulled her toward the bathroom. "My coffee. It's spilling," complained Fiona.

Twenty minutes later, they were dressed and on their way to Town Hall in Jamie's Prius. Fiona was reading the article and summarizing, as they moved through the traffic. "The police have turned the evidence over to the prosecutor, and they expect Mayor Ceravolo to announce an indictment this morning. This guy sounds like a psycho. First, he kills Casandra, and then he beats his wife to a pulp in front of their daughter. What an asshole. That poor girl. I can't imagine being fifteen and watching my father try to kill my mother, and then having the smarts to call the police."

"Just imagine when she hears that her father killed his girl-friend, too. What a prize he must be. Hey, maybe I can get an interview...."

"Now you're talking crazy. Baby, I need a coffee. You spilled mine. Stop in at Starbucks. We have time," said Fiona, strug-gling to put on her large hoop earrings. Jamie glanced at the dashboard clock. She was right. They had 20 minutes before the press conference. He pulled into the Starbucks parking lot.

Once inside, they realized that DeShawn Fletcher and Latitia Blackman were on line in front of them. Jamie scowled when Fiona pointed them out, but Fiona called to Latitia.

"Hey, Lati! What's up? You scooping my man? Ruinin' my love life?" called Fiona.

Latitia turned around with a smile as big as Mick Jagger's, with maroon lipstick all over her front teeth.

"Baby," said DeShawn pointing to his front teeth.

"What?" said Latitia, rubbing her teeth with her finger. Finally, she turned her attention to Fiona and Jamie. "I scooped who? This little man?" she pointed to Jamie. "Since when is he your man?"

"He's big in the right places. Since when is big, black, and beautiful your man?" Fiona and Latitia had known each other since they were toddlers, when their mothers had put them in a play group together, so they felt more like sisters than friends. Jamie and DeShawn, not knowing this, felt violated, standing in Starbucks with their girlfriends describing them as if they weren't there.

"So anyway, Latitia, who's the loose lips down at police headquarters? I've been trailing Detective Bickford like a love-sick puppy. He hasn't told me squat," said Jamie with a pout.

"You! You're pissed? What about me? I wake up next to this woman and she hasn't shared shit with me. I read about it while she's taking a shower. Does she say, 'Baby, they found a video-tape and nude photos and a key to the dead girl's apartment. DeShawn, you better get yourself one of those photos for your newscast.' Does she say that as she throws me into bed last night and ravages me? No, not a word. I feel used," said DeShawn with a mock frown.

"Go back to your wife," said Latitia, poking DeShawn playfully in the ribs.

"Order your coffee, woman," said DeShawn.

DeShawn and Latitia ordered lattes and moved over so that Fiona and Jamie could order. "Really, Latitia, tell me who broke down and told you," whispered Jamie.

Latitia looked seriously at Jamie. "Listen you, you scoop us every day. We always have to read our stuff after yours. You'll just have to give us this one," she said, shaking her head at him. "He is cute, though, Fiona, well done." Then Latitia turned to DeShawn. "C'mon man, what you waitin' for?" She grabbed DeShawn by the tie and pulled him out the door.

"She's right. We never get the story before you and it's annoying sometimes. You always have the photo out there first. The headline. You name it, you got it first. I'm sure we won't scoop you again for a long time." Fiona smiled and looked up at Jamie, who was pouting. "Don't pout. You're too metrosexual to carry it off."

"What?" he exclaimed. But she was already on her way to the door, leaving him stranded in a line of people all pushing forward to spend $4.25 on espresso.

NINETY-ONE

❧

oren Elliot was already awake when the alarm went off. She felt drained and light-headed. She turned her head and saw Peter lying next to her, staring straight up at the ceiling.

"I hate this day," he said, letting his eyes trail over to the window. "Do you want to think about it? Babies are little. They don't eat much."

Loren sat up and swung her legs to the ground. She was wearing a sleeveless, light-green nightgown that was now too tight across her bosom, and her engorged breasts spilled out at the armholes. As she sat on the edge of the bed, a wave of nausea rose from her stomach to her throat. She closed her eyes and breathed in. When her stomach felt under control, she said, "Peter, this is our last day of health insurance. We have no choice. I'm going to take a shower."

Peter watched her walk slowly to the bathroom. He loved her so much, but how could they afford a baby? He was too old to raise another child. He was 47, almost 48. When the baby was 20, he would be almost 70. How would he ever put that one through college? He wearily got out of bed and went downstairs to make coffee. Loren couldn't drink coffee in her present state, it made her sick to her stomach. But he still needed his coffee so he could drive her to the clinic and sit there and wait for her. He felt guilty making the coffee. He knew she loved it. The first cup in the morning was her favorite. She always said after the first sip, "Ahh, it's all downhill from here," and they would laugh. Today, he knew she was right.

Peter had been worried all week about going to the clinic. How could it be that a pro-life demonstration would be happening there, at the very time his family needed the clinic services? He thought about the term "pro-life." He was pro-life. He had dedicated his whole life to the lives of his wife and two children. But he also believed that there were good times and bad times to bring a child into the world, and this was the worst possible time for him. He shook his head as he went back upstairs, carrying his coffee cup. He knew that he and Loren would get through this, but it was damn hard.

When he got upstairs, Loren was dressed and ready to go. She had pulled her red hair into a ponytail. Her eyes looked sad but determined. He wanted to hug her, but he was afraid he might start to cry.

"I'll take a quick shower," he said.

She gave him a half-smile and said, "I can't wait until tomorrow, when I can have all the coffee I can drink." Peter knew she was trying to lighten the mood.

"I'll get some French Vanilla. It's your favorite," he said.

They left Emily sleeping. She would get herself to work. Loren had debated over and over again if she wanted to tell Emily, but had decided against it. She didn't want Emily to worry, and she had to admit that she didn't want Emily to judge her. It was a private matter, between her and Peter.

As they drove to the clinic, they listened to the radio. The announcer was reading a report that the police had apparently found photographs, a videotape, and a key hidden in the house of the man who was being accused of killing the girl found in the Green Street Apartments. Loren forgot about her personal crisis for a moment, and allowed herself to feel encouraged by this news. After interviewing Molly and writing the story with Latitia, she was happy that the police now had evidence that linked Eduardo to the dead girl. She wanted him to be convicted. Yesterday, she knew that Greeley and Latitia were working on some breaking news, but she hadn't been told what it was.

As they turned onto Route 54, they saw the two burly security guards standing by the door of the clinic. "Jesus Christ," exclaimed Peter. He wanted to say that he told her they should have gone somewhere else, but he couldn't bring himself to berate her at this time.

"It makes me feel safer," she said, knowing what he was thinking. They pulled into the parking lot, and one of the security guards came over to walk them in. "The demonstration isn't until tomorrow. Is this really necessary?" asked Loren.

"Probably not," answered the hulking guard.

Once inside, Loren felt a little nervous. She signed in, and was given a clipboard with a few forms to fill out. Peter gave the receptionist their insurance information. As Loren sat down, two Hispanic women came in the front door. One was badly beaten with two black eyes, a healing split lip, and a broken nose. The bruised one sat down heavily in the first chair by the door, and the other one, who was well dressed and well coiffed, went over to the nurse's window and came back with a similar clipboard and forms. Loren looked over and involuntarily shuddered when she looked at the beaten woman's face. She quickly looked down.

Loren filled out her forms and waited. Finally, the receptionist called, "Mrs. Fernandez? Please come up to the desk for a moment."

Fernandez! Loren looked up again. Could that be the wife of Eduardo Fernandez? Latitia had seen the woman in the hospital and said that she was beaten to a pulp. That would surely describe this poor woman. She was the right age, but there were many women with the last name Fernandez. Loren looked at the battered woman in front of her. *Now, this is a woman who can't have a baby at this point in her life. Her husband is in jail. A murderer. Maybe she has nowhere to live. Other young children to worry about.* Loren compared her own life to what she knew of the battered woman's life. Loren was in a loving relationship. She knew she had one of the best marriages of any of her friends. She had wonderful relationships with her children. They had very little income right now, but that could change tomorrow. Peter could get a job any day. Maybe next week. Marshall and Emily would help. What was she doing?

"Peter..." she said picking up her purse. "Peter, let's get out of here."

Peter smiled—the first smile to grace his lips in days. He sprang out of his chair, took the clipboard out of Loren's hand, and walked over to the receptionist. "Mrs. Elliot is canceling her appointment."

Kathleen, the receptionist, looked up. "Are you sure?" she asked, looking at Loren.

"I'm sure," Loren said, putting her arm through Peter's and starting toward the door.

NINETY-TWO

❧

"He is *fiiiine*. Is that just a friend thing with benefits or more?" asked Latitia, as she and Fiona sat side-by-side in the two toilet stalls in the Town Hall ladies' room peeing out their $4.00 coffees.

"I'm not sure. We just hooked up yesterday, but it's been building for a few months. You know. The looks. The verbal jousting. The smiles. The insults that are really compliments. I felt really comfortable this morning. Not like I'd made a huge mistake. But, more importantly, what the hell? You and DeShawn? His baby's not even a year old," said Fiona.

Latitia flushed. "That is a problem," was all she said.

Both women came out of their stalls and headed to the sink. Fiona waited while Latitia washed her hands, and then they switched.

"Is he just stepping out, or did they break up?" asked Fiona.

"They had some fight and she took the baby and went home to Georgia, to her mother," explained Latitia, readjusting her yellow scarf. She was dressed in a form-fitting white spandex dress, gold belt, and yellow scarf, and with her three-inch heels, she stood 6' tall. Fiona felt tiny next to her.

"That's too bad," said Fiona. Latitia scowled. "You know what I mean. For the baby!" Latitia headed out into the hall. She checked her phone for the time.

"Ten minutes to go time. Let's get a seat. I can't stand in these shoes for an hour." Latitia sauntered down the hall. Assorted clerks, politicians, and security guards watched her. Fiona followed looking for Jamie. As they entered the Red Room, she spotted him in the third row, and took an empty seat next to him. Latitia grabbed a seat in the back, near DeShawn and his cameraman. Fiona noted that Helen and Gary, as well as Kit and Wren, were in the room. Although Fiona hadn't been covering this story, she felt she had a right to be there, because her beat was crime and women's issues.

At precisely ten o'clock, Mayor Ceravolo, Chief Chodor, and Detective Bickford entered the room from the door that led directly to the mayor's office. Their faces all wore the same serious expression. The mayor was hoping that this announcement would take some of the focus off of tomorrow's demonstration. After all, there hadn't been a murder in Litchfield since 1892. This was big news.

As the officials walked in, a hush fell over the room. The reporters all whipped out their iPads to take notes and photos. Jamie was taking video of the proceedings, and felt better already, because he knew that he would beat every other reporter with his story. An air of gravity permeated the room.

Mayor Ceravolo walked to the podium, looking dapper in a lime-green shirt with coordinating green-and-blue tie and pocket square. He looked straight into the Channel 6 camera in the back of the room and started, "Good morning. I want to announce that evidence has been found in the Casandra Keller murder case that directly links Eduardo Fernandez to the victim. Fernandez has been a person of interest in the case for some days, and after obtaining a warrant, Detective Bickford searched Fernandez's house and found, in a hidden, locked box, an incriminating video, photographs of the victim, and a key to Casandra Keller's apartment." The mayor stopped and looked sternly into the camera at the other end of the room.

"Fernandez will be indicted for murder in the first degree for the death of Casandra Keller, and for attempted murder in the presence of a minor for his assault on his wife, Pia Fernandez. He is being held without bail."

Quiet murmuring started amongst the reporters, and the mayor lifted his chunky hands to quiet them. "I'll take a few questions," he said.

Jamie's hand shot up. When the mayor nodded to him, he asked, "Have you seen the videotape?"

"No," said the mayor frowning and shaking his head. "Acker!" he called, when Helen raised her hand.

"Which case did you have a warrant to search the house for?"

The mayor stepped aside, and Detective Bickford took the microphone. "Helen, sorry to disappoint. This is not a case of "fruits of a poisonous tree" when we find something we're not supposed to be looking for. We had the proper warrant. We have a witness who will testify that he saw Fernandez at the Green Street Apartments on the day Miss Keller was murdered." All the reporters' hands flew up like birds stretching their wings. Bickford smiled. His pockmarked cheeks folded back on themselves like the pleats in an accordion as he held up his hand in anticipation of their question. "I am not at liberty at this time to disclose the name of the witness."

$\mathcal{N}$ INETY-$\mathcal{T}$ HREE

❧

$\mathcal{T}$rue to his word, at 8:25 Friday morning, Michael pulled up in front of Clara's house. The day matched his mood. The sky was overcast and gray, and the air was cool. Heavy clouds hung low, aching to rain. She had told him to wait in the car and she would come out. Absentmindedly, he chewed the inside of his cheek. What if something went wrong? Who would he contact? Just in case, he decided to ask her for her father's phone number, a request that he knew would freak her out, but it was the adult thing to do. The day before, at the bank, he had emptied out his accounts--$573 from savings and $50 from checking. Rent was due. He didn't know how he was going to pay it. Maybe he would have to ask Father O'Malley or Jay for a loan. He decided not to worry about it now. As he waited, he looked up at the house and thought he saw movement in one of the upstairs windows.

A few minutes later, Clara came out a side door, wearing a light-blue hoodie, jeans, and leather flip-flops. She did not smile when she greeted him. Looking scared to death, she climbed in the car. Her eyes were bloodshot, and dark circles stained her smooth skin.

"Hey," was all he could think to say. For the first time when he was with her, he wasn't turned on. All he felt was sorrow and guilt for having put her through this torment. "It'll all be over soon."

"Yeah," she said.

They drove silently through town and out to Route 54. As they turned into the clinic's parking lot, Clara noticed the two guards and then remembered tomorrow's demonstration. She looked around just to make sure that no protesters were there today. She was glad she hadn't scheduled her appointment for tomorrow. She looked at her watch: 8:50. In a few hours she would be back in the car on her way home, with all of this behind her. Her dad wouldn't be home until 6:30 this evening, so she could sleep all afternoon.

As she got out of the car, one of the security guards came over to walk her to the door of the clinic. She just wanted to get inside, so that no one driving by would see her. Michael followed along behind Clara and the guard. He could feel the bulging wad of money in his front pocket. Once inside the crowded waiting room, Clara checked in at the receptionist's window. "Kathleen," as the receptionist's name tag stated, handed Clara a clipboard with various forms to fill out, and asked how she intended to pay. Most teenagers paid in cash. Large stacks of all denominations put together from their allowance, odd jobs, money stolen from their parents, or borrowed from their friends.

"I'll be right back," she said, and walked over to Michael, who had taken a seat.

"She wants to know how I'm paying," she said flatly. Michael got up, fished in his pocket, and handed her the wad of bills. She took it without saying anything, and handed the wad of cash through the window to the receptionist.

"Is that $600 even?" Kathleen, the receptionist, asked.

"I don't know," said Clara. "Do you want me to count it?"

"Please."

As Clara opened the wad of bills, she fumbled and dropped it. Michael came over. "Here, let me do this. You go sit down and fill out the forms." He counted out $600 and handed it to Kathleen.

Kathleen inspected him over her reading glasses, and clearly didn't like what she saw. "Will you be staying with her? Waiting to take her home? She can't drive, you know, after the anesthetic."

"She can't..." *drive anyway,* Michael started to say, and then realized how bad that sounded. "Yes, I'll be waiting for her and taking her home. What time will that be?"

"If everything goes as expected, she will be ready to go home around noon," said Kathleen, still peering disapprovingly at Michael.

"Thanks." Michael wondered what he would do for three hours. He walked over to sit next to Clara on a mauve-and-baby-blue love seat.

"Michael, I have to list someone to call in case of an emergency. I'm putting you. What's your cell number again?" Clara asked.

"Clara, that's fine. But I was also thinking that maybe you should give me your dad's number. Not to put on the form, but, you know, just in case." He watched the nervous look on her face turn to one of horror.

"You are *not* calling my father," she said in a threatening whisper.

"No, I'm not. It would...just be...you know what? Forget it." He would just have to hope for the best.

Clara finished filling out the forms as well as she could. She didn't know the answers to some of the questions—usually when she went to the doctor her mother filled out the forms—but she put down what she knew and returned the clipboard to Kathleen. When she sat back down on the love seat, she heard squeals of children's laughter and looked around to see where they came from. In one of the back corners of the room, three little girls were taking all of the toys out of a toy box and putting them in a circle. As Clara watched them, they giggled with delight as the oldest girl pulled a pink elephant out of the box. Their tired-looking mother was trying to convince her husband to take them home and come back later. Clara could tell from their old, ill-fitting clothes that they were poor. The woman wore a pink sweatshirt with a hole in the sleeve. She couldn't remember ever being so close to anyone poor before, except for Michael, whom she assumed was poor. The woman's husband was afraid to leave her. They were arguing in hushed tones while their children played.

On the other side of the room were two Hispanic women holding hands. One was very beautiful with chestnut brown hair, but the other was the saddest woman that Clara had ever seen. Her face was bruised and misshapen from the beating she must have endured. Clara looked away quickly. The only other people in the waiting room were a teenage couple who sat staring straight ahead. Although they looked about Clara's age, she didn't know them. For that she was thankful. The high school had more than 4,000 students, so she didn't know everyone. They could even have come from another town. The blond-haired boy had an athletic air about him. Clara assumed he played tennis or soccer. The girl had straight, honey-colored hair and wide brown eyes. She wore a trendy dress and sandals. Her face was a pale shade of gray, even though her long legs were tan.

Clara looked at Michael and saw him through their eyes. He was a dirtbag. They probably thought she was a dirtbag, too. Even though she had allowed him to be with her last night— which in her mind was a survival tactic—she was glad that Michael didn't try to hold her hand or put his arm around her now. *Oh, why was the clinic so busy?* Clara felt like she wanted to scream. She just wanted to get it over with and go home. Just when she thought she couldn't stand waiting another minute, the door opened and a nurse called, "Clara. Clara Mahoney?"

NINETY-FOUR

᪐

riday's edition of *The Litchfield Press* was the most interesting local newspaper that Suzy Walker had ever read
in all her years in Litchfield. *The Press* was usually full of sleepy
articles on Rotary Awards and Rake and Hoe cake bakes, but
today's edition was sizzling with an article about a murder, a
demonstration and imported demonstrators, a debated mayoral race, and an informational piece on the Supreme Court's
abortion rulings. This was not *The Press* she knew and never
loved. As Suzy finished her morning coffee, she read the article
about the evidence found in Eduardo Fernandez's house, and
wondered if the wife, Pia, needed an attorney. Suzy liked to do
one or two *pro bono* cases a year—usually divorce cases that she
heard about from Nina Adler. But if Pia Fernandez needed an
attorney, and she might not, since the police were actual eyewitnesses, Suzy would gladly take on the case.

Suzy shook her head and started reading the coverage of
the demonstrators being bused in from Smithtown. Patricia
Castellano was quoted as saying, "Litchfield will merely serve
as a central meeting ground for all the people in the area

who support the sanctity of life." This was followed by Father O'Malley talking about Jesus's wanderings to preach the word. Suzy wanted to barf. The nerve of these people. And Antonio Ceravolo was going to pay the price. Suzy had hired the public relations firm of Seal & Waldman to help her reach out to the media for the press conference she was holding tomorrow morning to announce Dr. Norman Rubin's run for mayor of Litchfield. She wanted to draw as many reporters away from the demonstration as she could.

She had known Georgia Seal forever and had represented her in two divorces. Georgia was a colorful local character, and she knew everyone in the area who had a byline or a microphone. She probably also knew the new media kid in town with the laptop, Jamie Ross. Suzy's law firm, Walker & Walker, occasionally had to issue a press release in a case, and Suzy always called Georgia. Georgia was a neighbor in Dorian Estates and her office was in her expansive home. Suzy was due to meet with Georgia and Rachel Horowitz at ten o'clock today at Georgia's, to put the finishing touches on the press conference. She glanced at her watch and saw that she was running late. Folding the paper and leaving it on the breakfast table, she gathered her things and rushed out of the house.

Fog blanketed the neighborhood, so Suzy drove slowly up the winding private road to the Seal estate. During Georgia's last divorce it had been put on the market for $8.2 million. That was before Suzy had her way with Martin Seal, Georgia's last husband. The house never sold and now belonged to Georgia. Martin Seal had inherited his money from his mother, who had inherited her money from her father, who invented the plastic guitar pick and made millions.

Suzy rounded the bend and saw the huge Tudor mansion rise out of the mist like a castle on the moor. It was painted in the traditional Tudor way, with white stucco walls and brown beams and window frames. She parked and walked briskly up the front steps and was greeted by Sonia, the housekeeper.

"Good morning, Sonia," Suzy said with a smile, looking cool and crisp in her tan linen suit and navy silk blouse.

"Good morning, Ms. Walker. Ms. Horowitz is already here in the breakfast room. We thought you ladies might want coffee and a table to set your things on," said Sonia.

"Good thinking," said Suzy as she charged through the massive foyer, turned left into the massive hallway, and entered the massive kitchen and finally arrived in the massive breakfast nook. The large glass table was set for three at one end and Rachel and Georgia had already spread out iPads, binders, and cell phones.

"Good morning, ladies," beamed Suzy as she approached the table. "Rachel, you must have gotten an early start. I'm not late, am I?"

"No, no. Please sit down. Coffee?" asked Georgia.

"Please." Suzy looked at Georgia while she poured the coffee. At 55, she was still a looker, with her long blond hair parted in the middle, her black eyes and brows, long pointed nose, and high cheekbones. She looked like a cross between Meryl Streep and Cher. She wore a long, flowing, rose-colored caftan and silver sandals.

"We were putting a press list together," said Rachel.

"Our problem is *watch.com*. We want *watch.com*, because our news will go out instantaneously, but there's only one Jamie. Little Jamie can't be in two places at once. He'll certainly want to be where the action is, at the clinic. O'Malley is scheduled to speak at ten. Do we postpone until eleven, so that Jamie can make it to the Swan Club to cover Norman's speech?" Georgia held a slim silver pen, twirling it between her long, thin index and middle fingers as she strategized. Rachel and Suzy sat watching the pen, and waited for the media guru to speak. They were almost in a trance by the time Georgia stopped twirling the shiny implement and looked from one to the other for reaction. Neither said anything.

"We'll switch to eleven and wait for Jamie," Georgia decreed. "A part of the press herd will probably come with him, cutting down on the time they stay to get react from the demonstrators. It'll cut into Patricia's coverage. I hear O'Malley is very unhappy with the whole thing," said Georgia, smiling conspiratorially.

"Really?" asked Suzy and Rachel in unison.

Georgia nodded her head and her black eyes twinkled. "I'm very good friends with Elsa Martinson, and she said that Thomas, as she calls him, is very sorry that he got involved with all this, but Patricia is such a large church donor that he doesn't know what to do. He can't just pull out."

Suzy and Rachel looked at each other. They had always assumed that Father O'Malley, being a Catholic priest, was supportive of the church's view on abortion. Suzy was the first to speak. "Do you think I should call him? Try to reason with him? I know the demonstration is tomorrow, but it could still be stopped."

"I don't think it will do you any good. Antonio went to see him and got nowhere," confided Georgia. "Now, that's an interesting story. I hear that the mayor arrived at the rectory Wednesday night and found O'Malley out back in the work shed, stripped to the waist, hammering together a chair with that gorgeous little photographer who Greeley has running around town. Do you know who I mean?"

"Yes, Kit Stilton. I saw her at the Safe Haven event at the Swan Club," said Suzy.

"Well, she left St. Raymond's when Antonio got there, and then stopped to chat with his driver, who happens to be my driver's brother. It's a small town," said Georgia. "More coffee?" Georgia picked up the silver carafe and topped off Suzy's cup.

"That's quite an image," laughed Suzy. "Thank you," she said, adding a dribble of skim milk to her coffee.

"Sexy blond priest playing Jesus the carpenter for his beautiful and adoring disciple..." Georgia raised her eyebrows, smiled widely, and offered the carafe to Rachel. Rachel held up her hand signaling no. Georgia and Suzy laughed and shook their heads in amazement at the mental picture they were both enjoying of the sweaty, virile priest and the beautiful, young photographer. Rachel, however, frowned at her companions. She was not one to fantasize or gossip.

"Interesting, but let's move on to our announcement. How do we compete with the demonstration for coverage?" asked Rachel in her stern business tone.

As if they were chastised schoolgirls, Georgia and Suzy gave each other a little smile and a shrug of the shoulders. "Norman should issue a statement this afternoon, criticizing the mayor for allowing the demonstration to get out of hand. He'll come out very strong, and hopefully, Antonio will take the bait and by tomorrow they will be in a heated exchange and the press will want to cover us," said Georgia.

"Brilliant," exclaimed Suzy.

"Yes," agreed Rachel. "I think Antonio will *have* to respond."

"However, it *is* going to be hard to compete for coverage. The demonstration will have everything: the priest, the protesters, the abortion clinic, the girl? I wonder who she is?" Suzy pondered out loud.

"What girl?" asked Georgia.

"There's one patient, a young girl, who has an appointment at the clinic on Saturday morning. Dr. Friedberg asked her to come early, before the demonstrators will arrive, but she said she can only come at nine o'clock. The board debated closing the clinic for one day, but Dr. Friedberg is adamant about being there for this girl. She said it was too risky to turn her away," answered Suzy.

"We could ask Dr. Friedberg who she is," said Georgia.

"She'd never tell us. Patient confidentiality and she shouldn't tell us," said Rachel.

Georgia shrugged. "Dr. Friedberg told the girl about the demonstration and she's still coming?"

"Probably the only day she can get away from her parents," suggested Rachel.

"Yeah, but I wonder," Suzy said, but it was more of a statement than a question. Her attorney's mind was whirling, honing in on the myriad possible reasons why the girl would want to arrive in the middle of the storm.

NINETY-FIVE

❧

*P*ia stood and hugged Stella when Dr. Friedberg called her in for the procedure. Stella was surprised by the resolve in her sister's eyes. She had expected to see fear, even panic, but instead she saw determination and a solid will. Stella, feeling a little panicky herself, felt better when she saw this look on Pia's face. Pia turned from her sister's embrace and walked toward Dr. Friedberg, who looked gentle and sympathetic. Pia had blocked everything out of her mind, except the one thing she was here to do. *Don't overthink it. Stay on course.*

"Good morning, Mrs. Fernandez," said Dr. Friedberg. At the sound of her last name, Pia shuddered.

"Pia. Please, just call me Pia," she said.

"Yes, Pia. Please come this way." They walked down the well-lit corridor to Dr. Friedberg's office. Pia was staring at the repeating pattern on the wallpaper so intently that it made her a little dizzy. Dr. Friedberg held the door, and Pia went in and sat in the chair in front of Dr. Friedberg's desk. Instead of sitting behind her desk, Dr. Friedberg took the chair next to Pia. She looked compassionately at the beaten woman sitting beside her.

"How are you?" started Dr. Friedberg, a look of genuine concern on her face.

"I'm okay. My face and nose are sore, but these bruises will heal," answered Pia.

"How far along are you? Can we wait?"

"Nine, maybe ten weeks. No. I want to get this behind me," Pia stated.

"Pia, there are services available for women in your situation. I don't know where you are living or if you have help, but I know a good lawyer if you need one. I can put you in touch with the head of Safe Haven, a shelter for domestic-violence victims, if you..."

"No, I'm staying with my sister. She's very generous. Thank you. I really just want to get this over with," said Pia, playing with the strap of her purse.

Dr. Friedberg saw that she was making Pia uncomfortable and decided to move along. "I'm glad you have family to help you. In terms of the procedure, because of the damage to your nose, I'm afraid to give you general anesthetic. I'll give you Demerol to make you sleepy, but you won't actually be out. Is that okay?"

"Yes. Doctor, how long will it take me to recover? From this procedure, I mean?"

"You should feel fine tomorrow. Possibly some cramping. When you go home, rest in bed, but tomorrow you should be able to get up and go about your business. Pia...just one more thing, I also know a good counselor. A woman who works with women, but whose specialty is working with children. How is your daughter?"

Pia looked down at her hands. She wished that this well-meaning doctor would stop talking and just take her into an operating room and do whatever it was she was going to do.

"I'm sorry, Pia. Please know that I am only trying to help. I want you to know that there are people who can help you when you're ready."

Pia continued to look down, but nodded her head.

"Fine. Then let's proceed. Please follow me." Dr. Friedberg started to walk toward the door.

"Doctor," said Pia.

"Yes."

"Thank you. I know you're trying to help me. I'll call you when I'm ready." Pia stood in the center of Dr. Friedberg's office, looking small and bruised and vulnerable, but Dr. Friedberg also detected an inner strength, a resolve that she had not immediately seen in this woman. She smiled at Pia, and the corners of Pia's lips turned up slightly. However, the swelling and the slit in her bottom lip prevented much of a smile.

"I just want you to know that you are not alone," said Dr. Friedberg.

$\mathscr{N}$ INETY-$\mathscr{S}$IX

❧

$\mathscr{F}$ather O'Malley woke with the smell of her all over him. She had crept upstairs while he met with the young couple planning their wedding and waited for him in his room. She lay naked, with the sheets partially wrapped around her, exposing one tender breast and one shapely thigh. Her beautiful gold hair was splayed around her face, and her eyes were closed. He shed his clothes and got into bed beside her. They spoke not a word. She left when the sun went down on the long summer day. It was past nine o'clock when she stepped out into the darkness.

Between his anger at Patricia over tomorrow's demonstration, and his guilt about succumbing again to seduction, Father O'Malley had fallen into a tortured and fitful sleep that night after she left. He remembered tossing and turning, with images of her laughing, moaning, smiling at him with that look that made his skin tingle. When he woke, he needed to pray. Without opening his eyes, he crawled out of bed onto his knees. He leaned his elbows on the wrinkled bedclothes, clasped his hands together and prayed out loud, "Dear Father, I have sinned. I am weak. My flesh is weak. Father, I beseech you, send me strength in the face of temptation. She does not understand my relationship to you and the church. She is young and cannot see the error of our ways. I am the one who betrays you. She is troubled and we have too many secrets between us. Father, I am a fraud. I need guidance. Please help me…please help us," he sobbed.

$\mathcal{N}$INETY-$\mathcal{S}$EVEN

$\mathbf{S}$ tress was not good for the skin. Why Patricia had called an organizational meeting for Friday morning at 10 a.m., she couldn't really remember. She hadn't slept in days, her face was broken out, she needed a manicure, Salvatore was a beast, Antonio wasn't talking to her, she couldn't recall ever feeling like this. She was a person who always tried to be in the right. She always liked to have the moral high ground, but somehow, busing all these indigents into her beautiful town would make it difficult for her to hold her head high at the salon. She dared not go into HF Spa and Essentials having to explain why she, Patricia Castellano, was actually providing buses to bring the riffraff into town. She was just going to have to ask Alla, her manicurist, to come to the house.

Patricia sighed as she drove to the office in her Jaguar. The car had been a gift from Salvatore on her last birthday and the rich, tawny-colored leather still had that new car scent. The cherry wood dashboard was so highly polished that she could almost see her reflection in it. Usually, the car cheered her up, but nothing was going to raise her spirits until this awful weekend was behind her. After the demonstration on Saturday, Father O'Malley was expecting her to come and support him at mass on Sunday. Salvatore was threatening not to go to church with her. Antonio would surely snub her. It was unbearable. How had this backfired on her so completely? Sandra. That's how. She had trusted that sneaky little bitch. Patricia couldn't wait to fire her on Monday.

Parking in her secret spot in the alley behind her office building, she grabbed her purse and got out of the car. As she shut the door she caught her reflection in the window. She stopped and looked at the plump, unkempt woman staring back at her in the glass as if she was a stranger. No lipstick. She couldn't believe it. The last time she had been seen in public without lipstick was probably 1992. As she reached into her purse for her cosmetics bag, her index-finger nail caught on the teeth of the bag's zipper and ripped off down to the quick. "Ouch," she yelped, sticking her bleeding finger in her mouth. "Mmm," she moaned, as she decided to get into the office and deal with her bleeding nail—and her lack of lipstick—in the privacy of her office bathroom.

As she emerged from the small alley between the buildings, she ran right into Elsa Martinson and her daughter, Linda. The two women and the girl stood staring at each other. Elsa was the first to recover.

"Good morning, Patricia. Are you...all right?" Elsa asked. Patricia was still sucking on her bleeding finger and feeling worse now that she actually had to have a conversation with someone. Linda, who had always admired Patricia's sense of style, grimaced, as if she couldn't believe the disheveled state of the woman before her.

"Elsa," said Patricia, only half-removing her finger from her mouth.

"You're bleeding," Linda said flatly, stating the obvious.

Patricia tried to smile. She tried to gain control of herself. "Yes, I ripped my nail off and it really hurts. I need to get upstairs and wash it off and get a Band-Aid."

"Patricia, I just want to say...that I do think you're doing a good thing," said Elsa. Patricia steeled herself for the "but...." It never came. That was all Elsa wanted to say. No one had said anything supportive to Patricia for days now, and she was genuinely moved by the comment, so much, that she started to cry. All the pent-up frustration and fear of public scrutiny and familial discord gave way to huge, watery tears that ran down her flushed cheeks from under her Ray-Bans. Without thinking, she threw her arms around Elsa and sobbed. Linda took a step back from her mother and this woman. How embarrassing! She hoped no one saw them.

"There, there now, Patricia. Let us walk you to your door." Elsa tried to maneuver the larger woman toward the next building. She knew that Patricia would be mortified if certain people in town saw her in this state, and wanted to help her off the street. "I know it must be stressful, with the whole town watching your every move. Father O'Malley told me just yesterday that doing the right thing is always hard. Taking a stand takes courage. You have courage, Patricia." She had gently moved Patricia the 20 yards from the alley to the door that led up to the Stand Up for Life offices. "Here you go. Now go upstairs and wash your face. Get yourself a Band-Aid. Do you need Linda to help you up the stairs?" Elsa looked over at her daughter, who was angrily shaking her head "no."

But Patricia lifted her head from the crook of Elsa's neck, took a deep breath, looked into Elsa's deep-blue eyes, and said, "Elsa, you have no idea how much your kind words mean to me. Thank you. I really don't know what would have happened if I didn't run into you. Thank you again." Then she leaned in and kissed Elsa on the cheek. Not a peck or an air kiss, but a real kiss, with feeling and contact between lips and skin. She stepped back and looked at Elsa. "Just when you think you can't go on, God sends you a messenger. You have been his messenger here this morning, Elsa. Thank you." Without even acknowledging Linda, she turned, opened the door to Stand Up for Life, and climbed briskly up the stairs.

Elsa looked at her daughter, whose bright-blue eyes squinted in concentration as she glared at her mother. "I thought you said you believed in abortion," Linda said in an accusatory tone.

"Of course I do, Linda, but Mrs. Castellano is St. Raymond's biggest donor and she needed someone to say a kind word to her right now. Come along. We're running late for the dentist."

As Linda watched her mother walk away, she wondered if anyone ever told the truth about anything.

$\mathcal{N}$INETY-$\mathcal{E}$IGHT

⤴

$\mathcal{P}$ia's mind raced while she lay on the examination table in the clinic's operating room, looking up at a poster of beautiful clear-blue water and pinkish sand. The nurse had been thoughtful enough to pull out the extension of the table, so that Pia's legs wouldn't hang off the end. Her first instinct was to pray for God's forgiveness for what she was about to do and to ask him to watch over Maria and Carmen while she was away from them. Instead, before she could summon the words of prayer, her mind began to question how God had let her marry that animal she called her husband. How had God let her bring two children into the world who called Eduardo father? None of it made any sense.

She tried to call upon her faith. She wanted to believe that God was protecting her now, but why had he abandoned her the night Eduardo snapped? Had God prompted Maria to call the police? But why would he place such a heavy burden on one so young? Pia knew that Maria had an inner strength that she herself did not possess, but had Maria been called on too young to prove it? She tried to picture Maria and Carmen right now in Stella's kitchen, talking and laughing. Or they were worried that she was at the doctor, or sad that their entire life was in shreds. Maybe she should ask the nurse to tell Stella to go home and check on them. Where was the nurse? Where was the doctor? Why were they taking so long?

Okay, enough. You're making yourself crazy. She forced herself to pray. "Our Father, who art in heaven, hallowed be thy name..." The Lord's Prayer soothed her. She finished, said "amen" out loud, and felt a little better. She started reciting the Act of Contrition: "My God, I am sorry for my sins with all my heart. In choosing to do wrong..." she stopped and opened her eyes. Was she choosing to do wrong? She felt her hard, round belly. She thought of Maria's face distorted with pain and horror as she ran into the living room to open the door for the police. No, Pia had to use all of her strength to help her children who were already in this world.

She felt her determination begin to waver. What if something happened to her? What if she never woke up from this operation? Her palms began to sweat. She sat up. She fought the urge to run out of the room. She decided to go and get Stella to wait with her. As her feet hit the tile floor, the door opened, and Joy, the nurse, came in. Pia had gotten up too quickly, and she felt dizzy. She leaned back on the table.

"Whoa. Where are you going?" asked Joy, stepping forward to grasp Pia's shoulder and support her.

"I...when is the doctor coming? I can't wait anymore." Pia put her hand over her eyes and tried to stop her head from spinning.

"Here. Sit in the chair. Let me get you some water." Joy led Pia over to the chair beside the operating table. Pia sat down, and Joy handed her a cup of water. "Let's talk about the procedure. You're probably getting nervous. Everyone is nervous beforehand, but it's easier if you know what to expect." Pia nodded. Joy looked down at the battered woman in front of her and felt a hot rush of anger at the man who had done this to her. "First, are you sure you want to do this today? You can easily wait another week or even two. You're only nine weeks pregnant."

Pia looked up at Joy. The skin around her eyes was a patchwork of blue, purple, yellow, and brown. The cuts on her eyes and lips were healing, but her face was still swollen and disfigured. "Look at me," Pia said. "My children see these bruises every day. They are frightened and hurt. I have to do this now. To get beyond this so I can be there for them. Do you understand?"

Joy nodded. "I do. I do understand, Pia. I know that you feel that you must take your life back. I know, I've seen this before. Do you want to hear what to expect?"

"Yes."

"First, Dr. Friedberg will examine your uterus. In a minute I am going to set up an IV to give you a sedative that allows you to be conscious, but deeply relaxed. You'll doze off. You won't be able to remember the actual procedure."

"But I won't be completely out?"

"No, that's not necessary."

"Good. How long will it take?"

"The actual procedure will take about 10 minutes, but first we have to dilate your cervix. Then, Doctor Friedberg will insert a small tube, and she will empty your uterus. You can expect some cramping after, but by tomorrow you should feel fine. Do you have any questions?" Pia shook her head. "After the procedure, you'll have to rest here for about an hour. Okay? If you're ready, I need you to get back on the table so I can put in the IV. Are you ready?"

Joy helped Pia stand and get back up on the operating table. She expertly inserted the IV needle into Pia's arm. "Are you cold? Do you want a blanket for your legs while you wait? Dr. Friedberg should be with you in a few minutes."

"I am cold," Pia said. Joy left the room, Pia felt panic surfacing again. *Why do nurses and doctors always take so long when they leave the room?* She heard voices in the hall, and when the door opened again, Dr. Friedberg, two nurses, and a doctor who turned out to be the anesthesiologist came in. Each of them had a role in the procedure and quickly went about their specific task in prepping her and the equipment. Pia felt that she was no longer in control. She had come here and told them this was what she wanted, and now it was up to them.

The last thing Pia remembered, before drifting off to sleep, was Dr. Friedberg holding her hand as she counted backward from 10. When she woke up, and opened her eyes, she saw a yellow curtain with white and blue flowers. She had made it to the recovery room.

$\mathcal{N}$INETY-$\mathcal{N}$INE

❧

$\mathcal{T}$he walk out to his car from the safety of his office had become more and more problematic for Mayor Ceravolo as the demonstration day approached. Reporters with cameras, videocams, and recorders were everywhere, springing out from behind trees and parked cars, moving in packs, circling him to hold him in place while they asked their questions. No, today he was going to use the back door of Town Hall and sneak out without having to deal with the upcoming demonstration, the murder, or his reelection. It was late to be going for lunch—maybe the media pack would be sitting at their desks, lethargic from their McDonald's or their pizza. He called his driver on his cell and told him to meet him by the back door. He intercommed his secretary, who assured him that the hall was clear.

Now, feeling confident, he opened the back door of his office. As he stepped out of his office doorway, he heard the unmistakable voice of Helen Acker coming from behind him off to the right, where there was a small vestibule between two windows.

"Mayor Ceravolo. May I have a word?" she said.

The mayor fought an urge to run down the corridor, out the door, and into his waiting car. He knew he could run faster than Helen, with her Birkenstocks, but he couldn't tell if she was alone. *You can never really run away from the press.* The mayor's shoulders collapsed with the acceptance that he was caught.

"What do you want, Helen? I'm late for an appointment," he said, as he slowly turned around to face her. He was pleasantly surprised to see that she was alone. She was holding a piece of paper, from which she now started reading.

"This is a statement just emailed to me from Dr. Norman Rubin." Helen paused to look up over her glasses with her squinty little eyes and see the mayor's reaction. He stared at her like a man waiting to take a bullet: which catastrophe was Rubin blaming on him now? If Rubin was just announcing his candidacy no one would care. The election was more than a year away.

Helen continued, "'Mayor Ceravolo's support of tomorrow's anti-choice demonstration in front of the Litchfield Women's Center is unconscionable. This flagrant attack on the constitutional rights of the women and families of Litchfield shows the mayor's conservative agenda, which he tried to conceal during the last election. There will be no place to hide in the coming election...'"

The Mayor had heard enough. His hands were clenched into fists. His cheeks reddened and his eyes had begun to bulge out of their sockets, but he had been in public life long enough to know that a tirade against Rubin would only escalate the debate. He crisply turned on his heel and said over his retreating shoulder, "My people will call you with a statement, Helen. I'm going to my appointment."

Helen waddled back to Room 6 and slunk over to *The Press's* desk. Latitia, who was writing the story about the indictments of Eduardo Fernandez from the morning press conference, was pounding away on her laptop, while biting down on a pencil between her teeth. She could sense Helen's frustration. It was ruining Latitia's concentration.

"What is it, Helen?" she demanded in an annoyed tone with her eyes closed, her fingers still poised over the keys of her laptop. Helen tossed Rubin's statement onto Latitia's desk. Latitia read it without moving. "How did you get this?" she whispered. "Did everyone get it?" If not, she certainly didn't want Jamie to get it from them.

"Jamie has it," Helen said, reading Latitia's mind. "But, I just cornered Ceravolo sneaking out the back of the building. It was just me and him, and he didn't say anything when I read the statement to him. Except that he was late for an appointment. Now, his office will put together a well-worded reaction, and we'll all read it first on *watch.com*."

"Shit," consoled Latitia, shaking her head. "Did the mayor react physically? Did his face turn red? Did he punch the wall? Bare his teeth?"

Helen looked at Latitia, "Well, he did get kind of red in the face, and his hands were clenched in fists, but he didn't punch anything. His eyes kinda bulged a little..."

"Turn *that* into the lead of your article and then include the well-worded statement in graph three or four. Jamie will lead with the statement," Latitia watched as Helen's dour face lit up. She almost looked attractive for a second.

"Thanks, Latitia," she said as she turned on her own laptop.

ONE HUNDRED

❧

Clara followed Patty, the head nurse, down the corridor. The multi-colored cats on Patty's scrubs, smiling and jumping on colorful trampolines. They were red and yellow and purple and orange, and Clara was concentrating so hard on the cats that she bumped right into Patty's back when the nurse stopped to turn the knob and open a door to her right.

"I'm sorry," stammered Clara. "I was looking at your scrubs."

Patty turned to the young girl. Clara's shoulders were hunched and her chin was pulled into her chest, as if she were trying to make herself smaller. Patty reached out and squeezed Clara's hand. "You're going to be fine. It'll all be over before you know it. Tomorrow you'll do something fun." She looked into Clara's big blue eyes and saw fear. "Here, let me give you a hug." She pulled Clara into her arms. Patty's oldest daughter, Sammy, was about this girl's age. When she pulled back, Clara looked a little better. Patty opened the dressing-room door. "Take all of your clothes off, and put on one of the dressing gowns on the rack. Opening in the back. Put your clothes in this bag. Then put these warm socks on. No one feels good when their feet are cold. Last, put on a pair of those surgical slippers over the socks. Come out when you're done." Clara took the bag and went into the small room. Her hands were shaking. She tried to remember to do everything the nice nurse had said.

She came out of the room holding the bag and wearing the robe, socks, and slippers. Patty took the bag and led Clara down the corridor to an operating room. Patty told her to sit on a chair beside the operating table and wait for Dr. Friedberg. Clara looked around the room. Posters displaying various parts of the female anatomy were hung on the opposite wall. The breast. The vagina. The ovaries. The fallopian tubes. Each part was diagrammed and explained. On the ceiling over the operating table was a poster of a beautiful beach, with palm trees and light-blue water. Clara realized that music was playing. Paul McCartney's voice sang "Hey Jude" softly into the room. Clara tried to focus on his voice. She loved The Beatles, and Paul McCartney in particular. She had read on Wikipedia that Paul had written this song for John Lennon's son, Julian.

The door opened, bringing Clara back to reality. "Hello, Clara. I'm Dr. Friedberg. How are you?" Clara looked up at the woman in front of her and thought she looked like her mom. Clara closed her eyes to steady her nerves, and forced herself to think about the doctor's starched white coat.

"I'm okay," she said, her voice sounding shaky.

"Clara, I want to talk to you about birth control options for after the procedure. I want to recommend that we insert something called an IUD into your uterus to prevent future pregnancies. Have you ever heard of an IUD?" Dr. Friedberg had pulled a chair over to sit next to Clara.

"Yes, I've heard of them. In health class."

"Once the small object is inserted into your uterus, you don't have to do anything for five years. Then you have to replace it or use another method of birth control. You won't even know it's there, and it's pretty much one hundred percent effective. It's a simple and effortless form of birth control. Are you interested?"

"I guess so. I don't have sex that often. It was only my second time." Clara bit her lower lip and looked down at the surgical slipper on her foot.

"I see. Is that your boyfriend in the waiting room?"

"No. He's just...helping me," said Clara continuing to look at her foot.

"Clara, there are other alternatives, you know. Adoption, for example..."

Clara looked up and cut the doctor off. "No. There are no other options for me."

Dr. Friedberg hesitated. She guessed that there was a story here. "Clara, are you afraid of someone? That man in the waiting room? How do you know him?"

"No, I'm not afraid of him. He's...my friend. I've made up my mind to do this, and I don't really want to talk about it. I just want to get it over with. Please? Let's just go ahead." Clara's mouth was set in a line of determination.

"Okay. Do you know how far along you are?"

"About eight weeks."

"Clara, I recommend we use a local anesthesia. I will give you a shot in your cervix and then you won't feel a thing. You will, however, be aware of the procedure." Dr. Friedberg saw the blood drain out of Clara's face. "Or, we can use something called "conscious sedation." You'll fall asleep and you won't feel or remember anything. But the quickest recovery time would be with the local."

"Yes, just give me a local."

"All right. Do you have any questions?"

"No."

Dr. Friedberg waited a minute. "Then, Patty will be right in to get you ready. Don't worry. You might have a little cramping afterward, nothing worse than a regular period, but that's it. If it bothers you when you get home, just take two Advil. I don't want you to use tampons right after the procedure. Only sanitary napkins," Clara looked up at the doctor and nodded her head.

Dr. Friedberg smiled. "The nurse will be in shortly," she said. Clara watched the doctor exit the room and shut the door.

Clara felt hot and cold at the same time. Her palms, underarms, and feet were sweating, but her arms and legs felt cold from the air-conditioning. Her teeth started to chatter while she waited for the nurse to come. She went back to reading the posters. Instead of Paul McCartney, Sheryl Crow was singing. Finally, she heard footsteps coming down the hall, but they moved past her room. She studied the tile on the floor and the wire crates hung on the wall holding small plastic bags of tubing. The air from the ceiling vent blew down on her.

When Clara thought she couldn't wait any longer, Patty, the nurse came in. "How ya doing? First, we're going to take a blood test, and then we'll need some urine. Do you think you can go?" Clara nodded. "You've had blood taken before?" Clara nodded again. She closed her eyes as Patty swabbed her arm. "Now, make a fist." Clara closed her eyes when Patty inserted the needle and took the vial of blood. "All done." Patty put a small piece of white cotton and a Band-Aid on Clara's arm. "Now, go down the hall, last door on your left, and leave a specimen. Use the cup with your name on it. Leave it on the counter and come back here."

Clara opened the door, and a middle-aged woman in a hospital gown, just like hers, was walking back from the bathroom. The woman looked a little surprised when she saw Clara. Clara quickly scanned her brain to think if she knew the woman. No, she didn't think she did. Thank God. She hurried down the hall and into the bathroom.

Once Clara was back in the operating room, Patty told her to lie on the operating table. The nurse helped her put her feet in the metal stirrups. While Patty stood next to Clara with her hand comfortingly on her forearm, Dr. Friedberg entered the room and approached the table. She looked down at Clara from between the girl's legs. "Clara, are you ready?" Clara nodded. "You'll just feel a little pinch."

ONE HUNDRED

AND ONE

❦

On Fridays, the Baptist A.M.E. Church in Smithtown served lunch to the community. Pale chicken, mashed potatoes, collard greens, yellow gravy, and white bread were kept hot in aluminum warming trays for the women and children, seniors, and single men who came every week for a hot meal. Reverend Turnipseed tried to attend this lunch each week to show his support, to monitor some folks he was worried about, and to have something good to eat. Collard greens were the reverend's favorite vegetable, and the women who cooked and served the food knew it. They liked to watch the reverend's progress through the line. As he advanced toward the steaming trays, he would dispense advice, listen to parishioners' troubles, laugh at jokes, trade arthritis remedies, and counsel the unemployed. Reverend Turnipseed had one speed, and that was slow. He walked slow, he talked slow, he stopped and listened to his people as if he alone could stop time from marching forward. His movements were slow, but his mind was sharp. The inner sanctum of his brain recorded every remark, every look, every interaction, and put them in drawers in his memory to be taken out later, analyzed, and used another day.

The Friday before the demonstration was a very busy day for the reverend, but no one would know it, to see him on line in the church basement, with its gray and beige tile, rickety tables, and unmatched chairs. Even though he still had more than 50 white folks to recruit for the next morning, he was going to enjoy his greens. While he was on line listening to Bertha Deegan describe her cesarean section two weeks before for the birth of her seventh child, he looked around the room and saw a small flock of white faces at a table in the back. They belonged to tired-looking women in their late 40s or early 50s, sitting in a corner in the back of the basement near a collection of broken things, including a piano and a beach umbrella with silver, bent spokes. Bertha had finished the story of the birth of her newest child and was getting started on the birth of her twins two years ago, when the reverend realized that her monologue could go on for an hour or more. He politely excused himself, promising to drop by and discuss plans to baptize the youngest, and then he cut the line—which was his prerogative as the church leader—loaded up his tray and started to walk toward the white women.

"Good morning, ladies," said the reverend as he approached their table. "May I join you?" The group stared up at the tall black minister with their hollow eyes and unhealthy color. He knew immediately that they were recovering drug addicts and drunks.

"Sure," said the liveliest of the group. When she smiled up at him, the reverend could see that once she had been a beautiful woman, but now she was reduced to a faded, gray, wrinkled version of herself. She removed a dirty black backpack from the seat beside her and pointed to the chair, inviting him to sit down.

The reverend put his tray on the table and folded his large frame onto the small metal chair. He took a big bite of collard greens and chewed them with enthusiasm. The women watched him. They ate hardly anything. "So, welcome to our humble establishment. Where you ladies from? I don't think I've seen you here before." There was no reply. He looked down the line of faces. Each told a story of despair. They would be happy to get $50 if they could get here early for the bus tomorrow. He tried to figure out which one was the leader. He decided on the healthiest-looking one sitting right across from him, and stared at her as he said, "How'd you ladies like to make fifty bucks apiece?" Now there was movement. The flock perked up. The women made tiny sounds and eye contact, as he looked from one to the other.

The healthiest-looking one said, "We might be able to help you out, Reverend. What do you need?"

"Where do you ladies stand on the pro-choice movement? Do you believe in baby killing?"

Phrased in such a way, they knew how to answer. First the healthy one said "no," and then a chorus of "no's" went around the table. Reverend Turnipseed took another bite of greens. He closed his eyes as he savored the taste, then he swallowed and sucked his teeth. A tiny smile appeared on his face when he was done enjoying the rich flavor.

"Well, that's good, because tomorrow morning there's a demonstration in Litchfield, a few towns over, and we need folks to stand up for the lives of the unborn. Where you ladies stayin'?" he asked.

An uncomfortable silence settled over the table. The lively one, sitting next to him, said, "We're down the road at Miss Nancy's house. You know it?"

"Yes, I know Miss Nancy. She's a great lady," said Reverend Turnipseed. Miss Nancy's was a halfway house where recovering drug addicts and alcoholics went after rehab. They spent six weeks to six months living with Miss Nancy before they tried to reenter mainstream society. They were allowed to go out during the day, but they had to be home for dinner, and then they were expected to stay in the house. Evening hours were very dangerous hours for recovering addicts. The reverend just couldn't remember when Miss Nancy had any white women stay with her. "So, how many ladies are staying with Miss Nancy now?"

"There are fifty-six of us, just come in from Pennsylvania," said a small and meek young woman near the end of the table. "The houses in eastern Pennsylvania are full. Miss Nancy's was nearly empty, so we were bussed in."

"Fantastic," said Reverend Turnipseed which produced a shimmy down the flock. "I mean…I'm so glad we could help. Fifty-six of you, huh? Think everybody might want to come to the demonstration?" His question set the flock to clacking and chirping among themselves. "I'll stop by Miss Nancy's later with the specifics. Now tell me about Pennsylvania. What town are you all from?" Reverend Turnipseed took another big bite of collard greens, savoring the earthy goodness.

ONE HUNDRED AND TWO

⚬

Outside the clinic, and down the road a little way, two cars were parked on either side of Route 54. In one car sat Police Chief Chodor and Sergeant Staler, and in the other sat Sandra Stett. They couldn't see who was in the other car because they were parked on opposite sides of the street at opposite ends of the lot. However, they were aware of each other and the traffic entering and leaving the clinic parking lot.

"Sinners," muttered Sandra, as another car arrived in the clinic parking lot and was greeted by one of the security guards. "You are sealing your eternal fate. God forgive you," she hissed, as she watched a young couple walk into the clinic. Sandra was there to map out the logistics of where Father O'Malley and she would stand tomorrow morning to address the crowd. When she had found out that Patricia would not be attending the demonstration, she had realized that God was opening a door for her. She would stand next to Father O'Malley while he spoke out against the evil happening behind the clinic doors.

She was playing with the idea of telling him that Patricia had said that she—Sandra Stett—should take Patricia's place and introduce him to the crowd.

She surveyed the site while she waited for the men from Party City to arrive with the platform she had ordered. This was another expense that she would have to bury in the books. She wondered who was in the other car that was parked across the street. She squinted her eyes to try to bring them into focus. It looked like two men, but she couldn't be sure because of the glare from the sun. As she stared at the other car, the driver's door opened, and Sergeant Staler stepped out of the unmarked car into the street.

"Damn," she said. It was that sergeant from the police department who had interrogated her. She didn't want to see him, but it couldn't be helped. The Party City men were expected momentarily. When they arrived, she would have to get out of the car.

The car's other door opened, and she watched the police chief get out. The two men stood looking at the empty lot, which was owned by the town, and the police chief was glad that it did, because his goal was to keep the demonstrators as far away from the clinic as possible. Better contained in the lot than directly in front of the clinic. The mayor had made his sister promise to have the speeches made from the lot instead of the street. Stand Up for Life said it was expecting 400 protesters, but the police knew that there would be a 20 percent fall-off. That brought the crowd down to 320, and some would escape to the small diner, as the hours wore on. Chief Chodor had checked the weather and was sorry to see that it was going to be sunny and warm, not cloudy like today. Whatever happened, it was only three hours—three hours without incident—that's what Chief Chodor wanted. Stand Up for Life's permit allowed the street to be closed for three hours. The police would move in their sawhorses today to corral the protesters once they arrived.

As the two cops stood surveying the scene, a lilac Party City truck slowed down and pulled over in front of the lot. Sandra knew she had no choice but to go over and greet the truck drivers. To conceal her face as much as possible, she put on large dark glasses and a straw sunhat, and hoped that the sergeant wouldn't remember her. The delivery guys had already gotten out of their pastel-colored truck and were approaching Chief Chodor and Sergeant Staler. Sandra wished, for the first time in her life, that she had brought Simon or Lee with her. She had tried to use her southern charm that night at the police station—to no good effect—so she decided to act much more New Jersey now in an effort to block the sergeant's memory of her. As she approached the men, she turned her face away from the sergeant and looked at the older Party City driver, who was holding the paperwork for the delivery.

"Hello. Let me show you where to set up the platform," she said, indicating with a look and a nod that the driver should follow her. She had decided to strategically place the platform so that when the cameras were taking footage of O'Malley's speech, they would get the clinic in the background. The two deliverymen followed Sandra, and the two cops watched. Sandra laid out exactly where she wanted the platform to go, and the men went back to their truck to drive up to the spot to unload. While they were gone, Sandra stood with her back to the cops, busily reading every word of the delivery papers. She was unaware that the two cops were coming up behind her.

"Good afternoon, I'm Police Chief Chodor and this is Sergeant Staler," Chodor boomed in his most official police chief voice as he walked up next to her.

Sandra almost fell into her helpless, southern belle routine, but then caught herself. "Good afternoon, Chief, I'm the organizer from Stand Up for Life," was all she said, avoiding any eye contact with Sergeant Slater. The guys in the truck were backing up into the lot, and Sandra and the cops moved away to make room for them.

"This demonstration has surely caused the town a lot of up-set. We're really hoping the protesters will be peaceful and fol-low all the rules tomorrow, Miss...I didn't get your name," said Chief Chodor. "Will you be here tomorrow?"

"Yes, I'll be here. Just call me...Sandy," Sandra said in her best New Jersey accent.

"Okay, Sandy. What time will you be here?"

The question threw Sandra. She hadn't decided exactly how the morning was going to play out, with all the buses com-ing in from Smithtown. "What time? Let's see. So much to do in the morning. I guess I'll be here around seven-thirty. Father O'Malley will arrive at eight-thirty and he'll speak at ten. We are planning a peaceful event. We're not here to hurt anyone. The people doing harm are inside the clinic." With this decla-ration, Sandra started to walk away from the men, but as she turned, Sergeant Slater made the connection.

"Sandy. As in Sandra Stett. I knew you looked familiar," he called after her. "Wait a minute."

Sandra clenched her teeth, uttered a few curses under her breath, and turned around, deciding to just be herself. They knew who she was anyway. In her most charming southern sing-song, she lilted, "Officer, I was just waitin' for you to re-member me."

"I'll bet you were. I'll just bet you were *waitin' for me to remem-ber little 'ole you*. Drive carefully, Miss Stett," he said.

"I will Officer, you bet I will." Sandra turned, making her full skirt flair out, and sauntered over to the deliverymen like a young debutante. Chief Chodor just shook his head.

ONE HUNDRED

AND THREE

᷒

"Choice is the Sacred Cow of Liberalism, But This Time the Liberals are Right" was the title that Darius Greeley had decided upon for his Sunday editorial. Although he was known throughout town for his fiscally conservative views, he felt—in his gut—that the issue of abortion was a common sense issue. He had done some research into the U.S. Constitution and the Declaration of Independence, and found no mention of women's rights. Hell, he didn't think the founders had done much thinking about women at all. The Declaration of Independence clearly stated that "all *men* are created equal." He did, however, think that old Thomas Jefferson cared about individual rights, and now that women were considered "individuals" Greeley assumed that Jefferson would want women to have rights.

Then, jumping forward in history to 1973, Supreme Court Justice Harry Blackmun, the famous author of the landmark decision in abortion rights, *Roe v. Wade,* had been able to weave a rationale for a woman's right to choose when to become a parent out of the Fourteenth Amendment's concept of personal liberty. When the amendment states that no "state [shall] deprive any person of life, liberty, or property without due process of law," Justice Blackmun found that the right to terminate a pregnancy was essential to a woman's right to liberty. Greeley had to agree. Having raised five kids, Greeley knew what they did to a person's liberty. He also had to admit that his kids had been a greater burden on his wife's liberty than his own.

As for the upcoming demonstration, it was helping to breathe life into his little paper, and his staff, but publicly, in his editorial, he had to take a shot at Patricia Castellano and her anti-abortion stance. She should confine herself to the school board, the arts council, or the hospital's foundation. This issue was too big for her to dabble in. Now, she wasn't even going to show up! That poor bastard O'Malley! Wow, how had she manipulated him to the point where he would be all alone at the microphone? On the other side, Dr. Friedberg had comported herself with dignity and composure. Yes, in his editorial he would put in a good word for the doctor.

Eight hundred words later, he was done. He looked at his watch: 12:25. Just in time for the daily meeting. He was excited about all the events the next day. He leaned down and opened the bottom drawer in his credenza, rummaged around, and found the silver flask. A little nip would fortify him. "Ahh," he uttered, as the Black Bush whiskey burned his throat. Damn, he thought, he wanted another hit, but he decided against it. Greeley gathered his notes and left his office.

Once in the hall, he yelled "time!" and headed to the conference room. Most of the reporters were already assembled around the large conference table when he entered the room. Latitia was eating a yogurt, Helen was reviewing her notes, Fiona was reviewing her nails—everyone was accounted for except Kit Stilton and Bill Johnson. Greeley sat down heavily in his chair at the head of the table. He liked everyone to be present when he started. He did not condone lateness. His eyes squinted slightly as the clock struck 12:30 p.m. A certain nervousness was felt in the room as all eyes traveled up to the clock.

As silence filled the room, the sound of clicking heels, a faint, high-pitched laugh, and a deeper chuckle were heard. Everyone knew that Bill and Kit were coming down the hall. They waited for Greeley to explode. He stared at the clock as the two offending staff members burst into the room and quickly ran to their seats. They both mumbled "sorry," neither daring to look at Greeley. Everyone else stared at Greeley, waiting for him to punish the two in some way. He looked at each of them and then turned to Helen and said with venom, "Acker! Where are we?"

Helen opened her mouth to speak...

"That is, now that Ms. Stilton and Mr. Johnson have decided to join us," he continued, giving each member of the offending pair a harsh stare with his cold fish-gray eyes. Kit, who was dressed in her usual layered T-shirts, raised her eyes and stared back at Greeley. Bill examined his shoe. Greeley turned to Helen and nodded.

"Latitia, Fiona, Gary, Kit, Emily, and I will meet at eight a.m. at the clinic. Bill and Tom will cover Rubin's press conference," Helen said with authority.

"How are you breaking up the coverage at the demonstration?" demanded Greeley.

"Latitia will cover the protesters, Fiona will do the absence of Castellano, Gary will do crowd and police, I'll do O'Malley, Kit will get the speeches, and Emily will do the crowd," Helen responded.

Greeley gazed at the far wall with his lifeless gray eyes while the staff waited. "What does everyone think?" he asked, looking from one person to the next.

"Why do I have to go to the demonstration to write about the absence of Castellano?" blurted Fiona. "That's a story I can write today. I'll go over to Stand Up and see what's going on. Tomorrow I want to see what the woman who got arrested for vandalism is up to." Here, she flipped through her reporter's pad, looking at her notes, "Sandra Stett. I want to see what Sandra Stett is doing."

"Yes, I was wondering about her," said Greeley. "Write the Castellano piece today. Then get Stett tomorrow. What about Friedberg? Who's getting to Friedberg?"

The table was silent.

"She's not talking," Helen finally confessed. "I've called her every day. She won't take my calls."

Helen saw the wheels turning in Greeley's head. "I'll call Georgia Seal," he finally said. "I hear she's been hired to do P.R. by Walker and Horowitz. Which brings us to the press conference…"

"Wait. Why am I doing the protesters? Because I'm black and they're black?" asked Latitia with an indignant look on her face. Everyone looked at Helen for a response.

"Yeah, I thought they would feel more comfortable talking to you," replied Helen.

"Because I'm black?" cried Latitia.

"Yeah, because you're black. You *are* Black, Latitia," said Helen.

"I know I'm black," yelled Latitia.

"Good, then we're all in agreement," said Greeley. "Johnson, what's going on?"

Bill Johnson was the quintessential jock-turned-reporter. Tall and blond with broad shoulders, sleepy eyes, and a big, dopey grin, Johnson had sailed through life on good will and scholarships. Hailed as the conquering hero of Litchfield's football team, he had hidden his desire to be a journalist when he was recruited to Notre Dame. After four years of trying unsuccessfully to recapture his Litchfield High glory days in South Bend, he returned to Litchfield to pursue his other passion—reporting.

Johnson was not one to be rushed. He sat back in his chair, steepled his fingertips together, and inspected them. He was wearing a short-sleeve FCUK henley T-shirt, and his healthy biceps stretched the thin material. "Ceravolo is issuing a statement in response to Rubin's statement. Seal, Walker and company are trying to divert attention away from the clinic, and they have moved back the time of Rubin's press conference to eleven o'clock, so our little friend Jamie can cover both events, hence beating us to the public on both fronts. However, he can't write six or seven articles that quickly, so there must be something we can say before he says it," Johnson finished.

"Okay, anything on our murder?" Greeley looked at Latitia, who shook her head. Greeley frowned.

"Kit, I want a close-up of O'Malley speaking at the demonstration. Try to get him genuflecting or looking up to God. Something that reads religion," Greeley continued. "Baby Elliot, get me a wide-angle crowd shot of the Smithtown protesters. Supposed to be a Reverend Turnipseed in charge of recruitment, get him and get a bus shot. Folks getting off the bus. Any Litchfield notables. Milford, where's the three-headed monster in this? At the press conference, or are they sticking with Ceravolo as their candidate?"

"They haven't decided yet. Might split up," said Milford.

"Really?" said Greeley. "I thought they moved as one...."

"We'll see," said Milford.

"Another question for Georgia." Greeley made a note. "Anything else?"

Silence.

"Fine, tomorrow is an important day. I want everyone back here as soon as the action is over wherever you are. Everyone files from here so I have bodies if I need them. Got it?" Greeley scanned his troops, looking for weaknesses. It was a pretty good team, he thought. The group nodded their heads. An air of excitement filled the room as they collected their notes and trooped back to their cubicles.

ONE HUNDRED

AND FOUR

✦

Clara lay on the bed in the recovery room staring ahead at the yellow curtains with white and blue flowers. The stalls were so small that she could have reached out and touched them if her arms weren't swaddled in the soft, warm blanket that the nurse had wrapped around her body after the procedure. She was almost afraid to think that it was over. Afraid that there was more. More to get through before she could go home. She lay rigidly at first, but soon, she started to relax, hearing nurses consoling other patients, pushing other beds down the hall. The nurse had said Clara could stay in the recovery room for as long as she wanted. Then they would help her up and she would move to a room where she could sit up and have a snack to raise her blood sugar after a morning of fasting for the procedure.

Just as she was beginning to feel that she could get up, Joy, the head nurse, pulled the yellow curtains aside and smiled in at Clara. "How are you doing? Would you like to have some juice and cookies? Do you want to sit up?"

"Yes. I think so," said Clara.

Joy removed the warm blanket and Clara felt the cool air on her legs. "Here are your clothes. Do you need help?" Joy asked placing the bag with Clara's clothes on the bed beside her.

"No. I'll be fine," said Clara. Joy left and Clara found comfort in putting on her own clothes. When she was ready, she stood up and pulled the curtain aside. Joy came to escort her from the bed in the recovery room to an alcove, or the "Room of Second Chances," as the nurses called the brightly lit, colorfully painted lounge that was full of plants and comfortable furniture. The women sat and ate a cookie and drank their juice out of paper cups before they left the clinic.

Clara entered the lounge feeling a little weak and light-headed. She walked over to the food table, poured a cup of apple juice, picked up two cookies and a donut, and went to sit on one of the comfy chairs by the window. She closed her eyes and chewed. Relief spread through her torso. She literally felt lighter than she had felt in weeks. There was no stress in her shoulders. *I'm going to make it. I'm going to be okay. I'm going home. Spiro Agnew will jump on my legs. I'll curl up in my bed and take a nap. I'm going to be a senior in high school. I'm going to college. I'll have my life back.* It's over. It was over and she felt fine. Her future was clear. She felt a little giddy with relief. Even the tight cramping in her uterus felt good. Opening her eyes, she looked out the window. The gray morning clouds had burned off, and the sun was coming out.

What are you going to say to Michael to make him understand that it's over? Now that this was behind her, she knew she never wanted to see him again. She felt that she was getting a new beginning, and although she was willing to forgive him for what he had done to her that night, she was not willing to continue a relationship with him. When she said good-bye to him she meant good-bye forever. As she sat mulling over her situation, the terribly bruised woman she had seen in the waiting room that morning entered the room. Clara knew she was staring, but she couldn't make herself look away. The woman had bruises all over her face and walked slowly, as if putting one foot in front of the other was almost more than she could manage. She leaned heavily on a nurse, who led her to a couch across from Clara.

The bruised woman tilted her head back and rested it on a pillow that the nurse arranged for her, and then the nurse went to get her some juice and cookies. Clara knew she was being rude by staring, but she couldn't stop. Someone had beaten this woman up, punching her in the face and leaving her a disfigured mess. Clara's eyes welled up. For a minute, she forgot about her own problems, and her heart went out to the woman in front of her. When the nurse handed the woman her juice, the woman opened her one good eye and saw Clara staring at her. Clara quickly looked down.

Another woman, the poor woman Clara had seen in the waiting room, came in looking pale but relieved. Her pink sweatshirt was too big for her, and there was a hole in the toe of her sneaker. The woman poured herself a cup of apple juice and took a sip. She looked out the window as the cool liquid flowed down her parched throat. After she drank the entire cupful, she glanced at her watch. She poured more juice and took a donut and wrapped it in a napkin. She went to sit in a chair at the far end of the room.

All three women sat, silently chewing their sugary treats intently studying the uneaten portions. After a few minutes, the poor woman looked around the room. She looked at Clara and fought the urge to shake her head. *So young, but still, I wasn't that much older with my first child.* As she glanced around the room, she saw a needlepoint pillow on the unoccupied couch at the back of the room. On its front someone had woven the message, "Room of Second Chances."

Clara followed the woman's eyes to the pillow. Clara smiled. That was exactly how she felt—as if she'd been given a second chance. She knew she was different than she had been that morning; any vestige of childhood was gone. Today, when she went home, she would be an adult, able to take care of herself— when she had to. In a weird way, she felt more confident than she had before. Clara vowed to take her second chance and not ever let anything like this happen to her again.

She looked from the pillow to the woman's face. Their eyes met. They smiled shyly at each other, neither knowing the other's exact circumstances, but knowing enough to understand each other's feelings of relief. It was then that Clara realized that the other woman in the room, the one with the bruised face, was looking at her. Clara knew that this woman's challenges were not over, and for that she felt truly sad.

The poor woman in pink finished her donut and got up to leave. As the woman passed Pia's chair, Pia looked up at her. Without thinking, the poor woman reached down and gently squeezed the battered woman's shoulder. She stood back, and they took a moment to lock eyes and connect with each other. Finally, the poor woman said, "Good luck."

"Thank you," came Pia's reply, "and to you." Their eyes met for another moment, and the woman walked out of the room to meet her family in the outer room. Clara got up, went over to the couch, got the pillow with the saying, and took it to Pia.

Clara felt a rush of tenderness toward this battered woman. "I'm sorry you're hurt, and I hope that you will have a second chance now that this is behind you. I know I feel that way for myself," Clara confided.

"Yes, I feel that way, too," said Pia, taking the pillow from this young girl, who was maybe a little older than Maria, but not much. "I do feel that way." Pia reached up and took Clara's hand. "You take care of yourself." For a moment they shared a common experience without judgment.

"I will," said Clara with a determination that made Pia feel that this girl would be all right. Seeing Clara made her yearn for Maria, and suddenly, she couldn't wait to get out of here and go home with Stella to Maria and Carmen. She knew that her road ahead would be hard, but with the love and support of her girls and her sister, she felt that she could summon the courage to rebuild her life.

ONE $\mathcal{H}$UNDRED

AND $\mathcal{F}$IVE

❧

Simon felt Lee's compact little body nestled against his own as he opened his eyes on Saturday morning. They had been instructed by Sandra to meet Reverend Turnipseed at 6:30 a.m. at the Smithtown Diner, before the demonstration. This plan suited Simon just fine, because he had no intention of showing up at the demonstration. He would be Patricia's donkey and carry the money to old Turnipseed, but then he was going back to bed. His decision had already caused more than one fight with Lee. Simon hated the way Lee followed every little instruction given to him by Sandra and Patricia.

"Lee, we have to get up," he said, as he flung his legs over the side of the bed.

"Give me five more minutes," Lee mumbled into the duvet. Simon went into the bathroom and turned on the shower. When he came out, he found Lee in the kitchen making coffee.

"You better get in the shower. We don't want to be late for the good reverend," warned Simon.

"What do you care? I'm the one who's going to the demonstration and has to deal with all of this today. Simon, please help me," Lee looked at Simon with big sad eyes.

"Shit, Lee. You know how I feel about what's happening today. I don't want to be a part of it," argued Simon.

"You've been a part of it all along. It wouldn't even be happening without your work. I'm going to take a shower." Lee moved past Simon with a defiant uplifting of his chin.

Simon took a mug out of the cupboard and poured his coffee. He had to admit that Lee was right. Simon had done his job, which had resulted in the demonstration today. He was really only making Lee's job harder by not going. Damn!

They finished getting ready in silence. Once they were in the car, Simon drove out on Grant Avenue toward Smithtown. Lee took out their "To Do" list and started to read it out loud. "Meet with Reverend Turnipseed and deliver the money. Make sure buses arrive at the Baptist A.M.E. Church at eight a.m. Count the white people. Count the black people. Put the white people on the first bus." At this point, Lee stopped reading and turned to Simon. "Do you think that's going to cause a problem? Putting the white people on the bus first?"

Simon laughed. "Just don't put the black folks in the back of the bus and the white folks in the front. Put them on separate buses." Lee looked distressed. His forehead and nose were scrunched up. "Let Turnipseed put the people on the buses. He knows what Sandra wants."

Lee went back to his list. "I'm riding with the white folks and you're riding with the black folks...."

"Lee, baby, you know I'm not going. I've been telling you that for weeks."

"You're going to leave me all alone with all of this planning? Moving all these people? Keeping them segregated? Working the press?"

Lee knew that Simon was not going to change his mind. Lee just saw the demonstration as part of his job. He wasn't protesting the clinic. He was just earning a paycheck. Simon's absence doubled his workload. As they drove into Smithtown, Lee's scowl became more pronounced. By the time they reached the diner, he was positively fuming.

When they entered the old diner, they saw Reverend Turnipseed presiding at a table in the middle of the main room. He was sitting with a small group of parishioners, gesticulating and punctuating his sentences with his hands as he told them one of his many stories, and his listeners were hanging on his every lifted brow and raised finger. He had been telling the same stories for so many years that the tales had been reworked, revised, and embellished. If he didn't like the ending, he invented a new one, tailoring the story to his audience. He was just coming to the end of his tale when he saw Simon and Lee making their way through the diner. *Damn. They will surely throw off my punchline.* "...and she never saw him again," finished Reverend Turnipseed, to which his audience howled with laughter. *Saved it!*

"Good morning, gentlemen," the reverend greeted Simon and Lee, as they walked up to the table. He noted that the little Asian one carried a shopping bag and that the other one looked really pissed off.

"Good morning," said Simon. "May we have a few minutes of your time, Reverend?"

"If you all will excuse me, these good men are from Stand Up for Life, the pro-life organization coordinating our activities this morning. I'll see you over at the church," said Reverend Turnipseed as he got up and pointed to a vacant table in the back of the diner. Once they were all seated, he turned to Lee. "Is something the matter?"

"Everything's fine," Simon said, jumping in defensively. "We've brought the money. It's divided into envelopes with fifty dollars and envelopes with twenty dollars." A wave of annoyance flowed across Turnipseed's face. He had been hoping for a stack of bills, so he could quickly take his cut off the top. Now, he had to open each envelope.

"You're both staying with the buses?" he asked. Now it was Simon's turn to feel annoyance rise up into his face and turn it red.

"Well, only Lee is staying with the buses. I have other work to do," lied Simon.

"I'm sure Patricia won't mind if you answer the correspondence on Monday," said Lee in an overly sweet tone. Simon glowered at him.

"The first buses are due to arrive at seven-thirty. How many white people do you have?" asked Simon.

"Fifty-six, if they all show," said Reverend Turnipseed.

"And black?" asked Lee.

"Two hundred, give or take."

"Lunch will arrive at your church at eleven and be set up to be served when the buses return at approximately noon. You'll have staff on hand to distribute it. Is that right?" asked Lee, conferring with the notes that Sandra had given him.

"Yes, we'll take care of the lunch. There is one detail I wanted to iron out. I'd like to stand next to Father O'Malley, in unity, as he speaks this morning. Do you think that will be a problem? My people..." and here he paused for effect. "My people will expect me to be visible."

Lee and Simon exchanged a glance. This had not been the plan.

"I'm sure that will be fine, but I'll have to check with Sandra," said Lee.

"I'll stand with Father O'Malley, in unity, or the buses will not arrive. Are we clear?" said Reverend Turnipseed with a grin.

"We're clear," said Simon. Lee said nothing, but the lines in his forehead and the scrunch of his nose returned.

ONE HUNDRED

AND SIX

❦

$\mathcal{E}$lsa Martinson saw today as her turn to have her picture in the paper. She spent so much time volunteering for the church behind the scenes with no pay, no perks, and no thanks, that she had decided that today she would step forward at the demonstration and be recognized. She would stand by Father O'Malley as he spoke, and the photographers would take their picture, and the TV cameras would roll, and when she went to the supermarket on Monday, her neighbors would mention that they had seen her on the news. They would see her as important to the community, able to take a stand on an important church issue. She would gaze adoringly at Father O'Malley and clap ardently when he paused for emphasis. It didn't bother her that she didn't actually believe in the message he was extolling. For the occasion, she had bought a light-blue linen suit with white buttons, and white pumps with sensible heels. Her perfect blond hair hung in a pert bob to just under her pointy chin. She had visited Dr. Paige for her Botox injections, and she would choose sensible jewelry to complete her image.

Patricia had told Elsa that for political reasons regarding her brother, the mayor, she couldn't be at the demonstration, and so Elsa had chosen herself to stand next to the priest. Elsa dressed quietly, so as not to wake her children, and went downstairs to eat a quick breakfast. While she stood at the granite-topped island buttering her toast, she tried to decide whether to ask Father O'Malley's permission to stand with him, or to just follow him up the steps of the platform. She was leaning in the direction of just following him. That would take nerve—but he would never shoo her away in public.

As she pondered the best way to handle the situation, Linda walked into the kitchen, already dressed for the day in a bright-purple T-shirt and lime-green shorts. Large dangly earrings with purple and green beads hung from her ears.

"Wow! You would certainly stand out in a crowd!" Elsa said to her daughter. "What are you doing up so early?" It was 7:30 a.m.

"Couldn't sleep," said Linda. "The demonstration's today? You bought a new suit for it?" Linda looked her mother up and down with an expression Elsa couldn't read.

"Yes, the demonstration's today. I'll be home around one o'clock, unless Father O'Malley needs me back at the church."

Linda smiled a strange, closed-mouth smirk, more grimace than smile.

"Are you okay?" asked Elsa.

"Yes," Linda said flatly, as she poured herself a cup of milk.

"See you later then," Elsa said, as she grabbed a folder full of copies of Father O'Malley's speech.

"Yeah, see you soon," Linda said, as Elsa walked out the door.

ONE HUNDRED

AND SEVEN

The sweat dripped down Father O'Malley's back, and tiny beads of perspiration stood on his upper lip, as he drove through the quiet streets in the early-morning sun, waiting for the air conditioner to cool the car. It would all be over in a few hours, he kept telling himself. Just go through the motions. Read the speech, shake some hands, look pious and pure. Look holy and righteous. Just when he thought he would be all right, her voice would echo in his head. Her words reverberated in his mind. Over and over again, he repeated them to find their true meaning.

"I *will* see you tomorrow," she had said simply, putting the emphasis on "will." She had given him a hard look, turned her back abruptly on him, and walked out the door. After she left his room, the words seemed to hover over his bed. He shook his head. *Focus. Put her out of your head for now.*

Father O'Malley looked at the dashboard clock. 7:45 a.m. The police would be closing the road soon. Maybe it would be better to park a few blocks away from the clinic, so that he could leave before the crowd. Yes, that was a fine idea. A few blocks south of Route 54, he pulled to the curb. He looked in the rearview mirror and smoothed his unruly curls. *Should have gotten a haircut.* Studying his reflection, he felt like a fraud. *Thomas, you are not fit to wear the collar.* Shaking these thoughts out of his head, he grabbed his notes, folded them, and put them in his pocket. He took a deep breath and got out of the car.

Once out on the street in the morning air, he felt a little better. He walked up to Route 54 and looked across the highway at the front door of the women's center. Two burly security guards were stationed on either side of the door. Father O'Malley felt almost embarrassed to walk by them. Life had put them in adversary roles, but he had no quarrel with these two men. Would they even know who he was? And what he was here to do? He didn't know. He decided to walk on the opposite side of the street and cross over after he passed the clinic.

As he walked to the demonstration, he focused his attention on the parking lot next to the clinic and saw Sandra Stett ordering her volunteers around. A low platform had been erected, with a podium and microphone in the middle. A printed banner hung behind the podium between two poles proclaiming the morning's mission: "Stand Up for Life". The logo looked like a Madonna, who had a profile very much like Patricia's, holding an infant. The stage, which was decorated with colorful pots of flowers, could hold maybe six or seven people. Father O'Malley had not been told who else would stand beside him. He walked up to Sandra just as two police cars arrived to cordon off the street. Eight policemen got out of the cars.

"Good morning, Father." Sandra greeted Father O'Malley with a huge grin and her southern twang which got on northern people's nerves.

"Good morning, Sandra," Father O'Malley said mechanically. "Who will introduce me this morning?"

"I will have the honor of introducing you." Sandra's perky demeanor bothered the somber priest.

"Who else will be on the platform?"

"Would you like someone else to stand with us?" Her strangely shaped eyes looked concerned.

"No, I don't care. I was just wondering," he said. As they spoke, Elsa Martinson approached, looking over-dressed for the parking lot in her linen suit. Sandra looked down at her own pink dress and felt washed-out and frumpy next to Elsa. She noticed that Father O'Malley's tone improved abruptly when he greeted Elsa. "Good morning, Elsa. Thank you for coming so early," he said, smiling as he took her hand in both of his and gave her a priestly nod.

Over Elsa's shoulder, Sandra saw Helen Acker's form lurch forward through the parking lot. She was dressed all in gray, like a cloud approaching on this beautiful summer day. Her lifeless hair stuck to her forehead, and she was already sweating profusely. "Good morning, Father O'Malley. Mrs. Martinson… Sandra." She said the third name after waiting a few seconds, almost as an afterthought.

"Good mornings" were exchanged all around. "Do you have a copy of the speech?" Helen asked, looking from Sandra to Elsa, knowing that Father O'Malley would never distribute copies of his own speech. That would be far too undignified for a priest.

"After Father O'Malley delivers the speech we will make copies available, Helen," said Elsa.

"Okay," Helen said, clearly annoyed. Her frown deepened as she spied the handsome form of DeShawn Fletcher leading Latitia Blackman slowly toward the parking lot on the other side of the street, holding her hand and stopping to give her little kisses. *How unprofessional can you get?* Helen turned to look at the clinic and wondered if Dr. Friedberg was already inside. She glanced at her watch. It was 8:10. Turning back to O'Malley, she said, "Father, can I ask you a few questions while we wait for the demonstrators?"

She detected a wave of irritation cross over Father O'Malley's face, but he smiled and said, "Of course, Helen, how can I help?"

"What do you hope to accomplish here this morning?" asked Helen, opening a new reporter's notebook to a fresh page.

"Awareness. Yes, Helen, I think awareness of the fact that all life is sacred to God and that the life of an unborn child is no less sacred in God's eyes." The propaganda rolled so smoothly off his tongue that he impressed himself. He stood with his hands together, his fingertips gently touching, swaying forward onto the balls of his feet, and then back slowly onto his heels, nodding with his eyes half-closed.

"When are the buses arriving?" Helen asked next.

Father O'Malley's eyes opened wide. It had not occurred to him that he would be asked about the buses.

"We do have some folks arriving by bus. They should be here shortly," volunteered Sandra, who had never left the priest's side and didn't intend to for the duration of the event.

"Make sure I get a copy of the speech," Helen said, looking over her glasses at Sandra before trudging away.

Father O'Malley looked down at Sandra. "I want you to handle all questions regarding the buses," he sneered.

"Of course, Father," said Sandra, looking up at the priest innocently.

By 8:30, demonstrators had started to arrive in dribs and drabs. Sandra had set up a table with coffee, and pamphlets, buttons, and pens that said "Stand Up for Life." On the back of the pamphlet was a large photo of Patricia's smiling face, oozing money and sporting expensive hair. Jamie and Fiona arrived and went over to say hello to DeShawn and Latitia. It was awkward for the reporters to try to get even a crumb of news that the others wouldn't have. They had all resigned themselves to writing the same story. Jamie knew that his would run first online. DeShawn would be up second with the evening news, and then *The Press* would come in last place with tomorrow's morning edition, but with the most in-depth coverage.

As the group of young reporters stood around flirting with each other, a large bus turned onto Route 54. Every head in the parking lot followed its slow progression down the road to the police barricade and watched as it rolled through to park in front of the lot. The doors opened a few minutes later and out bounded Reverend Atlee Turnipseed. He was dressed in a long, flowing fuchsia cassock with scarlet satin cuffs. A large, bejeweled cross hung from a chain around his neck, like bling. The reporters all responded at once and turned en masse to follow Reverend Turnipseed, as he walked with purpose toward Father O'Malley.

Emily Elliot focused her camera and started to move into place to get a shot of the handshake. Like the black king and the white king on a chess board, the two clergymen traversed the space between them, each hoping for dominance over the other. Emily raised her Canon and half-clicked for focus, as the robed arms of the priest and the reverend reached out for the greeting. She wondered where Kit was and why she wasn't getting this moment. Emily was a little nervous about taking shots of Father O'Malley, knowing that Kit was supposed to cover the priest, but Kit was nowhere in sight and this was a great shot.

ONE HUNDRED

AND EIGHT

❧

Inside the clinic, Dr. Friedberg and Rachel Horowitz huddled near the kitchen window that looked out toward the vacant lot. They watched silently as the tall, black pastor crossed the lot. He stretched his long legs and moved like a tribal king toward the platform, his brisk steps causing clouds of dust to puff up and hang in the air behind him. In his wake followed the sorriest-looking stream of washed-out white women that the doctor had ever seen. Dr. Friedberg knew immediately that they were recovering drug addicts and alcoholics.

"Oh my God! Patricia has really lost her mind," mumbled Rachel, clutching the rope of pearls around her neck.

"They're all addicts. They must have been let out of rehab for the day. This demonstration isn't even real. It's a show," snapped Dr. Friedberg. She watched the flamboyantly dressed reverend reach out his large hand to the handsome priest, who was dressed somberly in a traditional black cassock and white collar. They made a striking pair. *Actors on Patricia Castellano's stage. Disgusting.*

"Here comes another bus," said Rachel.

"What time is it? I wish that girl would get here," said Dr. Friedberg, looking at her watch. "Eight-forty-five. I hope she gets here soon," she said. As she turned back to the window, the other bus opened its doors, and a stream of black demonstrators, led by a small white man, started to descend from the bus. A U-Haul van had arrived, and men were unloading signs and handing them out to the demonstrators. Dr. Friedberg and Rachel noted a woman with short blond hair in a pink dress who seemed to be directing all the action.

"What a coward Patricia is," Rachel said with a snort, "to cause all this upset and then to hide in her Jacuzzi. That woman, you see who I mean?" Rachel held the curtain back and pointed. "The one in the pink dress? She looks like she's in charge. She must work for Patricia..." As the women watched the event unfolding outside, they were startled by a knock at the front door. Dr. Friedberg went to see who it was. It was Joy, who never worked on Saturday, but who had agreed to come in because some of the younger nurses were afraid.

As Dr. Friedberg opened the front door for Joy, Helen Acker seemed to materialize from behind a bush to the right of the door. Joy stepped quickly into the clinic, followed by Helen's Birkenstocked big toe.

"Good morning, Dr. Friedberg," she said. "May I come in and ask you a few questions?"

Dr. Friedberg, clearly annoyed, looked at Helen and couldn't decide what to do. "Just for a minute," she finally said. Helen lumbered in through the doorway and felt the cool air-conditioning embrace her. "Let's go to my office," the doctor said. Helen followed the doctor down the hall. Dr. Friedberg wanted to get Helen away from the door, because the girl with the appointment was supposed to arrive any minute.

When they were settled in Dr. Friedberg's office, Helen asked, "What are you feeling right now, Dr. Friedberg?"

Dr. Friedberg took her time. She ran various responses through her head. She tried to picture them in print. "I'm just here to do my job, Helen. Today is just like any other day."

Helen smirked as she wrote the doctor's words down. "Do you have any patients coming in today?"

"Helen, you know better than that. I'm not going to discuss my patients with you or anyone else."

"If you could say one thing to Patricia Castellano this morning, what would it be?"

"I'm not planning to speak with Ms. Castellano this morning."

"If you were?" Helen persisted, peering over her glasses at the doctor.

"Helen, do you have any questions that you think I will answer? Because I have work to do..."

"What is your reaction to the demonstration?"

"The demonstration this morning is a staged effort to start a debate on a topic that was decided more than forty years ago with *Roe v. Wade*. I can't imagine that we are going to hear anything new this morning. Now Helen, there's your quote. I have to get back to work." Dr. Friedberg stood up to signal the end of the interview. As she walked Helen to the door, she glanced at her watch. 9:15. The girl was late. The doctor hoped that she had changed her mind and wasn't coming.

ONE HUNDRED
AND NINE

❧

Father O'Malley's facial muscles were tired from looking pious and self-righteous for the cameras, but he was
inspired by his own rhetoric and that of Reverend Turnipseed.
Although he had come to the demonstration this morning prepared to shun Reverend Turnipseed if he showed up, he found
himself in awe of the reverend's showmanship—his fuchsia
robes, his booming oratory, his colorful metaphors. Here was
a man who could excite a crowd. A gifted speaker who took
some of the pressure off Father O'Malley. Turnipseed had giv-
en him a heads-up that he would like to say a few words, so they
had agreed that he would follow O'Malley up to the podium.
O'Malley knew that Patricia would cringe when she saw the two
of them together on the news, but he didn't care. *Patricia isn't
here. I'm running this show now.*

O'Malley knew that Turnipseed would deliver a Baptist-
style sermon that would whip his parishioners into a frenzy.
Addressing a crowd was sport for Turnipseed. Like a great

Shakespearean actor, Turnipseed would use comedy and trage-dy to reach his people. While his costume and physical presence made a spectacle, he would raise his powerful voice and engage his people in a call and response. These were techniques that Catholic priests were not taught. Priests were supposed to be above the people, not with the people. Father O'Malley knew that Reverend Turnipseed would be more quotable than he was, and that was fine. He knew that Turnipseed wanted the spotlight. *Let him take it!*

Ten minutes to go before the speeches. Father O'Malley felt pumped. The demonstrators were putting on a real show for the cameras, walking in a circle and holding their signs up high, and an air of excitement floated through the crowd. He surveyed the demonstrators, and he had to hand it to Sandra, she had rounded up the troops. Even though he knew that most of them came from Smithtown, as he scanned the faces, he saw members of his own youth group and a contingent from his senior choir standing under a shade tree in the back of the lot. He noted that Channel 6 was over there interview-ing them.

Father O'Malley realized that his own motives were even less pure than Turnipseed's motives—whatever they were. O'Malley had to admit to himself that he was here because of the politics of fundraising. He was here to open Patricia and Salvatore Castellano's checkbook. Not to put money in his own pocket, but for the prestige the money brought to the church and to him as head of the church. That's just the way it worked. Of course, he was also supposed to believe in this cause. O'Malley looked over and saw Sandra Stett looking smug and self-satisfied. There was something about that woman that he just didn't like.

Sandra saw Father O'Malley watching her, and she tried to keep a professional face to hide how thrilled she was with the way things were going. By her count, more than 300 dem-onstrators had shown up. Father O'Malley and Reverend

Turnipseed were bonding. Cameras for print, video, and TV recorded every nuance, even Darius Greeley himself was lurking in the background. Now, it was show time. She beckoned to Father O'Malley to come to the podium and saw Reverend Turnipseed follow him through the crowd to meet her. Feeling triumphant, she realized she didn't care if the reverend came up on stage. Let it be a spectacle. She had worked hard to create this event to spread God's word. Now, she would take her place beside God's servants and feel the passion of the people. As she and Father O'Malley walked to the platform, she saw that Elsa Martinson was standing by the steps that they would have to climb to get to the podium. She thought, with annoyance, that Elsa was planning to stand next to Father O'Malley on the platform. Sandra wanted that coveted spot.

She looked for Lee and gave him the signal to move the crowd toward the platform. Earlier, she had instructed Lee to "start with the Litchfieldians, then the white trash, and then the blacks." Lee had recruited a few of the members of the St. Raymond's youth group to help him. She noted with pleasure that the formation was shaping up perfectly. With a tight camera shot, the crowd would look all white. Long shots were visually boring, so she hoped and prayed that the papers would run a photo that focused on the action on the platform, with only the back of a few heads for crowd perspective.

Reverend Turnipseed had fallen in step beside Father O'Malley and Sandra as they approached the platform. The press was already jostling for good places down in front. Jamie Ross had positioned himself just to the right of the podium, so he could video-stream the speech in real time. DeShawn's cameraman had set up a tripod, and two radio reporters were plugging their microphones into the sound system.

The two men of God and the two blond women mounted the steps to the platform, and the crowd formed behind the press. As everyone settled in and jockeyed for position, Sandra noted with displeasure that the black matrons who were about to hear God's word could not be stopped from pushing the wounded flock from Miss Nancy's to the side. Sandra stood at the podium and pointed the situation out to Lee with a finger and a nod, and Lee rushed over to try to rearrange the women. She waited until the crowd had fully assembled to introduce Father O'Malley. Anticipation filled the air. When the crowd grew quiet, she welcomed everyone and gave a short and inspired introduction of the Litchfield-born-and-raised priest. As she finished, Lee started the crowd clapping, and she smiled for the cameras.

Now it was Father O'Malley's turn. He took his place in front of the podium and raised his hands to calm the wildly applauding demonstrators. As he did, he saw *her* crossing the street. He froze. What was she doing here? Her words from the night before filled his head. "I *will* see you tomorrow." He watched her small form navigate through the crowd and walk purposefully toward the platform. He was not the only one who saw her. Elsa Martinson, who stood to his left, had spotted her, too. The protesters were still applauding, so he took a minute to compose himself. He looked down at his notes. When he looked up again, she was lost in the crowd. He closed his eyes and lifted his arms, palms to the heavens, and a hush flowed through the crowd.

"Almighty Father, who art in heaven," he began. He dared not open his eyes. "Hallowed be thy name," he continued. The crowd took up the rest of the prayer. When their chanting ended, he looked down at his notes. He couldn't scan the crowd. He didn't want to see her flowing golden hair or her bright-blue eyes. Instead, he looked directly into the Channel 6 camera and spoke to it, pausing in a priestly way between sentences. "We are here today to rejoice in the wonders of life. Life is sacred. The church teaches us that life is sacred from the moment of conception to the moment of natural death. Every unborn child has the same rights, privileges, and protections as the child sleeping peacefully in his crib right now," he said, never looking away from the camera. He preached his memorized speech, unaware that she had made her way up to the side of the platform.

As he said his final "amen" and turned to relinquish his spot at the podium to Reverend Turnipseed, out of the corner of his eye he caught a flash of purple and lime green and a ribbon of flaxen hair blowing gently on the breeze as Linda skipped up the steps to the platform. She went straight to her mother and whispered in her ear. Elsa Martinson's expression went from concerned to horrified as she turned toward Father O'Malley.

"Father O'Malley is the father of my baby," Linda said to her mother, loud enough for those close by to hear. "I'm on my way into the clinic."

Father O'Malley put his hand over the microphone to drown out the sound of Elsa Martinson's screams. He grabbed Reverend Turnipseed by the forearm and pulled him to center stage. As O'Malley put his long arms around both Elsa and Linda and tried to move them off the stage, he was suddenly very aware of Jamie Ross standing in front of the platform, recording the priest's downfall for all of Litchfield. As Elsa started to descend the stairs, and DeShawn's cameraman was running over to the side of the platform, Reverend Turnipseed tried to distract the demonstrators, who were trying to figure out what was going on.

"*Pray with me,*" he commanded in a booming voice, raising his arms to heaven. The crowd was confused. Many of them turned their attention back to the podium, but the press was more interested in the sideshow. Elsa started down the platform steps, pulling Linda by the arm, with Father O'Malley right behind them. The three of them were tangled together, with Father O'Malley trying to shield Linda's face from Jamie Ross and Kit Stilton, who had materialized out of nowhere. Once they were down from the platform, there was really nowhere to hide. Father O'Malley looked up and saw the clinic.

He knew he had to seek refuge in the clinic. The guards would keep the press at bay. He took Linda by the hand and started to run with her through the parking lot toward the clinic. The press followed, screaming questions and taking pictures.

The guards watched the tall priest in his flowing black satin robe run toward them, dragging the little girl with the long blond hair streaming out behind her. A few yards behind them was a cackling pack of reporters.

"Father O'Malley, wait!" they shouted.

"Let us in," yelled Father O'Malley to the guards.

The guards looked at each other. They were not sure of what to do. Dr. Friedberg, who had been watching from the kitchen window, went to the lobby and opened the door of the clinic just as Father O'Malley and Linda reached it. They ran past her into the waiting room, both gasping for breath.

"Keep the press out," she said to the guards, and slammed and locked the door just as Jamie, DeShawn, and Kit reached the front walk. The guards moved to form a human blockade in front of the clinic door.

Linda Martinson looked at Father O'Malley with fearless eyes. She was totally in control of herself and the situation. "I'm here for my appointment," she said to Dr. Friedberg, never taking her eyes off of Father O'Malley. He slumped into one of the mauve chairs in the waiting room, his head falling down into his hands, a pained grimace tearing his lips back from his teeth. "My lover has joined me. Will you hold my hand during the procedure, Thomas? Is that allowed, Doctor?" Linda asked, with an edge in her voice that was as sharp as a scalpel. She looked at Dr. Friedberg for the first time.

Dr. Friedberg was clearly confused by this turn of events. She couldn't quite decide how to respond. She reached up and tucked her hair behind her ear. Rachel Horowitz found them this way as she walked into the waiting room.

"What is...Father O'Malley...who is..." she turned from Dr. Friedberg to Father O'Malley to Linda.

"I've brought the father of my baby to my appointment," Linda said smugly, pointing at the priest.

"The father..." echoed Rachel.

"Yes, I am the father," cried Father O'Malley, tears streaming down his cheeks. He pulled at his hair and ripped at the cleric's collar that was strangling him.

"Shall we begin?" asked Linda, cracking her gum. "Shall I pee in a cup? Take off my clothes? What's the drill?"

As Linda continued to torture Father O'Malley, they heard screaming outside the door. It was Elsa Martinson. "Linda! Linda! That's my daughter. Don't touch her. Let me in!" Dr. Friedberg walked to the window. Behind Mrs. Martinson, Dr. Friedberg could see the herd of reporters jostling for position, begging for a comment.

"I have to let her in," she said to Linda, who simply shrugged.

Dr. Friedberg walked over to the door and opened it a crack to instruct the guards to let Mrs. Martinson through. Elsa Martinson exploded into the room. "You hypocrite!" she yelled, seizing Father O'Malley by the shoulders and shaking him.

"Mother, please. Let's not have these histrionics. I'm here to get rid of it. It won't be a problem for long. You're never home long enough to know what I'm doing, anyway. I lost my virginity years ago to one of the teachers at St. Raymond's, and my lover here knew about it and was very eager to keep my secret. Isn't that right, Thomas? I call him Thomas when we're in bed," she said, looking straight into her mother's eyes.

Elsa Martinson let out an involuntary squeal and her hands went up to cover her eyes. Dr. Friedberg moved in to intervene.

"Okay. Okay, Linda and Mrs. Martinson, why don't we go into my office? Father O'Malley, you wait here." Dr. Friedberg put her arm around Linda's shoulders and started to lead her down the hallway. Elsa Martinson followed behind, mascara streaking her cheeks, her linen suit crumpled like a used napkin.

Rachel sat down next to the priest. His body was folded into itself and his face was buried in his hands. He shuddered from the waves of pain that coursed through his chest. His face contorted in horror as he saw his future and his past flash before him.

Rachel reached out and put her hand on his shoulder. "You see Father, you never know what's going to happen to you and who will be there when it does."

$\mathcal{A}$CKNOWLEDGMENTS

$\mathcal{I}$ want to thank all of the people who agreed to read the book at various stages and offer their input: Lois Elson, Joy Lara, Paula Horii, Rosanne Kurstedt, Eva Lesko Natiello and all the members of The Westfield Writers Group who read chapters. A huge round of thanks to my editor, Cheryl Sacra Paden, who went through the book with a fine-tooth comb and taught me a lot about punctuation! To Susan Cook, photographer, I never looked so good! Thanks for the photograph and your help with the cover art. I also want to thank Sergeant Ricerca of the Westfield Police Department who answered my questions about police procedure. And, of course, I am grateful to my family who had to endure countless hours of discussion about how the work was progressing and next steps. I'm glad to report it's done!

www.ingramcontent.com/pod-product-compliance
Lightning Source LLC
Chambersburg PA
CBHW051433260626
47162CB00001B/74